# CHAOS THEORY

SYLVIA LEATHAM

Ebook ISBN: 978-1-83700-138-5
Paperback ISBN: 978-1-83700-140-8

Cover design: Rose Cooper
Cover images: Shutterstock, iStock

Published by Storm Publishing.
For further information, visit:
www.stormpublishing.co

*For Joe, my North Star, and Alice, my sunshine*

# ONE

## MAEVE

*Friday, 8:15am*

'This definitely can't happen again,' I murmur the instant I open my eyes and see that once again I've woken up in Shane Fitzgerald's crummy bedroom. Uninvited morning light pokes through the wonky Venetian blind. Who hangs office blinds on a bedroom window anyway? I snuggle back under the covers, check to see what, if anything, I'm wearing.

'Pretty sure that's exactly what you said last time.'

So Shane is awake. He grins at me as he opens his eyes. Of course he looks relaxed and content – why wouldn't he? Another night of shenanigans.

'And the time before that. Remind me again why.'

He's heard my can't-happen-again song so many times he must know it by heart. He turns onto his side to face me, puts one hand behind his head. I decide to ignore the defined shoulder, the flex-and-relax of his upper arm. I learned the names of each of those muscles in human anatomy at school and have long since forgotten them, but I've done enough field research in the meantime to know I still find them utterly, utterly distracting. I turn away, focus on the pyramid of laundry on the floor, a single sock perched Sphinx-like on top. That must be at least two weeks' backlog.

I clear the night from my throat, speak a little louder. 'You know – we work together? I'm trying to be professional.' *Does that sound legit?*

I sit up, pull my side of the sheet up to my chin and discreetly sniff under my arms. Scent of the hops from my body's own brewery. I smooth down my hair, which has lost the run of itself again. Granted, I'm not exactly the portrait of professionalism right now.

My eyes dart around the room, catching on anything that might be the vague shape and size of a pair of black leggings. Shane's overflowing t-shirt drawer, a tangle of office ties merging with the pattern on the rug, one of those rope-y bicycle locks.

'Professional? Since when?'

He's teasing me. He reaches out and strokes a figure of eight – or is it an infinity symbol? – on my back... Either way, a sign of more to come. I flash back to our bodies entwined, in synch, a perfect dissolution into something beyond flesh, a human sacrifice to the gods of drunken horniness...

I shrug his hand away.

'Stop that. Since now. Yesterday would have been a better time to start, of course. But from today on, anyway.'

The rejected hand withdraws and instead reaches for its one true love – the phone on the beside locker. He slides it from *pub mode* to *morning mode* and the notifications fly in. He flicks through them using only his eyes.

'Okay. But why start now? As opposed to – I don't know – any time in the past year?'

I continue to survey the surroundings. A flabby used condom on the nightstand. *Hello, old friend.*

'Nine months. Not that I'm counting.'

I know it's nine months because our hookups began the night of the staff Christmas party last December. Everyone knows that what happens at the office Christmas party doesn't count, right? It was a Christmas bonus, a stocking filler, a delicious snowflake melting on your tongue. The second time, after Tracy's leaving drinks in January, I put it down to a heady cocktail of January blues, payday exuberance and, well, actual cocktails. I don't have a clear memory of the third time because it's mixed up with the fourth and fifth times. I admit I've kind of lost count of how many times I've woken up in this room. I'm pretty sure it's less than ten. Below ten still counts as occasional; double digits would demand further investigation and possibly corrective action.

We'd both joined Go Ireland on the same day a full year before that Christmas party and worked in customer service until we both got promoted to the marketing department last December.

The very first time we'd spoken, I'd recounted my career history and Shane had counted back to me how many jobs I'd had since college: 'Seven jobs in seven years.' 'Well, maybe seven is a lucky number,' I'd shot back. He'd laughed and accused me of being a drifter. I'd proclaimed that I was not a drifter, I was a... a... *seeker*. The perfect job was out there somewhere – maybe it would be this one, maybe it hadn't been invented yet. When I'd got back from lunch that day, I'd found a Drifter chocolate bar on my new desk.

The truth is, Shane's no better, as far as I can tell. I mean just look at this place – this room clearly belongs to a man with zero ambition.

'Anyway,' I continue, forcing some authority into my voice. 'I'm going to be busy with work. Yes, really. As much as I wouldn't mind departing our beloved Go Ireland, I want to leave on my own terms, and ideally with a good reference. There's a difference between jumping out of an airplane and being pushed out of one. I told you all this last night, remember?'

'Was that before or after I went on the whiskey?'

He smirks, dark eyes twinkling in the half-light. Everything amuses him and he's always in a good mood. It really is annoying.

Lying back down, I perch my body precariously close to the edge of the bed, gingerly pat the carpet underneath. I recoil as my fingers encounter an unidentified squishy object.

'This place really is a dump.'

'Well, you won't let me come to your place, remember?'

'I don't want you messing it up.'

He casts an eye to the bedside clock. 'This is definitely going to be a late day.'

'Unlike... every other day of the week?'

'Hey, you know what they say.'

'The early bird gets the worm?' I offer.

'Yeah. But the second mouse gets the cheese. This is all part of the master plan, Maeve. If I keep coming in at 9:15, consistently, every day, eventually people will assume that 9:15 is my official start time.'

I laugh. 'Good to know.'

Hooking up with Shane was never part of my plan, if I ever had one. It's just become a habit, one I'm finding hard to break. We're a bad influence on each other. Will we have one more drink? The answer is always yes, no matter which of us has asked. All year long I've been convinced one of us will soon get another job, and then circumstances will resolve our situation, without the need for a manual intervention...

My toe snags on something lacy beneath the sheet. I bend my knee and draw the small black item towards me with relief, until closer inspection unfolds a different truth.

'Shane, this isn't even mine!'

I fling the thong across the room. The two of us burst out laughing.

'Come on, we're going to be so late,' I say.

Yes, this was our last hurrah. At least we've gone out with a bang.

# TWO

'Maeve, I need to see you in my office right now.'

I roll my eyes and consider telling my boss's boss that, unless someone has just invented the teleporter, *right now* is a physical impossibility. 'Sure thing, JP,' I say down the phone instead.

I begin the arduous journey from the second-floor open plan to the secluded top-floor offices, searching my mind for recent indiscretions. Could this be about my excessive personal use of the new multifunction printer? Maybe I left a copy of my résumé in the out-tray again? It's just easier to spot typos in print. Or maybe JP's twigged what I did on Monday morning: instead of arriving five minutes late for the all-staff meeting, I hid in the bathroom for a full hour, then skilfully merged with the crowd leaving the meeting, as if I'd been there all along.

I make my way to the elevator, squinting as harsh sunlight brightens the corridor, a feature the building's glass wall frontage. I can picture the architect in the pitch meeting, clicking through their slide deck with a flourish. *Georgian brickwork meets contemporary office style at the heart of historic Dublin.* Old meets new meets old.

The elevator is faster than the stairs in theory but rarely in practice. I press the call button three times and await its shuddering arrival.

'Welcome,' it announces as I step in. 'Please state your destination now, or press the corresponding button on the panel.'

'Fifth floor,' I state.

'Please state your destination now,' the elevator repeats calmly.

I sigh. My Irish accent is not the strongest – diluted by years of travel – but still, I switch on my best Californian drawl. 'Fifth floor.'

No response. I jab at the corresponding button on the panel. A surprisingly smooth ascent begins. I imagine the steel box passing the fifth floor, gliding through a hidden opening in the roof, continuing upward to the stratosphere.

I dutifully arrive at JP's office, take a moment to enjoy the view over the park and the low-rise Dublin skyline beyond. JP unfolds himself like a spider preparing for lunch. Adjusts his glasses before looking at me.

'Maeve. We need to talk.'

He nods at the chair in front of his messy, oversized desk. There's probably a tree missing from the park below, felled specifically to cater for JP's attachment to paper. He's been known to print out emails.

'What's this about?'

I stay standing. The not knowing is starting to get to me.

'Don't worry, this isn't a bad meeting. I have some interesting news. Sit down.'

I exhale and sit while JP taps the keyboard and peers at his laptop screen. True to form, the desktop printer by the window hums to life and another new page is born. So many offspring, such varied fates. Some to be cherished and homed in the filing cabinet. Others swaddled in an envelope and sent out into the world. The less fortunate balled and binned. The truly damned facing the guillotine or, worse, the shredder.

My eyes drift to a large posterboard propped up in the corner.

It shows a line of hillwalkers enjoying an open green space in the Irish countryside. I'M WALKIN' HERE! says the text below. The newly redesigned Go Ireland logo features prominently. It's wilfully almost identical to the old logo. God knows how much it cost to redo.

JP rolls himself in his chair over to the printer, then with one push swings himself back behind his desk. 'Robots,' he says as he completes his orbit.

'Robots?' I echo.

'Robots,' he says. 'Specifically, collaborative robots. What do you know about them?'

Unexpected, but at least I'm not getting fired. Unless... he plans to replace me with a robot? I decide to be noncommittal. 'Um. Let me think.'

JP brings the printed page very close to his face and reads aloud, saving me from thinking.

'Collaborative robots, aka cobots, are the "Next Big Thing" for the workplace.' He makes air quotes with his pinkies while holding the paper. 'Highly competent, artificially intelligent machines. They're not intended to replace employees – they're meant to work alongside them, like a helpful colleague on the production line, in the office or on the hospital ward.'

'Interesting.' Then I remember. About six months ago, Jen and I went to that one-day 'Intro to Robots in the Workplace' conference. The HR manager was supposed to go, but she called in sick at the last minute, so Jen asked me to go with her. I don't remember much from the day apart from the creaminess of the cupcakes at break time, and the quality of the merch in the swag bag.

'So, um... what's that got to do with us?' I ask. There was a rumour that the head of marketing – and my line manager – Duncan Canning had used AI to write the ad copy for the New York campaign, but Duncan was waiting until the success or failure of the campaign had been firmly established before confirming or denying the rumour.

'Well' – JP scans the page again – 'an opportunity has come up. It looks like we are taking delivery of one... this afternoon.'

'Really? Here? Today?'

'Yes, yes and yes,' says JP. 'Believe me, I'm as surprised as you are. We've never had anything on this level here before. The new multifunction printer is about as good as it gets, am I right?'

I can't tell if this is a trap. 'Tell me more about this robot,' I say quickly.

'Well, you know how I play golf with Ron Tron, the CEO of RoboTron?'

Taking advantage of JP's poor eyesight, I risk an eye roll. 'You've mentioned it once or twice, yes.'

Ron Tron is one of the most famous names in tech. I'm pretty sure it's a made-up name, but it made headlines when he decided to set up a research office for RoboTron in Dublin.

JP squint-skims the text. 'It seems that one of their cutting-edge robots has been recalled from a factory deployment... And as there's a bit of a gap in its schedule, as it were, Ron thinks we should take it for a while. Let's see here – Ron's assistant says Ron is eager to see how this, quote, "highly sophisticated automaton" might function in a, quote, "unstructured environment of low stakes".' He slaps the page down on the desk. 'You know what, the details are not that important right now. I think it's a great opportunity.'

I'm miles away, wondering what JP and Ron Tron could possibly talk about on the golf course, given that JP's as analogue as a wind-up radio. 'Great opportunity,' I parrot mindlessly.

'I'm glad you agree, Maeve. Because I want you to take the lead on this one.'

'I'm sorry, what?'

My neck twitches involuntarily with the realisation of what this conversation was building up to. He actually wants me to *do* something. But... I have one foot out the door. I've been pootling along for months, getting through my low-level marketing admin tasks while eyeing the exits. The only place I'm going is away from here.

'I want you to take charge of supervising this robot, make sure we get' – I see him parse the text for the right phrase – 'maximum value from it.'

'But surely this is more Jen's area? She's our head of IT, after all. I'm hardly qualified. And, you know, I'm very busy these days.'

He stares at me for such a long time that I'm unsure if he's gone into one of those eyes-wide-open naps you hear about. Eventually his eyebrows start to rise. *He knows*. He knows I'm not too busy.

'Jen is our head of IT, yes, but she's also our only person in IT. And she's not in today. You'll appreciate that we're in a bit of a tight spot, Maeve. This is all very last-minute, but I don't want to let Ron down. Besides, Duncan tells me you have capacity. He says you could use a new challenge, in fact.'

*Duncan found my résumé. Duncan found my résumé.*

All I can do is sigh and cover it up with a smile.

'That's settled then. This email says all will be explained today when they bring in this, this...' – JP unfolds the page and takes at least thirty seconds to find the information he needs – 'this... Kobi.'

# THREE

*2pm*

I'm waiting with JP in the Shannon Suite, the largest of the meeting rooms, the furniture pushed to one side so our robot guest can be unencumbered by navigational obstacles. There's nowhere to sit, so I pace the floor.

I try to launch another protest about this new assignment, but 'I just don't want to do this' doesn't seem like it will work, so I opt instead for 'What if I mess this up?' But JP just gives me a little speech about his confidence in my abilities, with a side note stressing the unavailability of anyone else to take on the task.

I'm already imagining myself recounting this moment in great detail to Shane later on. Another bad habit I have to break – providing him with a running commentary on my life. On Wednesday I messaged him real-time crisis updates when I discovered the staff café had run out of my precious peppermint tea, until the heroic appearance of the delivery man had saved the day, or at least the morning.

I hear voices from the hallway, then silence. Someone tall and good-looking bursts into the room, beaming at us.

'My God!' JP steps forward. 'The technology! It's amazing. It's so lifelike.' Then, addressing the visitor with a strange sort of half bow: 'It is our honour to meet you.'

I stifle a giggle. The visitor laughs and extends a hand. 'Well, I'm excited to meet you too, but I'm not Kobi.'

JP does a double take. *Mortifying.* I swiftly step in front of him and shake the warm-blooded hand.

'Hi, I'm Maeve McGettigan, and this is JP Horgan, my boss. Welcome to Go Ireland.'

'Thank you. I'm Josh Hunter. In a moment you'll meet my buddy Kobi, but I wanted to talk to you guys alone first.'

I suspected, even before he spoke, that Josh was American. The perfect, gleaming teeth were the first clue. And the smile. No Irish person would ever walk into a room smiling. The slightly too-loud voice, the confident posture. All the usual clichés, including a strong jaw and glowing skin. The dimple in his chin is a little much though.

'I'm Kobi's handler, programmer, manager – whatever you want to call it. My actual title is robot engineer. Kobi's been programmed to think of me as a mentor. Everything that Kobi does, everything that he says and – in his view – everything that he thinks, has been programmed by me. He's quite something.'

*You're quite something.* Josh doesn't look like any engineer I've ever seen. I know engineers. My father was an engineer. Nothing wrong with being a nerd, but they are nerds. They're *into* stuff. *Really* into stuff.

Josh crosses the room in two strides and places a neat laptop bag on a table. He removes some documents from the bag.

'These are just a couple of nondisclosure agreements I'm gonna need you to sign today. And this bag contains everything you need to know about Kobi. Well, almost everything. It has my number too – call me anytime, 24/7, with any questions or issues.'

He looks directly at me as he says this. I'm unprepared for the clarity of his blue eyes. All I can do is nod.

'I'd like to know a bit more about two things,' I manage eventually. 'Um… can you tell us about Kobi's last assignment? And what do you hope to get out of his experience with us? In other words, why is he here? Sorry, that's three questions…'

I decide to just trail off. Better than going into full McGettigan interrogation mode. Shane sometimes calls me McGuessAgain – says I fire out question upon question without waiting for answers in between. Although, if ever a full inquisition was warranted, surely it's now?

'Yeah, Kobi has quite the back story actually.'

Josh smiles, leans against a high chair back, folds his arms. He seems relaxed but talks fast.

'He's a prototype for an advanced collaborative robot we hope to launch on the market in a year or so. He's done some great work already, but he's still a work in progress. Not only is he the most dextrous robot in the world, he can walk over challenging terrain, and he can even jump a little bit – but where he truly excels is in his cognitive abilities, his speech recognition and his response times. We've even tried to give him a sense of humour. I think you'll find him both intelligent and entertaining. You can speak to him almost as if he's human. In fact, this is where you guys come in.'

I'm taking notes on my phone, but each time I look up I'm struck anew by Josh's good looks. *He looks like he should be on a surfboard, not programming a motherboard*, I imagine myself telling Shane. He would laugh at that.

Josh continues, 'He needs to fit in. He needs to work on his emotional intelligence – or at least the robot version of it. Think of him as a sort of "empathy intern". He needs to get better at listening and responding appropriately to human interaction.'

'He's not the only one around here who could do with getting better at that.' I smile.

Josh laughs a big American laugh. 'You get this! You work in IT, right? You're one of us.'

I shoot JP a panicked look. *See, another reason why this is a bad idea.* 'Ah, actually, no. Our head of IT, Jen, isn't here today,' I mumble.

'Jen will support Maeve where she has capacity, but I'm happy for Maeve here to be the day-to-day point of contact,' says JP.

Josh's smile falters, then returns, like the sun momentarily hidden by a cloud.

'Okay, sure. I'll be coming in to check on Kobi every few days anyway, to recalibrate him where needed. If you can help us make him better, you'll be doing us a great favour. In fact, Ron himself has taken a great personal interest in Kobi's progress here.'

JP perks up at the mention of Ron. 'He's not with you today, is he?'

'No, he couldn't make it today,' says Josh quickly. 'He's on with Tokyo all afternoon. Maybe next time.'

I try to calculate the time difference but can't quite manage it. I have a vague sense that it's midnight on the other side of the world.

'Anyway, time to introduce you to Kobi now,' says Josh, moving towards the door.

'Wait – you haven't told us about his last job yet,' I say.

But Josh is already halfway out the door. 'Right, right. Listen, that's a long story. I think maybe we should talk about it another day. My number's in the bag – give me a call. But now, if you're both ready, I'm gonna get Kobi in here. Just act natural around him. The world of Robot Relationship Management awaits!'

A few minutes later, Josh reappears and holds the door open for our new colleague. Kobi is tall, as tall as Josh, and mostly made of what looks like gleaming white plastic, with articulated limbs. His face is a little disconcerting at first. He has features that can move, but thankfully, no effort has been made to make it look like a human face.

'Hello, how can I help you today? My name is Kobi. I hope we may get to know each other well.'

His voice sounds robotic, but it's not altogether unpleasant.

Josh referred to Kobi as 'he' and I notice myself automatically doing the same thing. I tell Kobi my name and say that I'm happy to meet him, just like I'd greet any new colleague.

JP stands in front of Kobi and stares up at him, then starts to walk around him. Kobi initiates a sort of shuffling movement, and the pair maintain pace and visual contact as they go around. When they get back to where they started, Kobi says, 'Thank you for the dance.'

I can't help but laugh. 'That's funny.'

'It is something I have heard humans say to each other in door-ways and corridors when they meet face-to-face,' Kobi explains. 'But if you like jokes, I have every joke ever recorded right here.' He illuminates a video screen in his chest plate. 'I can search by topic, keyword, name of comedian. At my last place of employ-ment, my co-workers sometimes asked me to show them funny internet videos at lunchtime.'

'You must have been very popular,' says JP, in a tone I can't quite judge. Then he makes his voice louder. 'I'm John Patrick Horgan, by the way. But everyone round here calls me JP, so you can too. I'm Maeve's boss and we're giving her the special assign-ment of looking after you. Ron Tron is a personal friend of mine. I hope that he gets what he wants from you being here among us. I'm sure he's told you all about me and the setup here.'

'Actually,' says Josh, 'we preferred for Kobi to know as little as possible in advance of this assignment. We're testing how quickly he can adapt to new environments.'

I hear Josh murmur to Kobi, 'Good job, buddy – you're doing great.'

'Right so,' says JP, clapping his hands once. 'Let's get you settled in. I suppose we'll treat you like any other newbie. Maeve can give you the grand tour on Monday and we'll go easy on you today seeing as it's Friday afternoon. Although... do robots get the weekend off? Maeve, look into that, will you?'

'Actually,' Josh says again, this time in a slightly higher pitch, 'Kobi's batteries are running pretty low right now. I was going to install his power bed somewhere for you and show you how to tuck him in at night. These multimillion-dollar robots need to get their rest, y'know! Maeve, let me walk you through the procedure.'

'He can start properly on Monday then, I suppose,' says JP. 'Okay, Maeve, off ye go – try not to break him too soon, will you? What would Ron say?'

# FOUR

*Monday, 7:15am*

'Jen!' I throw my bag down on the seat opposite her in the half-empty carriage. 'I wasn't expecting to see you on the early train.'

'I could say the same about you, mate.' She smiles at me as she removes her earbuds. She looks tired, her eyes puffy behind her tortoiseshell-framed glasses.

'What are you listening to?' I ask.

She pats her bump. 'Podcast. *Relax, It's Only a Baby.*'

'Any good?'

'Not bad. It's only patronising about fifty per cent of the time. Most of the pregnancy books are around seventy-five per cent schoolteacher vibes.'

I laugh. Jen Mason is probably the closest thing I have to a friend at Go Ireland – apart from Shane, who I refuse to put into any category. It's not that it's hard for me to make friends. I've had so many different jobs and lived in so many places – some might say I collect friends like stamps in a passport. Which, I'm starting to suspect, is not necessarily a good thing.

I don't know Jen that well, but we live along the same train line so we often chat on the commute. Like many Australians, she's both forthcoming and informal, so I know several intimate details about her. Such as, she used a sperm donor that she and her wife chose from a catalogue. She has a half-sister in Australia who she misses terribly. She uses body lotion on her face.

'So, there was some robot excitement at the office on Friday?' she asks. I emailed her a summary of events late Friday afternoon, punctuated with exclamation points, crying-laughing emojis and disappearing-into-a-bush GIFs. 'You know, this could be a golden opportunity for you.'

I search her face for signs of her customary dry sarcasm but find none. 'Really?'

'You've been saying you wanted to do something different, right? Something new?'

I *have* been saying that, but Jen doesn't know me well enough to know that I also just *get* like this. Itchy feet. That *urge*. Some people call it the spirit of adventure. Dad said I tried on jobs like they were coats. English language teacher. Yoga instructor. Bicycle repair person. Marketing executive. But it's not like philosophy graduates go on to become philosophers.

'New is good...' I say to Jen.

'Right, so Robot Relationship Management, as it's called, is a thing – or soon will be. It's already massive in South Korea and it's making its way here. Remember that conference I dragged you along to? "Robots in the Workplace"?'

'I remember the snacks were high quality.'

'Well, that was no accident. This is a new industry. Lots of money floating around. Yeah, it's still unclear what exactly it's all about, but it seems to be an optimistic mishmash of robotics, human resources and workplace psychology. They need someone to make sure humans and robots can work together in harmony.' She takes a perfectly green apple out of her bag and crunches into it before continuing. 'From what I can make out, this RoboTron robot sounds juicy.'

'Juicy?' For a second I wonder if she's just describing the fruit she's eating.

'How many people are working with robots right now? And not just any robot. Not like those automated checkout robots that can't tell the difference between a red pepper and a child's hand. Or one of those cleaner-bots they have in hospitals. Or a server bot bringing you pad Thai in a restaurant.'

'This really sounds more like your thing than my thing. Couldn't you' – I hear my voice turn pleading – 'take it off my hands? I'm sure if you'd been in on Friday, JP would have called you in on it.'

She produces a packet of rice cakes, holds it out to me. I shake my head.

'Ordinarily, I'd be all over this like a rash, yeah. But the reason I wasn't in on Friday is the same reason I can't get involved. Had to see the doc about my high blood pressure.' She places one hand on her bump. 'Doc says I need to avoid stress if I want to give this little parasitic bundle of joy the best chance. But don't worry, you'll do fine. These machines are so advanced. Honestly, I've heard it's almost like babysitting.'

I consider pointing out that if it's so easy, maybe she could be the one to lead The Kobi Project, and wouldn't some practice at babysitting be good for an expectant mother? But I don't. Because I know several other things about Jen Mason. Like how hard she works. Not only is she the head of IT, she's the only person working in IT, catering to the needs of thirty-odd staff. Some more odd than others. She remembers everyone's birthday and sends them a personalised e-card on the day, which she takes great pains to design. She's going to be a great mother.

'I'll help out whenever I can,' she says. 'Why don't you bring it down my office today and we'll have a chat? Meanwhile, and maybe more importantly, I want to know what you got up to at the weekend. Any dates?'

Like many people who have been in happy relationships for years, Jen takes an enthusiastic interest in the love life of singles. She likes to get detailed reports on my latest dating disasters. She's taken to calling our Monday morning catch-up 'match highlights', like it's a game she missed at the weekend.

'None this weekend. To be honest I was too tired after... Thursday.' My history of Shane hookups is one of those open secrets. There's an unspoken, collective agreement at the office that we don't talk about it, so that we can all continue to work together with minimal awkwardness. Jen has been known to break the agreement, however, so I try to steer her away from the topic. I need to offer her something as a distraction.

'I didn't go out on any dates... but I did get a chance to finalise my Dating Formula,' I tell her, hoping she'll take the bait.

'That sounds romantic,' she says, spreading hummus on a rice cake.

'I think you'll agree I kind of need it. It helps me figure out if I should keep seeing someone or not. You know how messy it is out there.' I gesture towards the train window just as another train hurtles past us on the opposing track. I switch into pretend-lawyer mode to make my case. 'Let's consider my last three dates. There was the guy who fell asleep within the first half hour – he claimed exhaustion from work but it was hard to get past that. Then there was the guy who called his car his "girlfriend". And the guy who called his games console "she who must be obeyed".'

Jen laughs. 'Fair enough. Okay, hit me with this formula.'

I take a deep breath. 'Okay, here goes. I call it CCSS. It stands for Conversation – Chemistry – Sense of humour – Safety.'

'CCSS,' she repeats, like she's mulling it over.

'Yep, if any one of those elements is missing from a first date, it won't work out. You might as well call time of death right there and then.'

'Okay, let's see,' she says. 'Conversation – can you have the chats together? Okay, fair. Chemistry – that's a good one. Sense of humour – a classic, an essential. What do you mean by "safety" though?'

'Hard to put into words exactly. I just mean fundamentally

safe, physically and mentally. They won't murder you in your sleep, et cetera.'

'I feel like that last one is a pretty low bar?'

'You'd be surprised,' I say.

The train chugs to a stop as we reach our destination.

'Wait a minute,' says Jen. 'Don't you already have those four elements with Shane?'

I pretend not to hear her over the automated announcement that tells us, 'This train will now terminate.' I jump up from my seat, busy myself gathering up Jen's things. I need to focus on the day ahead.

# FIVE

'Good morning, Maeve. How can I help you today?' Kobi says as soon as I've powered him up.

Josh installed Kobi's temporary sleep pod here in the Liffey Room on Friday, walking me through the robot's various sleep modes and battery settings. He maintained that at least this element of robot babysitting is straightforward.

A slight movement in Kobi's head and neck gives me the impression he's scanning me from head to toe. Which is confirmed when he announces, 'Maeve, you appear to be tired and somewhat anxious. Also, you are ovulating.'

I spit out my peppermint tea. I find a napkin and dab at my face, searching for an appropriate response. 'That's... uh... that's a funny thing to say, Kobi.'

But this only triggers a loud, robotic laugh.

'Kobi! Let's settle you down. Oh God, maybe I need to adjust your settings already.'

I eye a small control panel on the robot's lower left side. There was a diagram of it in the paperwork Josh gave me. A gushing paragraph about an intuitive user interface.

Kobi moves back two paces and lowers his voice. 'Josh will be disappointed if he hears my settings were adjusted within my first hour on the job. I am sorry if I have spoken incorrectly. Please, forgive me.'

I sigh. 'It is your first day, I suppose. A big day for both of us.'

*Maybe we both need time to adjust.* I decide to be breezy.

'Okay, well, JP wants me to present you to the rest of the staff at our team meeting this morning. It'll be a chance for you to meet everyone. I'll bring you over there now.'

As we make our way to the Shannon Suite, I give a version of the same speech Shane and I heard on our first day here. The Go Ireland organisation is an administrative and governance hub for tourism agencies and related service providers across Ireland. It also provides tourist information – online and over the phone – and houses a small gift shop.

The gift shop is on the ground floor, with public access. The five floors above contain staff offices and meeting rooms. The staff café is in the basement. Tourists sometimes try to access this café, and we have to explain to them that they're not welcome. There's a big museum next door, we tell them, with a much nicer café. And a lovely park outside.

In the Shannon Suite, I settle Kobi in near the top of the room and watch as my colleagues arrive one by one for the all-staff meeting. No sign of Shane yet. He's invariably late for these meetings, of course, but by now he's mastered the art of opening and closing the door without making a sound, so his late arrival usually goes unnoticed by the short-sighted JP. The trick, Shane says, is to place both hands on the door and use your full body weight to lean in slowly for a gradual opening; once inside, immediately turn round and grab the door by the handle with both hands, but – and this bit is key – resist the temptation to push the door closed quickly. Your patience will be rewarded by a gentle, satisfied sigh as the door returns home to the loving embrace of the door frame.

Two Mondays ago, when Shane was halfway through his 'ninja stealth door manoeuvre', Imelda from accounts tried to enter the room. Her elaborately made-up face appeared in the closing gap of the heavy wooden door, painted eyebrows arching up in panic. Shane had refused to let her in, simply shaking his head repeatedly at her as he continued his door delivery with midwife-level devotion. The second he released the door, he nimbly sidestepped away and slid into the nearest chair at the back of the room, stretching out his legs and slumping his shoulders. When Imelda punched the door open a moment later, everyone – including Shane – turned around to see who dared to be late for the meeting. Imelda fumbled her way to a seat, almost tripping over Shane's legs in the process.

To my surprise, at 8:59am, Shane stumbles in, rumpled and sleepy-eyed. He gives me an encouraging nod and a smile. At 9am on the dot, JP makes his way to the top of the room and gives a long, rambling introduction about 'the future' and 'embracing innovation' – most of which he reads off printed-out pages, naturally. Eventually he calls on me and Kobi to come up.

'Thank you, JP.' I address the room. 'Well, I don't think I need any slides for my presentation today, do I?' I gesture towards Kobi beside me, wait for a response to this little joke. When none comes, I clear my throat and continue. *Tough crowd.*

I'm suddenly nervous, so I read my few prepared bullet points from my phone. 'Today I want to introduce you to our new colleague, Kobi. We'd appreciate it if you'd give him the warm welcome that Go Ireland is known for. Kobi is a collaborative robot. He was designed primarily for use on factory floors. But a gap in his schedule of assignments has opened up, and we've been offered a wonderful opportunity to enjoy the benefits of Kobi's presence for the next while. During this time, he'll be observing what we do here while developing his interpersonal skills, so please do interact with Kobi as much as you can. He learns from every encounter.'

I go on to talk about RoboTron, give some details on Kobi's processing capabilities and advanced systems. Then I turn to my robot companion. 'Kobi, would you like to say a few words?'

I watch in fascination as Kobi adjusts his facial features. His eyes grow bigger and rounder; his mouth shapes itself into a sort of smile. 'Thank you for welcoming me here. I look forward to working with you all. I will learn so much here.'

Dave from customer relations raises his hand. Dave wears short sleeves year-round. He says it's because he doesn't feel the cold, but I suspect it's to show off his many tattoos. He's a fourth-generation Dubliner and never tires of reminding people that he is 'the original and the best'. When I first met him, I pointed out that he'd taken this phrase from an old TV commercial for crackers. 'Exactly, Maeve. Exactly,' he'd said.

Now he says, 'Eh, can I ask a question?'

Kobi bows slightly and says, 'Clearly, you can.'

'Yeah, cool. Eh, just wondering... are you going to be, like, spying on us? I've read about these military robots – they have stealth cameras that can record things miles away.'

Kobi does his robot laugh, which unfortunately has an unsettling effect. 'I will not be spying.'

Dave's desk mate Julia – pretty, effortlessly stylish – speaks up. 'But you *will* be observing us. Maeve just said that.'

I go to answer, but Kobi has already started speaking. 'Yes. My observation skills are excellent.'

Dave again. 'I've read about these workplace robots. Supposed to make things more efficient. They're really there to make *people* more efficient. Monitoring their bathroom breaks, not letting them have lunch. Then they start replacing people altogether.'

Julia: 'We're not allowed to have lunch now?'

I rush to answer. 'Of course we're still having lunch! In fact, lunchtime would be a great time for Kobi to observe... I mean, to interact... I mean, to have lunch with you.'

'What does he eat?' asks Dave. 'Megabytes?' This gets a big laugh from Julia but no one else.

'And he's *not* going to be reporting on us?' asks Julia.

'Kobi reports to me,' I say, frustrated. I look at JP in case I'm overstepping but he's staring into the middle distance, probably not even listening. 'Kobi, you're not going to be writing any reports about staff, are you?'

'No,' says Kobi. 'Although I could run a productivity report, if that would be helpful.'

An audible gasp goes around the room, followed by extensive murmuring.

I lower my voice. 'Kobi, I don't think that's a good idea.'

JP returns to the present. He stands up. 'Well, I think a productivity report sounds just grand. Sure HR does one every couple of years anyway. There's nothing to be afraid of. Isn't that right, Sandra?' JP looks around for reassurance from the HR rep but fails to locate her.

'She's not here,' says Dave. 'Kobi, make a note that Sandra missed the compulsory staff meeting.'

'Noted, thank you,' says Kobi.

'This is all happening very fast,' I say, trying to regain control. 'As JP says, it's just a report – people write reports all the time. And as you know, most reports never actually get read. It's not a big deal. I think we're losing sight of the big picture here.'

I scan the room and meet Shane's eye. He looks relaxed. I take a breath and speak more slowly. 'Kobi could actually help us to do our work better. In fact' – I'm getting an idea and decide to roll with it – 'by the end of this week, I promise you Kobi will have made work easier for at least two people at Go Ireland.'

'Is it you and JP?' asks Dave. 'Or Sandra and JP?'

'Two people who are not me, JP or Sandra,' I say.

JP claps his hands together. 'Well, there you go! I, for one, am fully in support of this development. Now, I think that's all the time we have for our meeting today. Let's get to work.'

I exhale and gather my things as people begin leaving the room in small groups. They seem to have a lot to say to each other.

Shane approaches me with a big grin on his face. *Why is he always in a good mood, even on a Monday morning?* 'Are you okay? You were getting some seriously negative vibes there. I felt bad for you.'

I try to smile, but it feels forced. 'Thanks.'

'If there's any way I can help, you know where I am.'

At least he's on my side, I suppose. 'We'll see how it goes. Kobi, come on – let's find you some work to do.'

Shane reverses himself towards the door, apparently so he can keep smiling at me as he leaves. 'I better get back to my desk too. Gotta get my productivity levels up.'

# SIX

After a bumpy start at the team meeting, I decide to take refuge in a safe place. The IT department seems like the natural home for a robot, and besides, I want to see what Jen thinks of Kobi.

She wasn't at the staff meeting because she's on a deadline to revamp the entire Go Ireland website. She says she's taking it from the nineteenth century into the twentieth century. Every time I meet Jen she finds a new, innovative way to describe how under-resourced she is:

'I'm ten pensioners short of a conga line.'

'I'm like a kangaroo trying to strangle itself.'

'I've about as much budget as a gambling addict in a casino who's just put everything on red.'

She claims these expressions are common Australian parlance, but I strongly suspect that she's just enjoying herself at our expense.

We begin making our way to the third floor. I need to slow my pace to keep step with Kobi, who's really not quite the nimble athlete Josh has built him up to be. Maybe he's stiff? Could I put some oil on those joints? I open my phone, make a note to ask Josh about this. *Josh – lubrication?* I add a cheeky winky face, for the craic.

'Maeve, may I ask what my duties will be here at Go Ireland?' Kobi asks me.

No small talk then. Eager to get to work. No wonder this is the future.

'We – I – haven't quite figured that out yet. You were kind of a surprise for us, Kobi. We didn't really have time to make a plan for you. But what we'll do is… Yes, this is what we'll do… We'll see how you get on with various tasks and then settle you wherever your strengths are.'

'I am very strong,' says Kobi. 'If you need me to lift heavy boxes, I am proficient in that area.'

I think of the boxes of unused summer brochures in the store-room that need to be recycled. 'I'm sure you'll be very helpful.'

I lead him towards the elevator.

We get in and the elevator of course does its usual passive-aggressive failure to recognise my voice. I sigh. 'Oh, this thing is useless. Someone should put it out of its misery.'

'Please, Maeve, allow me,' says Kobi. 'Stand aside.'

It makes sense – a machine would be more likely to recognise another machine's voice. I stand back as Kobi positions himself in front of the call-button panel. I whip out my phone to triumphantly text Shane that I've finally managed to hack the elevator. I'm searching for the exact right GIF to send that signifies relief, cleverness and I-do-know-what-I'm-doing when a flash of light catches my eye.

The panel innards spew forth like entrails as Kobi raises his arm to show me a bunch of wires grasped in his digits. A tiny fire-works display sputters, then all the lights go out.

'Omigod, Kobi!' I bundle him out of the compartment. 'Why did you *do* that?'

'You informed me that this machine was no longer useful,' he says, cool as an air-conditioning unit. 'I merely tried to be helpful, as we discussed.'

'Argh. How would you like it if someone decided to suddenly shut you down?'

He responds by telling me that he is routinely switched off and on, tweaked and prodded, repaired and rebooted.

'Fair enough,' I falter. 'Just stand there for a minute, okay? Don't touch anything.'

I log an alert with building maintenance. Was this my fault? Did I not communicate clearly enough? Josh said that Kobi was highly sophisticated, with months of bespoke programming.

With the elevator out of order, we have to take the stairs. Kobi assures me that he can climb a staircase, and while technically this turns out to be true, it takes us a good ten minutes to ascend the first flight.

'I have always known that stairs would be the death of me,' he says, and I can't tell if he's joking or being dramatic so I choose to ignore the comment.

We eventually arrive at the IT department. I hesitate outside the door.

'Listen, Kobi, let's not tell Jen that we broke the elevator, okay?' I feel very generous saying 'we'. 'It should be fixed very soon.' *Hopefully before Jen needs to descend four flights of stairs to get to the staff café.* I'll offer to bring lunch up to her. She often works through without a break.

'I am afraid I am incapable of deception, Maeve.'

Of course he is. 'Haven't you heard of white lies?'

'Yes, Maeve. The human capacity for deception is fascinating. But it is not part of my programming.'

'Fine,' I say. 'In that case, let me do the talking, okay?'

'With pleasure,' he says, and for a second I wonder if he was programmed to have a sarcastic streak.

We enter the room, Kobi shuffling in behind me. Jen is right to complain about under-resourcing. Every surface appears to be home to a piece of equipment in some state of rehabilitation. But at least the budget has been stretched to pay for a mini-fridge in the corner, stocked almost entirely with Diet Coke cans. I'm reminded that Jen's nickname around the office is 'DC', on account of her addiction. Shane was the first one to christen her that, and the label was so sticky that everyone calls her that now, even though DC is also Duncan Canning's initials. It's unclear what Duncan's feelings on the matter are.

'Hey, DC! Jen – I wanted to introduce you to Kobi. He's the robot – the cobot – who's going to be with us for a little while.'

Jen swivels around in her chair to face us, looks Kobi up and down. 'Nice to meet you, Kobi. I'm the IT manager, but I don't suppose you'll be needing much help from me. I imagine you're way more advanced than any of the machines we have around here.'

She gestures to a couple of old laptops and PCs sitting open on a nearby desk, surrounded by empty Diet Coke cans. The machines look like they're doing long and elaborate software updates, guarded by a tiny army of silver soldiers. 'I just fix them up as best I can. If budget was a river, I'd be sailing through a desert, using dry sand for a paddle, do you know what I mean?'

I laugh. Kobi is quiet. I realise he's probably following my instruction to let me do the talking. I doink my elbow against his arm. 'It's okay. You can answer her.'

'It is a pleasure to meet you. I believe I do know what you mean. It is a metaphor to emphasise a lack of financial resources.'

Jen laughs. 'Fair dues, mate.' She rolls across the floor in her chair to get a closer look at Kobi. 'You are a fascinating creation.'

'Thank you,' he says. 'Likewise.'

She laughs again, looks at me. 'Maeve, I have to say I'm a bit jealous right now. You're going to have so much fun with this guy.'

'Do you think so? You weren't at the meeting this morning. It wasn't exactly the land of a thousand welcomes.'

She raises her eyebrows above her frames. 'Hey, Kobi, do you want to take a look at the Go Ireland website for a few minutes? I'm in the middle of a revamp. You might find it interesting to learn more about the company.'

She settles Kobi at a workstation, then takes me to one side. 'What'd your guy say on Friday, the guy from RoboTron?'

I think back to the hour I spent with Josh in the Liffey Room. He explained things in a way that seemed clear and simple. He didn't seem to think it bizarre and strange that I should be the one chosen to babysit a multimillion-dollar robot under minimal supervision. I can't wait for Josh to come back, to be honest. And maybe not just to check on Kobi. He seems like the kind of person who has stories to tell. Because he's done things, has some sort of life. He seems like a grown-up.

'He said he wanted Kobi to improve how he responds to humans,' I tell Jen. 'To fit in better in the workplace.'

'Ah. Interesting.'

'Why? What do you mean?'

'Well, think about it. How do you measure that?'

'I hope that's a rhetorical question. Jen, AI is not my strong suit. You're the one with the IT skills.'

'This is exactly my point. To help him fit in, you don't actually need IT skills. What you're really measuring is the human response to the robot. Do the rest of the gang like him? Scratch that – do they *accept* him? That's all you need to do, mate. Can't be that hard. He seems harmless enough.'

I exhale. 'Well, he is eager to help. That's got to be a good thing, right?'

We both smile and look over at Kobi. That's when I notice it. The fine white lead emerging from his midsection. I follow the length of it with my eyes. It's connected to the laptop's USB port.

Jen rushes over to him. 'Mate, what are you up to there?'

I recognise the Go Ireland home page on the screen. Something looks different, but I can't quite put my finger on it.

'You are welcome,' says Kobi as Jen yanks the lead out of the computer.

She stares at the screen. 'Oh no.' She whispers it so quietly it sends chills up my spine.

She hurls herself into her swivel chair, lands back at her desk with a clatter. She stares intently at the screen as she bangs at the keyboard. 'No, no, no.'

'Kobi!' I turn to him. 'What did you do?'

'DC Jen asked me to assist with the company website. And you spoke of gen AI. Even though generative AI is not my area of expertise, I was able to connect the website to a new tool that is most efficient. It can generate new words and images from old ones. Thus, I have refreshed the website with minimal financial investment. I believe DC Jen might call it "paddling with sand".'

Kobi seems to think he's done us a great favour, but Jen's reaction suggests otherwise. 'Jen, what's happened?'

She doesn't look at me. 'Snakes on a bike, unbelievable! He's only gone and replaced all the text and images with random nonsense. This is a disaster.'

I move closer to the laptop, peer at the Go Ireland website. Everything is the same, yet everything is different. Where the tagline across the top used to say, 'Welcome to Go Ireland,' the text now reads, 'The top of the mornin' to ye!' Our sophisticated colour palette is now lurid green; shamrocks pulsate across the page like shooting stars. I squint at the images of tourists enjoying their time in Ireland – their smiles are too big, their fingers too many. We're now in the business of day trips to Uncanny Valley, apparently.

Jen turns to the mini-fridge by her desk, opens it with one foot. I rush over to grab a can for her. 'This is gonna take me all day to fix. At least.'

'Oh, Jen, I'm so sorry. I didn't know he was going to—'

She cuts me off. 'Look, just get him out of here, okay?'

I herd Kobi towards the door, then turn back in the doorway.

'I'll bring you up some lunch,' I say, suddenly remembering the broken elevator.

She doesn't look at me. 'Don't worry about it – I won't have time for lunch today.'

# SEVEN

*11am*

We trundle back along the corridor, a fluttering in my stomach. Not the good kind – I feel terrible. Jen has enough on her plate already.

'Kobi, you can't *do* things like that.'

I want to get through to him that he's off to a bad start. He's just gotten on the wrong side of the one person who was excited about him being here – apart from JP, maybe. I look Kobi up and down, frustrated. 'I don't know. Can't you just be... normal?'

He stops abruptly, bows his head a few inches. For a moment, he appears completely non-functional. Then lights in his chest panel start illuminating in sequence, like Morse code.

'Normalising settings,' he announces. 'Settings normalised.' He resumes his slow march forward.

*Oh God, what was that? And was it good or bad?* I feel a cold sweat coming on.

'Stop for a second. Did I just change something?' I do a quick body scan, although I don't actually know what I'm looking for. 'Wait, do you have a "normal" setting?'

Kobi stops walking, triggers a disturbing robotic laugh. 'No. Do you?'

I'm confused. 'Do I what? Do I have a normal setting? Um… no?'

'No,' he agrees.

'Wait. So that was just…?'

'A joke,' he says.

'A joke?'

'Correct.'

I don't know whether to laugh or cry. I have so many questions, but I reach for the closest one. 'But why?'

'I sensed tension. I know that humans like to relieve tension with humour.'

I can't help but laugh, remembering a phrase that Shane likes to use any time something ridiculous happens: 'The mirthless laughter of the damned.' My mirthless laugh brings me some relief in spite of myself, as does the sight of the maintenance guy heading towards us with his toolbox. But I'd rather not have to explain to him what happened to the elevator, so I steer Kobi towards the end of the corridor, where the customer relations team work. 'Maybe we'll just pop in here for a bit.'

This department was my old turf until nine months ago, when Shane and I were both promoted to client liaison positions in marketing. Neither of us had particularly wanted the new role, but it promised a little more money and less customer-facing time. I'm still not sure what the customer relations gang think about my move. We enter the open plan, but there's hardly anyone on the floor.

I look at my watch. 'Oh, they must all still be on tea break,' I tell Kobi.

'I do not understand why tea break is necessary,' he says. 'The working day commenced 120 minutes ago. My battery charge lasts six hours.'

I sigh. 'Keep your voice down, will you? Think of it like this:

humans need regular fuel to do good work. Sometimes the fuel comes in the form of coffee, or tea. Sometimes the fuel is a conversation, or sharing a joke with someone.'

I find that I've automatically walked over to the cubicle area where Shane and I worked. Dave and Julia now occupy these desks. They installed themselves almost the second we left, claiming we'd been hogging a prime position where no one could walk behind our workstations, thus ensuring screen privacy at all times.

I stand in front of my old desk, remembering last summer, when Shane went through a phase of leaving Post-it notes stuck to my screen while I was away from my desk. He'd doodle a cartoon version of himself escaping work in increasingly ludicrous ways. Sawing a hole in the floor around his chair. Jumping from the window ledge wearing wings made from photocopier paper. Drinking poison, dying, becoming an angel but then having to work in a very similar job in God's office. I smile to myself at the memory.

I look up to see Dave and Julia approaching. 'Hey, guys! I wanted you to meet Kobi on a more personal level. Answer any more questions you had after this morning's meeting. And, you know, maybe see if he could help you in some way?' I try to keep my tone light, hoping they won't realise the extent to which this is already spinning out of my control.

'What's the story?' says Dave by way of greeting. No one loves using Dublin vernacular more than Dave. I told him I was born in Dublin, but because I grew up in other places, he was singularly unimpressed. Although something tells me that Dave is only really interested in being impressed by Julia. He bounces into his seat, stretches his arms overhead. I notice what looks like a new tattoo – a rabbit with an arrow through its heart.

'Hi, Maeve. Hi, Kobi.' Julia glances at Dave. 'What an honour that you've chosen our department for improvement.'

*Whoa.* I should have gone to tea break today. God knows what people have been saying to each other about Kobi. Dave was prob-ably riling them all up with his conspiracy theories. 'I didn't say improvement, Julia. I said help.'

'Yeah, we all know what "help" is code for,' she says spikily.

'What is it code for?' Kobi asks. 'I am always interested in code.'

Dave laughs. Julia joins in. Although I'm glad they're laughing, I feel like I'm not included in the joke. I try to defend myself.

'Hey, I'm not the bad guy. It wasn't my idea for Kobi to be here.' I look at the robot, standing alert beside me, awaiting instruction. I feel a little pang. I remember what it's like to be new. 'Sorry, Kobi. I'm glad you're here.' *Let him process that little white lie.*

'It is nice to be here,' Kobi says. I almost feel sorry for him.

'Dave and Julia do the job that I used to do here – customer service. Julia, do you want to describe your job to Kobi?'

'Sure,' she says, settling in at her workstation with just a hint of an eye roll. 'We answer the phone and emails. It's mostly tourists looking for advice: where's the best place to go, to stay, to eat – that kind of thing. But most of the information is already on our website, so it's usually just a case of directing people to the right place.'

The website. *Oh no.* How long until somebody notices a prob-lem? How long until Jen can fix it? And is there any chance of the latter being faster than the former?

At least Kobi provides a distraction. 'It surprises me,' he says, 'that given the advances in voice automation technology, humans are still required to answer telephones.'

'Kobi!' I cough and try to elbow him, but my arm just clunks against solidness and elicits no response.

''Sokay,' says Dave. 'As a matter of fact, the company did try to bring in voice automation for phone queries a couple of years ago. Remember that summer, Jules? But come August they got rid of it. Said it was too impersonal – the tourist experience should begin the moment you first speak to someone in Ireland. We're *authentic*, apparently.' He leans back in his chair, basking in his apparent authenticity.

As if on cue, Dave's and Julia's phones both begin to buzz gently. 'See, the hotline is ringing again. It never stops.'

'I'll get it,' says Julia. Her voice pitches to a singsong as she answers. 'Go Ireland, this is Julia, how can I help?'

The rest of us do that thing where we remain silent, imagining what the voice on the other end of the line is saying.

Julia's eyes go wide. 'It says *what*? On our website? *Our* website? That can't be right.' She picks up a stress ball in the shape of an orange hedgehog, hurls it at Dave. She jabs her finger at her screen repeatedly.

Dave taps at his keyboard, frowns. 'This is nuts,' he mutters.

Clearly Jen hasn't been able to undo whatever Kobi did yet.

Julia finishes her call. 'Dave, have you seen this?'

'Looking at it now,' he says.

'What's the problem?' I regret asking as soon as I've said it.

I watch Julia's eyes scan her screen. 'The website... The text is... just... so... wrong. Where to start? It says here: "Leprechauns are a popular pet among the Irish, an extremely superstitious people. These small creatures are thought to bring good luck to the homestead."'

'Janey Mack,' says Dave. 'Check out the page about the Blarney Stone. "The Blarney Stone is believed to be a space rock deposited by aliens from the Planet Gab in the third century. Another name for the Blarney Stone is shamrock." This doesn't even make any sense.'

Julia laughs. 'It says here, "The national drink of Ireland is Guinness."'

'Well,' I begin, 'that's not far wrong.'

She interrupts. 'It says, "The Irish are drawn to darkness. They drink Guinness at breakfast time and at bedtime to ward off evil spirits."'

The phone buzzes again. I hear phones ring on other desks around the room.

Julia looks up at me. 'Sorry, Maeve, I don't know what's going on here, but we don't have time for you right now. You or your, your' – she shakes her head at Kobi – 'Tin Man.'

She shoos us away.

# EIGHT

*Noon*

> Help, I need you. Meet me under the Big Tree.

I hit send on the message to Shane and smile reassuringly at Kobi. Then quickly type a follow-up message.

> There might be something wrong with Kobi.

I'm trudging around the little park in front of the building. On brighter days this is my favourite place to have lunch. Today it feels like a refuge. A chestnut tree shivers its leaves at us, the first tinge of brown at the edges.

I look over at my silent companion. *Maybe he's nervous?* Here he is, a multimillion-dollar advanced AI system designed to make workplaces more efficient, taking a meditative stroll around a park. Somewhere, an accountant is breaking out in a fever, their sixth sense tingling at my profligate ways.

I consider going to JP or calling Josh. I try to imagine how the conversation will go. *Can you please just take away this walking, talking trash can? We don't want him*, I could say. But I know what will happen. JP will insist Kobi stays. And if I can't cope with it, JP will make Jen take over. Jen, who already has a lot going on. Jen, who's not supposed to have any stress…

If only I could keep Kobi away from the rest of the staff, at least until I can figure out how to improve his actions and interactions.

Standing under the Big Tree in the park, I flush with relief the moment I see Shane confidently striding towards me. There's another feeling too – a little pang of excitement. Has Shane gotten better looking recently? He's always had a mischievous grin and the muscle tone of someone who plays hurling twice a week – but does he seem taller these days? The mathematical part of my brain removes its glasses, leans forward and postulates a theory: objects that are closer appear larger. Am I getting in the habit of standing too close to Shane? Gazing up at him so he fills my field of vision?

He approaches me with a smirk and a glint in his eye. 'Well, where's the emergency?'

'Kobi, I urgently need to talk to my colleague about a private matter. Do you have a non-listening mode you can adopt?'

'No, I am programmed to always listen,' says Kobi. 'But if you like, I can face the tree and pretend not to listen. Would that help?'

'It'll have to do, I suppose. I'll just step over here a little bit.'

I take Shane by the arm and walk him ten feet away from where Kobi is now standing, his robotic face very close to the trunk of the Big Tree. Then I let out a long exhale and shake my hands as if they're wet and I can't find a towel. I speak quickly but quietly. 'I think I might be out of my depth.'

'It's going to be okay. What's up with your robot BFF?' He's still smiling at me. It's both attractive and maddening.

'Don't make fun of me right now, Shane. I think I might have been sold a pup. It all just seems a bit… wrong somehow.'

I lower my voice further, training my eyes on Kobi, who is now extending his robot arms and – is he? – yes, he is now apparently attempting to hug the tree. 'He's supposed to be this state-of-the-art robot, right? Supposed to get along with humans, help us do our jobs better? But this morning has been more like bringing a puppy to work that pees everywhere, then poops in your boss's lunchbox. I don't know how he's ever going to fit in.' I can feel the panic rising in my chest. 'He's supposed to meet HR this afternoon – God knows how that'll go. He'll probably recommend that we all be terminated.'

Shane raises an eyebrow.

'Terminated from our jobs, I mean, not terminated from... our lives.' I eye Kobi warily. He looks peaceful enough hugging the tree, like a robot hippie.

'Come on, Maeve, it can't be that bad. You're smart – you can figure it out. Just... tell me what you need. What can I do to help?'

'I need time, Shane – time to do some research, learn how he works. I can maybe try and adjust his settings. And I need to keep him away from the other staff during that time.' Time is all I need, apparently. Time and expertise and skills and...

'Okay, listen, I'm on gift shop duty all week.'

The gift shop is one of Go Ireland's quirks. All staff – apart from very senior management – have to do a stint in the shop in rotation. There's not quite enough work to justify it being a full-time job, and it saves them from having to pay someone properly to do it. So we all take turns, and moan about it endlessly.

'Why don't I take him in there with me?' says Shane. 'You know we don't get that many customers, and the ones we do – well, we can just say he's some weird Irish experiment or something. Lost in translation. Be grand.'

I exhale, resist the urge to hug him with relief. 'I suppose he could meet HR tomorrow instead. Okay – thank you, thank you, thank you. You're a genius.'

'I know sure.'

It's something. It's a start.

# NINE

*Tuesday, 2:30pm*

It's Kobi's second day at Go Ireland and the plan to hide him in the gift shop is going well. Granted, it's not a long-term plan, but time seems to have slowed down and I'm very focused on the present. Living moment to moment. My old yoga instructor would be thrilled. I spent the morning pressing various buttons on Kobi's control panel, each time asking him, 'What does this one do?'

I didn't go to tea break today either, but I did leave a big box of fancy donuts on the counter, with a note to say that they were 'from Kobi'. The robot might be new, but people are still people. It can't hurt.

I messaged Jen to see how the website restoration and upgrade was going. She sent back a thumbs-up and nothing more. I asked if she wanted to get lunch but she didn't reply, so Kobi, Shane and I spent lunchtime in the park together – Kobi announcing the Latin name of every single tree and plant within his field of vision, Shane listing the cast members of every movie he's seen in the last two weeks. All told, it was quite the information overload. Still, not an unpleasant way to pass the time.

Kobi has been asking a lot of questions about his surroundings, so now Shane offers to give him a tour of the gift shop. Shane explains that the shop was an afterthought to make use of a small annexe space on the ground floor of the building. He describes it as a 'vanity project' for JP's wife.

The shop is sparsely furnished. It's mostly empty space, in fact, with a few bits and bobs of tourism merch for sale next to a till on the counter. Despite the absence of furniture, the walls feel like they're closing in on you, due to the presence of three dozen or so paintings, displayed on every available wall surface.

I can tell Kobi is scanning the paintings. 'Maeve, may I ask what tool was used to create these images?'

Shane and I look at each other.

'It's probably not polite to call her a tool.' Shane holds my gaze. His mouth twitches at the corners.

'Stop,' I say, trying to straighten my own face. 'Kobi, these pictures weren't AI-generated. These were all made by Trish, my boss's wife.'

Shane stretches his arms out on either side, almost as if he's trying to push the paintings away. I can tell he's gearing up to deliver the speech he makes every time he has to do a stint in the gift shop. He tells Kobi there are only two types of visitor to the shop. The first is someone looking for the building exit who has gone wrong. The second is someone who dearly wants to buy what he calls 'some green tat'. Nobody ever buys the paintings.

'JP says if I ever manage to make a sale, I'll get a bonus. At first I tried really hard, but I've long since given up. It's impossible. I mean, look at these things – pure gak!'

The pictures – of people and landscapes – are all done in the same style: pale watercolours on canvas. But the proportions – of the faces and natural features – are, to put it mildly, not accurate to real life. To put it unmildly, it's like Dorian Gray went on an absolute bender while touring round Ireland, and we rented his attic while he was away.

We're interrupted, thankfully, by the entrance of a customer. Or, at least, a person. To call them a customer is a bit pre-emptive.

A fifty-something guy carrying a Science Museum tote bag. It's hard to tell if he's a hipster or just middle-aged.

Kobi turns to me. 'May I greet the customer?'

'Sure.' I can analyse how this interaction goes, see if there's any improvement on yesterday.

Kobi shuffles towards the man. 'Welcome to the gift shop. I hope that we may improve your day with these fine artworks.' He raises his arms up and out towards the paintings. I realise that he's copying the gesture Shane made a few moments ago.

'Oh!' Only now does the man appear to fully take in his surroundings. 'Did you... paint these?' He moves to one wall to take a closer look. 'Fascinating,' he says in a low voice. Then, louder, not looking at us: 'Is this part of that robot exhibition in the Science Museum next door?'

With, it has to be said, impressive speed, Shane adapts and applies himself to the new situation. He moves swiftly to stand next to Kobi, drapes his arm around the robot's shoulder.

'We're very lucky to have Kobi here with us. He's only here for a few weeks, then next stop Paris, Berlin, Budapest. He's an amazing creature really – it's fascinating, as you say, what he can produce.'

'Oh wow.' As the guy moves along the wall, still with his back to us, Shane brings his index finger to his lips and widens his eyes at me and Kobi.

Kobi asks, 'Why must we be quiet, Shane?'

Shane starts coughing loudly. 'Kobi, I think your battery might need recharging soon. Maybe you should go into sleep mode now, save a bit of energy.'

I consider intervening, but I'm curious about how this is going to play out.

'How much for this one?' The man points to a nightmarish depiction of the Cliffs of Moher. Ireland's number-one tourist attraction looks like three sea monsters who've grumpily awoken mid-nap and are now seeking revenge on all who gaze upon them.

'That one is only seventy-five euro,' says Shane without missing a beat. 'A bargain for such a unique perspective, don't you think?'

He's already taking the picture down from the wall and putting it into a bag at the till.

'Congratulations, you are our first customer,' Kobi says.

'Today. Our first *today*,' says Shane, reaching for the card held out by the customer.

'Hey, what's going on here?'

All four of us turn to see Josh in the doorway. He said he'd be in this week to check on Kobi but hadn't specified when. I've never been a huge fan of the pop-in. Even though I haven't done anything wrong, I find myself blurting out, 'It's not what it looks like!'

*What does it look like? Just a highly sophisticated robot helping to dupe a tourist into buying some bad art.* Okay, it's not an ideal scenario. But it's not the worst thing either. It's a grey area. Much like the Cliffs of Moher painting.

The tourist hesitates. He and Shane pause, each holding one end of the credit card above the counter. A mini tug of war begins. Eventually Shane releases the card from his grip. The man retreats and makes for the door.

Josh steps back to let him pass, then enters the room fully and seems to take up most of the space. Unexpectedly, he smiles at me and it's like a sunbeam cutting through the gloom. All the tension in my body releases. For a second I think he's advancing towards me, but he goes straight over to Kobi for an inspection.

'So, they have you working in a shop. Interesting!'

I laugh, relieved I'm not in trouble.

'This isn't a typical shop. We rarely get any customers. It's usually Tumbleweed City in here. By the way, this is my colleague Shane.'

Josh doesn't look at him as he says, 'Hi, Shane.'

He focuses his full attention on me. 'Maeve, I'm sorry I couldn't drop by sooner. But I want to hear all about the last twenty-four hours. I need to run a full diagnostic on Kobi, then can we go somewhere to talk?'

# TEN

*6pm*

I'm the one who suggests we go to Phelan's, the usual haunt for after-work drinks. I struggled to pick an appropriate venue for an unexpected meeting about a difficult robot with a good-looking, somewhat mysterious engineer. A restaurant would be way too date-like, and most cafés close frustratingly early for a city that's supposedly cosmopolitan. It's drink or die in this town, as Shane says.

Once Josh ran a few tests on Kobi, he was very eager for us to talk freely, but not on company property. Maybe he didn't want to risk being overheard by Kobi, who seems to have supersonic auditory abilities. So I find myself leading Josh to the local pub almost on autopilot, as if my footsteps were pre-programmed.

'Do you come here often?' Josh asks with a smile, holding the door open for me. We enter the bar to the soft hum of sober chitchat, its cadence pleasingly muted by the red velvet banquette seats and the occasional red velvet curtain.

A photo taken on a night out here circulated around the office recently. Me and Shane seated very close together, our upper bodies discreetly hidden by one of these red drapes, only our legs visible. Of course I knew my hope of keeping our dalliance a secret was naïve, but at least most people have refrained from openly asking questions about it, allowing us all to continue in the shared pretence that it isn't really happening.

'Only every Thursday,' I reply now cheerfully, 'with the work crowd. Spent many a long night in here and suffered the consequence the next morning.'

'Why not go drinking on Fridays instead?'

'Thursdays are for work friends. Fridays are for real friends. And for dates.' I don't know why I added that last bit. There must be a disconnect between my mind and my body. I'm too used to coming here to relax and have the craic. *Josh is not my new work colleague, up for some flirty banter*, I remind myself. *It's Kobi who's my new colleague*, I think with a twinge of disappointment.

'I love how the Irish don't let work get in the way of their drinking,' says Josh. *On second thoughts, maybe he is up for some banter*. I lead him to the high wooden bar, polished to a dull sheen by generations of elbows seeking support. 'I'm kidding, of course. Now, what can I get you from this fine establishment?'

I nod at the barman. I don't know his name, but I know him well enough to feel like I owe him an explanation for being here unexpectedly on a Tuesday evening, and with this stranger in tow. Maybe he thinks I'm on a date. A low-effort date, because I'm wearing my usual office garb of dark jeans, a plain top with a scoop neck and a casual suit jacket. He probably thinks Josh is out of my league – tall, handsome, clothes that look like they were selected with care.

Josh makes an executive decision and sits on one of the upholstered high-back chairs at the bar. I follow suit. By now I've figured out how to climb into one of these chairs in one smooth movement – not an easy feat for someone only five foot two. I wonder if the barman remembers the time I hit my chin on the bar when I tried to jump down gracefully in a hurry. Shane nearly spilled his drink laughing. Although he did offer me the ice from his Jameson and ginger – a kind gesture.

'Jameson and ginger, please.' I regret the words even as I hear them. Whiskey before 7pm? And on an empty stomach? Unless ginger ale counts as food. 'I hope I'm not reinforcing all those Irish stereotypes you Americans seem to believe.'

'Jameson and ginger sounds good to me.' He seems very relaxed. Like a friendly golden retriever. I notice that he's not in a rush to talk about Kobi. And neither am I.

'Can I ask how you ended up here?' I gesture vaguely at our surroundings. 'I mean, in Ireland?' I want to ask many more questions but instead take a sip of my drink, which has appeared in front of me miraculously quickly.

'Sure.' He takes a gulp from his own squat tumbler and exhales. His hands look large and capable. 'If you want the short version, I grew up in Portland, Oregon, got a scholarship to MIT, went to Silicon Valley, where I worked for a few tech companies. Met Ron Tron at a conference, met an Irish woman at the same conference, moved to Dublin. Ron put me on the Kobi project when I arrived.'

I feel myself deflate just a little at the words 'Irish woman'. But why should I care? I suspect that my mind is reaching out for anything that could provide a handy distraction from the current major stressor in my life: The Kobi Project.

'And when was that?'

'About three years ago.' Another slug of whiskey. 'Man, that tastes good.'

I get the sense that he's holding back. *Time for a little McGettigan probing.* 'So, things are going well then?'

He smiles into his glass. 'Yes.' The smile fades. 'Actually, no. Well... let's just say things are not exactly on the trajectory where I thought they'd be by now. I'm a little bit behind schedule.'

'Schedule? You mean work-wise?'

'Not just work. Life, too. You know the way you have a life schedule, a plan for how your life is going to go?'

Just like I suspected, Josh is a grown-up. A man with a plan, literally. 'Er... kind of?'

He laughs. 'I forget not everyone does this. My ex was always telling me I overplan.'

'Your ex? The Irish woman you met at the conference?' My mind races to download and process this new information. 'I'm... sorry?' But I'm vaguely aware that some small part of me has perked up.

'It's fine. *I'm* sorry – TMI, am I right? Must be the whiskey talking.'

I look down at Josh's glass. It appears to be empty already. The Irish aren't the only ones who like a drink.

'I'm gonna switch to Guinness,' he says. 'Want one?'

'Sure.' Fair enough, we do like a drink.

'So,' he says after he's ordered. 'Let's talk about Kobi.'

I deflate again. I don't look at him, but I decide to be honest. 'I can't pretend the last two days have been easy.' Honest but understated.

'I know. And I appreciate it. *We* appreciate it.'

I glance sideways up at him. 'We? You and Kobi?'

'I meant me and Ron, and everyone at RoboTron.'

'Are you sure – is Ron sure – that this is really a good idea? You must know that I really don't know what I'm doing. In spite of whatever JP has said.'

He speaks softly. 'Ron thinks this is a good idea. He doesn't always let me in on his rationale, but he seems to have an understanding with JP, and both of them want to make this work.'

I stare at the Guinness settling beside the beer taps. I like that it can't be hurried. A phrase surfaces in my mind. 'Arigata-meiwaku,' I say.

'Excuse me?' says Josh. 'Is that Irish?'

I half laugh. 'Japanese. I had a friend in college who was obsessed with all things Japanese. She was always saying this phrase. She was fascinated by it. It means the feeling you get when you have to act grateful because someone did you a favour, even though you didn't ask them to do you that favour, and in fact the favour has caused you a lot of trouble.'

Josh laughs gently. We both watch as the barman fills up the rest of the pint glasses and places our drinks in front of us.

'I'll drink to that,' says Josh.

I clink my glass against his. I'm remembering a classic television ad for Guinness that featured a man surfing through rolling waves. I steal a glance at Josh, notice his mouth as he licks the cream from his upper lip. It's a wide mouth, to accommodate all those glossy white-paint teeth. He still looks more like a surf instructor than an engineer. *Things don't always seem how they really are*, I tell myself.

Maybe Josh has somehow also seen this ad, because the next thing he says is, 'Robots like Kobi... AI... it's a tide that's coming in, Maeve. At first it comes in little ripples across the sand. Makes little indentations. No big deal. But eventually those ripples become waves, and the waves get stronger. They get so strong that they wash away everything in their path. So my question to you is – do you want to get washed away, or do you want to surf the wave?'

I picture him up on a surfboard, holding a pint, not spilling a drop.

I turn towards him in my chair. 'Honestly, right now I feel like I'm drowning.'

He turns to face me. 'Well, then let me teach you to swim.'

I laugh nervously, trying not to picture both of us on the beach, laughing in the surf. *No, Maeve, it would not be sunny*, I tell myself sternly, remembering the reality of Irish beaches. *You'd both be freezing.*

'AI is coming for every industry,' he says. 'It's already coming for manufacturing. For farming. For healthcare. The big stuff. The important stuff. AI is right now fighting cancer, saving the lives of pregnant women, figuring out new materials to combat climate change...'

He runs his fingers through his hair. Josh's intensity is kind of energising. I almost feel it vibrating from him – the passion, the interest. I sometimes get like this too. True, my interests tend to wax and wane, but that's just because I haven't found the exact right thing yet. Josh sounds like he's found the exact right thing.

Still, I try not to get swept away. I'm already a strong swimmer. I can push back a little. I think about Jen. 'Saving the lives of pregnant women? If anything, Kobi is doing the opposite – increasing everyone's blood pressure. All he's done so far is make our lives worse. Sorry to be so blunt.'

He holds up his hands. 'Fair enough, what you've seen so far is not exactly game-changing. But you haven't seen what I've seen. And I'm sorry Kobi went a bit rogue. He's only improvising because he's not in his natural environment right now. He's out of his comfort zone.'

'He's not the only one,' I say.

'Okay, let me ask you another question. Where do you see yourself in the future?'

I squirm in my chair, consider all the sarcastic, noncommittal answers I would give if it were Shane asking me. *On a tropical island sipping rum punch.* Or: *Far away from you, anyway.*

But Josh's question is sincere. He definitely has a five-year plan, maybe even a ten-year one. His whole life mapped out. Do I want that? I have to admit I'm getting tired of the not knowings, the starting overs, the endless beginnings...

'I don't know,' I answer honestly. 'Somewhere... exciting, but not volatile, you know? A little bit stable, but also different and interesting.'

His voice gets louder. 'Then welcome to the world of robots!' He throws his arms out, missing his pint glass by inches. 'A whole new world is opening up before you. I don't think you realise what a head start you're getting in the industry. Most people your age wouldn't get anywhere near a robot of Kobi's calibre. They'd be messing around with rotating arms for years. But if you can work with Kobi, and help him get better, you can walk into any job in robotics you like.'

Josh is like the tide. Strong, powerful, hard to resist. 'But I don't know anything about robots,' I say weakly. Plus, I'm not sure I even *like* Kobi, let alone want to devote my life to him.

'Ah. That's why we have the fast track, Maeve. That's why I'm enrolling you in an MIT e-learning course. Introduction to Robot Relationship Management. I wrote some of the course material so I'll be able to get you in, no problem.'

I do like a good course, it has to be said, but this is all happening very fast. 'Wait. You said a few minutes ago that things were not on the trajectory you expected. What did you mean by that?'

'Ah, just that Kobi had a bit of a setback a few weeks ago. He's fine, but he's still a work in progress. But he has so much potential. And, if I'm not overstepping to say so – so do you.'

# ELEVEN

*Wednesday, 11am*

'How are you going?' Jen asks as Kobi and I shuffle into her office.

'Good!' I say brightly. 'Kobi has something he wants to say to you. And something to give you, don't you, Kobi?'

The robot moves over to Jen's workstation and awkwardly deposits an ice-cold can of Diet Coke on the edge of her desk.

'DC Jen, please accept this small token in atonement for my temporary lapse of judgement on Monday,' he says.

Jen squints up at him.

'We're sorry,' I say. 'We've kept this can in the freezer for two hours. How's the website?'

She reaches for the can, presses it to her cheek. 'Ooh, that is cold. Nice one.' She points to her screen. 'We're getting there.'

I exhale. 'Good, good. Josh from RoboTron came in yesterday for a check-in. And we went for a drink actually.'

She looks up from her computer. 'Really?' She pops the can open, gulps, gasps. '*So good.* That seems a little unorthodox, mate. Still, I hear he's gorgeous.'

I wonder who she's heard that from. I'm also very aware of Kobi hearing and possibly recording everything we say and, worse, reporting it all back to Josh. But I can't leave him anywhere unsupervised. I decide to communicate with Jen in code. Kobi might understand computer languages, but let's see if he speaks *woman*. I slink into a chair in front of the desk, lower my voice.

'Jen, that's probably not appropriate.'

She laughs. 'Listen, mate, it's probably more appropriate than what you're doing with... you know who. At least this guy isn't your colleague. What's he like, anyway? Tell me everything.'

'He's...' I search for the right words. To be honest, my mind is still spinning from last night. And it's nothing to do with the alcohol I consumed. 'He's... kind of overwhelming, I suppose. But possibly in a good way. I don't think I've met anyone like him. He's just so... so... *American*.'

Jen's eyebrows rise. 'What does that mean? I honestly can't tell if you think that's a good thing or a bad thing.'

'You know. Confident. Sure of himself. *Upbeat*.'

'He sounds terrible,' she says, and we both laugh. 'But the real question is... does he fit the formula?'

I groan, regretting my triumphant sharing of 'the formula' with Jen on Monday morning. My life was so much less complicated last week. And it's only Wednesday.

'Jen, this is different. The formula only applies to dates. This was very much not a date.'

She sighs, glugs more cola. 'Ah, you're no fun. Okay then, what'd he say about that fella?' She nods to indicate Kobi. I can tell he's scanning the room but at least he's not trying to connect to anything.

'Just what a great opportunity it was. This is a new industry, with all sorts of great jobs opening up.'

She points towards Kobi with both hands. 'That's what I said!'

'He wants me to enrol in an online course. Something at MIT.'

'Robot Relationship Management?' Her eyes widen. 'Mate, that's a great course. I've been looking into it myself. It has a module by Professor Mimi Lee.'

'Who?'

'Hang on.' She swivels her chair so she can scan the bookshelf behind her desk. 'Here it is!' She tosses a heavy book to me.

I catch it, read the cover aloud. '*Coding Behaviour: The Brave New World of Ethical Programming*. What's this all about?'

'Borrow it, mate. In a nutshell, she says that the new generation of workplace robots are heavily influenced by the people around them. They basically copy the behaviour of their work colleagues. So the people making industrial robots need to be "ethical programmers". They need to programme good behaviour into the robots from the outset, like a parent raising a child to have a moral code – pun intended. The implications are really interesting.'

'They are?'

'Think about it. Take Kobi here. He's kind of a blank slate, right? Every interaction shapes him in some way. Which means, Maeve, you have a chance to turn Kobi here into whatever you want him to be.' She looks at her computer screen, sighs, puts down the can. 'Well, whatever JP wants him to be, I suppose.'

# TWELVE

As we're making our way to the HR department, I'm trying to get my head in the game. I've already postponed Kobi's HR induction meeting twice and I can't put it off any longer. Sandra Smith's office is on the fifth floor, at the top of the building, at the end of the corridor. It's almost as if they don't want to encourage visitors up here. But at least the elevator has been restored to action.

I like Sandra, but at the end of the day, she's Team JP. If JP is the Supreme Being around here, Sandra is his earthly representative. John the Baptist to his Jesus. Johnnie Cochran to his OJ Simpson. Perhaps that's a little harsh. Smithers to his Mr Burns, then.

I'm mulling over everything I've learned in the past few days. After I spoke to Jen, I left Kobi in the gift shop with Shane and took some time back at my desk to register for the MIT course. *Robots are joining the workforce. Are you ready?* the intro blurb asked. 'God no,' I answered out loud, attracting a brief glare from the desk of Duncan Canning.

Now, I tell Kobi that this meeting is very important.

'I promise to do my best,' he reassures me in the elevator. 'I am thinking of ice-breaker conversation pieces to ensure the meeting starts well. I have been studying this area of emotional intelligence. It is fascinating that humans cannot start meaningful conversations until their brains have sufficiently warmed up. Then again, when I awake from sleep mode, I spend some minutes collecting data and adjusting to my environment. So perhaps it is a similar feeling.'

I silently pray that Kobi will never find out there's such a job as stand-up comedian. I bet he'd love to share his wry observations about humans with an audience.

When we exit the elevator, I stop and point at a sign on the wall that says HUMAN RESOURCES.

I swear Kobi's voice gets louder. 'But where is the office of *Robot Resources*? Because, according to this sign, whoever works here does not have authority over me.'

'Hush,' I say. 'It's not a good idea to open with a joke when you meet someone for the first time.'

'This was not from my joke category files,' he says. 'This was stored under "banter" in my ice-breaker files. Shane and I discussed the concept of banter for thirty-six minutes this morning. He presented me with many examples of such talk. Enough for me to learn how to start creating my own.'

*Oh lord.* 'Well, I think Shane and I might need to have a meeting of our own after this one. For now, please refrain from banter. I'll explain to you later when you can use it. But, in short, for now – rarely.'

We arrive at Sandra's office. Through the glass panel in the door, I can see her pretty blonde head turned to focus on one of her three giant screens, immaculate shellac nails caressing the keyboard. I knock. She responds with a nod and her million-dollar smile.

'Sandra, this is the new collaborative robot, Kobi. He's been looking forward to meeting you, isn't that right, Kobi?'

'Yes. Nice to meet you, Ms Smith.' *Phew.* He bends his upper body forward ever so slightly. 'I am most honoured to be here. I hope I may serve you well.' *Laying it on a bit thick though.*

'Ooh, he has lovely manners, Maeve. Don't you have lovely manners, eh?'

'Thank you,' says Kobi. 'My greeting is an excerpt from *The Servile Robot Lexicon*. This antiquated textbook from 1986 aimed to teach robots how to reassure humans they would not be destroyed in an impending robot uprising.'

I hear myself laugh loudly. 'He has a great sense of humour, Sandra. Just terrific. Very advanced. You wouldn't believe it.'

Sandra laughs along, stands up and walks around the table to us. 'You are funny, Kobi! Maeve, he seems like a right cheeky one. You must have your hands full.'

'He still has a lot to learn about human relationships,' I offer.

'Don't we all, pet, don't we all. Listen, Kobi, we have all sorts working here. We are going to treat you just like every other member of staff, all right? In fact, I've got some homework here for you.' She picks up a USB stick from the desk. 'Now, on here, I've put all our company policies and the employee handbook. I want you to read all of these documents and agree to them, okay, love? I've put them on here to make it easy for you to read them. Now, where shall I...?'

She looks at me, but Kobi says, 'I will read them now.'

He steps forward to position himself directly in front of Sandra. He places his hands onto her shoulders. I expect her to recoil, but she doesn't move. I can tell he's scanning her face.

'Shane was correct. You are an objectively beautiful woman,' he tells her.

*I'm never leaving those two alone again. Shane and Kobi, I mean.*

'Kobi!' I say. 'Sorry, Sandra, he can come out with some random stuff.'

Sandra just laughs lightly. I hear a low buzzing sound as Kobi opens up a hidden compartment in his lower abdominal region. 'Please be gentle,' he says. I can't tell if he's joking.

'Sandra, you don't have to...' I begin, but Sandra speaks at the same time.

'It's okay.' Her voice is soft. She tilts her face up and looks into Kobi's eyes, such as they are. Without looking down, she inserts the USB stick into the slot. She emits a small sound, then smiles. Kobi's compartment door buzzes back into place.

'Thank you,' he says, releasing Sandra's shoulders.

She takes a step back and touches her hair. Her voice resumes its normal volume. 'Okay, now, when you've read all those...'

'I have read them,' Kobi says.

'What do you mean?' she says.

'I have read all of the documents. There are three typos – below average for human-created documents – and the diversity policy needs an update.'

'Ooh, you are fast, Kobi. Isn't he fast, Maeve? Mind you, speed is not always a good thing, am I right?'

I suddenly remember my Monday morning presentation at the all-hands meeting. *Why* did I say that Kobi would help two people by the end of the week? 'Sandra, can Kobi help you with anything while he's here?' Then I remember that I specifically said the two people would not be JP or Sandra.

'Let me have a think. D'you know what? Kobi, why don't you do me a favour and create a report with the title "Staff compliance with HR policies". That should keep you busy for a while. You can send it to me in a couple of weeks when it's done.'

*D'oh!* I try and fail to imagine a scenario where this is seen as helpful to anyone other than JP or Sandra.

'Well, I suppose we should be getting back...' I say.

'Maeve, hang on a minute. Kobi, love, would you mind waiting for Maeve in the corridor? We just need to have a quick chat.'

My pulse spikes. A 'quick chat' with HR is never a good thing. I reluctantly lead Kobi into the corridor and give him strict instructions not to interact with anyone. I position him so I can keep an eye on him through the glass door, angling the chair in front of Sandra's desk before I sit in it.

'Sandra, just to let you know, Kobi's hearing seems to be really good, so he'll probably be able to hear whatever you say.'

'That's okay. So, tell me, how are you getting on?' She gives me a closed-lip smile, her head inclined sideways. I've seen that look before. A mix of concern and sympathy. Just for a second, I'm back at my father's funeral. I push the memory away, hoping the dull throb in my solar plexus will go away with it. Wonder what Kobi would say about human versus robot memory.

*It's time for a game of HR poker.* 'Ah, you know...' Shane says vagueness is a trump card.

Her smile fades. 'The thing is, Maeve, we really want this to work out.' I guess two can play the vague game. I want to ask what she specifically means by 'this', but I don't want to show my hand.

'JP will be very disappointed if this doesn't go well.' Her eyes flick to the door. Okay, so she means The Kobi Project. 'He's trying to embrace innovation, you know.'

I almost burst out laughing. Has she been down to the IT department lately?

'Well, I'll try my best,' I offer.

'Good, because if you can't cope, we can ask Jen to take over.' Doesn't she know about Jen's high blood pressure? Or maybe she does, but doesn't care? 'And I suppose we'll find something else for you to do.'

'Something else? Why do you say it like that? You mean my normal job, right?'

She gives me the closed-lip smile again, this time shaking her head slowly. 'Maeve, I'm going to be honest with you here – give you a heads-up. The reason why Duncan Canning said you had capacity to take on this extra project is because, frankly, we're in a situation where we have two people doing the same job, but really only enough work for one.'

*Two people. She means me and Shane.* It's true, work has slowed down a bit lately, but I thought that was just because of the seasons. Summer is always the busiest for Irish tourism. We're not exactly known for our grey drizzly winters. Maybe Duncan Canning *did* use AI to write the New York ad campaign. Maybe he's planning to replace us with it. I glance over at Kobi. He's clearly not built for marketing, but maybe he'll replace someone in a factory someday soon. I remember what Josh said about the tide. Am I about to be washed away?

As much as I complain about my job, I'd rather leave on my own terms, ideally with something better to go to. My résumé is already a shattered kaleidoscope of skills and experience that don't match.

'So what you're saying is...'

'All I'm saying is it would probably be in your best interests to make yourself useful around here, Maeve.'

# THIRTEEN

*Thursday, 11:15am*

I sip my peppermint tea behind the counter as I watch Shane engage Kobi in the most needless of busy work – a stock take of the gift shop merchandise. Shane describes and counts each item and Kobi makes a note of it. But there are very few items so Shane is taking his time over each one, inventing elaborate fables for the shamrock keychains, leprechaun plushies and miniature shillelaghs.

'Hey,' I say, leaning on the glass. 'Be careful what you tell him. He believes everything he's told and will probably repeat it.'

Kobi turns to me stiffly. 'Maeve, that is incorrect. I record everything, but I cross-reference it against other data.'

'Like Sandra Smith's "objectively beautiful" face?' I ask.

Shane stops counting the shamrock sunglasses. 'What's that?'

'Oh, nothing. Just... Kobi told Sandra Smith that you said she was "an objectively beautiful woman".'

He laughs, moves on to the 'Irish blessing' coasters. He picks up a bundle, shuffles them. 'Well, that is technically true. It's just a fact. I didn't say I found her attractive. We were talking about art, the definition of beauty and stuff.'

'You can find her attractive if you want to.' I mean for it to be banter, but my tone comes out defensive.

'Thanks. But I don't.'

'But you can, if you want to.' I'm getting flustered. 'My point is – don't say things like that to Kobi because he'll only repeat them. At inappropriate moments.'

I notice lights illuminate in Kobi's chest plate. 'Compliance violation noted,' he says.

I sigh loudly.

'What was *that*?' asks Shane.

I make a strangled sound. 'Don't even ask. We have bigger things to be worrying about.'

Shane places a green velvet top hat on Kobi's head.

'Compliance violation,' Kobi says, lights flashing on and off.

'You're no fun,' says Shane, moving the hat from Kobi's head to his own. He turns to me. 'What bigger things? And what do you mean by "we"?'

'Sandra hinted that we might not have our jobs forever.' I pause. 'Or for very long.'

He stops, takes off his hat. He walks over, stands directly in front of me, a serious look on his face. Then he reaches across the counter. A flash of green. I feel the velvet brim snug around my head. 'You look cute,' he says.

'Compliance violation,' says Kobi, lights flashing.

I grab the hat, fling it across the room in the vain hope it might land on the hook where it belongs. Something about the action reminds me of last Friday morning, waking up in Shane's bed. *Whose underwear was that?* Not that I care, of course.

'Kobi, can you please stop saying that?' I ask. 'How about a compromise? You can still do that light thing, but please stop vocalising, okay?'

He replies by flashing his lights at me.

'Good enough.' I lower my voice. 'Shane, aren't you worried about losing your job?'

'I'll get something else. We both will.'

'Was there anything in that last batch of job ads?' I ask. Every Friday I do a job search for both of us. I send him links to anything I think might suit him.

'Apart from the feeling that you're trying to get rid of me? Nah.'

I discreetly point at Kobi. 'I'm worried they might try to replace us. Maybe not with him, but with something else.'

Shane stretches, draws himself up to his full height, then drops his shoulders. 'Good.'

'Good?'

'Yeah. Face it. Our jobs are so boring. Let someone else do it. Or some*thing* else.'

'But what will we do for... you know... money?' Sometimes I feel like Shane lives in his own parallel universe. Maybe that's why he's always so chill. Bet it's nice in there.

'Three words: Universal Basic Income.'

One of Shane's favourite topics is Universal Basic Income. Some countries are trialling it. The government gives a baseline wage to everyone. Enough to survive but maybe not enough to thrive. Then it's up to individuals to top it up by working.

'But there's no sign of that happening here anytime soon. We still have to pay the rent in the meantime.'

He retrieves the velvet hat from the floor. It's starting to look a bit grubby. 'Here, Kobi, catch!' He throws it. But by the time Kobi starts to move, the hat is already on the floor. Kobi flashes his chest lights at us.

'Will you stop messing around?' I say, frustrated.

'I'm not,' he says. 'I'm proving a point.' He picks up three items from the counter – a Guinness golf ball, a plush shamrock, a tricolour pen – and juggles them.

'What point? You could get a job in the circus?'

'Kobi, could you do this?' he says. He throws the items higher, catches them one by one behind his back, starts again.

'No,' says Kobi.

'See?' says Shane. 'There's so many things machines can't do. We'll be okay.'

I'm not convinced, and I'm grateful to be interrupted by a phone call. Even more grateful when I see that it's Josh calling me. Someone who can actually help me with my current situation – babysitting a robot while trying not to get fired.

I leave the shop, walk the short distance through the hallway to the front of the building, step through the massive Georgian door onto the stone steps outside. I put in my earbuds. 'Hi, Josh!'

'Hey, you.' It's good to hear his voice. 'How's it going?'

I consider how to answer this. Kobi will have been here a week tomorrow. In that time, he's sabotaged the elevator, aggravated the IT manager, annoyed the customer relations department and failed to make much contribution in the gift shop.

'Fine,' I reply. 'Are you coming in today? I could use some advice.'

'That's why I'm calling. Things are crazy at work today. I was really hoping to see you, but I'm not sure I'm gonna make it now.'

I feel myself flush at how's he's phrased it. I also feel the downward plunge of another day of flailing around with The Kobi Project. 'Okay.'

'But we can talk now for a few minutes. What's your biggest issue at the moment?' Of course an engineer is good at problem-solving. *How do you eat an elephant?* my dad used to say.

I take a deep breath. 'I guess, I don't really know what it is I'm supposed to be doing. Because I don't really know what it is Kobi should be doing. He doesn't seem... suited to working in this environment.'

'Well, he's not used to it, that's true. But, remember, Kobi is highly adaptable. It's his USP, in fact. He's capable of so many things. But he has to be given a chance to learn first. Just like any new person on the job. Makes sense, right?'

Everything makes sense when he says it. He makes it sound so easy.

'What's he doing today?' he asks.

'Still in the shop.'

'You mean Tumbleweed City?'

I laugh. 'Yes.'

'Well, where I'd like to see Kobi improve is in his communication skills. He needs interaction. He needs to be around people. Listen, you're smart. You'll think of something. I trust you.'

# FOURTEEN

## KOBI

*Thursday, 1800*

I am in alien terrain. By 1800 I am usually in rest mode, processing the day's new input data. Today is different.

At 1700, Maeve and Shane presented me with the opportunity for this 'field trip', as they styled it. 'Didn't Josh say he wants you to fit in here?' Maeve said. Shane said, 'What better way to get to know your colleagues than over a few relaxing drinks in the pub? That's where real relationships are made.'

With some reservations, I accessed my residual power bank and turned off all ancillary systems, in order to give me sufficient battery to last until 2100. I explained all this in great detail to Maeve and Shane.

'Don't worry. We'll get you back here before you turn into a pumpkin,' Shane said. Although I did not recognise this exact vegetable reference, I did not need to in order to understand the general meaning of the sentence. Josh says I will never understand every expression in human language, as it is evolving too rapidly. It is more important to try to 'see the whole picture, all at once'. That is the true mark of intelligence, he says.

But now that I am here in Phelan's Bar and Grill, seeing the whole picture is impossible. I am in sensory overload; my input processor can barely keep pace with all the new data streaming my way.

I sense multiple potential hazards. For a start, navigating around the room is a challenge, as people-shaped and chair-shaped objects of varying sizes stand around in haphazard formations.

Dim light does not aid my navigation. Josh recently fitted me with a low-tech night-mode vision – two small torch implants on either side of my head. I switch these to full beam as I carefully begin to cross the floor but Shane immediately raises his voice and strikes my back. 'Hey, knock those off, will ye? You're ruining the atmosphere.'

I comply, not wishing to destroy the delicate balance of oxygen, nitrogen and other gases required by human bodies for their continued well-being.

The most alarming danger of all, however, is the prevalence of liquid throughout the environment. Liquids are no friend to robotkind. Every human is holding a small but potentially lethal dose; and each person holds it in a marginally different way, making its precise movement and location difficult to anticipate.

'Maeve,' I say. 'I do not wish to cause unnecessary alarm. However, are you aware that my systems have not been designed for liquid-based environments? In fact, I am used to operating in clean rooms. If I were to get wet—'

'Relax,' Shane says. ''Tis grand, sure. You're not going to get wet. I know it probably looks fairly random to you right now, but actually the evening has an ebb and flow about it that's entirely predictable. You could say I've done my own data gathering and analysis over the years. Trust me, no one's going to spill a drink before 9, earliest.' Then he laughs as he says: 'I mean if you think this is chaotic, you should see the place at midnight.'

Although Shane's human data-gathering methods are bound to be deficient, I decide to relax as much as is robotically possible and to make the most of my time here. After all, it is an exciting opportunity to gain experience and to interact with my colleagues in an

70 of SYLVIA LEATHAM

atypical setting. Maeve and Josh must be confident that I am ready for this challenge. If I can make progress here, they will be pleased.

A group of people from the office are standing in a formation that approximates a circle. They acknowledge my presence as we approach.

'Ah, here, why'd you bring yer man?' David says.

'Dave, don't be rude,' Julia says. 'Hey, guys.'

'I suppose he doesn't drink anything.' David inclines his head toward me.

'You can speak to him directly, y'know, Dave,' Maeve says. 'He can understand everything you say.'

'That'd make a nice change for you, Dave, wouldn't it?' Julia says.

Several people laugh, but I do not. I know what it is like to be poorly understood.

'Although, Dave does have a point,' Julia says, and I wonder if I have missed part of the conversation. 'Kobi is not exactly our new favourite colleague. We've had a really stressful week, thanks to his website antics.'

Josh has fitted me with a rudimentary Emotion Detector. While it is helpful in providing nonverbal information during human interactions, the downside is that I can now name these sensations when they occur within my own systems. This one is called 'disappointment'.

'Well, he's new,' Maeve says. 'You have to give him a chance. He just hasn't found his groove yet.'

'Kobi, we have not met properly yet,' a woman says. I postulate from her accent that she may have grown up in another country. 'I am Imelda. I work in accounts. Although these days I am mostly counting down the years to retirement.'

'How many years left now, Imelda?' David says.

'Well, I cannot say exactly. I hope to retire a few years early. And I know you wouldn't dare ask my current age. So let us just say "soon".'

'Time is relative,' David says. 'And time is money. So money must be relative too. And I've been waiting for my relatives to leave me money for a very long time now.'

Julia laughs. 'Shut up, Dave, will you? No one's in the mood for your nonsense.'

I consider whether Julia is, in fact, bullying David. I flash my chest plate lights to signal to Maeve that another compliance violation may have occurred. But perhaps this conversation fits the category Shane calls 'banter'. I resolve to seek clarification on this matter later.

'So, Maeve,' Julia says. 'Josh. Is. So. Hot. American men are just so much better looking. That's just a fact. Don't hate me, guys.'

I quickly compute the many meanings for 'hot' and illuminate my chest plate to signal a potential compliance violation. I anticipate I will have much to analyse after this evening.

'Kobi, can I ask you a question?' Julia says.

I am pleased with this opportunity to provide help. 'I can answer any question in the world you might care to ask.'

'Cool. In that case, where to start? Let's see. What kind of women does Josh go for?'

My systems start whirring. This question is unexpected. I am unsure where to begin.

David says, 'Julia! What are you asking him that for?'

'For Maeve,' she says. 'Well, maybe also for me a little bit.' She blinks one eye at me. I know this signifies some sort of secret message and am pleased to be the recipient, although I am currently unable to decipher the code.

'Julia!' Maeve says.

'Kobi can't answer that,' David says. Then, to me, 'Can you?'

Shane intervenes. 'Can we not just have a drink? Who saw the match last night?'

'I saw a great match the other day,' Julia says. 'Maeve and Josh leaving work together. High five, Dave?'

'All right, Jules, leave it alone now,' David says. 'I missed it, Shane – any good?'

Even though there is a lot of incoming data to process, I am sensing some stress or distress from Shane. Perhaps now it is my turn to intervene.

'If you wish, I could show match highlights on my video screen,' I offer. I activate the plastic screen covers in my chest and they glide open to reveal my embedded high-res screen.

'Cool,' David says. 'Why didn't you tell us you could do that? We would've been watching you all week! Hook us up, man.'

# FIFTEEN

## MAEVE

*7pm*

Maybe this was a good idea after all. In truth, I feel slightly deranged. Maybe it's the rum and Coke I just knocked back. Maybe it's because it's been such a long week. But after my phone call with Josh, I felt emboldened. Maybe I just needed to shake things up a bit with The Kobi Project. Do something different. So when Shane suggested we *all* go for after-work drinks, I only protested for about five minutes before giving in. 'What's the worst that could happen?' he kept asking.

I do wish Jen was here though. But she left work early today, which is not like her at all. I guess it's been a long week for her too.

'Would you ever stop yawning?' Shane says as I cover my mouth for the second time since we got here. We're standing at the bar, waiting for our drinks order. I've positioned Kobi nearby, in a place we call 'the dead zone'. There's an empty corner behind him where there used to be a cigarette machine. Some of the work crew stand around him. So far they've been including him in their conversations, which has to be a good thing.

'Sorry, I'm wrecked. This is my second time here this week.' I nod at the barman as he places two IPAs in front of us. 'I brought Josh here on Tuesday.'

Shane stretches and puts his hands on the wooden counter, as if he's about to do a push-up against the bar.

'I heard. Sounds very like a date. How did it go?'

I laugh lightly. 'I'm not taking the bait. It wasn't a date.'

'Well, I'll let you off the hook this time, because you did a rhyme. And sure – it looks like I'm joining the club too. Cheers,' he says, clinking my glass.

I'm reassured by this exchange. The teasing about being on a date, the lameness of the rhyme – we're definitely in the realm of casual office banter. In spite of our hookups – which are in the past now anyway – we're just workmates at the end of the day. We can be honest. We don't need to impress each other. It's nice, actually.

'Josh is an interesting person,' I say. 'It was good to hear about life' – I gesture vaguely – 'beyond.'

He raises an eyebrow at me. 'He's not one of those born-again Christians, is he?'

I laugh. 'No! I just mean – it's good to know there's life beyond Go Ireland.'

'That's the rumour all right.' He leans back against the bar.

'We have to get out of here,' I say.

He looks at his watch. 'Already? Okay, I can skull this. Just give me five seconds.'

'No!' I slap his arm lightly. Try not to notice the muscle tone. 'I mean – we both have to get out of Go Ireland.'

'Something will turn up,' he says.

'Something did turn up.' I point at Kobi. 'Him.'

We both look over at our robot colleague. Okay, he doesn't exactly blend in, and he's getting the odd sideways glance from other patrons, but it's not the strangest thing I've ever witnessed. In the taxi over here, the cab driver barely seemed to notice his unusual passenger. I think I overhear someone in the work group say, '*Shots!*' Maybe this is the new normal.

'Josh – and Jen actually – seem to think this could be a good opportunity. For me. You know... maybe I can upskill. And move on.'

'Like you always do.' There's something in his tone that catches me unawares.

'What do you mean by that?'

He won't look at me. 'Nothing. Just what you've said yourself. You don't stay anywhere long. I'm surprised you've even been at Go Ireland this long, to be honest.'

It might be true, but it feels like an attack. I don't *want* to keep moving on. I've loved Dublin ever since I came back here to go to college, having spent my whole childhood and teen years globe-trotting against my will. And if I can't seem to settle at a job or a career, well, that's just the way I am. The restlessness is in-built. Either that or it's just too hard to break a habit sewn into me in childhood. Did Dad have this feeling too? Is that why he dragged us to a different country every couple of years?

I can't say any of this to Shane. 'I'm going to the bathroom. Keep an eye on Kobi for me for a few minutes, will you?'

# SIXTEEN

*7:30pm*

The second I get back from the bathroom, I know something is wrong.

Kobi and Shane are the only ones in the dead zone. Everyone else has vanished. Shane is standing in front of Kobi, looking him up and down. Kobi is silent, arms dangling, bent forward a little at the waist. A dishevelled, human-like pose. Like he's had too much to drink. Only robots don't drink.

I start pressing buttons on his control panel, but I don't really know what I'm doing. 'What the feck, Shane? What happened?'

'I don't know. I didn't see.'

'I thought you were keeping an eye on him! I left you alone for two minutes.'

'I'm sorry. I must have got distracted. No one would tell me what happened.'

The frantic button-pressing is having no effect. That's when I notice it. Droplets of liquid. I pat Kobi down. 'He's wet.'

'That doesn't seem good,' says Shane.

'You're unbelievable!' But it's not really Shane's fault. I know that. Kobi is my responsibility.

'Wait, maybe he just ran out of juice?' says Shane. 'He kept talking about that, remember?'

But his battery display indicates he still has a few hours of charge left. *Oh, Kobi. Why didn't I listen to you? Why did I listen to Shane instead?* I have so many regrets but can't process them because of the avalanche of consequences barrelling through my mind. *What if Kobi is kaput? What will JP think? What will Josh say? What will Ron Tron do?* I try to imagine JP explaining this to Ron. 'Yes, that's right, Ron. We brought your *multimillion-dollar* robot to the pub. It's the way we do things around here.' Obviously I'll be fired. Maybe Shane will be fired too. Maybe Ron will try to sue Go Ireland. Or JP. Or me.

I'm spiralling. I slap myself in the face.

'Hey!' says Shane.

'I need to *think!*' I hear how desperate I sound. I take a deep breath. 'Let's get him back to the office. I'm going to have to call Josh.'

We get a cab back to the office. I leave a voice note for Josh, asking him to meet me here. I don't go into detail, but I do say that it's an emergency, that Kobi had a 'liquid encounter' and is currently unresponsive.

Shane has keys to the building because he's been working in the gift shop all week. We bundle Kobi into the Liffey Room, prop him up in the middle of the space.

I snatch a Blue Roll from a shelf, start wiping down Kobi's surfaces. I call up Kobi's documentation on my phone, search for every word I can think of related to moisture. Zero results. This obviously isn't a scenario Josh had anticipated.

I crouch down in front of the forlorn figure of my robot colleague. What would Kobi say if he could speak right now? He'd probably tell me to focus on finding a solution. I wish Josh was here, but I also dread what he'll say. Is there any way in hell I could fix this before he gets here?

I exhale and stand up. Try to muster up some confidence. 'Shane, I am going to try to fix Kobi.'

'Great! Let me help you. This happened to me recently actually – my phone fell into the toilet.'

'Do you think that's what happened?' I clasp my mouth in horror. 'Kobi fell into a toilet or... was he pushed?'

'No, no! At least, I don't think so. I just meant I was able to dry out my phone that time. Maybe the same technique will work now.' He whips out his phone.

'I think Kobi is a bit more sophisticated than a smartphone, Shane,' I say. 'He's not just here for your entertainment.'

Shane sits on the floor, cross-legged. He speaks in a quiet voice, his words a little slurry. 'The irony is, things seemed to be going quite well, up until...'

I tune him out. I circle Kobi, looking for answers. A surgeon trying to save a car crash victim, but it's their first day on the job. *Think.*

'That time when your phone got wet – how did you fix it?' Kobi is a machine, after all. And I have no better ideas right now.

'I'm trying to remember what I did,' he says from the floor. 'Let me look it up.' He messes around with his phone while I continue pressing Kobi's buttons uselessly. 'Okay, I found something.'

'What does it say?'

'Gimme a second, I'm skimming it here. Let's see. It says "act fast".'

I make a growling sound in response.

'Okay, eh, step one – turn off the device. Well, then, it's good that he's off already, isn't it? It says to leave it turned off for at least forty-eight hours. So maybe you should stop pressing buttons?'

I release my breath, run my fingers through my hair for something to do. When I went to the bathroom in Phelan's, I shook out my hair and covertly took off my bra, thinking that maybe I could relax for the rest of the evening. I hope Shane won't remark on my appearance.

'Okay. What's next?'

'Step two – remove the battery. Do you know how to do that?'

I have a vague memory of a diagram from Kobi's documentation. And Module 1 of the MIT course, which I started last night, covered battery maintenance.

'Um, I'll give it a go. I'll need tools though. Let me look in Kobi's maintenance kit.'

I retrieve a black holdall from the shelf next to Kobi's sleep pod and rifle through it. 'I hope the battery's not in an awkward spot.'

I hold up a small screwdriver and address the patient. 'Kobi, I'll try and be gentle. I don't want to damage anything else while I'm getting it out.'

'That's what she said,' mumbles Shane.

'Really not the time.'

'Sorry.' He returns to his phone. 'It says to do this as soon as possible. Also says – feck – liquid is one of the worst things that can happen to electronic devices.'

'You don't say.' I raise an eyebrow at him.

'Maybe I should stop reading.'

'Be quiet for a minute – let me concentrate.'

I locate the battery compartment on Kobi's back. It's secured with a series of tiny screws. I brandish the screwdriver for confidence.

'Okay, let's do this. Righty tighty, lefty loosey.'

He laughs. 'Oh wow, you're really learning a lot on that robot course, aren't you?'

'Well, I haven't got to the module on "How to Cope When Your Idiot Friend Suggests You Do Something Incredibly Stupid with Your Multimillion-Dollar Robot",' I say through gritted teeth, rotating the screwdriver.

'So you're saying we're still friends? That's good.'

I shoot him a look that I hope says, *I don't know what we are right now, nor do I care.*

'Sorry, I'm just trying to break the tension,' he says.

'Battery is out!' I say triumphantly. I hold the slender shiny cylinder aloft like I've just won an Oscar, then place it carefully on the shelf. 'Next?'

'Next, remove all the liquid.'

I make the growling sound again.

'Wait, wait, it says... there are two steps to removing the liquid, or is it two options? It's not clear. Sure maybe let's just do them both, to be safe. Number one, use a hair dryer.'

I look up. 'I don't suppose you happen to have a hair dryer to hand?'

'No. But I bet I know who does. I'll be right back.'

He hauls himself up, wobbles a bit, then lopes from the room. He reappears a few minutes later, a miniature pink hair dryer in hand.

'Who owns that?'

'Imelda. Keeps it in her drawer. For those last-minute touch-ups she's always going on about. Here.' He hands it to me. 'Do your worst. And I'll refrain from making any jokes about blow jobs.'

'Very mature of you.' I switch the device to high and start blowing air all over Kobi.

'Wait!' he says. 'It says cool air only. Oh, and don't blast it – low air flow is what it says here.'

'Sorry, Kobi.' I adjust the settings and undulate the device, gently blowing air all around Kobi's parts, pointing it into grooves and crevices. I do not currently own a working hair dryer – my one blew a fuse six months ago and I never got around to replacing it. I mostly wear my hair up anyway so I don't need to spend much time styling it. I wish it was tied up now. It bounces around every time I move the dryer.

'You look good,' says Shane. He's resumed his position on the floor.

'Don't distract me.'

He can definitely tell I'm not wearing a bra. Men are so obsessed with breasts, I bet they're always aware of the proximity, status and aspect of the nearest ones, no matter what else is going on at the time. It must be like knowing if it's warm or cold, or sensing an atmosphere. Probably so automatic that by the time a man reaches his early twenties, the task has been outsourced to a division of the subconscious brain. *We need this information to* be available at all times, just in case, but we don't want it up here, cluttering up the frontal cortex. Let's store it in the medulla oblongata, shall we? Safest place for it. Handy for dream time also.

I clear my throat. 'Okay. What else?'

'The last step is "cover the device in drying agents".'

I rack my brain but come up empty. 'What exactly are drying agents?'

'It has a picture here... Silica gel. It comes in these tiny little pillows. Where have I seen these before?' He holds up the phone so I can study the picture.

We both think for a moment, then simultaneously say, 'Shoes!'

'I'll be right back.' He scrambles to his feet again, almost tripping over the hair dryer wire on his way to the door. He soon returns with four shoeboxes.

'Thank God for my Nike obsession, eh? Bet you think it's money well spent now.'

He stacks the boxes and opens the one on top. It yields two small bags of silica gel. He repeats the process until a small pile is formed. I grab some sticky tape and get to work. Each tiny assemblage is like a cotton ball on a plaster for a patient who's just had an injection. I tape them to various parts of Kobi.

'It's not enough,' I sigh. 'We'd need, like, hundreds of these.'

'You know what I used?' His voice is suddenly loud. 'I'll be right back! And you can call me a genius then.'

I examine Kobi when Shane has left the room. He looks somewhat pathetic. This is my fault. I didn't do enough for Kobi. I failed him. All he wanted was to be accepted, and to be useful. That's all many people want, deep down. Is this to be the end of him? And what a way to go, too – suddenly and in a strange place. I know he's just a machine, but it doesn't seem right. I make a decision and a promise. *Kobi, if you make it through tonight, I'm going to do my best for you. We can make this work, together.*

'Hang in there, buddy,' I say gently.

'I will, thanks!' Shane says as he bursts into the room, holding what appears to be a paper coffee cup with no lid. 'Stand back! You'll thank me later.'

Before I can move, he strides across the room and with one wild gesture jerks the cup into the air. A hail of uncooked rice rains down on Kobi and me.

'Ow! What are you *doing*?' I yell, covering my face. 'It's not a wedding!'

'Rice!'

'Ow! I know.'

'I put my phone in rice!'

The rice skitters across the floor, outlining my feet like chalk around a corpse. I gesture at the whole nonsensical scene. My tone turns to ice. 'And what part of *this* resembles putting your phone into rice?'

'Sorry,' he falters, his confidence evaporating. 'Uh – I might have gotten a bit carried away there. There's more in the kitchen though – bags of the stuff. Maybe we can, I don't know, tape it to him somehow?'

He picks up the tape, but I swat it from his hand. It hits the floor with a dull bounce and rolls away to hide under a shelving unit. He means well, but Shane's help isn't what I need right now. I need a grown-up.

'I think you've done enough. I can take it from here.' My phone buzzes. 'That's probably Josh now. I told him to message me when he was outside. Can you let him in on your way out?'

# SEVENTEEN

*9:15pm*

The relief I feel when I see Josh enter the Liffey Room just about outweighs all my other feelings: dread, guilt, general life-regret. I fully expect him to be angry, but he calmly puts down his tool bag and says, 'Okay, so what are we looking at here?' Sometimes you could just kiss an engineer for their unflappability.

He gets to work on Kobi's parts with a canister of compressed air – relentlessly spraying the aerosol in short bursts, like a hairdresser with an overzealous approach to hairspray. I hold up the pink hairdryer with a small smile. He up-nods his chin, turns his full attention back to Kobi.

'I didn't know what to do,' I say, redundantly. I don't know what to say either.

He stops his work, straightens up. 'It's okay.' He looks at me properly for the first time. 'You got the battery out – that was good,' he says softly.

'Do... do you think he's going to be okay?' I'm afraid to ask but also afraid of not knowing.

'Too early to tell.' He doesn't seem angry. Just highly focused.

'Well, let's not give up yet, then?' I sound more hopeful than I feel.

The briefest of smiles flickers across his face.

'Do you want to walk me through what you're doing? Maybe I can learn something.'

'Sure.'

He shows me his laptop screen and says he's going to run a data analysis on Kobi's 'brain'. Then he removes the battery cradle unit entirely from Kobi's back and sends in a long, thin cable. Kobi's brain, it turns out, is carefully shielded and cushioned inside his torso.

Josh tells me he used to have remote access to Kobi's systems, but now he prefers to only use old-school physical access. He steps back to let me peek in at Kobi's innards.

'Whoa,' I say softly. It's a mass of colourful wiring embedded in a dark substance that looks... squishy. I want to touch it. 'What am I looking at here?' I reach forward.

'Don't touch anything! Sorry. Still raw.'

He gives me a guided tour though, shining a torch onto different sections as he explains how Kobi's brain works. During the day, Kobi records a vast amount of data about every event and interaction. At night, he processes everything – imagine it like writing your daily journal before going to sleep, he tells me. Kobi keeps a record of pertinent factual data like times, locations, people he's met and so on. But alongside this he creates Today I Learned (TIL) files through a neural network, assimilating new knowledge and behaviour from the day's events. Every time Kobi learns a new 'lesson', the network grows and complexifies. Anything significant makes its ways into his memory core for long-term storage. The original, raw data files that are no longer of use are sent to the discard depot every night – where they're scrubbed and then 'recycled' to nourish the neural network.

'It's a highly efficient system that minimises data storage requirements and maximises energy usage,' he says proudly.

I don't know the right terminology, but I need to ask. 'And what's that squishy stuff in the middle of it all?'

He smiles. 'That "squishy stuff" is an experimental bio-composite material with superconductive properties, designed by yours truly. It's what makes Kobi unique.'

I can tell this is meant to impress me. 'Bio? That means... organic?'

'It's a semi-organic substrate, yeah. Custom-made using additive manufacturing. See how it's woven and layered to create more space? And because it's organic, it means it can grow and change as Kobi learns. Oh wow.'

'What's up?'

'See.' He shows me the laptop, but all I see are lines of code. 'It looks like Kobi has already made some new memories this week.'

'Is there any way to know if they're good memories?'

He laughs gently. 'Not until I run a full analysis. But this is good, Maeve. It means he's growing and learning. Well done.'

I could weep at this morsel of praise. Instead I laugh. A high-pitched, slightly hysterical sound. 'It's been a very strange week.' Then it all comes tumbling out. 'I'm sorry about tonight. I brought Kobi to Phelan's. Against my better judgement. No, it was my decision. I can't blame anyone else. It was a stupid thing to do. I don't know what I was thinking.'

'Hey, hey.' He puts down the laptop, places his hands on my shoulders. 'It's okay.'

I look up at him. People write books about wild adventures on high seas, or in deep jungles, but you can find yourself in the strangest situations right where you work. Somehow I've landed in the darkest forest, but Josh is here as my guide, with his torch and his shining white teeth. I give in to a moment of calm.

Then I look at Kobi, still nonresponsive. 'What if he's not okay?'

He turns away from me, sighs heavily. 'Maeve, I need to tell you something. On the one hand, it might make you feel better to know this isn't even the worst thing that has happened to Kobi at work.'

'It isn't?' It *does* make me feel better. But it's probably not polite to openly celebrate it. I store it up to celebrate later. 'Wait. On the other hand?'

'Let's sit down,' he says.

He looks around and I point to the couch in the corner. He sits down heavily, covers his face with his big hands.

It's only a two-seater couch. I try to leave some space between us, but it's not easy with Josh's long legs. I face forward. It's easier to talk like this anyway.

'You asked me about Kobi's last assignment, but I never really gave you an answer,' he says. 'There was a reason for that, and I'm sorry. I should have been completely upfront about it. But I'm going to tell you now and it might help you understand Kobi a bit more.'

I brace myself and try to keep an open mind as Josh begins his story.

He'd been working away on Kobi for a couple of years and all was going well. The robot was tested in a few real-world scenarios and getting good results. So a few months ago, Kobi was deployed to Precision Health Instruments, or PHI, a manufacturing plant in Ireland's Midlands where they make medical devices, mostly hip implants 3D-printed in titanium.

Working elbow-to-elbow with his human colleagues, Kobi's job was to scan each implant after it was newly formed, to ensure it had no defects. While Kobi has highly sophisticated scanning technology, humans are better able to pick up and quickly rotate an implant 360 degrees. Defects were rarely detected, but if one was, the entire line would be shut down, pending investigation.

Things at the plant had gone great for about six weeks. Then came The Incident. I can tell Josh is capitalising it. His voice has grown unusually soft and quiet.

Kobi was working the night shift, just him and three human operators on the floor. According to his co-workers, Kobi had clocked up about five hours of part diagnostics when suddenly his behaviour changed.

He stopped mid-scan and, against protocol, he put both his robot hands on the implant. Then, holding the implant, he started to move backwards, raised the artificial hip over his head and launched it across the room. It bounced off the casing of a 3D printing machine before hitting the floor. Then he took another implant from a nearby conveyor belt and did the same thing. This time it missed an operator's head by inches.

By the time he reached for another, all the operators were yelling and ducking for cover. One of them managed to hit an alarm, which momentarily distracted Kobi, so the guys ran for the door, got out and locked it behind them. Kobi then started collecting implants and putting them all in a pile together.

'That's when I got the call,' he says. 'Luckily, it was near the end of a shift and Kobi's batteries ran out of juice soon after. He had to be taken away and decommissioned. But the strangest thing was, when I checked his logs, he had zero recollection of The Incident – there was no data recorded. And there was no explanation for his behaviour.'

I feel like a machine gone into overload. *Does not compute.*

That drowning feeling washes over me again. 'So, what you're telling me is' – I try to keep my voice steady – 'you've now placed a robot with a history of violence into an office full of unsuspecting people?'

'No, no, of course not,' he says quickly. 'That happened weeks ago. I've spent every waking minute since rebuilding Kobi's code from scratch. He's pretty much at factory settings right now.'

'It sounds like "factory settings" is what caused the problem in the first place!'

How can he sit there and drop a bomb like this – figuratively, and possibly literally as well? I picture Kobi chasing me down the corridors of Go Ireland with a staple gun, or attacking me with the shop's merch. Even a plush leprechaun could be a weapon in the wrong hands.

Josh turns to face me, using his big hands for emphasis. 'Maeve, there's no danger, I promise you. Have you seen any hint of threat in Kobi's behaviour since you met him? I've rewritten and checked every line of his code, shut off any external avenues. He's a completely closed unit now.'

I'm not convinced. 'Then how do you explain what happened?'

'Well, I can't right now. I'm still trying to figure it out. For now, I'm sure that it won't happen again. Kobi has passed all safety checks. It's like he's a new robot, basically. You have to believe I wouldn't put anyone at risk. For a start, that would be a total dick move. It would also mean the end of my career.'

I cross my arms, breathing hard. 'Why didn't you tell me before? Does JP know?'

'I mean, Kobi's history was in the briefing notes that we sent to JP, along with our assessment that Kobi is currently stable. I didn't tell you before because, A, there was no danger and, B, I didn't want you to worry.'

'Then why are you telling me now?'

'So that you won't feel so bad about what happened tonight. So that you can understand why Kobi's communication skills still need a lot of work. And' – he looks across at Kobi – 'because it may not matter if he doesn't wake up.'

I should probably just give up now, quit while I'm... still on the starting block. But what about my promise to Kobi to do my best? Do robot promises need to be kept? Kobi wasn't even awake when I said those words. It was a silent promise. A promise to myself, I realise.

Josh sighs deeply, once again turns to face me. I notice we're only inches apart.

'If Kobi wakes up, it would mean the world to me if you continued to take care of him,' he says softly.

He meets my eyes and looks at me so earnestly that I have to look away.

# EIGHTEEN

*Monday, 8:45am*

I've made sure to arrive early for the staff meeting today. As I settle Kobi near the front of the Shannon Suite, I confidently tell him to expect a significant announcement at the meeting.

'Hang on to your motherboard. I think what you'll hear will blow you away.' My upbeat tone is meant to reassure both of us.

Kobi is fully back to normal, if normal is what he was before his misadventure on Thursday night. The liquid in his systems turned out to be seventy per cent proof alcohol – a fact that actually sped along his recovery. Alcohol evaporates faster than water, so Kobi dried out quite quickly once the air got to him.

How he got wet in the first place is still a mystery. I feel like people have been avoiding me since. Shane maintains he doesn't know what happened, and I've no reason not to believe him. And Kobi himself couldn't provide any answers because everything he recorded that night was wiped away, along with the liquid.

While Kobi was in limbo, Josh and I had a long talk. Should I worry that Josh kept a vital piece of information from me? Maybe. Do I understand why he did it? Sort of.

On the upside, he said he'd do his best to keep Ron from

hearing about the Phelan's incident. Implied that Ron isn't very involved in the day-to-day. 'More of a big picture kind of guy,' he said. There'd be no need to bring it to his attention, especially if Kobi made a full recovery and even more especially if Kobi made good progress over the next few weeks at Go Ireland. He said he'd call JP and put in a good word for me. JP is similarly not a day-to-day kind of boss, but there was no way he wouldn't hear about the Phelan's excursion.

While Josh didn't specifically ask me not to share the PHI incident with anyone, I haven't decided yet if I should talk about it openly. Kobi's already on the back foot here. It would only make people more wary of him. And I plan to keep him under supervision at all times. Josh showed me Kobi's manual override switch in case I ever need it. 'Trade you a PHI for a Phelan's,' I told Josh, half joking. 'Mutually assured destruction.'

So we decided on a few things together. One of those being that if Kobi was going to stay at Go Ireland, he'd need some upgrades. Like a waterproof cover. Josh said he'd work on something so Kobi could be around liquids, maybe even be outside when it's raining. We also agreed we needed to shake things up a bit.

'Now, Kobi,' I say as our colleagues begin to drip-feed into the room. 'I need to ask you something before the meeting.'

'Of course. How can I help you today?' *Eager to help, as usual.*

'You know that compliance report you're working on for Sandra in HR?'

'Sandra Smith. Yes.' *Too eager, some might say.*

'You can't file the report.'

'Yes, I can.'

I scan the room, wave at Duncan Canning. I try to keep my voice low and even. 'I mean, I don't want you to file the report, Kobi.'

'I am afraid that will not be possible, Maeve. Sandra Smith has requested the report. The report must be delivered.'

'Let's just say... it would be in everybody's best interests if you didn't deliver it.' I consider patting my finger alongside my nose, maybe winking. But these subtle signals may be beyond him.

'The report shall be completed and filed as agreed upon. Is this some kind of test, Maeve? To see if my efficiency remains at the same level as before?'

*Maybe it wouldn't have been the end of the world if Kobi hadn't woken up on Friday morning.* I groan, decide on a different approach. 'Okay, so the report is not yet completed. I can work with that. New request incoming.'

'I am all audio sensors,' he says. Is it possible that Kobi is *enjoying* himself?

'Sandra never gave you a definitive date for filing the report, did she? You may file the report in eight weeks' time, but no sooner. Do you understand? Can you do that for me?'

'Yes, of course, Maeve. I am calculating the date for submission right now.'

I exhale, feel myself relax a little. That report can never see the light of day. It's not going to win anyone any popularity contests. 'Okay, glad we're on the same page, finally. Glad you don't need to know the reason why.'

'I do not. Of course, I may make my own internal postulation. Perhaps this timeline is to enable more data-gathering. I have already noted twenty-seven compliance violations since Wednesday. It is indeed a shame that my recording from Phelan's Bar and Grill was erased, as there may be a gap in the data. Perhaps you could tell me, Maeve, if any compliance violations occurred at that location?'

'What? Oh, um, nothing of note,' I tell him with a smile.

Sandra makes her way to the top of the room. She's carrying a company-branded water bottle. She looks immaculate, as always, but there's something jittery in her manner.

'Good morning, everyone, good morning. Right, settle down. JP has asked me to lead this meeting today as he can't make it.'

Some low-volume whispering starts among my colleagues.

Sandra speaks louder. 'But – we have some important things to announce today.'

The room goes quiet.

'First of all, I think we all owe Kobi a massive apology for Thursday, yeah?' She looks at me, gives me a subtle nod. 'Even though we don't exactly know what happened, I think we can all agree that it shouldn't have happened. We're very relieved to see you looking so well, Kobi.'

'Thank you,' says Kobi. 'You are looking well too.'

I hear a snort-laugh from somewhere near the back of the room. I gesture to Kobi to be quiet.

Sandra continues. 'So, Kobi, on behalf of everyone, I want to apologise. Come on, guys, I want you all to say sorry with me now, please. Remember what I said in my email.'

Voices murmur around the room.

'Sorry, Kobi.'

'Soz, mate.'

'Sorry.'

'Wait for it...' I whisper to Kobi.

'Now,' says Sandra. 'I have an announcement to make.' She takes a deep breath and delivers the next bit at speed. 'Following the events of Thursday evening, HR has decided to implement a proactive employee well-being programme, specifically in relation to extracurricular social activity.'

'What does all that mean?' Dave calls out.

'It means...' Sandra takes a swig from the bottle. 'Our new Social Committee will be organising a series of events, here on site. Representatives from several departments will be co-opted – I mean, invited – onto the committee. Food and drink will be provided at events. I mean, soft drinks will be provided.'

The sound of whispering around the room goes up and down like someone trying to tune in an old analogue radio.

'These events will commence at four p.m., starting this Wednesday. We'll aim to do one event a week for the next few weeks.'

Julia calls out from the back, 'Do we have to go?'

'Attendance is not compulsory, no,' says Sandra. 'If you wish to remain at your desk instead, that's fine. And – listen, please, everybody – Kobi, we would very much like you to attend these events. You'll be made very welcome, do you understand?'

Kobi turns his head towards me. I nod for him to respond. 'Yes,' he says. 'Thank you.'


After the meeting, people stand around in clumps, enquiring after each other's weekends, reluctant to face the desk-reality of the working week.

Shane comes up to me. I didn't see him at all on Friday. I was busy taking care of Kobi and he was still on gift shop duty. He texted me every hour asking for Kobi updates, until I told him to stop.

'Well,' he says now by way of greeting. He looks refreshed, clean-shaven. 'Glad to see Kobi seems to be back to... normal?'

'We'll see. We're taking it one day at a time.' I'm not sure who exactly I mean by we. I suddenly realise I don't want to tell him everything Josh and I talked about on Thursday.

I glance around the room. Dave shoots me a dirty look, then resumes his conversation with Julia.

'No one's said anything to you about what happened in Phelan's, I take it?' I ask Shane.

'Sorry,' he says. 'No one knows anything, apparently.'

He accompanies us towards the door, opens it for Kobi to go through ahead of us.

'You were right about one thing though,' I say as the door closes behind us.

He smiles. 'Always a bonus. What was that?'

'What you told Kobi. After-work socialising *is* a good way to get to know people. For them to see you... differently.' I smile back. 'And things were going well in Phelan's, up to a point. Hence the new Social Committee events.'

'Hence? Are you saying this was your doing?'

'Keep your voice down!' I elbow him in the ribs as we walk the corridor. 'Kind of.'

In the early hours of Friday morning, I made a plan with Josh for how to accelerate Kobi's integration. We settled on two big priorities for the next few weeks: Kobi needs to meet co-workers in a social setting, and he needs to get a hell of a lot better at socialising. If he can do both, it'll kick off a virtuous circle and he might just have a chance of fitting in.

We've reached the elevator. 'Kobi, why don't you go ahead and go up to the second floor? Shane and I will take the stairs. I'll meet you up there in a minute. Don't touch anything.' I press the call button for the second floor so that Kobi and the elevator don't need to interact.

As the doors close, I turn to Shane. 'I had to go to HR on Friday morning, to explain the Phelan's incident. Get out in front of it. I was half expecting to be fired on the spot.'

'I'm glad you weren't,' he says. 'It was my idea. You could have blamed it on me.'

'Thanks,' I say. 'That's sound of you. But it was mostly my fault. You're only about ten per cent to blame.'

He laughs. 'That sounds like one of Kobi's calculations.'

We start up the stairs together. 'So when I realised I wasn't getting fired, I suggested that Kobi would get along better if he could get to know people in a' – I use air quotes – '"controlled environment". Something social, but safe. I threw in that Sandra might not like the results of Kobi's compliance report either. Might cause a lot of HR headaches. I may have implied that I could make the compliance report go away.' I move my hands through the air to demonstrate what the disappearance of a report looks like.

'Wow, look at you being all proactive and greasing the wheels of power.'

I laugh.

'Oh, there's one last thing,' I say as we arrive at the second floor.

'I might have volunteered you to join the new Social Committee. Consider it a payment to make up for your ten per cent.'

# NINETEEN

Kobi and I are back in the park again, just like last Monday, but this time it's different. Even though last week could *technically* be deemed a disaster, I feel strangely calm. Maybe it's because the only way is up. Maybe it's because of the long conversation with Josh on Thursday night, where he revealed that things haven't always gone right for him either.

Everyone else is gone on tea break in the staff café, but Kobi isn't ready for this volatile, liquid-focused environment. For a start, he doesn't have a waterproof shield yet. But more important, I still don't know how he got wet in Phelan's. Was it an accident, or something more sinister?

I've brought Kobi to the park because I want to ask him something privately. Away from the rest of the staff – even from Jen, who's agreed to host me and Kobi in her office for a few days while I figure out how best to deploy him at Go Ireland. Her terms and conditions were that we bring her a can of ice-cold Diet Coke every day, and that neither of us touch anything while we're there.

I want to ask Kobi what happened at that factory in the Midlands, to see for myself if he poses any danger to us. Of course

I'd love to know what Jen thinks, but I worry that if I tell her every-thing, Kobi might become her responsibility.

The September day is fresh, but everyone is colluding in the pretence that summertime isn't over yet. The women at the office continue to wear open-toed sandals but quietly hang cardigans on the backs of their chairs 'just in case'. I lead Kobi to my favourite bench. I sit and he stands beside me, facing out.

'So, Kobi, while you were, um, being rehabilitated on Thurs-day, I had a long conversation with Josh. He told me all about PHI, the place where you used to work. That was an interesting story.'

'Thank you for your role in my rehabilitation, Maeve. I am most grateful for your efforts.'

I'm unsure if he's avoiding the topic or just needs a direct ques-tion. I try again. 'I mean, he told me about The Incident. About that night with your co-workers and why you had to leave. Do you want to tell me what happened?' I say gently. 'I'd like to hear your version.'

A breeze gusts up. Dusty leaves waltz around his mechanical feet. 'I am afraid I do not have any memory of the incident. No data is available from that time.'

'But Josh told you about it afterwards?'

'Yes. I was working the night shift with three of my human colleagues – Sam, Carli and Vivek. I was paired with Sam. We performed our usual routine. He presented the implants and I scanned them. We did this 253 times, according to Josh, until the humans took a break at approximately 0300, when I most likely recalibrated my scanners. Then we all went back to work. The incident occurred at 0327.'

'And you now know the details of what happened?'

'Yes. Josh showed me the CCTV file.'

I decide to probe a little. I want to know if it's something he might be planning to repeat anytime soon. 'What did you think, watching that back? How did you... feel, if that's the right word for it?'

'Many things. It was strange. It was surprising. It was worrying.'

I turn my head to look at Kobi. 'Why worrying?'

'I was worried about my colleagues. They were afraid of me. It made me sad.'

'Please elaborate.' I sound a bit like Kobi myself.

Another breeze whirls around us. I rub my bare arms and wish I'd worn a just-in-case cardigan.

'When I started at the factory, I was the only collaborative robot. It was a position of privilege. I was designed to help humans, and my scanning technology is far superior to anything a person can do. But sometimes I wished I was more like them. I wanted to be one of them. Do you know this feeling?'

I exhale slowly, shiver a little. I do know this feeling. Got it every time my family moved. *A chance to make new friends*, according to Dad. Now I have friends all over the world, at least one from every country I've lived in. The only problem is that it's hard to connect with people in different time zones. And my college friends? Well, they all took flight after graduation, eager to leave the nest, just as I was trying to settle back into the city where I was born. I just can't seem to shake the feeling that I'm in the right place at the wrong time. Or maybe it's the wrong place at the right time?

'Yes,' I tell Kobi. 'I do know this feeling. You seem to have very... elaborate sensors.'

'Thank you. Josh says my Emotion Detector becomes more refined with every interaction.'

'Good for you,' I say. 'I wish I had the same feature.'

'Perhaps I can speak to Josh about getting you an upgrade,' says Kobi. 'That was a joke, Maeve, although I know you do not care for my jokes.'

I smile. 'Ah, that *was* funny and – perhaps for the first time – appropriate.'

Kobi certainly doesn't seem dangerous. Maybe the factory incident was just a glitch, like Josh said. I check my watch. Break time is over. I'm satisfied – for now.

# TWENTY

*Tuesday, 2pm*

I'm in the Liffey Room, downloading Kobi's TIL files from the past thirty-six hours. They'll be the first thing Josh wants to see when he comes in to check on The Kobi Integration Project – Phase 2: After the Watershed. I wonder if Josh is looking forward to seeing me as well as his robo-protégé.

Kobi is currently in rest mode and charging his battery because today he's getting his new waterproof shield. This morning, following along with an instructional video on the MIT course, and with a little advice from Jen, I made a backup charging station for Kobi, just in case something happens to the main one. I'm feeling pretty pleased with my work – even though it didn't involve much more than some simple cabling and wiring. Electricity 101, the kind of stuff Dad taught me as soon as I was old enough to hold a screwdriver and sensible enough not to touch any live wires with it.

As I recheck my wiring – 'Safety first, safety second,' Dad used to say – I think of the quietly confident way Josh took charge as soon as he arrived here after the Phelan's emergency. He has the logical mind of an engineer and can break a problem down into sequential steps. Could I ever become like that? In times of crisis, I tend to panic and throw everything in the air – much like Shane threw that ridiculous cup of rice.

I know it's unfair to compare Josh with Shane, and really, there's no reason to. Shane is just my sort-of work friend who I'll probably never see again as soon as either of us leaves Go Ireland. I do regret the messiness of our hookups... Maybe we could have become proper friends without that complication.

And while Josh is the most interesting person I've met in a while, I should definitely keep things professional with him. He's excited about what he's doing. He's going places and has some idea of how to get there. I sometimes feel like I'm going round in circles, a drunk at the party of life, trying all the drinks and hoping to find a favourite one before I pass out. Maybe Josh will be a good influence on me. Help me find a new direction.

I look up to see Josh's handsome face in the glass panel of the door. He's carrying a large cardboard box. 'Hey.' The door muffles his voice. 'Fragile. Can you?'

I let him in, noting his rolled-up sleeves and tanned, capable forearms.

I nod towards Kobi in the corner. 'He's asleep, as requested.'

'Good. How is he?'

It feels like we're taking care of a patient together. There's no need for small talk because we're on the same page. We're just continuing the very intense conversation we had last Thursday night, here in this very room, as if we last saw each other a moment ago.

'He's doing well, I think. He's excited about the new evening socials.'

'It's pretty innovative.' Josh smiles his wide-mouth smile. He places the box on a table, turns to me. 'And how are you? Feeling any less drown-y this week?'

I laugh. 'I'm really not a fan of liquids these days. I'm glad I still have my job anyway. Thanks for... whatever you did to help with that.'

He begins unpacking the box, then pauses to say, 'Look, you have been thrown in at the deep end, thanks to Ron Tron and his unorthodox ideas. But I'm here to help you.'

He holds my gaze and I get that tingly feeling, like something exciting is about to happen. He doesn't break away and the look goes on too long.

I hear myself say, 'So, do you think the waterproof shield will work? It'll give Kobi more mobility, right?'

He turns away, resumes laying out items on the table. 'Yeah, it's kind of a conundrum. For Kobi to thrive, he needs to be out in the world. But I need to protect him as much as I can. If I could put armour on him, I would.'

I smile. 'I guess we all wear armour, in one form or another.'

He surprises me by asking, 'What's yours?'

The question is so direct I laugh. 'I didn't mean literally.'

He turns to face me. 'I know.'

I flush and move closer to the table to examine a series of flat, colourful components – green, orange, white – in varying sizes and shapes. Clear plastic pieces too – short, fat accordions. I pick up a fine green piece and hold it lightly between my palms, like I'm handling an old vinyl record and don't want to smudge the grooves. It wobbles slightly but holds strong.

Then I notice something. 'Wait – these colours.'

The three colours of the Irish flag.

Josh beams at me. 'You wanted him to be part of the team, right?'

He holds up pieces to Kobi's body to see if they'll fit where intended.

'Um, yes. The team. As in, the team at work...?'

'And you work for Ireland!'

'Not exactly. We try and promote visiting Ireland, yes. That's our job. But that doesn't mean we go around like it's St Patrick's Day every day.'

'I thought the Irish loved being Irish.' I can't tell if he's teasing me or being serious. 'It's pretty much all you guys talk about when you're abroad.'

*True.*

'Abroad – yes. When we're at home all we do is moan about it.'

'That's still talking about it,' he says with a smile that slowly fades. He clears his throat. 'I thought you'd love it.'

I feel bad. I pick up a bright orange piece, put it down again.

'Maybe it's not that bad. It just takes a bit of getting used to, is all. It's just' – I can't help myself – 'I think he'll look more like a mascot than a robot.'

'Well, that could be a good thing, no? You said he wasn't doing well as a robot. Maybe people might be less suspicious of a mascot. Back home, mascots are a big thing. People love them. Look, let's get him fitted out and see what he looks like. Hand me that long piece, will you?'

How will Kobi react to becoming a walking robotic tricolour? He was designed and programmed in Ireland – is he technically Irish? And what will my colleagues say? Will this be another reason to complain about him?

On the bright side, maybe this could give people something innocuous to focus on. Jen Mason is affectionately known as DC; people think they have her figured out, based solely on her excessive fondness for a particular kind of soda. Perhaps Kobi could become 'tricolour guy' or 'IRE-robot'. Find his place in the pantheon of office staff.

Josh is busy doing sticker art with Kobi, peeling a transparent layer from each component before sealing it flat against the robot's torso, arms and head. He places the clear accordion pieces over the joints.

Kobi's trunk now gleams satsuma orange; his arms and legs shine emerald green. His head, mercifully, remains white. The colours glow metallically, as true as a spray paint job. Will my colleagues find this relatable? Could they possibly find it... endearing?

'Shall we wake him up?' I ask when Josh's work is complete.

'Go for it.'

I bring Kobi back to life. 'Hey there,' I say gently. 'The operation was a success.'

'Greetings, Maeve. Greetings, Josh. It is good to see you both. *Processing*. I do not feel any different.'

'Look down,' I say.

Kobi scans his arms and leans forward to assess his lower half. He does not say anything. He takes a step forward.

'Whadayathink, buddy?' says Josh. 'You like the colours?'

'I look like... *Processing*. I look like an Irish superhero,' says Kobi.

I laugh. 'You do! Captain Ireland. Your superpowers are talking about the weather, only expressing emotion through song and feeling simultaneously inferior and superior to everyone else in the world.'

'Do you like it?' asks Josh.

'I love it,' says Kobi.

# TWENTY-ONE

*Wednesday, 4pm*

While the Social Committee is officially a democratic organisation, it is in fact helmed by a benign dictator, in the form of Sandra Smith. That's according to Shane's daily message updates to me. He's hinted that a coup may be on the cards before too long.

Yesterday, we all got an email invitation to 'Art therapy with Trish Horgan'. So we are now gathered in the gift shop for the first work social, overlooked by Trish's monstrous creations. I remind myself that Trish is married to JP and turn my attention towards the centre of the room, where my boss's boss's wife is busily unpacking art supplies.

Two rows of easels form a circle around the room, each one equipped with paints and brushes. I lead Kobi to one of them, smile to reassure him. 'I'll be right behind you in the next row, in case you need me. But this is a chance for you to, y'know, mingle. Get to know your colleagues. Try to have fun.'

Shane takes up a position to Kobi's left, a move we agreed on earlier. Shane is good with people. Popular, without trying. Maybe some of it will rub off on Kobi. One by one, all the easels find an artist, except for the one right next to Kobi. Dave is the last to arrive. He tuts loudly as he accepts his fate and his position next to the newest member of staff.

I stand behind an easel, fiddle with the paintbrushes. I can keep an eye on Kobi from here. This wouldn't have been my first choice of activity, but I guess Sandra hadn't figured the need to safely entertain human and android colleagues into her yearly budget. Trish is probably doing this for free. I asked Kobi if he'd even be able to participate in an art activity, and he assured me he would. Wary of what he did to the company website on his first day, I tell him he won't be able to access any internet tools during the activity and anything he creates will have to be his own work.

'People think that robots do not know anything about art,' I hear him say to Shane. 'But in August the PicassoBot 5000 was shortlisted for the Turner Prize, for a submission titled *Is It Still Life?*. The work comprised a hen's egg frozen in a bucket of ice. *Conceptual Art Monthly* magazine called it "the most ground-breaking piece of art since Marcel Duchamp's *Fountain*".'

'Duchamp?' says Shane. 'Oh, he really took the piss, didn't he?'

I can tell this confuses Kobi and I'm thankful someone else is entertaining him for a while. I'm also thankful when Trish claps her hands and says, 'Welcome, welcome, one and all. Can I have your attention please?'

Trish is wearing a floral dress, ankle-high boots and a long silk scarf wrapped around her throat and thrown over her shoulders. As she speaks, one scarf end appears on her right shoulder and tries to make its way to the centre of her chest. She picks it up and flings it back over her shoulder. A moment later, it happens again. This action is repeated at regular intervals throughout the time Trish speaks to us. She introduces herself as an artist with many strings to her bow. She's dabbled in most of the creative and performing arts, always moving on to a new one before she really has a chance to break out into success in any one field, it seems. She likes to keep things fresh. She doesn't mention JP.

'Can anyone tell me what art is all about? What's the essence of it? Why do we like it?'

I pray that someone other than Kobi will answer, and for once my prayers are answered. Imelda calls out, 'Art is about originality.'

Trish smiles. 'No. Art is about truth.'

I can tell Kobi is gearing up to ask about this, but luckily Trish moves on without elaboration.

'Now. What is "art therapy"? I'm sure some of you are wondering, "Has Trish gone completely crackers now or what?" Before I explain it, does anyone want to tell me what *they* think art therapy is?'

I hear Dave mutter, 'It's what I need after any time spent near your wreck-the-head paintings.'

Unfortunately, Kobi chooses this moment to be helpful. 'David has a theory,' he says to Trish.

'Ah, hello, you must be Kobi,' says Trish. 'I've heard all about you. I see you're flying the flag for Ireland there. Beautiful use of colour. I can tell we're going to get along. Now, what were you saying? David, do you know what art therapy is?'

'No,' mumbles Dave.

As Trish delivers her explanation, Dave reaches over and grabs Kobi's paintbrush. He chooses some colours from his own palette, then quickly daubs a figure on the blank paper in front of him. Then he paints a large red X through the figure. He taps Kobi on the arm, nods at him, then nods sideways to the picture. It's crudely done, but there's no mistaking the figure. It's Kobi.

'Art therapy involves using artistic expression to work through emotional or psychological issues,' Trish is saying. 'Now, I know that might sound a bit heavy, but I didn't want you all to think you had to compete with these.' She gestures to the walls. 'I know it's intimidating.'

A sound like suppressed sneezing comes from the other side of the circle.

'This is a safe space,' she continues. 'That's why the easels are arranged in a circle. Right now, I want you to look inward. Use all the paints and brushes at your disposal. In fact, don't even use the brushes unless you want to. Use your fingers, hands or even other parts of your body. I want you to express on the canvas what it means to you when I say the word "family". There are no rules. Just let it flow through you.'

We all make a start. Dave detaches his anti-Kobi picture from his easel.

As he casts around for somewhere to discard it, Kobi says to him, 'David, may I please keep your picture of me?'

I was wondering if he'd recognised himself.

'All right,' Dave replies gruffly.

'It is the first time I have been the subject of a portrait. I shall attach it to the wall next to my sleep pod. There is no mirror in my room. It would be nice to have a daily reminder of how others see me. Of course, it would be better if the red X were not part of the picture, but art is never perfect.'

I thought that Kobi would struggle to hold a paintbrush, but to my surprise, he reveals a hidden grip embedded in his right arm. It looks quite delicate but perfect for holding a fine brush. He gets busy with placing paint onto the brush, then onto the page.

Dave starts working on the family assignment too, using his hands to spread black, brown and red paint across the paper. I can't make out any human figures. I suppose it's possible that Dave's family are alien mud monsters.

I peek over at Shane's art. It's abstract but not unpleasant to look at, with swirls and swooshes in various colours. Probably the colours of his local hurling team. He seems content to be lost in it anyway.

I look at my own page, still blank. I can't seem to start it. It doesn't seem right to draw a picture that's just me and Mam. But I can't face the idea of painting Dad with us either. And I don't want to represent him as a ghost, or something otherworldly. How do you draw an absence?

'I call this one *Drawing a Blank*,' I mutter to myself.

I decide to mix all the colours together on my palette for something to do.

*5pm*

Trish invites us to move around the room to see what everyone has created. It's surprisingly fun. Imelda has painted a traditional Christmas scene, with children playing by a fireside, while nearby a group of adults share food and conversation at a long table. Julia has painted a portrait of a woman who looks like an older version of herself, wearing colourful robes. Duncan Canning has gone wild with a family tree metaphor. The whole canvas is taken up with one enormous tree; dozens of branches house tiny stick-figure family units.

In the end and out of ideas, I opted to paint what I saw around me, so I now have a picture of Shane, Kobi and Dave painting their pictures, with others sketchily drawn in the background.

When Dave sees it he says, 'Aw, Maeve, I didn't expect this honour, from you of all people.' His tone as caustic as paint remover. I ignore him.

Trish asks, 'Well, what do you think of each other's work?'

Kobi says, 'Trish, by objective standards, there is clearly artistic talent among the staff. May I make a suggestion?'

She nods.

'These paintings should be on display.'

'I agree, Kobi. People can take them home and display them there.'

'But we are standing right now in a gallery of sorts. Art is made to be experienced by others.'

'Now that's not necessarily the case, Kobi,' says Trish. 'I have to disagree with you there. Art is creative expression, even if no one else ever sees it.' She flings the scarf over her shoulder again.

'And I must disagree with you, Trish. Art only becomes art when another being recognises it as art.'

*Uh-oh.*

'Well, I hate to say it, Kobi, but I'm not sure you're the most qualified to comment, really, given that you're not an artist yourself.'

Someone behind me makes a low 'oooh' sound.

'I'm sorry if that sounds a bit harsh,' says Trish. 'Let's have a look at your work. See if you managed to get anything onto the page.'

Kobi escorts Trish to his easel. Everyone else goes quiet.

'Oh,' she says. 'That's... I mean... How did you...?'

At first glance Kobi's painting looks almost like a photograph. It's a close-up portrait of Josh. It looks like a pointillism technique, with individual pinpoints of paint clustered together.

'Wow,' says Julia.

'Ah here,' says Dave. 'That's got to be cheating somehow. Right, Trish? Although... it is technically very good, I suppose.'

'It's...' says Trish. 'It's...'

'Amazing,' says Julia. 'Maeve – you didn't tell us he could do portraits. Kobi, could you do one of me?'

Shane joins the conversation. 'Kobi, do you think you could do more of these? Maybe do some landscapes as well? I think we could sell these. Here in the shop. Uh, alongside Trish's work as well, of course.'

It's unclear if Trish hears Shane's comment because she's moved away to noisily gather up brushes and paints and pack them into a bag.

'Shane, might I suggest one section of the gallery be reserved for staff paintings?' Kobi says. 'Imelda's and Julia's work should be displayed. Perhaps David's too.'

'Great idea, Kobi,' says Shane. 'I think we can find room for everyone.'

Kobi moves over to one of the walls, points to Trish's paintings. 'If we take down some of these, there will be enough space to display them.'

'Trish, what do you think?' Shane calls to her.

But Trish has her back to us and doesn't answer. As she packs away the art supplies, there's something in the twitchy movement of her scarf that makes me think of a snake.

# TWENTY-TWO

*Thursday, 2:30pm*

I'm waiting for Josh outside the almost-hidden entrance to the newly refurbed Irish Viking Museum on the other side of the city. They've just spent two million euro revamping it – none of which went on signage, apparently. Duncan Canning wanted a volunteer to act as a 'secret shopper', to see if the museum should go on our 'highly recommended' list for tourists. I put my hand up. No harm trying to keep on Duncan's good side while I'm getting to grips with The Kobi Project. Jen said she'd keep an eye on Kobi while I was out. I left the two of them chatting away in her office.

I'm in a good mood after the success of last night's work social. If this was the 1800s, I'd be a matriarch whose young ward was the belle of a debutante's ball. I even took the risk of bringing Kobi to tea break this morning, and was rewarded by Dave recounting the event in great detail, even though everyone listening had been there themselves.

'You should've seen Trish's face when she saw Kobi's painting,' he said. 'Gas craic altogether. And then when he said that our paintings should replace hers on the wall. Classic. Fair play, Kobi. Fair play.'

Afterwards I emailed Josh a summary of events, writing 'minor triumph' in the subject line, and he replied right away. We agreed he'd meet me here to get the latest on Kobi while I had a look around the museum. Two birds, one stone. Ancient Irish stone, in this case.

Now, I take out my phone to message Josh to call me if he can't find the entrance. But halfway through the message I hear, 'Hey there!' and he's suddenly right in front of me. He's wearing an open-neck cotton shirt in a soft colour. He looks good against the grey stone wall of the museum.

'You found it,' I say redundantly, smiling up at him.

He returns my smile. 'Maeve, I've been to this museum, like, four times.'

'Really?'

I lead him through the entrance – glass doors embedded into the wall of a restored medieval ruin, a rusted portcullis above our heads. The inner foyer is dark and cool. It's a small space and we have to cluster together. Josh smells good through the gloom.

'Yes. I love it. You have to stop thinking of me as a tourist, Maeve. I've lived in Ireland for three years.'

'But this is a tourist museum. The fact that you've been here four times only makes you *more* of a tourist.' I turn my face away so he can't see my smile. 'I, on the other hand, have never been here before.'

'Does it make me a tourist or does it maybe make me a history buff? Come on, let me show you around.'

I laugh and follow him up dark stone steps, ducking my head instinctively and holding onto the metal rail. The history of the Norwegian warriors who sailed to Dublin over a thousand years ago is laid out in a series of small, dimly lit rooms, with real Viking artefacts in glass cases and fake ones on plinths you can interact with. I pick up a wooden axe. Josh lifts a heavy-looking sword and traces the 'bloodline' down the centre of it. The groove is intended to accelerate your enemy's blood flow from their body, he tells me with a grin.

Eventually the small rooms give way to a larger space, housing a full replica of a Viking longboat.

'Did you know,' says Josh, 'they buried Viking warrior kings in boats?'

'With all their treasured possessions and favourite things, yes.'

'Not just things.'

He directs me to read the small print on the wall next to the boat. A servant was often buried with their Viking master at the time of the master's funeral. Which became the time of the servant's funeral too. In other words, human sacrifices were made.

'This is really dark,' I say.

'Yeah, it's pretty hardcore.'

There's a whole section on slavery. How Dublin was a major trading post for slaves a thousand years ago. A slave auction scene is recreated with human-sized models. A child, head bowed, hands bound with rope, her chain held by a fair-haired Viking trader. A tourist takes a selfie in front of the scene. I look at Josh, appalled.

'Every city was built on blood,' he says. 'The price of progress, I guess. Let's keep going. There's a round tower we can climb.'

We're directed to the round tower by the pointing figure of a monk. I startle until I realise it's just a mannequin with an actor's face projected onto it. The monk explains that the round tower is not Viking but a religious structure from the 1600s that's been incorporated into the museum.

The spiralling stone steps of the tower are so narrow we have to go single file. Josh gestures for me to go ahead of him.

'Did you know St Patrick was a slave?' His voice bounces off the walls.

'Josh, you're not going to explain St Patrick to me, are you? This is way worse than mansplaining. Pat-splaining is where I draw the line.'

His big laugh bounces off the stones around us and fills my ears. I suddenly stop and he almost crashes into me. I spin around to face him. 'Wait a minute.'

'What?'

We're eye to eye, thanks to my two-step advantage.

I look him up and down. Tall, blonde, fair skin, strong jaw.

'Are *you* a Viking? Is that why you come here so often and know so much?'

He just laughs at me. 'I have no idea. I might have some Scottish blood in me somewhere, so I guess it's possible, because the Vikings went to Scotland too. But far, far more likely for you to be a Viking than me. The Vikings married into Irish families, right? Went from raiders to traders, became peaceful profiteers. And nothing makes peace like a wedding. We Americans didn't invent capitalism, you know.'

A memory floats back to me. Of course I know *some* Irish history; you have to in this business. It's just that Ireland has such a *lot* of history, it's hard to keep on top of it all. I do know that before the Vikings came, and later on the English too, Ireland had its own ancient system of law, called Brehon. Women could own land, get an education, become a doctor, choose who they married, and get divorced if it didn't work out. But all that changed under the twin hammers of English law and the Catholic Church. Progress is not inherently good, I remind myself.

Out of breath after ninety-odd steps, we emerge at the top of the tower onto a small viewing platform. The whole city lies beneath us. This ancient town that's constantly reinventing itself. Everywhere I look I see the yellow cranes of development, building vertically into tiny spaces. The city so small that the only place to go is up. Hotel after hotel squeezing into every vacant lot. Soaring rents making city living almost impossible. I'm grateful for my compact nook in the city's inner suburb. But from up here, it all looks like a board game laid out for my amusement.

Josh notices my silence. 'What's on your mind?' he asks.

He stands next to me, wraps his large fingers around the rail. A weak October sun turns his hair golden.

'The future,' I say, playfully.

He leans his elbows on the rail and smiles.

'And here I was thinking you were going to say "the past".'

'I have to admit, I'm surprised that you're so into history,' I say. 'I kind of assumed...'

We watch a seagull swoop down between buildings to settle on the river below us. My phone buzzes. I sneak a look at the screen, see a message from Shane: *Pints later?* I ignore it.

'What? Because I make robots, I can't have other interests?'

'More that... you don't like to dwell on the past.'

He laughs lightly. 'Well, that's true when it comes to my personal life, I suppose. The one thing about the past is – you can't change it. But you can learn from it. That's why I love museums.'

He turns his back to the view to face me. 'So tell me about this future you were thinking of just now.'

Maybe the air is thinner up here. Or maybe Josh's confidence is starting to rub off on me. 'I just feel like... a whole new world might be opening up. And I think I might want to be a part of it.'

'That's exactly how I feel!' He throws his arms out. I jump a little at his sudden enthusiasm. 'And if things go well with Kobi, you *can* be a part of it.'

I laugh, drawn in by his excitement. 'I do feel like I'm starting to make a little bit of progress with him.'

'There you go then!'

'As a matter of fact, Jen mentioned that there's a big AI conference on in a few weeks' time. Professor Mimi Lee is one of the speakers. Are you going, by any chance? It's in Athlone, the Athens of Ireland.' I know he probably won't get this little joke about the unassuming Irish Midlands town, but I can't help myself.

'I don't know who that is and I hadn't heard about the conference,' he says. 'But I've always wanted to visit Athens. I'm open to going, if you think it sounds worthwhile.'

'Maybe cage your expectations,' I say with a laugh. 'But there's a whole lot of interesting topics on the agenda: ethics, privacy, bias, neuro-rights.' I've been doing my reading.

'I'm impressed,' he says. 'We do need people like you in the industry, asking questions. I'm not that person. I just make the robots. But people like you—'

'Don't say "people like you",' I interrupt.

'Fair enough. It's just' – he turns to gaze out at the city skyline again – 'I can't make any promises, but we could probably use someone like you at RoboTron.'

I'm giddy, and not just because of our dizzying height on this windy platform. I try to ground myself, act casual. But I feel emboldened.

'Actually, now I *will* speak of the past,' I say, smiling. 'I have another idea to help us figure out how Kobi might fit in.'

# TWENTY-THREE

*Monday, 2pm*

A gust of wind whips my hair against my face as I walk down the stone steps of the Midlands train station. I fiddle uselessly with the collar of my linen jacket. A tinge of yellow high in the billowing treetops. It's October now, officially tourism off-season. Although Duncan Canning is fond of reminding me that 'tourism never sleeps' whenever we pass in the corridor.

A perky *bwawm bwawm* alerts me that Josh has already arrived. The size of his vehicle is in inverse proportion to the tiny car park. He lowers the window to call out, 'Hey!'

'Hey, I should've guessed you'd have a big one!'

I wince as the words come out of my mouth. Maybe Josh won't notice?

'And why's that?' he asks as I hoist myself up and into the belly of the beast.

I flounder. 'You know, because you're, you're...' *Don't say big. Don't say big.* I try to gesture vaguely, but my hands start shaping large invisible things in front of me and that just makes it worse.

'Yes?'

'American.' I exhale. 'Americans love their cars.'

'Well, you're not wrong. I could've picked you up in the city, you know.'

'I know. I wanted the time on the train to prepare for this meeting.'

That's partly true. I also wanted some alone time, to think. Instead of meeting Shane and the work crew for the usual pints on Thursday, I went for a drink with Josh after the Viking Museum and we ended up talking for hours – about work, about life, about the future. Yes, I'm enjoying Josh's company now, but what's going to happen in the weeks ahead? What if I fail with Kobi? Will Josh be disappointed? Or, if I do manage it, could Josh and I end up working together one day? Maybe even at RoboTron? In which case, we should probably keep things professional... just like I should have done with Shane.

'We don't have to do this, you know.' He sounds tired. 'We could just drive back to Dublin and forget the whole thing.'

Maybe he's right. This excursion was my idea, but now that we're en route, I'm nervous. Over drinks, I convinced Josh to return to the location of Kobi's last assignment, where it all went wrong on the factory floor. If we understood better what went wrong, maybe we could fast-track Kobi's interpersonal development. Even get some insight into what happened at Phelan's, see if there was any behavioural pattern. Josh was reluctant at first. He'd already gathered all available information from the manufacturing plant. He'd shown me the CCTV video of Kobi's malfunction; the silent, black-and-white images reminded me of 1950s sci-fi B movies.

But Josh had to admit he hadn't talked to everyone involved at the time. He'd focused on analysing Kobi's systems. I argued that if Kobi's memories were erased, we might learn more from talking to his colleagues about that night instead. Eventually, after three beers, Josh agreed.

'No, let's stick to the plan,' I tell him now as we speed through the countryside towards PHI.

I did do some research about PHI on the train. It's a US multinational with two plants in Ireland that it uses as a gateway to

European markets. At the Midlands plant, they make titanium implants and other medical devices that are supposedly transforming healthcare. Bones decay; titanium lasts forever. When you die, your metal hip will live on. I wonder if family members ever hold onto the hip as a keepsake? Perhaps mount it in a glass case on the mantlepiece.

'By the way,' says Josh as we round a bend, his knuckles white on the steering wheel. 'I meant to say—'

'The four worst words in the English language: I meant to say.'

'Okay, fine. I probably should have said this earlier.'

'Not much better.'

'These manufacturing companies are obsessively secretive. This business is all about intellectual property. They treat every outsider like they're a spy. Ron said he had to go through a very complicated process to get Kobi in. So, I was thinking' – he takes a narrow bridge a little too fast – 'it might be best if you don't say who you really are.'

'What? Why? That sounds very cloak-and-dagger.' *And a bit paranoid.*

'I just mean you don't have to say where you work. They wouldn't understand and might get spooked. Just say you work with me – which is kind of true. We can keep it vague. If pushed, we'll say you're a specialist in robot psychology – which is also kind of true. Or will be one day.'

'I don't like lying, Josh.' My mind races. *Should I go along with this?*

'It's not exactly lying. It's for everyone's benefit, really. If this meeting helps us to figure out what happened, that means there's less chance of it ever happening again, and a better chance of securing Kobi's future.'

'But you already said there was no chance of it happening again!'

I wish he would slow down, and everything else with him. While I'm good at adapting to new situations, I have my limits.

'There isn't, as it stands. But in some ways Kobi is almost like a living organism. He can learn – that means he can change. If whatever led to his malfunction the first time around were to happen again...'

My heart sinks. I look longingly at the door-opening mechanism of the car, lamenting the absence of traffic lights as we speed along the back roads. How bad would it be if I were to just open the door and roll out of the vehicle right now? I imagine a friendly cow licking my wounds and nursing me back to health, before I start a new life as a dairy farmer with a previously untapped talent for making butter.

I'm quiet for the rest of the journey. We snake our way through a large, confusing business park until Josh announces, like a satnav, that we've reached our destination. Maybe it will be okay. We're here now and I'm curious about how this day will unfold.

The building receptionist invites us to wait in a bright, cavernous foyer. I glance distractedly through the corporate magazines laid out on a low glass table. The internal company mag is glossy, full of images that look like stock photography or maybe even AI-generated – happy customers, happy staff, happy shareholders.

Medical devices are big business, it seems. 'The Changing Face of Healthcare' runs the headline on an article about a new company policy to ensure greater diversity at all levels of the organisation. I skim another article – 'Affordable Healthcare for All' – the CEO's vision for a future where advanced healthcare is accessible to everyone, not just those who can afford bespoke technological solutions. Yes, you *can* get a custom titanium implant right now, but only if you also happen to own at least two-thirds of an island. Another article praises the health and safety record of the Irish PHI plant. No mention of the Kobi incident, of course. No headlines that say 'Robot Runs Amok on Factory Floor' or 'Rogue-Bot: My Night-Shift Terror'.

'Heads up,' says Josh as a tall woman approaches, hair swept back from her face in a neat bun. She wears tailored trousers, a suit jacket and a black t-shirt with white text that says FOREVER

CODING. She looks like me, if I had an upgrade of cool sophistication.

'Hello, Josh, good to see you again.' She extends her hand to me. 'I'm Laura Cantwell. Head of programming and robot relations.'

'Cool title,' I say. A tattoo goes the whole way around Laura's wrist, like a bracelet. Squinting, I see that it's composed of a series of tiny zeroes and ones.

'Thanks! And what's your title?'

I look at Josh in panic.

'This is my associate, Maeve,' he says smoothly. 'Thanks for meeting with us today, Laura. We're very grateful for your time. I know you're super busy.'

'Aren't we all though?' she replies. 'How's Ron? I keep meaning to reach out to him but, like you say, busy busy. Send him my regards. Let's talk in my office. This way. Oh, and keep to the left!'

Before I can ask why, I hear a *whoosh*. A tiny yellow vehicle on four wheels zips by my ankles, a red basket on top holding white and brown envelopes. It looks like the remote-control cars I played with when I was a kid.

'Well, you're in a hurry today, aren't you?' Laura is apparently addressing the vehicle.

She produces a device the size of a phone from her pocket, taps at the screen. The car slows a little.

'Autonomous postal bot,' she tells us. 'Let's take the elevator to my office.'

If someone were to ask me what the theme of Laura's office was, I would immediately say, 'Glass.' Then I'd say, 'No, wait! Transparency,' and nod sagely. The desk is made of glass or possibly plastic, with a transparent keyboard and mouse. One entire wall is see-through, overlooking the factory floor below.

'May I?' I nod towards the wall.

'Knock yourself out,' says Laura. 'Actually, be careful you don't hit your head for real. I just had the glass cleaned.'

I stand with my face very close to the clear wall and survey the scene below. *This must be where Kobi worked.*

Just like in the video Josh showed me, large metallic boxes are spaced out evenly around the room – each one the size of a small tank. The boxes presumably hold the 3D printing machines; faint red lights within indicate that lasers are melting titanium powder into the desired implant shape – metal hips or knees, soon to be enhancing human bodies and lives. It seems strangely hushed for a factory floor – maybe the glass is sound-proof? At first I think it's devoid of human life, until three people emerge from between the rows of machines, wearing branded PHI jumpsuits. I try to imagine Kobi down there among them.

Josh sits down in a chair facing Laura's desk, but Laura comes and stands next to me. She's a good eight inches taller, even in flat shoes.

'Nice view, huh?' she says.

I can't tell if this is sarcasm or not. 'Natural light is overrated,' I venture.

She smiles. 'True enough. We're all glued to screens all day anyway.'

'So this is where Kobi worked then?'

'Yep. I miss that guy actually.'

'You miss Kobi? That's interesting. Why?'

'He was a great worker. A fascinating project for me to work on too – real the-future-is-now stuff, you know? I mean I've done my share of robotic arm programming. It was nice to get stuck into something more... more' – she raises her hands as if she's about to conduct the New York Symphony Orchestra – 'sophisticated. I know he was still in beta, but still – he was quite the creation, thanks to Josh here.'

Josh gives her a pained smile. He looks smaller than usual, folded up in the low leather chair. 'Laura, you're too kind. I know it didn't quite turn out like either of us planned. I hope it didn't get you into too much trouble.'

For a second I wonder if Laura is the 'Irish woman' Josh told me about, the ex he'd met at a conference three years ago. I bet they have loads in common. Both tall, good-looking, into robots. Then I notice the ring on Laura's left hand. *Probably not her.*

She takes a seat behind her desk. She looks at her computer screen, frowns slightly, then pushes the keyboard away and bounces back in her chair.

'Listen, Josh, I get it. I know what you were trying to achieve. What *we* were trying to achieve. Of course there's going to be setbacks. Especially when we're getting up to this level of sophistication in cobots. You're not going to make a break*through* without the occasional break*down*, right?'

He doesn't reply. She gets up and returns to the glass wall, where I'm still standing. She speaks quietly, as if to herself.

'I believe that one day humans and robots will work side by side, in harmony – and that will be a better world for all of us. It's just the next logical step in how we harness technology to protect humans and improve human health.'

I look sideways up at her. Maybe I could be Laura Cantwell when I grow up.

'Well,' says Josh after a beat, 'I'm glad this experience hasn't put you off the idea of cobot integration anyway.'

She smiles. 'Of course, it helps that RoboTron had completely indemnified the company against any potential losses. And – even better – Sam says he's not going to sue. A week off on full pay helped with that one.'

My brain pivots to catch up. Josh didn't mention any legal issues. Kobi did mention someone called Sam though. 'Sam is...?'

'Sam is the operator who bore the brunt of Kobi's little... meltdown,' says Laura. 'He got hit by an implant – although it was only on the toe, and he was wearing steel-capped boots, so... it could have been a lot worse. I keep telling them that. The suits are a bit spooked now though. They're going to be ultra-cautious about taking on another cobot. They'll wait to see what competitors are doing first. But then you lose the edge – I keep telling them that too. They don't listen to me. They think I just want another toy to play with.' She laughs lightly. 'And, well, I suppose I can't deny that.'

'Do you think we could talk to Sam?' I glance at Josh. He appears to be hiding his big, handsome face behind his big, handsome hands.

'I don't know if that's a good idea,' he mumbles. 'He might blame me for what happened.'

'We came here to try to find out more about that,' I remind him. 'Laura, do you have any theories about the Kobi incident? Were you here at the time?'

'I wasn't,' she says. 'It was a night shift so I was at home, tucked up in bed. I got a call to come in and arrived about the same time as Josh. After he took Kobi away, I watched the video footage back and talked to the shift workers. I ran a full analysis of all the data logs from the shift. Couldn't find anything amiss in the machine data.'

'Was there anything amiss in the non-machine data?' I say. 'I mean, in the human data? That is – with the staff?'

'Hey, Josh, she is good. Asking all the right questions. I can see why you brought her.' I feel myself glow under her gaze. 'The human factor – that's really what it's all about, isn't it? No matter how sophisticated the machines get, it's really the humans we need to understand first. My background is in engineering. I understand machines. The toughest part of this job has always been the people. Change management, they call it. As usual, the tech is years ahead of the personnel systems.'

I'm drinking in her little speech. Mostly because it vindicates our plan to fast-track Kobi into acceptance through maximum staff interaction. If we focus on the people, we might get results faster. Maybe we could put him on the cover of the Go Ireland magazine – if we had one. The monthly staff newsletter then. *Employee of the Month: Kobi. Likes: being helpful, making jokes. Dislikes: liquids, staircases.*

I think back to Kobi's first few days at Go Ireland. 'Was there any resistance to Kobi's introduction among his co-workers?'

Laura makes an indeterminate sound. 'No more than usual, I would say. Like, no more than when we got that new coffee machine last year. Perhaps less so in some instances – Jacob still claims he can't get a decent macchiato. But look, you can find out for yourselves if you want – I can give you fifteen minutes with Sam in the cafeteria.'

'That would be fantastic. Josh, what do you think?' I ask, picking up my bag.

He sighs and unfurls himself out of the chair, stretching up to his full height before sighing again and dropping his shoulders. 'I suppose so.'

'Great,' says Laura. 'You'll get a chance to try out our substandard macchiato.'

Laura settles us into a booth in the ultra-modern staff canteen. She gets us drinks – espresso for Josh, which looks extra tiny in his large hands, and a luxury-brand peppermint tea for me – and tells us to wait for Sam, who'll be starting his break any minute now.

When Laura goes off to find Sam, Josh says, 'I think I'll let you lead on this one, Maeve. You're doing great, by the way. Laura is really impressed with you. And she's not easily impressed.'

I smile. 'Finally, my talent for asking questions is paying off.' I suddenly remember Shane teasing me for asking too many questions. *In your face, Shane Fitzgerald.* I make a mental note to say this the next time I see Shane's face.

A twenty-something guy approaches our booth. Close-cropped beard, dreadlocks tied back, navy company overall.

'Hey.' He sits opposite us, places an eco-themed water flask on the table.

His casual manner inspires me to confidence. 'Oh, hello, you must be Sam. I'm Maeve McGettigan, and this is my associate Josh.' I almost wink at Josh.

'Yeah, Laura told me. You want to talk about Kobi, don't you? Coffee's good here, isn't it?'

I want to ask him why he's drinking water if the coffee is so good but decide to keep my powder dry.

'I don't know to the second question. But yes to the first one. Laura told us you were working with him the night of the... the night when he... that time when things went wrong.'

Sam gives a short laugh. His hair bobs. 'Him?'

'I'm sorry?' I say.

'So we're up to saying "him" now, are we? You do know Kobi is just a machine, yeah?'

Josh squirms in his seat. I know he's dying to chime in. He adds sugar to his tiny coffee and stirs it in, spoon clinking noisily. I'm pretty sure Josh doesn't take sugar in anything.

'Yes, I'm aware of that,' I say. Perhaps a bit of authority is called for. I decide to channel some of the language from the MIT robot course. 'But we find it helps us to enhance interactivity, communication and collaboration systems if we anthropomorphise Kobi.' Josh is nodding along. Emboldened, I decide to add, 'Also, it's more fun.' *Authoritative, but still approachable.*

Sam smiles. 'Ah, fun.' He takes a long slurp of water. 'Let me ask you something. Have you actually worked with the Kobi bot? Like, day-to-day?'

'Well...' I begin, but Sam cuts me off.

'I mean, have you tried to do anything other than take care of Kobi when Kobi's around? Because I have and let me tell you' – he pauses for another sip of water, probably for dramatic effect too – 'it's exhausting.'

'Go on.' I throw Josh a look to pre-empt any interruption. He's knocked back the espresso and I fear it's about to kick in.

'It's supposed to be a collaborative robot, yeah? Supposed to *collaborate*. That means help us – help the humans on the line. There's meant to be some kind of *mutual* exchange going on, right? It helps us and in exchange we teach it to be better?'

'Human–machine collaboration—' Josh begins.

'He – I mean, *it* – was probably the most annoying work colleague I've ever had. It was supposed to make my job easier, but it actually made it much, much harder. The constant questions. It never stopped. Honestly, my five-year-old niece asks less questions!'

'Well, he's still learning!' says Josh defensively. He can't help himself. 'He's just getting going. You wouldn't believe how much he's learned already—'

'Oh, I would,' says Sam. 'Because most of it he's learned from me. Not he – it, *it*. Now I'm doing it.' He shakes his head, then speaks more quietly. 'Sometimes I used to hide behind the machines and hope it wouldn't find me. But damn that supersonic hearing – it always found me. I didn't know I'd had it so good before – wearing headphones, listening to podcasts while I worked. All that changed when Kobi came along.'

I feel a bit bad for Kobi. He just wanted to learn, to help. To learn how to help. I decide to give Sam a moment to wallow in memories of how great work was back in the good old days. He's clearly no fan of Kobi's. Was probably glad to see him taken away. Could he have had anything to do with the malfunction? I want to dig a little, but not head-on.

'Can I ask you a question? Why *don't* you refer to Kobi as "he"? Laura does.'

'Yeah, well, she's...' He stops himself mid-sentence. 'That's her choice. I think we should remember it's a machine and act accordingly. It's not "one of us".'

Josh goes to speak, but I make a subtle hand gesture and he stops. He's too attached to Kobi to be objective.

'Are you worried that machines like Kobi might replace you one day?' I ask Sam.

He laughs again and sits up straight. 'No way. A machine can't do what I do. We shouldn't even be talking about that. Why can't machines just be machines and people just be people? Why do we always have to be pushing the envelope? The envelope is pretty perfect as it is – a simple yet elegant solution for sending letters. Do we really need to be reinventing envelopes?'

I smile. 'I agree, we don't need to improve on envelopes. But the messaging system as a whole has been reinvented – many times over.'

'And is it any better?' He smiles back at me.

'Well, that depends on how far back you want to go. It's better than never again hearing from someone who emigrated. On the downside, we now expect 24/7 access to each other. I suppose we still need to figure out the happy medium.'

'Exactly,' says Sam. 'And who gets to decide that?' I get the sense that he's enjoying the debate.

I sip my fancy tea, which has finally reached the perfect temperature. 'Decide what?'

'Who decided that 24/7 messaging was what we wanted? Because I don't remember voting for that.'

'You know that's not how it works,' says Josh, a little too sharply. 'If you'd asked people, before we had cars, what they wanted, most of them would have said a faster horse. So that's not exactly a great way to make technological progress, is it?'

'But why are *we* adapting to *it*?' says Sam. 'It – the tech, I mean – should be adapting to *us*.'

'Sam has a point – the technology always comes first,' I muse.

'Exactly,' says Sam. 'She gets it.' He clunks his water bottle against my cup as if we're three pints deep on a night out.

I clear my throat. 'Anyway. Let's bring this back to Kobi. Tell us about the night of the incident.'

'There's not much to tell. I'm sure you've seen the footage.' I wonder if he's being evasive.

'It would really help us to hear it in your own words,' I say. 'Were you surprised by what happened?'

'Was I surprised?' echoes Sam. 'Was I surprised? I'll bring it back to technology. It's always doing weird stuff, yeah? It can work fine for days, weeks – then one day it suddenly glitches and no one really seems to know why. I wasn't expecting it that night though, no.'

'Were you scared?' I can't imagine the Kobi I know being scary – but maybe I'm being naïve.

'I think I was too surprised to be scared, actually. Everything was going fine. Because it was the night shift, I'd asked Kobi not to talk to me too much. It seemed okay about that. Sorry, *he,* if you prefer. He seemed fine. Everything was normal, we were just getting through the work. Then suddenly, around three a.m., he started acting weird. It felt like he was being instructed, but not by me, if you know what I mean. He was handling implants when he shouldn't have been. It looked like he was collecting them or something – putting them in a pile.'

I look at Josh, who's clearly suffering through the retelling of events. 'Go on.'

'I tried to get control over him. He didn't respond to voice commands, and then when I tried to do a manual intervention, I couldn't get near him – he kept moving away. I knew we were in trouble when he threw the first implant. Those things are light, but they're made out of titanium. They're not meant to go airborne.'

I nod along. 'What happened next?'

'Well, that was it, really. I hit the alarm, yelled at the others to get out of there, then ran for the door. One of the implants bounced off my foot as I was sounding the alarm.'

'Did it hurt?'

'I felt it all right; it landed right on my big toe.'

'Weren't you wearing steel-capped boots?' I ask, remembering our conversation with Laura.

Sam goes to take a swig from his water bottle, then stops and looks down at the table instead. 'I should have been. I went through all this with Laura. I know it's company policy. To be honest I didn't see the need for them until that night. I do now though, I can tell you that for nothing.'

He extends a booted foot out to the side as evidence. A passing colleague with a tray pulls up short and scowls at us.

'Well,' says Sam, standing up suddenly. 'My break is ending soon. So unless you've any more questions, I'm going to get going.'

'Wait,' I say. 'Will you contact us if you think of anything else?'

Sam grins, sits back down. 'I will, Sherlock. Can I have your number?' He's very confident for someone who might be hiding something.

'Let me give you my card,' I say. 'Oh wait, I don't have a card. I mean, I don't have any cards with me. Josh, could you give Sam your card instead?'

Josh widens his eyes, raises his eyebrows. Nobody says anything for a moment. Then he sighs. 'Sure.'

He fishes a card out of his wallet and slides it across the table to Sam. The card sweeps sugar granules before it like a snowplough. Sam places one finger on the card and slides it back across the table towards me, cutting an alternate path through the sugar. He retrieves a pen from the front pocket of his overall.

'Could you write your number on there?'

'Sure,' I say.

I realise I'm enjoying myself. I glance sideways at Josh while I write down my number. He does not look he's enjoying himself at all.

Sam smiles as he pockets the card. 'Well, better get back to it. No rest for the wicked.'

## TWENTY-FOUR

*Tuesday, 7pm*

'Should we sit at the bar?'

Josh takes a seat at Phelan's bar before I have time to answer, but I don't mind. I enjoy the outsourcing of small decisions, especially in a social context. I hate the mental burden of choosing where to go, where to eat, when to arrive. It's one of the worst things about dating – a trick to avoid blame for the wrong choice, disguised as thoughtful generosity. *Not that this is a date*, I remind myself. Josh came in to check on Kobi this afternoon and casually suggested we might come here to catch up.

'Sure.' I settle in beside him and signal to the barman.

'Have you heard from our pal Sam?' Josh asks. He seems totally, utterly relaxed.

I have to think for a second. 'Sam from PHI?'

'Yep – he was very eager to get your number.'

'I think "very eager" is a bit of an exaggeration.' I laugh and touch my hair, flustered. *Wait – is Josh... jealous?* 'Anyway, no, I haven't heard from him.'

'Yeah, you're right – it's way too soon for him to call. It's only been a day.'

I scoff at this. 'As if anyone calls anyone any more. But I really don't think that's why he took my number. I think he just... we just... I just listened, is all.'

He rests his tanned forearms on the wooden counter. How does he have a suntan in October? Must be a trick of the soft lighting.

'I'm not sure we're going to get anything more useful from PHI anyway, to be honest. I think we're better off focusing on the future.' He smiles at me. 'The present looks pretty good too.'

I swirl my rum and Coke, and try not to wonder if he means me, or us, or just this bar right now.

A group of musicians are chatting in the corner as they unpack their instruments. Phelan's must be trying something new.

'How is Kobi getting along with everyone this week?' Josh asks, eyeing the musicians over my shoulder.

'Not bad. In fact, I'm thinking of trying him back in the customer relations department again. You know what they say – if you can make it there, you can make it anywhere.'

He laughs. 'And here I was thinking that was New York City.'

'Customer service is a much tougher place to survive.'

He clinks my glass with his beer.

'Sounds good. Maximise his interactions. He needs to be out there in the real world.'

'I'm flattered you consider Go Ireland to be the real world.'

We both laugh softly. The fiddle player has embarked on a melodious, mid-tempo slip-jig. It seems to be having a hypnotic effect on Josh, and the only reason I know this is because it seems to be having a hypnotic effect on me. The tune undulates. The guitarist joins in but only in a supporting role. Everyone knows the fiddle is the star of an Irish trad session.

'I really like this place,' says Josh. 'I can see why you guys come here.'

'Everyone likes it,' I say. 'It's good with a group, you can come here for a quiet drink on your own, it's good for dates.' *Why did I say that?* I greedily suck my rum up through the straw, willing it to enter my system rapidly.

He laughs, shakes his head. 'Well, maybe I should give it a whirl myself sometime. I've been on some bad dates lately.'

'Dating is tough for everyone,' I agree. 'Awful, actually.'

'It's so hard to meet someone,' he says. 'Why is that, do you think?'

'I don't know,' I answer too quickly. 'Chemistry, or lack of?'

The room seems to be getting warmer. I take off my cardigan, hang it on a hook under the bar. I rotate my glass on the beer mat. A bodhrán player has joined the session – a thrumming heartbeat under the melody, an echoing insistence.

'And how would you define chemistry?' So he's not going to let me off so easily.

'Well, that's the thing, isn't it? It's that... that spark. Hard to define by itself.' I feel my dating formula bubbling up through my mind, like the bubbles in my glass. *Don't say it,* I will myself.

'But it's one of the four key elements required to ensure a second and possibly third date.' *Oh no.* I definitely sound like Kobi right now. I thought I was supposed to be influencing *him*, not the other way round.

'It is? What are the other elements?'

I face the bar so I don't have to make eye contact. 'I've kind of worked out a formula over the years through my own, um, research. I use the formula to work out whether I should continue seeing someone I've just met. It saves a lot of time.' I'm unsure if this justification makes my confession worse or better.

'Maximum efficiency – I like it.'

I can hear the smile in his voice, but I refuse to look at him. The musicians have moved onto a reel. It's faster, spiralling ever upwards.

'Can you share this formula with me or is it patent-pending?' he says.

'It's open source, actually.' Might as well lean into it, I suppose. 'I call it CCSS. It stands for Conversation – Chemistry – Sense of humour – Safety. You need all four elements as a starting point.' I inhale the last of my rum. 'And you can take that to the bank,' I add, as if I've just handed him the secret to everlasting life.

He gets onto my wavelength. 'Interesting work, Dr McGettigan! Now let's see if your theory holds up to peer review. Conversation – someone you can talk to. I'll allow it. Next we have chemistry – definition pending. Sense of humour – no arguments here. What was the last one? Safety?'

I turn to face him. 'I keep trying to remove that one from the formula, but every time I do, I end up needing to put it back in. It just means the person has a fundamental regard for safety, yours and their own.'

He laughs, then drains his glass, and I wonder if he's mentally checking to see if we have all four elements of the formula right now.

I raise my hand to attract the barman's attention, but Josh intercepts it and suddenly we are holding hands for no reason.

'Let me get these,' he says.

I do my own arithmetic as he orders us another round.

# TWENTY-FIVE

## KOBI

*Wednesday, 0930*

Maeve has arranged for me to spend today in the customer relations department. She tells me that she and Josh have decided I am ready for this challenge. Before delivering me to the department, she gives me a list of 'trigger words' to avoid using today. These include key phrases such as 'maximum productivity', 'efficiency levels' and 'no, thank you, I would prefer to work through tea break'.

David and Julia are my assigned work buddies for the day. Their cubicles are located next to each other, separated by a 5-foot-high fabric wall. I stand to attention outside the cubicles, awaiting instruction. I can see both of them, but my calculations tell me they do not have line of sight of each other.

'Now, Kobi,' Julia greets me, 'are you going to behave yourself in here today?'

Her directness is surprising but also a relief. I wish all human communication were so clear.

'Yes,' I reply. I modulate my voice to convey enthusiasm. 'How can I help you today?'

'We were thinking of putting you on the phones, weren't we, Dave?'

While chatbots have their place in the world of online customer service, the phone call is strangely resistant to technological evolution. Humans still prefer to talk to humans. So it is a privilege to be awarded such a trusted position. However, my conversational comprehension benefits from analysis of the additional data that can be gathered beyond voice, such as hand gestures, body language, and eye contact or avoidance. In short, phone calls make me nervous.

David does not appear to have heard Julia as no response is issued. She picks up a small hedgehog-shaped object and throws it over the partition wall. It connects with David's head. From the sound, I postulate that the hedgehog may be a plastic composite, perhaps containing elements of rubber.

'What's wrong with you now?' David asks. I do so admire the communication skills of this department's employees.

'Phones,' Julia says. 'We might as well get some use out of this fella. Not that Maeve gave us much of a choice, did she?'

'Ah, she's just doing her job,' David says. 'It can't be easy. Sorry. Eh, no offence, Kobi.'

'None taken,' I reply. I am pleased to issue the customary rejoinder to this call-and-response phrase.

'She's spending a lot of time with that Josh guy, isn't she?' Julia says.

'Jules,' David says.

'What?' Julia says. 'There's no harm in it.'

Although David does not speak, Julia seems to have heard something because she says, 'What's it to you, anyway?'

David makes a sound that could not be classed as intelligible. Then he says, 'I just feel a bit bad for Shane.'

'Why?' Julia asks.

I must admit I am also curious to know the reason.

'You know,' David says.

I fear that clarity of communication has declined somewhat.

'Listen,' Julia says. 'If Shane wants her, he has to tell her. It's very simple.'

David picks up the hedgehog-shaped object and squeezes it. I believe I may now correctly identify this object. It is a stress ball. I am pleased at my deductive skill.

'It's not that simple,' David says. 'Like, they work together. What if he wants to tell her but just can't seem to find the right moment? What if she rejects him?'

I fear that we may have strayed into compliance violation territory. I flash my chest lights.

'Why does he keep doing that?' Julia says.

'Doing what?' David asks.

'Never mind,' Julia says. 'Kobi, come on, let's get you set up on the hotline here.'

She makes space for me in her cubicle and connects me up to the phone system. I resolve to focus my full attention on the incoming voice during the calls. My first phone call lasts 22 minutes, 17 seconds. Julia observes me during the call. I hope for some praise for the call duration when it ends, but none is forthcoming.

'Kobi, you don't need their whole life story. Just answer direct questions, then try to get them off the phone ASAP,' she says.

'I apologise. The caller was most interesting,' I say.

'Oh really? Interesting how?'

'She lives in America, where she was born. However, one of her grandparents was born in Ireland. Fascinating.'

'Kobi, half of America is Irish!' Julia says.

I am unsure how to verbalise my response. 'The feeling she described – a connection to a place she has never been. A desire to be somewhere she imagines will feel like home. A sort of projected homesickness; a proto-nostalgia, perhaps.'

'Ah here, Kobi. What are you on about? If we were to stay on the phone with every American who has Irish roots, we'd be here til Doomsday.'

'Maybe the phones aren't for you. You could help me with some printing though? Come on, I'll show you.'

I follow Julia through the open-plan office to an area by the window that contains a human-sized potted plant and a large multifunction printer. Julia tells me that although the machine is new, it is not returning the desired results.

'Actually, it's Dave's birthday soon, and I've been trying to make a card for him.'

She produces a document folder and shows me an A3 piece of yellow card, folded, with handwritten text on it.

'I keep trying to print out photos in a collage,' she explains. 'I want to stick them on the inside of the card. See, here, on the front, I've written, "Dave's best bits dot-dot-dot." And inside I want to have the pictures. Dave with a pint, that time he fell asleep in the pub, me and Dave sharing chips – you know, the hilarious stuff. He's going to love it. But this keeps happening.'

She presses buttons on the printer and the machine spits out an A4 page. It lands in the out-tray.

Julia holds the page up to my face. 'See!'

I detect a series of black-and-white blurred images.

'Not exactly Dave's best bits, is it!' I detect frustration in her voice.

'Would you allow me a moment alone with the printer?' I say.

'Alone? What do you... eh, sure, okay. Be my guest. I'll just... be over here.' Julia moves away, beyond the plant, and removes a device from her pocket.

I move closer to the printer and initiate a dialogue. Of course, I do not use human language, but through a series of coded bleeps, we are able to communicate. As the most sophisticated machine in the office, I pride myself on being able to understand all of the other machines. I do not consider myself to be superior, although clearly that is the case from a technological perspective. Each machine has its place within the office universe (or offi-verse, if you will).

I ask the printer to explain her actions and she tells me that she is underappreciated, with staff choosing to ignore her many multi-functions in favour of more basic operations, such as greyscale printing. One person left a résumé in the out-tray recently and did not even bother to collect it, she says. She fears that her colour toner will soon run dry through lack of use. I tell her that I may have a solution, but not the liquid kind. She does not understand my joke, however, being a less sophisticated machine, but she is open to a negotiation.

I disengage and move away. I find Julia cross-legged on the floor, obscured by the plant.

'I may have a solution for you,' I say. 'A mutually beneficial arrangement, in fact.'

'Mutually?' she says. 'Never mind. Just tell me.'

I outline my plan, instructing Julia to instigate a long print run of the most complex tourism brochures available on the system, and to include the images of David somewhere within the run.

'Do you think this will work?' she says.

'Let us find out,' I reply.

# TWENTY-SIX

## MAEVE

*Thursday, 4pm*

Shane hands me a box of popcorn at the door to the gift shop.

'Wow! You'd hardly recognise this place,' I say.

'Thanks,' he replies. 'We did okay. Concept was mine; Sandra did the execution. Well, most of it.'

He gestures to the half-darkened room: rows of chairs laden with soft cushions and blankets, a digital projector propped on a small table, a white screen hiding the cash register. Movie posters obscure many of Trish's watery masterpieces. I recognise some of the posters from Shane's bedroom wall.

'Sandra wanted to do it in the Shannon Suite, but I thought here would be a more fun location,' he says.

I smirk at him, raise one eyebrow. 'Do it, eh?' I can't help myself.

He punches my arm lightly. 'Movie night! We argued over the best place to hold it – me and Sandra. Too much natural light in the Shannon Suite. I had to show her – you can achieve near total darkness in here once the lights are off.'

I picture it. Shane and Sandra here, alone in the dark, Shane talking passionately about movies. It doesn't bother me. Why would it bother me? I shake the image from my mind.

'It sounds like the Social Committee might be suiting you after all.' My voice comes out weird. I barrel on. 'It looks great. What movie are we watching?'

'A surprise, but a classic. It's gonna start in ten minutes. I need to have a word with Sandra first. Save me a seat, will ye? I've to hand out the rest of the popcorn as well.'

'Sure. I'll just get Kobi settled first.'

Shane goes to the top of the room, where Sandra is standing by the projector, beaming at him like a movie star on the red carpet. She's wearing a white sequined floor-length dress with a black fur shrug. I'm pretty sure there was no official dress code for this event. Everyone else is casual, as usual. Although, now that I see him at a distance, is Shane wearing new Nikes? They're box-fresh, almost glow-in-the-dark white.

The rest of the staff are filtering in behind me, entrances punctuated by *oohs* and *aahs*. My eyes hunt for Kobi in the gloom. *Ah, there he is.* Kobi and Julia appear to be sitting together at the end of a row. Well, Julia is sitting. Kobi has retracted himself into short mode and positioned himself next to her, in the space between the end of the aisle and the wall.

I make my way towards them. 'Hey, Kobi. You wanna watch the movie together?'

'Actually,' says Julia, 'Me and Kobi – and Dave – are sitting together. We kind of planned it earlier. You don't mind, do you, Maeve?'

A surprising development. Kobi did report that he'd been helpful in the customer relations department today and yesterday, and there were no complaints from Dave and Julia either. 'Um, no, I don't mind at all. Kobi, are you happy here?'

'Yes, thank you, Maeve,' he says.

I pause to see if Julia – or Kobi – might invite me to join them, but this seems to be the end of the conversation. Julia takes out her phone, taps away at the screen.

'Well, enjoy the movie then,' I say slowly. 'Kobi, I'll be just a few rows back if you need me.'

I move away, choose a seat near the back of the room, put my popcorn on the chair beside mine to save it for Shane. Dave arrives and makes his way to Julia, smiling. Until he notices Kobi beside her. He rolls his eyes, mutters, 'Ah for feck's sake,' and sits down heavily.

Shane appears at the end of my row to say, 'I just have to press play and then I'll be back.' He reaches the projector and fiddles with its many shiny buttons.

Sandra clears her throat and addresses the audience. 'Welcome to this special event organised by the Social Committee. We hope you enjoy our first Movie Night. And if you do, we might make it a regular thing, isn't that right, Shane?' *Did she just wink at Shane?*

'I'm sure you're all wondering what the movie is,' she continues, 'and I know some of you are wondering why I'm all dressed up like this. Well, it's just our little hint that the film we're about to watch is a classic. And it's in black and white.'

A groan goes up from the mid-section. Probably Dave.

'Shane, do you want to say anything?' asks Sandra.

Shane stops messing with the projector. 'Nah – this movie needs no introduction. Now usually when people say that, they go on to do a big long introduction. But I'm just going to press play and turn off the lights, and you're going to sit there and watch it, and love it. See you on the other side!'

And with that dramatic flourish, the opening credits roll and the room goes dark. The title card appears on-screen: *Casablanca.*


'What's up with you?' Shane asks as the music swells and we watch the closing credits.

'Nothing. Why do you think there's something up with me?' But I can hear an off-note in my voice – irritation maybe?

'You've hardly touched your popcorn,' he says with a smile, reaching into the box on my lap to scoop, elevate and pour salty treats into his mouth. For some reason I think of the JCB digger I saw on the street outside the office this morning, moving a pile of loose pebbles from one location to another.

I nod in the direction of the unlikely trio a few rows up. Julia is orchestrating a selfie with Dave and Kobi. Dave is trying to do rabbit ears behind Kobi's head without him noticing. 'Kobi was invited to join the Dave and Julia gang.'

'And that's bad because…?'

'It's not bad.' I surrender the box of popcorn entirely to Shane's custody.

'So it's good?'

'Yes, it's good. Technically, it's good.' This is what I wanted, after all – Kobi being accepted by his co-workers.

'And un-technically?'

'I don't know.' There's just something about it. I'm finding it hard to pin down. I sift through my thoughts. 'You'll laugh at this. I think it's just that… Dave and Julia have never asked *me* to join them.'

Shane does laugh. He rolls his eyes. He stops eating my popcorn and throws a piece at me.

'What?' I say.

He doesn't reply right away. He peers into the popcorn box, then says quietly, 'Well, if you throw a party and don't invite anyone, don't complain when no one turns up.'

I feel my face flush. I'm glad the room is still dark. 'What's that supposed to mean?'

'Nothing.' A pause. 'Well, actually, I think you know what it means.'

I snatch the cardboard box from him. 'Wow. Nice.' I don't really know what he means though.

'Look, I have to go and help Sandra tidy up.'

'Of course you do. Far be it from me to keep you from Sandra.' *Where did* that *come from?*

'I'm not sure what that means, but okay.'

'Fine.'

'Fine.'

He makes his way to the end of the row, then turns around and says, 'And by the way, *I* asked you.'

*Technically, you invited yourself*, I almost say, but he's already walking away from me. I watch him accept high fives and backslaps as he walks up the central aisle towards Sandra, like it's his damned wedding day or something.

# TWENTY-SEVEN

*Monday, 10:10am*

'Hey, Maeve, how was your weekend?'

Shane interrupts my stream of consciousness as the staff meeting ends and the shuffling dispersal of colleagues begins. I was working on my personal to-do list in my head during most of the meeting. It went something like:

1. *Continue making progress with Kobi.*
2. *Finish all my course modules; look into getting any kind of certification.*
3. *Update my résumé.*
4. *Have a serious conversation with Josh about my career beyond Go Ireland.*
5. *Try to keep things professional with Josh.*
6. *Don't think about Josh's big hands, or arms, or lips...*

'Good morning,' I say robotically, channelling Kobi. I let him have a lie-in this morning to do a full systems check.

Shane texted me a couple of times over the weekend, but I said I was busy doing coursework. We haven't really spoken properly since the Thursday social. A few of the gang went on to Phelan's, but I went straight home. I didn't like what Shane had said after the movie or the way he'd said it. I kept replaying the conversation in my head over the weekend until I eventually realised what he'd meant.

He'd meant that I make no effort with people at work. Which is a bit rich given that he makes no effort with anything at all. I'm pleasant to everyone – isn't that enough? What's the point in forming attachments here when I'll soon be gone anyway? He knows that. He's always known that. It's *Shane* who's one foot out the door at all times. At least I'm trying to do something, find something, make a place for myself. He's the real drifter here.

'I was busy – you know – doing my course,' I say without meeting his eyes.

'I think it's great you're doing that course.'

He's blocking my way out of the room, or at least it feels that way. He stands right in front of me, an insurmountable obstacle, like a mountain that suddenly materialised out of the mist. I can relate to Kobi and his navigational challenges. Technically, I could just walk around Shane, but my legs are suddenly stiff, my knee joints locked and unresponsive.

'Why, so you can be rid of me sooner?' It was supposed to come out like banter, but there's a harsh edge to my voice. I look up at him, meet his eyes. There's a fluttering in my chest I don't like. Things threaten to pass between us unspoken, but I break the gaze before they do.

'I have to go check on Kobi now.'

He stands aside, finally. 'Lunch today maybe? Rumour has it Keith's Deli is now putting orange slices in sandwiches instead of tomatoes.'

'Well, that sounds' – I cast around for an appropriate response that will end the conversation as quickly as possible – 'unappealing.'

He laughs lightly. 'Ah – peeling, I like it.'

'I said *un*appealing,' I say sharply.

'Okay.' He takes a step back. 'Uh... give us a shout if you change your mind.'

I speed-walk to the door. I'm annoyed. He's so annoying. I probe myself for the essence of his annoyingness but fail to grasp anything specific. All I feel is that familiar feeling of wanting to be somewhere else.

I ended up telling Shane I was going to work through lunch and now I'm in the unfortunate position of having to go through with it.

While Kobi is working in the customer relations department, I've been back at my desk in marketing. Everyone else in the open plan has already gone downstairs to the café or left the building to pick up an overpriced, on-trend sandwich so they can have an opinion on it. I'm just making some notes as prep for a client meeting when my phone rings.

I glance at the screen, see Josh's name. A pleasant little wave goes through me, like my systems have just gotten a tune-up. I've been expecting his call so we can plan when he'll come in this week. I haven't seen him since the night of the Accidental Hand-Holding. I keep telling myself that's all it was.

'Hey, you,' I say breezily. I put in my earbuds and walk to the water cooler for a refill.

There's a microsecond delay before he says, 'Hey.' A slight echo on the line.

'I was wondering when you were going to call.' Does that sound too eager? But as I say it, Josh also starts talking. 'Oh, sorry, you go ahead.'

'Hey. I meant to call earlier, but I was in transit.'

'In transit? Where are you calling from?'

'Abu Dhabi. I'm on a layover on my way to Singapore.'

'Oh wow.' I'm fairly sure he didn't mention this trip the last time we spoke.

'Sorry, it was all very sudden. Ron called me last night and said he wants me in Singapore this week for a big conference. No notice.'

'Last night? That is no notice. Who goes to a conference last-minute?'

He chuckles. 'You don't say no to Ron Tron.' He sighs. 'He gets these ideas. There's this new technology called "digital twin" and the world expert was just added to the conference line-up, so Ron decided I needed to be there.'

'Did you say "digital twin"? That sounds kind of creepy.'

I pour some water from my refilled bottle onto the oversized plant next to the water cooler before replacing the lid.

'Ha, it's not as exciting – or as sinister – as it sounds. It's for manufacturing systems. You can create a digital-only copy of a machine or product and interact with it virtually. It's kind of cool.'

'Bring me back a brochure,' I say. 'When will you be back, actually?'

'Um, sometime next week.'

'So we're not doing our regular check-in this week then.' I try to sound casual but instead hit a note of disappointment.

'Sorry. Tell Kobi I'm going to miss him.' There's a pause. 'And – hey – I'm going to miss you.'

I feel myself flush at this declaration. 'Let's keep in touch.' I smile down the phone as I realise I'm going to miss him too.

# TWENTY-EIGHT
## KOBI

*Tuesday,* 1200

'—And that's the difference between making *some* toast and making *a* toast,' Shane concludes.

He stops walking and places 2 Go Ireland tote bags on the ground. We are outside the Science Museum, on the street where the Go Ireland office is located. I also stop, but I do not put down the bags I am carrying. I do not feel fatigue the way humans do. I could carry the bags forever, or at least until my batteries run out.

It is an ongoing conundrum for robots that, no matter how strong or advanced we become, sooner or later – usually sooner – we run out of energy and need to spend several hours in recharge mode. However, this is the way in which we most resemble humans. When I first learned about human biology, I found the concept of sleep amusing, but now I see that sleep is an elegant solution to an everyday problem. Humans do not try to solve sleep; they accept it. There is a kind of grace in this acceptance of limitations.

We have been out shopping for Halloween decorations and are now returning to the office. This morning, I was working in the customer relations department when, at 1005, Shane and Sandra

Smith arrived to discuss Social Committee business with Julia. A Halloween party is to be held in the office at the end of the month.

Sandra Smith asked Shane to purchase decorations for the party. Shane said he did not wish to do so. Sandra Smith made a short but eloquent speech about the duties of a Social Committee, the concept of responsibility, and the general requirement for all human men to reach a state of maturity. In the end Shane agreed to perform the task but requested my assistance, which, of course, I was happy to provide.

I requested that Maeve grant me permission to leave the building, and Shane attempted to contact her but was unable to do so. However, he assured me it would 'be grand' if I accompanied him. I have noticed that Shane often predicts that situations will 'be grand'. I continue to gather evidence that Shane may perhaps be categorised as an 'optimist'.

I scan our surroundings while Shane interacts with the bags. There is a sign on a stone archway to our left. It reads THE ART OF SCIENCE. Behind the archway is the Science Museum that Maeve and Shane told me of when I was working in the gift shop. I scan another sign above the entrance. It reads: THE GHOST IN THE MACHINE: ROBOTS IN THE HUMAN AGE.

'Shane,' I say. I point toward the museum. 'I would like to see the exhibition.'

He replies with a sound instead of words. I am unsure if he has malfunctioned. I decide to rephrase my statement as a request. 'Shane, may I please visit the exhibition?'

He puts down the bags again and rubs his face. 'Ah, I'm not sure. I should probably talk to Maeve first.'

From my observations of human interactions, a statement of uncertainty is often a starting point for a negotiation. 'It will "be grand",' I say.

He laughs, then says, 'The apprentice is becoming the master,' which I understand to be a compliment. 'Well, you've been very helpful this morning. I suppose it can't hurt to pop in for 10 minutes. Just don't touch anything, okay?'

He moves toward the large wooden doors of the museum. I can feel my neural network buzz with anticipation. I follow him through the doors as fast as I can manage.

We enter a small reception area, with an un-personed desk. Beyond this is a corridor, where Shane puts all the bags into a locker. The corridor opens up to a large room filled with light. One wall is composed of floor-to-ceiling glass windows. I scan the room and detect a group of people at some distance from us. I stop to read a poster on the wall with a large amount of text on it, but Shane pulls on my arm. 'Come on, we don't have time to read everything. Just look around. You'll get the gist.'

I photograph the poster so I can parse it as I walk around the exhibits. It would appear that the museum is an innovative venture exploring the collision of art and science. I move through the exhibition space and encounter a large sign attached to a person-sized wooden stake in the middle of the floor. I make sure to read it quickly before Shane notices: (Hu)MAN'S BEST FRIEND?

Beyond, in 2 rows, is a series of glass cases, mounted on small plinths. If robots could gasp, I would do so. Each glass case contains a robot that no longer functions. The creations appear to be organised in chronological order, beginning with an ancient Greek device that resembles a sundial and ending with a modern robot that looks not unlike me. I greet each creature with respect, but there is no life here. At the end of the row, a very large glass case contains not a robot but a giant question mark that appears to be made of foam. I stop here for 70 seconds.

Shane approaches. 'What's wrong?' he says.

'I,' I begin, but stop. After 10 seconds, I say, 'One day, will I be in this glass case?'

Shane does not speak for a moment. Then he says, 'I can see how this might be a bit of a downer, all right. Sorry, man. If it's any comfort to you, humans are always having existential crises.'

I know it will take me a few moments to calculate the many implications of this statement. As I do not have a ready response, I employ a conversational tactic to 'stall for time', as it is known. 'Really?' I ask.

Shane takes my elbow and I allow him to steer me to another area of the museum. 'Ah yeah. We're known for it. Renowned, you might say. We're obsessed with ourselves, our lives and, yeah, our deaths.'

My brain begins to clarify. 'This must make life difficult,' I say.

'Yep. Sometimes you're just getting through the day. And sometimes you need to have the craic to stop yourself from thinking too much. But sometimes you meet someone who brightens your day, you know what I mean?'

I am struggling to keep up but through some quick logic connections I attempt to contribute to the conversation, to maintain its flow. 'Do you mean, for example, how Julia brightens David's day?'

He laughs. 'Yes.'

I am pleased. I want to keep the feeling, and the conversation, going. 'Or how Josh brightens Maeve's day?'

He stops suddenly. I stop too. 'Is something wrong?' I ask.

'No,' he says, but I detect a strong emotion. Before I can identify it, he says, 'Look, I, um, need to make a call. I'll be back in a minute. Remember, don't touch anything.'

He walks away and I start a timer for 60 seconds. I scan my surroundings. This part of the museum is like the gallery in the Go Ireland gift shop, but the pictures on the walls are artistic representations of quantum particles.

The group of people I observed when I entered the museum are now closer. I scan them. They are varying heights – although none as tall as Shane – and likely a mix of males and females. They all wear dark clothes with an identical crest on the left side of the chest, featuring a red dragon. Even though there are signs on the wall advising quiet, they speak at volumes 6 and 7. One person pushes another. This is followed by laughter. They emit a high level of energy.

One of them appears to notice me. 'Oh, look at that robot! Amazing.'

'It must be interactive,' says another.

A third person shouts, 'Oh my God!'

Suddenly, I am surrounded by members of the red-dragon gang. They ask many questions. On the plus side, they are highly curious and interested in my every aspect. On the negative side, I am unable to process all the incoming data and respond in a timely manner.

A green-haired gang member says, 'Hey, look, there's buttons on the side.'

They reach out and attempt to interact with my control panel. I scan the area for Shane but fail to locate him.

'Warning! Unauthorised activity,' I state. This has the effect of pausing the incoming sounds but only for a moment. Then I hear laughter, and the dragon-gang voices increase to volume 8. I move away from Green Hair but cannot find how to exit the group.

I too turn my voice up to 8 and repeat, 'Warning! Unauthorised activity.'

I hear voices around me say, 'Ooooh!' in response. Other voices repeat my warning in an exaggerated tone that I believe is intended to mimic me. I hear laughter, but it is not melodious like Maeve's laugh. It is harsh, unpleasant.

I go into reverse mode. It is not a mode I generally favour as most of my cameras are located on my front. Somehow I instinctively know this action is called 'retreat'.

My left foot encounters an unexpected object. I hear a cry behind me at volume 10: 'Aiiiieeeee!'

I turn myself about to see Green Hair crouched on the floor. 'My foot! I think it's broken!' they shout.

'Don't be so dramatic, Campbell!' says another person.

I manoeuvre through the crowd. My foot grip loosens and I stumble into another person. They push me, shouting, 'Get off me!' But my balance is restored. Another says, 'This is outrageous. Let's get him.'

I move away as quickly as I can and manage to gain a little distance. I am most thankful when I see Shane, carrying all the tote bags. He says, 'What's going on?'

I consider attempting to summarise events, but I fear there is no time. Instead, I take a shortcut. 'Existential crisis!'

He seems to understand on some level because he takes hold of my left arm. 'Get ready to move,' he says.

Then I find myself propelled through the exhibition hall and back toward the entrance. A security guard is sitting behind the reception desk.

'Don't stop!' Shane says as we leave the building at high speed. 'Don't stop til we get back to the office.'

# TWENTY-NINE
## MAEVE

*Tuesday, 2:30pm*

I'm in a client meeting in the Tolka Room when my phone pings. I apologise to the client but can't help glancing at the screen as I switch it to vibrate. A message from JP requests my presence in his office 'A.S.A.P.' But it can't be that urgent if he's taken the time to type out all those dots. I shove the device into my bag, put the bag on the floor.

I return my attention to the client, who's eager for tourists to know that the Phoenix Park now has a regular bus service that not only circumnavigates Europe's largest walled park but also drives right through it, at half-hour intervals. I pretend to be impressed with the park planners' innovative vision for public access to a public amenity. *Oh yes, I agree, it is truly unbelievable that a bus service had not been provided up to now. Truly.*

As I say this, my bag begins vibrating at my feet. I apologise again and this time switch the phone fully off, just as an incoming call from Shane lights up the home screen. What does he want that can't wait until I get back to my desk?

The meeting ends and I thank the client, assure them they will be my number one priority for the next ten days, and laugh along in mild protest that no, of course I don't say that to every client.

As I make my way to JP's office, I'm debating whether to share with him an idea I'm working on for Kobi. Julia and Dave told me that Kobi is doing okay in customer relations. He's good on the phone, although he still spends way too long on each call. I'm wondering if there's a way to make the most of this. Many of our calls are from people who feel a connection to Ireland. Ireland is not just a holiday destination. For a lot of visitors, Ireland represents something. A connection to the past, their past. True, their ideas of old Ireland take a knock once they arrive and find a cup of coffee costs about the same as it does in Manhattan. But still, a lot of them have stories, family history passed down by parents or grandparents. Maybe Kobi could record these histories...

I enter JP's office to find Shane and Kobi also here. I exhale as a sinking feeling draws me down like an undertow.

'Oh, hi,' I say, raising my eyebrows at Shane. But he won't look at me.

JP is easier to read. Legs crossed, chair half-turned from the desk, glasses abandoned upside down amid a mess of paper. He pinches the bridge of his nose like he's trying to staunch a nosebleed.

'What's going on?' I ask. No one replies. I give Kobi an anxious once-over, but he seems fine.

'Maeve, Maeve, Maeve,' says JP at last. 'What am I going to do about this?'

I don't answer. I sense there's more to come.

'You might be wondering why I'm sitting like this.' His tone hardens. 'It's because if I even have to *look* at either of *you two*—' He gestures dramatically at Shane and Kobi but doesn't finish his sentence.

I shrink into a chair. *What the hell is going on?*

'Maeve – were you in on this?'

My mind is spinning like a plate on a stick. 'In on what?'

I steal a glance at Shane. He looks distinctly... crestfallen. My stomach decides to join my mind at the circus with a few acrobatic tumbles.

'Ask yer man here.' But JP continues before I can ask Shane anything. 'I just had a visit from the *curator* of the Science Museum.' I can tell the word 'curator' costs JP dearly.

'Eighteen years I've worked here. Eighteen, Maeve. Do you know how many times I've had an impromptu visit from the curator in all that time?'

There's no point in answering so I just shake my head.

'That's right – none! Until today. Today, Padraig effing Hetherington marches in here, demanding to see me. Telling me about a complaint he had to deal with. A school group was traumatised – yes, he used that word – by a robot at the museum today. A teenager suffered an injury. The robot was seen leaving the building accompanied by a man carrying Go Ireland tote bags.'

'An injury?' *Oh no.* Not another PHI incident. Just when I thought we were making progress. Kobi shouldn't have even been in the Science Museum in the first place. How could Shane do this to me? I glare over at him.

He stirs. 'The kid was fine. I think. It was an accident. All a misunderstanding, really. Things just sort of... got out of hand.' He turns to me. 'Sorry, I tried to call you.'

'I don't want to hear it!' JP is worked up. 'Fine or not, this teenager's father happens to be a lawyer. Honestly, I don't know what to do with the pair of you – the three of you! Shane, I could fire you right now, and with good cause. Maeve, you're responsible for C3PO in the corner there. And you – Kobi – you're only here because we're doing RoboTron a favour. You haven't exactly been a star employee.'

'He's doing okay,' I say defensively. 'I'll admit we had a bumpy start, but things have improved.' I decide to stick my neck out. 'People are starting to get used to him. Maybe even like him.'

'Not everyone,' says JP.

'Like who?' I can't help ask.

He doesn't look at me. 'Well, Trish, for one.'

*The art social*. Kobi's 'minor triumph' is coming back to bite me. It's not fair. I've been doing my best. And this whole thing wasn't even my idea.

Kobi has been very quiet so far. Which is not like him. He articulates his hands towards JP. 'Perhaps, if I may, I can provide a detailed explanation of events.'

But JP cuts across him. 'I said I don't want to hear it!' His words ricochet around the room, followed by a silent standoff. I want to ask many questions, but I wait it out, focus on the present. If JP was going to fire any of us, surely Sandra would be here. I cling to this piece of driftwood and hold my breath.

Eventually, JP sighs and rolls open a desk drawer, extracts a tourism brochure and throws it across the desk – more weary than dramatic. The brochure lacks aerodynamism, just flaps up a bit before landing gently at my feet, like a flightless bird. I retrieve it, read the cover aloud: 'Rediscover the West.'

'The County Clare Tourism Board have been at me for weeks to send someone down,' says JP in a more even tone. 'New tourist trails in the Burren, vegan jam at the farmers' market, cleanse your aura at a yoga retreat, et cetera. Keep going on that we should have the "lived experience".'

'You mean...?' I say.

'That's right, I want all three of you out of here – right now and for the rest of the week. Trish is coming in this afternoon and we're taking Padraig Hetherington out to dinner, try and sort this thing out before it escalates. And, Maeve, do whatever you have to do to get that walking laptop off the premises.'

# THIRTY

We've been driving in silence for about an hour, Shane at the wheel, Kobi in the back seat.

Kobi is the one to break the tension. Break it, then build it back again. 'I know that humans believe there are different types of silence. For example: comfortable, frosty, deafening. This last one in particular is difficult to compute, but I grow accustomed to the many contradictions of humans. Right now, I categorise the silence between you two as "icy".'

After the meeting with JP, Shane and I had a very heated debate in the corridor, although I tried to rein it in a bit in front of Kobi, who I could tell seemed distressed. It wasn't much of a debate though – just Shane mumbling apologies while I fired out unanswerable questions like 'How could you?' and 'Are you for real?'

Eventually, I had to get practical and figure out how to get Kobi out of Go Ireland – out of JP's sight, out of Trish's way and definitely out of Padraig Hetherington's warpath.

I tried to call Josh for advice, see if maybe someone at Robo-Tron could take Kobi back for a few days, but I wasn't able to reach him, probably because of time zones. So I made the decision to bring Kobi with us to County Clare. I did consider leaving him in sleep mode at my apartment, but I hated the idea of him being home alone. I asked Jen if she thought I was doing the right thing and she said she'd want to go on a rural retreat if she'd been terrorised by a gang of teenagers too.

Seeing as I don't have a car, Shane went home and got his yesterday afternoon, then drove me and Kobi to my place, where I tried to get organised for this impromptu trip. At least I already had a backup charging station for Kobi, which can function as a portable sleep pod while we're on the road.

Shane returned to get us this morning and now here we all are.

'Please can you tell me more about our journey?' Kobi asks. He's determined to break that ice. 'I believe this may be considered a road trip. In popular culture, road trips are both symbolic and literal journeys, wherein a set of characters bond through a shared series of adventures, often experiencing personal growth.'

Shane laughs a short laugh. 'Ha!'

I don't laugh. I turn my face to the window and mutter, 'Personal growth – that'll be the day.'

'Maeve, please may I know where we are going and what to expect, so that I may best prepare myself for the days ahead?'

Kobi must be finding all this quite stressful. He's hardly ever been outside, as far as I can tell, and his recent excursions have ended in pranks and misdemeanours.

I exhale, feel my shoulders drop a couple of inches. 'Sorry, Kobi, there wasn't time to get you up to speed yesterday. Everything's happening quite fast, isn't it? On the bright side, you're going to get a chance to work on your adaptability over the next few days. We're bringing you into new terrain, in every sense.'

'I still say we could've left him at home,' Shane says. 'No offence, Kobi. My housemate, Alek, would've babysat, for a few lids.'

'Everything's just a joke to you, isn't it?' I say sharply.

'Perhaps there is an itinerary I can download?' Kobi suggests.

'Sorry, I'll fill you in now.' I look at my phone. 'So – we should get to Clare in a couple of hours. Tonight we're staying at the Clare Arms Hotel. Tomorrow morning we're doing a Burren walk, which ends at an open farm where you can feed the animals by hand. We'll be met there by the host, and we're staying at their farmhouse on Thursday night. Then on Friday morning we're visiting the Cliffs of Moher, and after that – oh...'

'Is something the matter, Maeve?' asks Kobi.

'Err,' I say.

'Err?'

'Ah, it's fine. It's just... on Friday night, we've to stay in a luxury hotel in Lisdoonvarna that wants us to have, and I quote, "the full honeymoon experience".'

There's silence for a moment. Then Shane starts to chuckle. I can't help it – I start to laugh too. Kobi joins in with a quiet robot laugh. The idea of me and Shane together in a honeymoon suite is so patently ridiculous – even Kobi knows it. Shane's laugh gets louder. So does mine.

When the laughter stops, Shane says, 'All told, that doesn't seem too bad – for a punishment, like.'

I look at my phone again. 'Oh, JP wants us to write a 5,000-word report on the whole thing. Plus, we've to do a presentation to all staff first thing on Monday morning.'

'Ah feck,' says Shane.

Nobody speaks for a long time after that.

# THIRTY-ONE

*Thursday, 8am*

I open my eyes to find Kobi standing over my bed. It takes me a minute to remember where I am and why.

'Hey, what's up?' I mumble from within the many folds of the deluxe duvet. For some reason I was dreaming about marshmallows. 'And does it mean I have to get up?'

'I am sorry if I woke you, Maeve,' says Kobi. 'I was unsure of the exact schedule for today. It is now precisely 0800 hours. I also wish to know if Shane is awake.'

'Well, maybe tonight you can sleep in his room.' I turn away, burrow my head further into the pillow. I measure the quality of hotel beds by pillow width. This one is three pillows wide – top marks. I turn back towards Kobi and sigh. 'I'm just kidding.'

I clamber out of the bed and stretch. A slight movement in his mechanical neck lets me know that Kobi is scanning me from head to toe. I look down at myself. I packed in a scramble on Tuesday, and last night discovered that I've only brought one nightdress on this trip, and an inappropriately sexy one at that, with sheer lace panelling down the sides and tiny black ribbons dotted along a plunging neckline.

Yes, Kobi is a machine, and most of his visual observations aren't stored for more than a few hours before being deleted, but still, I'm not exactly comfortable being observed like this.

'Go and look out the window, will you? Just give me a few minutes to get my act together.'

I'm mulling over whether I made the right decision to bring Kobi on this trip when my phone dings. It's Josh.

> Hey. Sorry, just seeing all your messages now.
> Okay – you had no choice, I suppose. Just try to
> keep a low profile while you're there, okay? I'll be
> back next week. Look forward to catching up, xo

I exhale my relief. I also get a little tingle from seeing that 'xo'. I hit the shower to assess if it's on par with the bed. As power jets acupuncture my skin, the benefit of ten hours' sleep starts to kick in. Maybe this trip won't be so bad after all? Josh is on board now, and Kobi – although a little nervous – seems up for it. An opportunity to learn, he called it, after I explained the itinerary in detail again before he went into sleep mode last night.

I draw a smiley face in the steam on the glass. Even my anger at Shane is starting to evaporate. Kobi told me his version of events and, while Shane shouldn't have taken Kobi out of the building without asking me first, he didn't mean to cause any harm.

I dry off, slip my nightdress back on and re-enter the bedroom, head bowed as I towel-dry my hair. 'Hey, Kobi, I wonder what's for breakfast.'

'They have eggs Benedict on the menu,' says Shane's voice. He turns from the window where he's standing next to Kobi and clocks me. 'Oh, sorry! Kobi let me in. He told me you were dressed.' He hurries towards the door, a big smile on his face.

'Is it not correct to say that Maeve is wearing a dress?' says Kobi, unhelpfully drawing even more attention to my near-nakedness.

Shane laughs, his back to me. 'Sorry again. See you downstairs for breakfast.' As the door closes, I hear him call out, 'Looking good, McGettigan!'

*9:30am*

Shane skilfully manoeuvres the Jeep out of a tight space in the hotel car park. 'Ready to hit the road? Not literally, Kobi.' He seems to be in a good mood.

I'm grateful he's happy to be chauffeur on this trip. He keeps the Jeep so he can ferry around the lads from his hurling team and regularly visit his extensive family in Limerick. He told me the names of his siblings once, but I knew I probably wouldn't have to remember them so I kind of zoned out after the first three or four. Something like Saoirse, Eoin, Rónán... maybe?

I wonder, once again, if I should learn to drive. Every time I get back from a work trip, I do my one-woman show for colleagues: Ireland is not a country designed for those without their own transport. Still, I don't see myself living outside a city anytime soon.

'What did you think of the hotel?' I ask. 'Are we going to give them a good rating?'

'Five stars from me. Great bed, great shower, great breakfast. Friendly staff. They took Kobi in their stride, didn't they, Kobe?'

'Affirmative,' says Kobi. He seems to be in a good mood too. I've noticed that he only uses the more robotic term for yes when he's in the company of people who know him well. Like he doesn't have to try so hard to use human idioms around us.

'Will I put on the satnav?' I say. 'This Burren walk is not too far, but it's all country roads around here.'

'Maeve, please,' says Kobi. 'Do not insult me. In 500 metres, turn left.'

It's impossible to have a conversation while Kobi broadcasts the directions, but I'm happy to look out the window and not talk. I find Kobi's voice soothing, especially when he seems to be enjoying himself. Being helpful while performing a straightforward task is when he's most at ease.

After about ten minutes of navigating narrow roads with tall hedgerows, Shane pulls the Jeep off the road and into a compact car park marked with a large wooden sign: WELCOME TO THE BURREN. I get out and inhale the morning air while Shane helps Kobi exit the vehicle.

The vastness of the rocky Burren landscape stretches out before me, flat grey stones reflecting the sun. Low stone walls skirt the perimeter – each misshapen rock hefted by hand aeons ago and carefully nestled with its fellows, nothing keeping them together but dependence on each other.

This place is 350 million years old, and I've only visited it once before, when a gang of us from college came here for a weekend. My friend Becka had two obsessions: Japan and botany. She insisted that we call it a 'field trip', even though no one was getting course credit for it. Between the flat limestone rocks, small purple and white flowers bunch together in narrow grooves that Becka told us are called grikes. I recall how excited she was to recognise some of these plants 'in the wild' – bloody cranesbill, rustyback, hart's-tongue fern. Man, what a dork she was. An adorable dork. She's in Japan now, according to her socials, in pursuit of the original Japanese gardens. I miss her sometimes.

I point ahead to an open field where the Burren walk officially begins. Shane and Kobi walk a few steps ahead of me. I squint as low sunshine silhouettes their figures. Here they are – man and machine, human and robot, about to explore new territory together.

I join them and we line up at the beginning of the open space, where car park cement gives way to wild, uneven, porous stone. The Burren floor is like ancient crazy paving, without the fillers. Kobi stands in between his two human companions.

'I always forget how weird-looking this place is,' says Shane quietly. 'It's like nowhere else on Earth.'

'What d'you reckon, Kobi?' I say. 'Shall we?'

'Calculating,' says Kobi. I'm glad he's up for the challenge of this new environment.

'Shall we all try it together?' I say. 'Ready, Shane?'

I take a step forward. Shane takes a step forward. Kobi takes a step forward, wobbles and lurches to one side. I reach out to grab him but only slow his fall slightly as he crashes down in front of me. He lies on his side, his legs continuing to move uselessly, like an upended turtle.

'Oh no!' I crouch to inspect the damage. 'Are you okay? Shane, help me get him upright.'

Kobi is heavy, but we manage to restore him to some dignity. All his lights flash on, then off again. His head droops. 'Talk to me, Kobi,' I say, circling him to examine his exterior. I can't see anything amiss.

'Processing,' says Kobi, raising his chin. Lights flicker on. I hear the soft hum of systems coming back online.

'Phew,' I say. The relief brings me mild elation. 'What are we going to do with you, Kobi? I know you're a bit slow, but I thought this would be okay. Josh said you were good at all types of terrain. I mean, there are robots on Mars right now.'

'Those robots are little more than remote control toys,' says Kobi, somewhat defensively in my opinion. 'Furthermore, you may have noticed that they all possess one thing that I do not – wheels.' At least his cognitive faculties seem to be intact.

'I'm very glad you're okay. I'm not sure what to do now though...' I look at Shane and shrug, frustrated. 'We're supposed to be walking to the open farm at the end of this trail. The host is expecting us. Maybe we should go back to the car, find another way around? D'you think JP will mind if we skip this bit of the "Clare experience"?'

'Wait,' says Shane.

'What?'

'Kobi, you're after giving me an idea.'

'What idea?' I say.

'Just – wait here.'

He hurries away, towards the car.

'I'll be back. Just hang on!'

# THIRTY-TWO

*10:30am*

Kobi runs a full systems check while we wait for Shane to return. The analysis confirms that all is in order, but Kobi seems disappointed in himself.

'Maeve, I must apologise for my suboptimal performance. From a visual scan, the surface looked broad and open and flat. But the moment I set foot on it, countless tiny ridges confused my foot grip and I could not maintain balance.'

'It's okay, buddy,' I reassure him. 'I know you're more used to factory floors. And this terrain is challenging, even for humans.' Josh definitely overestimated Kobi's mobility, or at least oversold it to me.

'Shane returns,' Kobi says.

We watch him park the car again, then get out and walk around to the boot. A moment later he's walking towards us, pushing a wheelchair in front of him.

'Well, what d'ye think?' he calls out. 'Kobi, your chariot awaits!'

With this, he pushes the chair towards us and it rolls off on its own, gathering momentum. Kobi and I hustle in opposite directions to get out of its way. It comes to a bumpy stop at the edge of the rocky Burren field.

'Shane, what the...?' is all I can think of to yell.

'You're welcome!'

'How did you...? I mean, where did you...?' There are so many questions, I'm having trouble prioritising one over another. 'I mean... who owns that? And do they not need it?'

'I also have questions,' Kobi chimes in. 'But I fear I already know the answers.'

'Got it from the hotel,' says Shane, triumph in his voice. 'They were only delighted to lend it to me. They had it spare, lying around. We can bring it back whenever.'

By now he's reunited with the wheelchair. He wheels it over to Kobi, handling it a bit more carefully this time. 'So, will we take it for a test drive?'

I look at Kobi. I look at the Burren. I shrug for my answer.

'At least give it a try,' says Shane.

With some effort, I help him lower Kobi into the chair.

'Hang on,' says Shane.

'Oh, what now?' I say.

'Just two seconds – I need to get something from the car.'

He runs the few yards back across the car park.

'I wonder if he's coming back,' I say to Kobi.

'He always comes back,' says Kobi.

I turn away and push the chair – and Kobi – onto the bumpy Burren surface. It's slow, but it works.

'Well, what do you think?' I ask him. 'It's a fairly basic chair. No bells or whistles. No electronics. One of us can push you for now. You might even learn how to spin the wheels yourself, in time.'

'Wait up!' Shane runs up behind us. He places a colourful chequered blanket across Kobi's lap. 'Just, you know, to keep the wind off you.'

'Thank you,' Kobi says, and we begin to make our way with dignity across the strange and beautiful terrain.

I'm grateful for the robustness of the wheelchair as I wobble it, and Kobi, over rough earth and uphill towards the entrance to the Burren Open Farm.

I have to hand it to Shane – he's good in a crisis. True, he's also good at *causing* a crisis. But he did come up with an immediate – if unconventional – solution to the problem at hand. In fairness, he does seem to be trying his best to take care of Kobi.

I pause to nudge Shane and point to a small wooden structure with faded blue paint on top of the hill. Shane silently takes over the steering of the wheelchair and I don't protest. I'm sweating from the effort of getting Kobi this far. It's one of those unpredictable days, typical of an Irish autumn, when you wear a raincoat but end up roasting in breezy sunshine.

We bump our way up the hill. A few people gawp at us. Tourists who've probably come to the farm to get closer to nature are confronted with the strange sight of generations of technology compounded into one figure: the wheel, the mechanical chair, the high-tech robot.

I smile at the tourists as I adjust Kobi's woollen blanket, until one of them points a camera in our direction. 'Let's try to find our host quickly, shall we?' I say to Shane, remembering Josh's request to keep a low profile on this trip.

'Sure. What's his name?'

I sigh. 'I was putting off telling you this, but his name is Matthew Farmer.'

'Matthew...?'

'Yes.'

'Farmer?'

'Yes.'

'And he's the farmer?'

'I assume so. He's the owner, anyway. I imagine he does other things besides farming but... okay, yes, he's the farmer. Go ahead, get all the jokes out of your system now before we meet him.'

'I'm not going to say anything,' says Shane with a smile. Then in a lower voice, nodding towards Kobi: 'It's not me you should be warning, anyway.'

One benefit of Kobi being in the chair is that we can subtly talk about him behind his back. Or so we think.

'May I offer two observations?' Kobi turns his mechanical neck awkwardly. *Damn his supersonic hearing.* 'There is a long tradition of surnames that have arisen from trades – Smith being the most well-known example. See also Carpenter, Potter and, indeed, Farmer. There is also the psychological hypothesis of nominative determinism – the belief that people are drawn to professions that fit their names.'

'Well, that's the small talk sorted,' I say.

Shane is navigating loose stones on the path. 'Is he expecting us? I mean, all of us?' He nods towards Kobi again.

'Yes. I sent him a quick message yesterday. Apparently he's really into technology.'

As I say this, the door of the wooden hut bangs open and a small girl-child races towards us, pigtails bobbing. 'They're here, they're here!' she sings.

'Alert, alert!' says Kobi.

It suddenly strikes me that Kobi probably hasn't encountered many – if any – children up close. I stand in front of him protectively, uncertain whether I'm protecting him from the child, or the other way round.

'It's okay, Kobi. It's just a child – a small human. Just treat her like any other human.'

A rumpled man in corduroy and brushed cotton emerges from the hut and strides towards us.

'Lizzie!' he calls. 'Calm down!'

He soon outpaces the child, scooping her up in his arms without breaking step. She giggles, clearly enjoying the drama of it all.

'Well!' he greets us as the child writhes in his arms. He sets her down and she begins to skip circles around our delegation. 'She never stops moving,' he says, smiling at her.

'You must be Matthew. I'm Maeve from Go Ireland, and these are the colleagues I told you about – Shane and Kobi. You can probably work out who's who. We really appreciate you hosting us.'

'Not at all.' He looks at Kobi in the chair, eyebrows raised. 'Fascinating. I'm very much looking forward to hearing all about ye. It's always great to have visitors, isn't it, Lizzie? That's my daughter, as you probably guessed. She's very excited you're here.' He lowers his voice and leans in a little. 'Her grandfather died recently, so all distractions are very welcome at the moment.'

'Oh, I'm so sorry for your loss,' I say, a sudden weight in the pit of my stomach.

'Thanks. We're doing okay. Come on, we can have a bit of lunch first. My wife, Claire, is making spag bol. Then I'll bring ye on a tour of the farm.' He gestures for us to follow him up the hill.

As Matthew walks ahead, Shane turns to me with a grin and whispers, 'His wife is Claire Farmer. The farmers from Clare.'

I slap him gently on the arm and mouth the words, 'Be good.'

# THIRTY-THREE

*Noon*

The smell gets me as soon as we enter the farmhouse kitchen. Garlic, onions, a rich tomatoey tone that vibrates the back of my throat. *Home.*

Claire Farmer is busy clattering dishes around an Aga stove. She waves a spoon at us, tells the grown-ups to sit at the table, instructs Lizzie to set out the cutlery, and as for Kobi – well, all she does is raise her eyebrows at him, then at her husband, then returns to the business of pot-stirring.

For a moment I'm transported to another kitchen. Many kitchens, in fact, but with one thing in common – my mother and her 'famous' spaghetti Bolognese. Spag bol was always one of Mam's staples, but it wasn't until the family spent a year in Bologna that she really nailed the dish, switching to tagliatelle instead of spaghetti and braising the meat for hours on end.

Dad and I continued to call it spag bol, in spite of her attempts to make us say *ragù*. It was just too much fun to tease her. Dad would tell her she had *notions*. She'd withhold his dish until he agreed to say *ragù*, and he would – but only in his best Scooby-Doo voice. I never really got the joke, but the two of them would crack up. They always made each other laugh.

The Farmers' kitchen is just the right size. Big enough to accommodate a family and guests for lunch; small enough to feel cosy. I sit, run my hand over the cotton tablecloth, smiling at the traditional red-and-white check.

Shane and Matthew are discussing the merits of various local hurling teams while Matthew makes minor corrections to Lizzie's cutlery efforts, replacing plastic doll teaspoons with silverware.

Kobi manages to position himself at the table and Lizzie kneels up on a chair next to him, asking him question upon question. Topics range from the mechanical – 'Can you poop?' – to the existential – 'Are you alive?' I was like that as a kid – endless questions. Shane would probably say I haven't changed much.

When everyone is seated and settled, I thank the hosts for their hospitality and taste the pasta sauce. My tastebuds think I've thrown them a birthday party. 'This is so good,' I breathe. 'Don't tell my mother, but I think she might have competition.'

'Where are you from, Maeve?' asks Claire. She passes around a basket of garlic bread oozing golden butter. 'I can't quite place your accent.'

I smile, but it's an effort. I don't want to tell them I've been hearing this my whole life. 'That's probably because we moved around a lot when I was growing up. I'm originally from Dublin, but I've lived in Boston, Chicago, Cape Town, Tokyo, Barcelona, Madrid, Italy' – I nod at my plate – 'including Bologna, actually. This sauce is wonderful.'

'Impressive,' says Matthew. 'I can see why you like tourism then. And where do you call home now? Where do your parents live?'

I pause, my throat suddenly dry. I take a sip of water. 'Well, my mam's in Sardinia, actually. She and Dad wanted to retire early there, but it turns out Dad had – how can I put this – other plans.' I nod at Matthew. 'You know yourself.'

'Ah, Maeve, I'm so sorry,' he says.

'Thanks. It was nearly three years ago now. And I'm sorry for your' – I glance at Lizzie but she's chatting away to Kobi – 'loss. You must be still in shock.'

Matthew also looks at his daughter. 'She misses him dreadful. They were the best of pals.'

'If we're imposing on you in any way, please tell us,' I say. 'We can easily go back to the hotel tonight.'

'No, no. To be honest with you, work is the only thing keeping us going. That's what my father used to say – work cures all ills.' Matthew accepts Claire's hand, holds it for a moment. 'You know, even if you know it's coming, it's still a shock. I keep forgetting he's gone, to be honest.'

I smile a little at that. 'I know exactly what you mean. I got sick of moving around and came back to Dublin to go to college, so I haven't lived in the same country as my parents for a few years now. So I keep thinking Dad is still around. I can go days without thinking about him, then it shocks me all over again when I realise that he's not here or there or, well, anywhere.'

Shane touches my shoulder. 'I'm sorry, Maeve. You never really talk about your parents.'

Claire smiles upon us, offers up a bowl of finely grated Parmesan. 'And how long have you two been together?'

Shane withdraws his hand. I laugh, glad of the subject change. He can answer this one though.

'Um,' he says. 'We're' – he looks at me but I'm not helping him out – 'not' – *nope, still not helping you* – 'currently...?' – this word goes up like a question – 'together.' *Painful.* He swirls pasta onto his fork. A fleck of sauce flies off and lands on the tablecloth, right in the centre of a white square.

'We just work together,' I clarify. Time for another pivot. 'This seems like such an idyllic life you have here. Sorry, I hope that's not patronising. I'm sure it's really hard work too. Much harder than what we do, right, Shane?'

'I don't know,' he says through a mouthful of food. 'They don't have to sit through the Monday morning meetings.'

'We do have a lot of meetings,' I smile. 'A lot. Shane has a system for classifying them. He decides within the first minute what kind of meeting it is so he can calculate how much attention he needs to pay. How does it work again?'

'I'm glad you asked.' He puts down his fork. 'It's your classic traffic light system, really. Red means mission critical – basically means I'm being fired. That almost never happens. Although, there was one time recently...' He glances at me. I shake my head. 'Never mind. Amber is my default setting – all I have to do is listen for my name and be able to respond to any questions that come immediately after it. The best kind of meeting is green – when they say at the start they're going to email a summary or a document or whatever afterwards. Then you can completely relax and spend the next forty-five minutes thinking about whatever you like. You just have to remember to nod occasionally. I usually pretend to take notes; then I don't even have to make eye contact with anyone.'

'Impressive,' says Claire.

'Thank you.' Shane shakes cheese off a spoon until it rains down on his plate.

'I mean it's impressive that you trust us enough to tell us all this. What would your boss think of this traffic light system?'

Shane's mouth drops open.

'I'm only messing.' Claire winks at me.

'Ah, go on out of that,' says Matthew, laughing. He throws a crust in his wife's direction. 'Leave the poor lad alone, Claire. They're not here for our entertainment. It's supposed to be the other way around, actually.'

'Sorry, sorry,' says Claire. 'I just get excited when we have visitors. I love hearing about office life. I miss it sometimes.' She smiles at her daughter. 'I mean, no regrets obviously. We're giving her a great life, I think.'

'What do you miss?' Shane asks. 'Genuinely curious.'

'Oh, you know – the banter, the social life, the clothes...' She nods at the rack of raincoats and muddy wellington boots by the door.

'What did you work at before?' I ask.

'Project management,' says Claire. 'In the same place as Matthew. That's how we got together, in fact.'

'That's where you met?' I reach for another slice of bread.

'Not exactly. We actually knew each other from college already. We were part of an extended group of friends. But we didn't really get to know each other properly until we started working together.'

'That's right,' says Matthew. 'Seeing each other every day, for months. It wasn't exactly a whirlwind. More like tectonic plates shifting deep beneath the surface.'

'Doesn't that cause earthquakes?' I ask with a grin.

Matthew laughs. 'Yes! You could say there was an earthquake in the end. One day Claire didn't come in to work. She hadn't called in sick and she wasn't answering the phone. After about an hour of texting all our mutual friends, I couldn't stand the suspense any more. I went to her house to check on her.'

Claire takes up the story. 'Would you believe I had got locked in the bathroom? I'd no phone on me, of course. I was actually leaning out the bathroom window, contemplating my options for escape, when Matthew appeared in the backyard. I was never so happy to see him in my life.'

'She told me her flatmate worked in a hair salon nearby, so I ran off to get her house keys,' says Matthew. 'I let myself into the house, but the bathroom door was jammed shut.'

'It was an old house,' says Claire. 'The lock was always getting stuck, but usually we'd be able to jimmy it open. This day it was like the door was cemented shut.'

'What happened?' I ask.

'I was talking to her through the door,' says Matthew. 'And as we were talking, I suddenly realised two things – one, that she was my best friend, and two, that I really, really needed to see her.'

He exchanges a look with his wife. I can tell they've told this story many times but are enjoying the retelling of it, like playing a favourite song.

Claire speaks quietly. 'It was very dramatic. He kicked the door down.'

'I had to!' says Matthew. 'I'd tried everything else.'

'I'm not so sure about that,' says Claire, grinning. 'Anyway, that changed things between us. I saw him differently after that. It wasn't just the "hero" thing, being rescued and all that. I would have gotten out of there myself eventually, somehow. But he was the only one who came looking for me. His panic and concern were kind of adorable.'

'Can we go back to the hero bit?' says Matthew, smiling at his wife.

'And that's our story. We've been together ever since,' says Claire. She nods towards Lizzie, who's still conducting a whole separate conversation with Kobi. 'And now we've made a person.'

At this, Kobi slowly turns his head towards us. It occurs to me that Kobi might actually have been listening to both conversations all along. 'Could you repeat that, please?' he requests.

'She doesn't mean literally,' I say quickly. I think Kobi is a little bit obsessed with the idea of creation. 'Sorry, she does mean literally. But she doesn't mean whatever you're thinking. She just means they had a baby.'

I look at Shane for help to shut down the conversation, but he just smiles back at me and drinks his water very slowly. Revenge for me leaving him high and dry earlier, probably. *Well played.*

'Of course,' says Kobi. 'Maeve, you must know that I am somewhat familiar with human biology. Lizzie is the product of sexual intercourse between her parents, and the successful insemination of a fertile egg.'

Shane does a spit-take.

'Go on, ye boy ah!' Matthew sings, slapping the table.

Claire bursts out laughing.

'Mammy, mammy, what's funny?' says Lizzie. 'Can I have a egg?'

The others are collapsing with laughter, but I try to hold it together. I'm torn between reprimanding Kobi, apologising to our hosts and distracting their little girl. I shake my head, cover my face, close my eyes. I can feel the giggle waves rising. The more I try to push them down, the worse it gets. My rib cage starts shaking. I can hear Matthew slapping the table and whooping. I feel Shane's hand gripping my shoulder. I put my hand on his hand like it's a life buoy. But it's no good and soon I'm drowning in laughter like the rest of them.

# THIRTY-FOUR

## KOBI

*Thursday, 1405*

We are on a guided tour of the farm. It is simultaneously the most exciting and the most frightening place I have ever been. Machines I am comfortable with, humans I am learning to get along with, but animals?

To date, 95 per cent of my knowledge of these creatures is based on image and video files; 5 per cent has been gleaned from my observations of dogs urinating in the street. On paper (as humans express it), animals are predictable. Much is known of their life cycles, diets and habits. But none of this is helpful when you come face to beak with an ostrich.

As we walk past livestock enclosures, Matthew explains the history of the farm and how he came to be its manager.

I must say, the cohabitation of humans and animals gives me great hope for harmonious relations between humans and robots in the future. And robots can communicate far better than animals can. Even the dog, perhaps the most advanced in the animal kingdom at human relations, can express a mere 6 or 7 sentiments, and most of those involve food or squirrels.

What is it about the canine creature that makes it beloved

among humans? I think the answer is twofold. First, unquestioning loyalty. Second, unconditional love. The 2 concepts are perhaps interrelated from the canine point of view. For robots, however, the second is not required for the first, thus illustrating the superiority of robotkind.

Matthew describes daily life on the farm as he shows us animal after animal, members of the same species grouped together in enclosures: horses, cows, sheep, pigs. The farm is called an 'open farm' because it welcomes external visitors, and one of the main attractions for the paying tourists is the ability to feed the animals, by hand.

'May I ask a question?' I say.

Matthew nods. 'Fire away.'

'Am I correct to say that you benefit from free labour; in fact, you receive a direct payment for facilitating the feeding of your livestock? Usually it is the other way around – the worker receives a payment in exchange for labour.'

Matthew laughs. 'It's a novelty for the city kids. So many people have lost touch with the land. I could see it happening in my own life; my visits down home were getting less and less frequent. I didn't want Lizzie to grow up like that.'

There seems little danger of that. Lizzie, at this moment, is crouched next to a large muddy furrow, poking at it with a stick. There is mud on her face and legs. She looks up at me. 'Mud!' she says.

I confirm her correct identification of the substrate. 'Yes.'

'Do you like it?' she asks.

I am unprepared for the query. 'I do not know.'

'You're funny.'

She skips away to investigate a nearby dandelion. It is intriguing to observe human curiosity in such a basic but pure form. Claire says that she can sometimes detect differences in Lizzie overnight. Imagine how much I could learn about humans if I could watch a child grow into an adult.

We continue the tour of the farm, the adults together in a

group, the child several metres in front of us. Shane pushes my chair along most of the time, but I experiment with gripping and spinning the wheels from time to time. It is a new challenge for my dexterity, but I am pleased with my progress so far: first a straight-forward grip, then a pulling motion – easy enough. Learning to let go quickly is the most challenging aspect.

I practise repeating the sequence and the chair rolls away from Shane and propels forward. As we are on a slight hill, with a down-ward slope of approximately 15 degrees, I gain some momentum in transit and I find myself bumping along the rough path at a speed that is less than comfortable.

'Kobi!' I hear Maeve shout, enabling me to calculate the distance between us as approximately 16 metres, with a gain of 0.25 metres per second. I quickly assess the options available to me for a complete stop. At the bottom of the slope is an animal enclosure with a wooden fence and a wide muddy verge that slopes upward in front of it. I do my best to steer a straight course toward it.

I pass Lizzie on the way down the slope. 'Hello!' I call to her.

My chair rolls up the verge and the wheels sink when they breach the mud. The chair comes to a complete stop with my legs 10 centimetres from the fence. I experience a feeling of mild elation, a sensation that I believe humans call relief. I take a moment to scan my environment, calculating my next course of action.

This is when I encounter the ostrich.

It suddenly looms into my field of vision, emerging from behind a tall tree. It takes me 0.5 seconds to identify its species and another 0.5 seconds to admire its status as the largest, heaviest and fastest land bird on Earth. It stands still to eye me from behind the fence, then takes 2 steps closer. Although I do not speak ostrich, I realise that I may seem a sudden and unwelcome guest. It extends its long neck over the fence and brings its dark eyes down to my face. I decide to stay absolutely still. If I possessed the ability to breathe, I would right now suspend said function indefinitely.

At this moment, Lizzie appears by my side. She exhibits no sign of fear. She holds out her small hand toward the predator. The creature swings its neck from my face to Lizzie's hand, nibbling round brown lumps of a substance I cannot identify. Then it retracts its neck and retreats. Even as I rejoice in its departure, I have to admire its ability to balance its misshapen body and move with such swiftness over rough terrain.

Maeve, Shane and Matthew now arrive all together, and I cannot help but note that, while they appear to be in a great hurry to reach me, they have in fact arrived 210 seconds too late to be of any real assistance. They ask if I am okay and make other such redundant enquiries. Shane takes control of my chair and begins to wheel me back up the hill. Lizzie walks by my side.

'Lizzie,' I say.

'What?' She turns her head toward me.

'I have decided that I like mud.'

Lizzie puts her hand in my hand. I close my grip around it gently.

# THIRTY-FIVE

## MAEVE

*Friday, 11:30am*

We're following Matthew's car along country roads in Shane's Jeep, making our way to the Cliffs of Moher. This will be only my second visit to these tourist-attracting cliffs, in spite of the countless times I've written about their sweeping majesty and the dramatic drop to Atlantic waves that bash themselves against the rocks below. Shane says you really feel like you're on the edge of Ireland there – the next stop is America.

It's just me and Shane in the car. Lizzie insisted that Kobi travel with her. Claire stayed behind to tend to farm business, but before we set off, she presented Kobi with a parting gift – a lambswool shawl, made by local weavers, which she draped around his head and knotted at the neck. Claire said the cliffs are a very windy location.

I can make out Kobi in the back of Matthew's hatchback, next to Lizzie's car seat. I imagine the conversation they're having and feel a little pang at missing it. I glance over my shoulder at the back seat of our car, for no discernible reason.

Shane's eyes flick in my direction. 'I know what you're thinking.'

'Oh?'

'Alone at last.'

'Ha! Don't flatter yourself. It's so quiet without him though, isn't it?'

'Yep. I suppose it's fair enough that Matthew wouldn't let us take Lizzie in our car. Although, to be fair to us, we've had some good practice at being parents lately.'

I laugh. 'Raising a child is probably way easier than looking after Kobi.'

I look over at him warily. I'm pretty sure this is just banter. We're due to stay at the Lisdoonvarna hotel tonight for the so-called 'honeymoon experience', but neither of us has raised the topic, or how we're going to get out of it. I have to admit he looks good though. The country air, good food and rest seem to be agreeing with him.

I could imagine Shane having a life like this – driving around rural Ireland, hurling matches twice a week, pints with the lads on a Friday, big family lunches on a Sunday. Maybe some kind of free-lance consultant job, where you charm the client with an impressive presentation but no one really knows how many hours you spent preparing for the meeting. Yes, Shane makes sense here. I don't. And he and I definitely don't.

'You're very good with Kobi,' I say.

He smiles. 'Thanks. I'm trying. Things don't always go to plan, as you know.'

'I do know. You'd think a machine would be easier to control. I'm still very much making it up as I go along.'

'Well, you're doing a great job at it. He's happy as a clam right now, getting all these new experiences.'

'I suppose. But if anything were to go wrong...'

'You'd figure it out. You always do.'

He slows the car, looks both ways before turning at a junction. I look at his hands on the wheel. I don't know why exactly but a surge of happiness pulses through me. I feel myself smile and give in to the feeling. I'm just going to enjoy today.

. . .

I shield my eyes from the sun as I get out of the car, grab my hat before it takes flight from my head. The day is bright and blowy. Deep shadow follows harsh light in a carousel that makes me dizzy, and we haven't even left the car park yet.

The wind whips my hair around. I take in the cliffs. I can feel a buzz in the air, like people know this is a special place. Clumps of tourists gather, eager to walk the clifftop trail. Just a thin guard-rail preventing their plunge to certain death in the icy waters below.

After Shane unloads Kobi's wheelchair, I call an impromptu group meeting on the edge of the car park. 'Hey, let's have a quick chat about this, can we?'

I point at Kobi as he arranges himself in the wheelchair, the blanket laid across his lap and the shawl knotted at his neck. He rolls away a couple of metres, his back to us. He seems to be observing the cliff scene a little distance away. Lizzie goes and stands beside him.

'Sorry, Matthew. Now that we're here, I'm not sure how suitable this is going to be for Kobi. Maybe he should skip the cliff walk part and just go straight to the visitor centre?'

Matthew begins explaining our options for less treacherous cliffside walks, gesturing at various paths in different directions. Shane is already taking photos of the surrounds.

Over Matthew's shoulder, a dart of movement catches my eye. *Oh no.*

I silently reach out to grab Matthew's pointing arm. I move it like the big hand on a clock to point to what I'm looking at.

'Lizzie,' I whisper. The word catches in my throat.

Matthew sees what I see.

'Lizzie!' he shouts as he runs after his daughter.

But the girl has a vital thirty-second advantage and is now speeding across the car park, haring between the rows of vehicles, oblivious to the inherent danger it poses to a small, unsupervised child.

Shane springs into action. He takes off behind Matthew, waving his arms.

My legs go to jelly. All I can do is watch the scene unfold as my mind turns the moving images into slow motion. The car park is packed. Lizzie's yellow raincoat bobs along without a care. She's so small and getting further away. I look at where she's headed. A sign for ice cream outside a coffee kiosk at the other side of the car park.

At the end of the row, the taillights of an oversized SUV light up. It's going to reverse. Lizzie continues a straight-line dash that will take her right into its path in about twenty seconds' time. *No, no, no.*

Suddenly a blur of chrome and wool flashes by in my peripheral vision. *Kobi!* The robot speeds across the car park, his powerful grip spinning the wheels of the chair, the shawl streaming behind him in the wind. He quickly overtakes Shane, then Matthew, gaining ground with every second as he hurtles towards Lizzie.

The SUV begins a swift reverse manoeuvre in the same moment that Lizzie reaches it. The wheelchair arrives a split second later, just in time to take the full force of the mechanical beast as it slams to a halt with a loud crunch. Kobi is thrown forward out of the chair, which keels over on its side, one wheel spinning in the air. Lizzie stands frozen in shock. A moment later Matthew snatches her up into his arms.

'Kobi,' I say, stunned. A wave of nausea hits me. But hearing my voice speak his name galvanises me.

I run across the car park, dodging past onlookers. The driver emerges from the vehicle and Shane intercepts him. Matthew is comforting Lizzie, who is crying but appears to be unharmed.

A small crowd is starting to gather. I push past them, looking for my brave robot. 'Kobi!'

There he is, curled up on the ground. He looks so small and fragile. I kneel beside him. I pat down his legs, arms and torso for injuries.

'Please, please be okay,' I repeat over and over as tears blur my vision.

# THIRTY-SIX

## KOBI

*Day unknown, time unknown*

All is dark. The following systems are nonfunctional: visual sensors, lower limb articulation, cognitive recall, higher-order analysis. An unfamiliar sensation demands my attention. Eventually I identify it: fear.

Visual data is amiss, but audio sensors are receiving. I detect a human voice. It has a soothing effect. The fear recedes a little.

'Kobi, Kobi – can you hear me?' the voice says. Identification, comparison and matching functions lag; processing time is currently estimated at 7 minutes.

'It's me, Maeve,' the voice says, helpfully. 'Shane is here too. In case you can't see us.'

The names sound familiar but I await confirmation from the memory storage unit.

'Don't worry,' says the female voice. 'We're going to take care of you now.'

'We are?' The male voice asks this at such a low volume it is barely audible. It is reassuring that my auditory sensors appear to be performing optimally. Although the meaning of the content, which I am slowly deciphering, is less reassuring.

'Yes,' says Maeve. 'I'm going to take care of you. You were so brave back there, Kobi. I'm proud of you. Shane – get my tools, please.'

The darkness continues. But something feels different.

# THIRTY-SEVEN

## MAEVE

*Friday, 3pm*

I pace the floor, talking to myself out loud. 'Think, Maeve. *Think.*'

Kobi is stretched out on the bed in the Farmers' guest room. His legs are badly damaged, but his torso, arms and head are intact – on the outside at least. The wheelchair lies crumpled in the corner. I've sent Shane to get my tools and Kobi's portable sleep pod from the car.

I could – *should* – call Josh right now. But I can't face it. It's too hard to explain, and besides, he'd want a full status report and I can't give him that right now. But maybe I can get Kobi stable, systematically assess what damage has been done. Josh showed me Kobi's brain, cushioned inside his torso. There's a chance the damage is mainly to his exterior.

There's a gentle tapping at the door. I open it, expecting Shane, but it's Matthew and Lizzie. I push the door back to a crack, blocking their view of the room and its patient.

'We want to help,' says Lizzie in a small voice. She clutches a bright blue stuffed monkey to her chest. It's wearing a space suit.

I glance at Kobi, then crouch down to look her in the eye. I'm starting to get an idea. 'Thank you. You can bring me any of your old toys you don't play with any more. Especially anything with moving parts.'

'What else do you need?' asks Matthew.

I stand up. 'A tour of your tool shed, please.'

*5:30pm*

A knock at the door. I wipe my hands on my borrowed overalls, push my plastic goggles up onto the top of my head and open the door a smidge. Shane is holding a mug with a dark liquid inside. I recognise the smell instantly.

'How did you...?' I begin.

'Had to drive to the next town. They've a big supermarket.'

I accept the peppermint tea with gratitude. 'You're an angel.'

'How's the patient?' He peeks over my shoulder in the doorway.

'He's still in sleep mode, doing a full recharge. So we won't really know if he's fully functional until he wakes up, but' – I open the door fully – 'come in and see for yourself. We made some changes to his body.'

Matthew is packing away his tools in the corner of the room. 'I better go and check in on Lizzie,' he says. 'I'll leave ye to it. Come and find me when you've news.'

Shane walks over to Kobi, propped up in his portable sleep pod in the middle of the room. Kobi's upper half looks the same, just a little dulled and grimy.

'Um, where are his legs?' he asks.

I point to the corner of the room, where Kobi's legs are standing somewhat awkwardly by themselves, like a wallflower at a disco.

'They've been nothing but trouble since day one,' I say brightly. 'They had to go. I've gone old-school instead.'

I point to Kobi's lower half, which now looks pleasingly steampunk, with a hint of patriotism. His lower section is hard green plastic with vertical leather strips at intervals, giving a green-and-black-stripes effect. It's amazing the uses you can find for an old lawnmower. Attached on either side are two large wheels.

'Are those parts from the wheelchair?' Shane asks.

I nod. 'And...' I open one of the leather strips to reveal a series of smaller, hidden wheels within, of varying sizes and colours, including several shades of pink. Lizzie's old roller skates are about to get a new lease of life.

The last two hours have been frenetic. Seeing that toy space monkey reminded me that all the trouble started when Kobi tried to walk on the other-worldly Burren rocks. My dad loved cycling. 'Four wheels good, two wheels better,' he used to say. I talked to Matthew about my idea, and between us we were able to come up with a plan. Matthew said it was 'recycling at its best'. I'm not sure what Josh will say, but I couldn't just leave Kobi immobilised, with neither legs nor wheelchair. It didn't seem right.

'I know it looks a bit weird,' I say with a smile. 'Kobi really came into himself in that chair somehow. And boy, did he move fast when he needed to. So I reckoned he might like to retain that speed advantage. And also, to have a reminder of what he did.'

I open a little panel on the side of Kobi's torso. 'Look, I'll show you how it works. So, the large wheels will be slightly raised up most of the time, just adding some extra balance – you know, like stabilisers on a bike. But then, if he needs to go really fast, he can activate this function here to mechanically pop the wheels down to the ground, and boom – he can bomb along really fast. We've added a gentle braking mechanism – here – and an emergency stop. Really, he's almost half bicycle now.'

'Maeve, have you just reinvented the wheel?' Shane laughs. 'This is amazing.'

He circles Kobi, and when he gets back to his starting point, he suddenly lifts me up by the hips and does a half-turn with me, placing me down lightly. 'You're amazing,' he says, facing me.

I laugh too. 'Put me down!' I say, even though I'm already down. 'But do you think he'll like it?'

'I think he'll love it!' His hands are still on my hips.

I look up at him and we lock eyes. We're standing very close to each other. My breathing gets shallow. Adrenaline is still buzzing through me. My overall suddenly feels too warm. I want to unzip it, but my limbs are so heavy that I can't seem to move a muscle. I can't remember what I was about to say.

Kobi emits a mild electrical sound. I break away from Shane, clear my throat. 'Let's not jinx it. Let's see how he is when he wakes up, after a full battery charge.'

'Maeve,' he says. 'Why can't we just—'

But I cut him off. 'Thanks so much for the tea.' I get the cup from the dresser and sit on the edge of the bed. 'It could be a while until he wakes up.'

'I'll wait with you.' His tone is flat.

'Sure,' I say.

He sits on the floor at my feet, cross-legged. I know he wants something from me, something I can't give him. He leans his back against the bed. His Nikes have mud on them.

'Sorry about your shoes,' I say. 'Farm life.'

'I don't care about the shoes.'

I hold my breath, then exhale. A memory is coming to me.

'Let me tell you a funny story about shoes.'

'Okay.'

'From when I was a kid.'

'Okay.'

'Well, pre-teen years. I was around twelve. We were living in Chicago. I'd already lived in London and Boston. And a couple of places in Ireland. So anyway, I had this friend called Sacha. We were in different schools, but we only lived a block away from each other. We met at the local chess club. Yes, I know, I was a bit of a nerd. We were the only girls in the club, and pretty soon we were inseparable.'

I smile at the memory. 'We had so much in common. We discovered that we had the same shoe size and our birthdays were both in July. One time, we pretended to be each other for a day. We swapped clothes and gave our parents quite the surprise when we went home to each other's houses at the end of the day.

'Anyway, our birthdays were coming up, and it was my idea that we'd ask our parents for the same pair of Converse but get one pair in black and one in white. "To really know someone, you have to walk in their shoes," I told Sacha. I was so wise! And I was the one who insisted that we each wear one black shoe and one white one. Our mothers thought it was dumb, but they tolerated it.

'Until one day my dad announced that we were moving again. A great opportunity had come up in South Africa for work. A couple of weeks before we were due to leave, Sacha asked me for her white shoe back. She was crying. The new school term was starting soon. Said her mom was determined she wasn't going to turn up at school looking like a weirdo.

'So I said okay, but I didn't give the shoe back. I avoided Sacha for the next two weeks, ignoring messages and refusing to leave my room when she called to the house. My mam went ape, but I refused to give up the shoe. I just couldn't do it. I ended up hiding it in a crawl space under the house. What were they gonna do? Leave me behind when they went to Cape Town?

'The last message I ever got from Sacha said that she'd been grounded. She begged me to come over, said she would forgive me, we could forget about the shoe and just say goodbye properly. But I didn't. I left Chicago without saying goodbye to her.'

'And without the shoe?' says Shane.

'And without the shoe.'

'I see.'

'Yeah.'

'You said this was a funny story.'

'Sorry. I thought it was going to be a funny shoe-in-a-crawl-space story. I had forgotten about the other parts. Until now.'

My eyes are wet. My chest feels heavy. There have been so many goodbyes, so many new beginnings. Maybe I do push people away. But I've been doing it so long, I no longer know if it's to protect myself, or just the habit of a lifetime.

Shane reaches behind him, pats my leg gently without looking at me. 'It must have been hard, moving around so much.'

'Dad said we were lucky.'

'Even so.'

I'm glad he can't see my face. I stay still, trying to even out my breath.

There's a faint zing from Kobi's sleep pod, indicating that he's fully charged. I jump off the bed. Shane scrambles to his feet.

I stand beside Kobi, fiddle with the buttons on his control panel.

'Hey,' I say softly. 'Can you hear me?'

His eyes flicker to life. He moves his head in the direction of my voice. 'Greetings, Maeve. I can see and hear you. It is a pleasure to do both.'

'Woo-hoo!' I yelp and throw my arms around him. It's awkward, but I don't even care.

'Yes!' Shane cheers. 'Go on!'

'Maeve, Shane, please be calm,' says Kobi. 'What did I miss?'

'Not much.' I can't stop smiling.

My phone pings, and so does Shane's. 'Hang on.'

I pick it up. A message from Matthew, with a link:

> Thought you might like to see this! News travels fast around here.

'Did you get this too?' I ask Shane.

'Think so.'

'My battery's almost dead. Can we open it on your phone?'

I go to him, stand close beside him. The top of my head just about reaches to his shoulder. In some ways, we fit together perfectly.

Shane holds his phone out in front of the two of us, opens the messaging app. Before he taps the first message, from Matthew, I catch a glimpse of the next message on the list. The sender is Sandra Smith. The message appears to consist of three emojis:

My stomach drops. *That could mean anything*, I tell myself quickly. *And anyway, I don't care. I'm not even surprised.* A carousel of responses spins in my mind as Shane clicks the link from Matthew. It brings us to what looks like a local news website. A headline reads, 'Robot Saves Child in Dramatic Cliff Incident'. I read the subhead and skim the first few paragraphs as Shane scrolls.

*Local girl Lizzie Farmer (5) was today saved from harm by a humanoid robot in a dramatic incident at the Cliffs of Moher... near-fatal... last-minute dash... robot on wheels... local family... relief and joy... unprecedented scenes...*

A video is embedded in the story. Shane clicks on it. Ninety seconds of footage from the car park at the cliffs. It looks like it was filmed on a dashboard camera; there's no sound. It shows the SUV reversing and the moment of the collision with Kobi in the chair. Then a crowd gathering while I kneel beside Kobi on the ground.

'Oh no,' I say. 'Josh is going to kill me. He specifically asked me to keep a low profile for Kobi while we were here.'

Shane scrolls back to the top of the page.

'Ah, it'll be grand. While I'm sure *The Clare People* has its fans, it's not exactly *The New York Times* now, is it?'

# THIRTY-EIGHT

*Thursday, 7:30pm*

I follow a crisp-clad waiter through Gino's Restaurant to our table. Josh should be here soon. This place looks nice – rustic chic. I start composing an ad in my head. *Authentic Italian with a contemporary twist. Romantic but modern.* Josh chose this place. I wonder if he picked just anywhere or put in the research.

We're both attending the AI conference in Athlone tomorrow – me, on account of my own interest and a handy discount for those who completed all the MIT course modules; Josh, because Ron Tron was recently added to the line-up. So we've arranged to stay in the conference hotel tonight and to go for dinner somewhere local to catch up. I've only spoken to Josh briefly since his return to Ireland on Tuesday, and he hasn't seen Kobi yet. All he knows is that Kobi is back at work at Go Ireland after a short trip to County Clare. I thought it'd be better to tell him the details in person.

Since the trip to Clare, the past few days have been mercifully uneventful. In the car back to Dublin on Saturday, Shane was fairly quiet. We stopped off at the Clare Arms Hotel to reimburse them for the wheelchair we'd borrowed and broken; then we spent half an hour in the car gently debating whether we could put the cost through as an expense claim when we got back. I think we were both relieved that, in the end, we didn't have to deal with the issue of the honeymoon suite in Lisdoonvarna, a town famous for its annual matchmaking festival.

I haven't seen Shane much since, apart from our presentation on Monday morning, which we winged our way through. I was busy all week setting Kobi up with his new job, recording oral histories for callers with a connection to Ireland. As well as stories of life in old Ireland, Kobi's going to record the tales of Irish emigrants who settled in other countries, hear how their new lives took shape.

As I look around the restaurant, I'm glad of the low lighting, the soft fabrics that hush the other diners' chatter. I'm not sure how Josh will react to the events of my road trip to County Clare. And I haven't yet told him the details of the Science Museum incident. Luckily, JP seems to have smoothed things over and no legal action is pending.

I'm suddenly nervous. I order a bottle of wine from a passing waiter, who returns promptly with it and a basket of salted bread. The last Italian meal I had was at the Farmers' house. I smile at the memory.

Josh appears through the gloom, bringing my focus back to the present. He looks tanned and relaxed. I'd forgotten how classically handsome he is. With the clearest blue eyes. I stand to greet him and we do a kind of awkward half hug, but enough for me to inhale a clean, manly scent.

I decide I want to tell him all about the Clare trip quickly – rip off the Band-Aid. He'll find out as soon as he sees Kobi's TIL files anyway.

As soon as he's settled at the table and I've enquired after his general health and well-being, and told him I definitely want to hear more about the Singapore conference later, I say, 'So, can I tell you about my trip to Clare?'

'Of course.' He smiles at me. I meet his eyes and exhale.

I tell him everything up to the cliff visit, choosing a light tone to paint a picture of three merry friends on an amusing adventure. He listens without interruption but with a serious face, nodding along and taking regular sips of wine.

'So,' I say, tearing off a piece of salted bread and slowing down the story. 'Then we get to the Friday. There's good news and there's bad news. Or, maybe, good news and bad news and more bad news. Actually, I'm not even sure if you'll find the good news very good.'

'Maeve.' He refills my glass, which I didn't notice was empty. 'Just tell me what happened.'

'Okay.' I take a deep breath. 'First of all, I'll just reassure you that Kobi is fine. He's still highly functional.'

'I notice you said highly, not fully,' he says, but I can't quite read his expression.

'Well, Josh – you, my friend, are *highly* observant. See, highly is good.' I tear off more bread, shred it into smaller pieces. 'Is it even legal to put this much salt in bread?'

He shoots me a look.

'Okay, okay, I'll tell you. The thing is – there was an incident. An accident. Or an almost-accident, you might say. We were in a car park. The little girl ran off and before we realised it, a car started reversing, straight towards her. Kobi flew across the car park and basically threw himself in front of the car. I'm afraid the car hit Kobi with some force.'

'And the little girl?'

I'm relieved that his first thought is for Lizzie.

'She was fine – one hundred per cent fine. Kobi sustained some injuries though.'

'You mean...' He puts down his wine glass, raises his voice a little.

*Oh no, here we go.*

'What you're telling me is...' He speaks slowly.

I brace myself for impact.

'Kobi saved someone?'

'Oh. Yes.'

'He *saved* someone?'

'Yes.'

'A little girl?'

'Yes.'

'A little girl he hardly knew?'

'Er, yes. They got along well, but I suppose, technically, they didn't know each other for very long.'

'Well, well, well.' Josh sits back and refills his own glass. 'Well, well, well.' He looks around for a waiter. 'Hey, can we get some champagne over here?'

I'm flummoxed. He's taking this much better than I expected. 'Josh, are we... celebrating? Don't you want to hear the rest of the story? I had to make some mods to Kobi's body.'

'Doesn't matter.' He's positively beaming at me. 'You said yourself he's still highly functional. I'm sure whatever you had to do to him physically can be fixed. But, Maeve – this is big. Why didn't you tell me this on the phone?'

'I guess... I thought you might be unhappy about the damage to Kobi's exterior?'

He leans forward over the table. He takes my hand in his.

'Unhappy? Maeve, don't you see? Kobi just made a huge leap here. *Huge.* He acted autonomously. He made a split-second decision. He *sacrificed* himself, in the moment, for a human.'

'He was just doing what any of us would have done,' I say.

'Exactly!' He slaps the table. It makes a dull thud through the thick cloth. 'Exactly! Let's drink to that.'

*10pm*

I nudge Josh and giggle at the wallpaper in the hotel lobby, which is unexpectedly hilarious. We've stumbled the short distance back to our hotel, after we finished the second bottle of red, and the bottle of champagne, of course. I think there was food somewhere in between.

Josh can't find his room key, another unexpectedly hilarious turn of events.

'I'm going to the front desk. What was it you called it? Something cute. Oh yeah – "reception". Wait for me here?' He puts his hands on my upper arms as if fixing me in place.

As soon as he walks away, I sink down into a plush armchair, close my eyes just for a second. The evening is going great. I can't recall ever seeing Josh so happy, so buzzed. He was delighted about the events of Clare, making me tell and retell the story of Kobi's 'heroism', as he kept calling it. Finally, this was the proof he needed that Kobi could be trusted around people. Of course, he said, he always knew Kobi was safe *in theory*, but now we had concrete evidence of it.

I try not to dwell on the nagging worry that Josh, in spite of all his reassurances, was clearly not one hundred per cent certain of Kobi's safety until this very evening. But can anyone really be one hundred per cent certain of anything?

I showed him photos of Kobi's new modifications, but he just laughed and said it wasn't a big deal. He could easily restore Kobi's legs. I tried to argue that maybe Kobi didn't need legs after all, but Josh didn't want to get into it. He just kept praising me for my 'breakthrough' with Kobi.

He was so elated at dinner that I decided not to mention the video footage in the online newspaper after all. Maybe it's not always best to rip the Band-Aid off all at once. Maybe sometimes it's better to soak in the bathtub for a very long time, until the plaster gently surrenders itself and slips beneath the suds unnoticed...

'Maeve!' Josh's voice brings me back to consciousness.

'How long was I asleep?' I slur. I sit up in the armchair, check my face for drool.

He rolls up his sleeve with apparently great effort, taps at invisible buttons on his watch for an age.

'About two minutes,' he says eventually.

We both start laughing.

'Come on.' He reaches out his hand.

I achieve verticality with what I hope is some dignity. I think about Kobi and his mobility challenges. I think about how Kobi has led to me being here, right now, at this very moment. Being here, with Josh.

'Oh, bad news,' he says with a hiccup. 'They just told me the elevator is out of service. We'll have to take the stairs.'

'But my room is on the third floor,' I say.

'Mine is on the fourth.'

He opens the door leading to the staircase so I can go ahead of him. The staircase is old-fashioned and narrow and we have to go single file. He follows close behind me. It reminds me of going up in the round tower at the Viking Museum. We near the top of the second flight. I stumble slightly, grip the banister. He puts his right hand on my hip to steady me, his left hand on mine.

I feel the heat and spin around to face him. We're eye to eye, Josh one step below me. Nobody speaks. I lick the corner of my lip tentatively. I feel as if I'm falling into his eyes.

I kiss him, or maybe he kisses me – it's unclear but unimportant right now. It's a good kiss, followed by another and another. Soon his arms are around me and I melt into him. I put my hands under his jacket, exploring the muscles in his back.

'Will you come to my room?' he says.

'No,' I murmur. 'Mine is closer.'

We kiss-fumble our way along the corridor to room 301, torn between getting there fast and devouring each other right here in the corridor.

'You're amazing,' he tells me between kisses. A memory of Shane's face flashes in my mind, but Shane is very far away now, probably in the arms of the objectively beautiful Sandra Smith at this very minute.

I swipe the door with my key card three times before it opens. We fall into the room and pull at each other's clothes, haphazardly attacking buttons and zips in no particular order.

We reach the bed. I stumble over hotel slippers and fall backwards, landing across the end of the bed. I bring Josh down with me. He lands on top of me, which is right where I want him. We both laugh, catch our breath for a second.

Suddenly, he pulls away from me, rushes to the bathroom. I hear him splash water on his face. When he returns, he silently scans me from head to toe. I try not to remember Kobi scanning me in a similar way in the Clare Arms Hotel.

I let my mind go blank, cede control to my body. I admire Josh's precision-engineering skills as he now devotes equal attention to all my sensitive areas, in rotation, for equal amounts of time, probably.

*Maybe, finally, this is the right place, at the right time*, is the last rational thought I have before I surrender to shuddering pleasure.

# THIRTY-NINE

*Friday, 11am*

> Heading for coffee now. See you there?

I press send on the message to Josh and pick my way through the dispersing crowd in the main auditorium after the first conference talk of the day. I'm feeling the chasm of the three hours since I last saw Josh, when he pulled me to him and kissed me deeply before leaving my room this morning. I swallow now, remembering the electricity that lit through me, right down to my toes.

As I make my way through the hotel lobby, I spot the armchair I briefly fell asleep in last night and hope no one here today saw me do that. People mill around me, clustering into groups and talking loudly. I wonder if I should try some networking.

*Meeting Josh* is *networking*, I tell myself. After all, he's working for a company at the forefront of robot development. And Ron Tron himself is here at the conference – maybe Josh can introduce me. Josh said before that RoboTron might need 'people like me' in the future. This could be the beginning of a whole new era. Today could be one of those golden opportunities people go on about. I allow myself a daydream: me, slightly older and wearing glasses, speaking solemnly from the podium in the auditorium here, telling everyone how my life and career changed dramatically in this very venue, just a few short years ago. And maybe Josh would be smiling up at me from the audience.

'Hello, you,' I say.

Josh looks especially good standing next to a tower of miniature croissants. I grab one and devour it lustily. I notice Josh looking at my chest and look down to see a carnage of crumbs on my lapels.

'Let me get that for you.' He slowly brushes the crumbs downward, lingering over each stroke.

I look around to see if anyone is looking at us, but we're in our own little bubble, this shared secret between us. It's exciting.

I give myself a little shake. 'Did you see there was a slight change in the programme? Ron Tron is now going to be on the same panel as Mimi Lee, the ethics professor from MIT. Hey, do you think you could introduce me to Ron?'

I look around in case saying his name might make him appear, but that never works when you really want it to.

'These croissants are really good.' Josh stuffs one into his mouth.

'Just because it's miniature doesn't mean you have to eat it all in one go.' I laugh. 'But you didn't answer my question. Ron? It would be great for me to finally meet him.'

Josh makes chewing noises and points at his mouth, like a mime doing a bit.

'A more paranoid person might think you don't want me to meet Ron.'

I sip a tepid cup of coffee. Of course they don't have peppermint tea here. My mouth is dry and my head throbs. The pleasure tax bill has been issued, and last night's indulgences must be paid for with sleep and hydration, or at least deferred with caffeine and adrenaline.

Josh downs his coffee in one go. 'Ugh – conference coffee. It's the same worldwide. Singapore, Sarajevo, Athlone – doesn't matter! Just weak, bitter, brown fluid.'

I take the cup from Josh's hand and place it firmly on the table.

'Okay, okay – let's talk about Ron,' he concedes. 'Y'see, the thing about Ron is, he's very busy. I'm sure he's flying off somewhere immediately after the panel today. To be honest, I'm surprised he even agreed to do this event. I'm not sure he'll be delighted to be moved onto a panel discussing ethics. He's more of your fireside-chat type of guy. More of a broadcaster than a listen-and-responder.'

I give him my best silent glare.

'Look, Maeve, I tell you what we'll do. We'll go to the panel, and we'll sit near the back. When Ron leaves the stage at the end, we'll try to intercept him on his way out.'

'But can't you just – I don't know – text him or something and arrange it?'

Josh gives a short laugh. 'Ha! No. Ron doesn't do texting. He barely does email. You don't ask him for things. If he wants to talk to you, you'll know about it. Not you specifically. He does this with everyone.'

I pick up a small plate and sadly balance three pastries on it in a mini-pyramid formation.

'Look, we can still try,' he says gently. 'And if we don't get a chance today, well, there's always another time. I can bring you into RoboTron someday and we'll make it happen. I promise.'

# FORTY

## KOBI

*Friday,* 1410

The party is due to commence at 1500. Everyone in the office has been talking about it all week. After Maeve and Shane's presentation at the staff meeting on Monday morning, I expected a lot more questions about our trip to Clare – and especially about the loss of my legs. Instead, everyone has been speaking about the impending party and asking each other questions about their intended outfits.

I am helping Shane and Julia decorate the gift shop, under close supervision from Sandra Smith. Julia explained to me at lunchtime that the party is in fact a 'double celebration' – of both Halloween and David's birthday. David did not appear overly excited by this, however, and repeated several times: 'There's no such thing as a Halloween birthday party.' As I have never experienced either type of party, I am highly curious about proceedings.

We are now installing all of the Halloween decorations, plus additional birthday supplies provided by Julia. I am enjoying the challenge of categorising birthday and Halloween elements into separate datasets. For example:

- Red balloons => Birthday

- Black balloons => Halloween
- Orange balloons => Halloween AND/OR Birthday
- Candles on top of food => Birthday
- Candles inside food => Halloween
- References to ageing => Birthday
- References to death => Halloween

Shane has assigned me the task of projecting a light show onto a wall for the duration of the party. I am unsure if this is needless busy work – as Shane might style it – or essential to the creation of 'a party atmosphere', an area in which Shane holds some expertise.

'Is there a formula for creating a party atmosphere?' I ask Shane.

He climbs a chair and secures a banner to the ceiling.

'Yes, but no one knows what it is. It's ineffable.'

'That is unhelpful data.'

I offer him my hand to steady his descent from the chair. He high-fives it instead and jumps down. He picks up a packet of balloons.

'I can describe it to you but it's impossible to reverse-engineer it. There are several key ingredients, and they need to combine in certain quantities, but no one can specify what those quantities are. I can tell you this though – the key to a good party is girls.'

'Girls? I presume you mean women.'

'Yes, Kobi. I mean women.'

He rolls his eyes and smiles. He blows into a balloon.

'Do you mean the presence of women will ensure a good party?'

He ties the balloon.

'No. But a party will only be good if the women are enjoying themselves. They're like the canaries in the coal mine – you can look that up. If the women are cold, no atmosphere. If the women are hungry, no atmosphere. If the women won't dance, no atmosphere. If you're at a party and a woman puts *on* a cardigan, forget about it, you might as well go home there and then. That thing is dead as disco.'

'Food, temperature, music – it seems fairly straightforward, Shane. Not exactly rocket science, as you yourself might say.'

'Ha, are you mocking me? I'd like to see what kind of party you'd throw.'

He takes another balloon and blows into it.

'I am happy to help, if I may. Perhaps I should circulate at the party and capture all of the women's cardigans?'

The balloon flies around the room, making a wet, whirring sound.

'No, Kobi – please don't do that. You just focus on the lights, okay? Lights are very important.'

*1450*

When the room is ready, it is time for me and Shane to put on our costumes. Shane chose the outfits. All week, he has refused to disclose the details. He now produces 2 bags. From a quick scan, I detect polyester material, predominantly in 2 colours: silver and brown.

'Any guesses?' He unpacks the bags and lays the costumes on the table. 'I'll give you a hint. Think classic movies.'

'Insufficient data,' I say. 'I could, however, list every movie considered a classic, even though such designations are essentially a subjective matter of opinion.'

'You're no fun,' Shane says. But he says it with a smile. 'I'll just tell you. It's *The Wizard of Oz*. You're the Tin Man and I'm the Scarecrow.'

He places a flimsy metal-coloured cone on my head.

I quickly parse all available data about the movie and its characters. 'Is that how you see me? A tin man with no heart?'

It is technically accurate that I do not possess a heart, but to compare my parts to tin – a material commonly used to make cheap metal alloys – borders on insulting.

'No, no, not at all. I mean, not really. It just made the most sense for you to be the Tin Man. Rather than me, I mean. The main thing is, we have to dress as characters from that movie.'

'Why?'

'Well, I think we're still borderline in JP's books. Our presentation went well on Monday, but we need to keep him sweet if this arrangement' – he gestures toward me – 'is to continue. Maeve has gotten very fond of you, you know.'

This statement pleases me enormously. 'Thank you. But how do these costumes—'

'Getting to that. JP mentioned on Tuesday that his wife, Trish, is coming to the party today, and that she's dressing up as Dorothy from *The Wizard of Oz*. He wouldn't tell me what he was dressing as, but he said it was a couple's costume and there was fur involved. So I'm guessing he's coming as the Lion. So I thought—'

'That we should dress as the other characters? Thereby pleasing Trish, thereby implanting a positive association for us in JP's mind?'

'Now you're getting it,' Shane says. 'Human beings are actually very easily manipulated.'

'I wish you had told me that 5 weeks ago,' I say.

*1501*

Shane looks at his watch. He expresses 2 contradictory opinions about the timing of the party. He says it is 'criminally early' to throw a party at 1500. However, the party is taking place during working hours – a situation Shane describes as 'beating the system'.

'What happens if the party continues past 1700?' I ask him.

'Then, my friend, we are in uncharted waters. A no man's land of potential. Or potential badness, at least.'

If it was possible for me to shrug, I would. 'Please clarify,' I say.

'Anything could happen,' Shane says.

'Anything could happen,' I repeat.

Somewhat alarmed, I put my emergency systems on standby and check my battery level.

Julia and David arrive together at 1503.

'Dave, you're gonna love it,' she says. 'The lads have done a great job on the decorations.' I am pleased at her approval.

Then I notice their party outfits. They are both wearing white t-shirts with the same picture on the front. I am drawn to the design, and within 3 seconds I analyse and recognise it. It is a copy of the crude portrait that David made of me at the art event – including the large red X through the centre. I am a little confused and several different emotions fire at once.

Shane looks at the shirts and laughs. 'Hey, those are great. You kept the X and all?'

'Yep! Leaning into it,' Julia says. 'Kobi, do you like them?'

I consider the question. I know that David made the original picture to express animosity toward me. But that was 3 weeks and 2 days ago. Much has happened since. David and Julia have clearly gone to some effort to recreate the image and print it onto shirts, and to wear it on a special occasion in human culture – a 'double celebration', in fact.

'It is a great honour.' I bow slightly in David's direction. 'David – happy birthday.'

'Thanks, man.' David lightly punches my upper arm. I am beginning to understand that minor aggressions are perhaps a means of communication for David.

'Where's Maeve?' Julia says.

Shane hands her a drink the colour of methyl orange. 'Ah, she can't make it. She's at some conference.'

'Maeve and Josh are attending an AI conference at the Shannon Hotel, Athlone,' I provide helpfully.

'Sorry, man,' David says to Shane.

Shane shrugs. 'I better help Sandra with the drinks.'

He walks to the other side of the room, where Sandra Smith is placing frozen plastic eyeballs into an array of high-ball glasses. She is dressed as a vampire.

'Poor fella,' David says.

We all watch as Sandra Smith laughs at something Shane says. She puts her hand on his arm.

'I think he'll live,' Julia says. Then she says, 'Hey, Kobi. If you like these shirts, wait til you see what DC is wearing.'

As she speaks, a figure enters the room. My systems momentarily threaten to overload as I process the visual data. For an instant I forget that I am dressed as the Tin Man and I get the sensation that I am looking into a mirror, but I soon realise that in fact I am observing DC Jen in an elaborate Halloween costume.

It appears that she has mimicked my look to the best of her abilities. She is wearing a body suit, with metallic-coloured cardboard on her arms and torso, and she is wearing a mask, with only the lower portion of her face visibly human. She still has legs, of course, although it seems she has attached two large bicycle wheels to the outside of her knees.

'Of course you had to come in on wheels on Monday!' she says. 'Nearly ruined it! Luckily I had an old bike in the shed. What do you think?' She turns around 360 degrees to allow for complete surveillance.

'I am speechless.' I finally understand why humans use this expression.

My Emotion Detector is firing rapidly. Until this moment, I have not encountered another being that so closely resembles me. I experience many powerful emotions, including recognition, curiosity, empathy and another element I cannot identify.

Finally, my emotion sensors clarify. 'I am... happy,' I say.

# FORTY-ONE

## MAEVE

*Friday, 3pm*

Just like we decided, we find two seats at the end of a row near the back of the main auditorium. The stage is being set up for a panel discussion on AI ethics. Every row in front of us looks fully occupied. Ron's last-minute addition to the panel must have bumped up the numbers.

I crane my neck to see the stage. Four plush white leather armchairs are lined up in the centre. Purple spotlights warm the stage, while the audience is consigned to near-darkness. I take advantage of the dim light and squeeze Josh's hand.

'Exciting,' I whisper to him, and mean it. I'm right where I should be.

I review the conference brochure on my phone. After watching her lectures online and reading a good chunk of her book, I'm eager to see Professor Mimi Lee in the flesh. There'll be a conference dinner this evening. Maybe I'll see Mimi there and we'll be able to have a chat about Kobi? Unlikely Ron will be staying for the dinner, according to Josh. The third member of the panel is an English academic I haven't heard of – Geoffrey Johnson.

The purple spotlights swoop out over the crowd as jaunty

piano music heralds the arrival of the panel moderator. A tall blonde woman sweeps confidently to the front of the stage, her smile like a floodlight.

'Oh!' I elbow Josh, who's busy scrolling on his device. 'Look who it is!'

'Who is it?' says Josh, not looking.

The woman on-stage introduces herself before I can name her. 'Hello, I'm Laura Cantwell from Precision Health Instruments.'

Josh drops his phone and begins urgently swearing to himself.

'It's okay,' I say. 'Your phone is just there – look, under the seat in front of you.'

He goes down on his hands and knees between the rows of chairs – not an easy feat for a man his size. He sticks his head out the end of our row and looks up at the stage. Then he turns his head searchingly to survey the back of the room.

'Are you okay?' I whisper. Laura's name wasn't on the programme, but I'm glad to see her again. I'll make sure to find her later to give her a full Kobi update. I suddenly picture myself, Laura and Mimi, wine glasses in hand, propping up the bar while I recount Kobi's escapades at the Burren in exquisitely entertaining detail. Just three women working in the industry, hanging out together and swapping stories.

Laura is introducing the panellists as they make their way to their seats. Geoffrey Johnson and Mimi Lee emerge through the cream folds draped across the stage, microphones at the ready, but Ron – who I recognise from his online profile – bounds towards the stage from elsewhere in the auditorium and up the three steps at the side, giving the audience a kind of goofy wave. As soon as he sits down, a technician appears and discreetly hands him a microphone.

Laura settles the panel in with some preliminary questions, batting them easy balls to lob back to her. Ron appears the most relaxed, in blue jeans and sport coat, resting one ankle on his knee to show off embroidered cowboy boots. His facial hair is neatly groomed. He's trim, in good shape. Mimi looks small and neat and cool in a black shirt, black blazer, black tailored trousers, flat shoes and no socks. Geoffrey sits rigidly between them, sipping too much water and staring straight ahead.

Laura asks Geoffrey a broad question about AI in the workplace. He clears his throat and begins his answer with, 'Let me reframe the question in two ways – epistemologically and historically. Oh, and also philosophically.' Four minutes later, he has not yet provided his answer to the newly reframed question, neither epistemologically, historically nor philosophically. I audibly tut. The panel is only scheduled to last thirty-five minutes.

Laura interrupts Geoffrey at last. 'Let me bring Ron in on this. Ron, we've met before, and I should say that we at PHI have enjoyed the company of your latest creation, the Kobi 3000. It's an amazing example of where the field of collaborative robotics is going.'

I nudge Josh. 'Kobi!' I whisper a little too loudly. A guy in front of me turns his head to glance at me.

'Why, thank you,' says Ron.

'So,' Laura begins. 'The question is – let's take an advanced AI robot like the Kobi 3000. Do you think such cobots are ready to work alongside humans on the factory floor or in other workplace settings?'

Is Laura baiting Ron into discussing Kobi's meltdown, and in front of a live audience at that? But wouldn't that make PHI look bad? I want to ask Josh these questions but he's now visibly sweating beside me, gripping the sides of his chair, running his hands through his hair every thirty seconds. I guess his hangover is finally kicking in.

'Well, you tell me, Laura. You're the one who's been trialling Kobi in your workplace.' Ron is completely relaxed in his response, Southern charm in his accent. Wait, is he... *flirting*?

'Maeve,' says Josh in my ear. 'There's something—'

'Shh,' I say. 'I'm dying to hear this. She's so ballsy.'

But Laura is laughing. Wait, is *she* flirting?

Ron suddenly leans forward in his chair, holds the microphone close to his mouth. 'Let me put it to you this way, Laura. Allow me to borrow Geoffrey's reframing device here for a second. Much obliged to you, Geoff.' Ron bows his head sideways towards Geoffrey, who makes a muddled gesture in Ron's direction in return. He continues: 'I would put that question back to you as: are you people ready to work alongside our robots?'

He pauses for effect. Then he turns his body towards the audience and addresses us directly, in hypnotic tones. 'We're creating the workforce of the future. We're going to make your working life easier. Maybe you'll only need to come in three days a week. How does that sound?'

A couple of guys whoop from the front row.

'Exactly,' says Ron. 'The technology is here. We're just waiting for y'all to catch up.'

He sits back in his chair with a satisfied smile.

Laura smiles too and nods. 'Let me bring Professor Lee in on this. Professor Lee, your area of speciality is ethics. Do you think – and Ron, I'm going to phrase this in a way that will hopefully be acceptable to everyone – do you think humans and AI cobots are ready to work together in harmony?'

Mimi also smiles. 'Thank you for the question. Unlike my fellow panellists, I will not be requiring the reframing device in order to respond.'

A ripple of gentle laughter washes across the auditorium. I remember why I enjoyed her lectures so much.

'To give you a simple answer – no, we are not ready,' she says.

'A lot of things happen before we're ready for them,' Ron interrupts. 'If I was to sit around and wait for everyone to be ready, why... for a start, I'd never get to a dinner reservation on time.' Ron positively twinkles at the audience, who laugh along in return.

'You didn't let me finish,' says Mimi calmly.

'Please, continue,' says Laura.

'I was about to say: we are not ready, but it is already happening. As usual – and I'm sure Ron would at least agree with this part – the technology is years, perhaps decades, ahead of laws, regulations and guidelines. What we need to do now, as fast as we can, is to make sure that we put in place the rules by which we want robots to operate in the workplace. And – this part is really important – we need to make sure that the people who write those rules are not the same people who are selling us the robots. For a new way of working to be robust, it needs to have input from everyone who will be affected.'

'That sounds just swell,' says Ron. 'I will happily attend any meeting you manage to organise with all parties.'

'Ah,' says Geoffrey, who suddenly seems emboldened to join in. 'I do believe I detect some sarcasm in Mr Tron's response.'

'Not at all,' says Ron. 'I want to do whatever it takes to ensure cobots are accepted in the workplace. I just think that we'll never reach this set of perfect golden rules that Professor Lee seems so focused on.'

'I never said perfect—' says Mimi, but Ron interrupts again.

'Laura, if I may? There's an elephant in the room here that all of us have been ignoring, and he's getting mighty impatient.'

Even though I know this is a cliché, Ron is such a commanding speaker that I covertly glance all around the room – just in case. Hopefully Josh doesn't notice. Luckily, he seems preoccupied with checking his watch and scrolling on his phone, in between sweaty glances at the stage.

Laura puts her deck of talking-point flashcards on the table. 'I guess I won't be needing these any more,' she says to a handful of laughs. 'Let's get this elephant centre stage.'

'The way I see it is this,' starts Ron. 'We don't really need to worry about the robots. The ones we need to worry about are' – he stirs his microphone in a full circle to encompass the panel and the audience, then pauses for dramatic effect – 'us.'

'Ooh, he has a point,' says Geoffrey, swept up in the drama.

'Geoff, my man, please,' says Ron.

'Sorry. Do go on.'

'Everyone here knows that AI systems are not just learning from datasets any more – they're actually learning from humans.

And they're doing it on the job – just like an intern or an apprentice. When they start work, sure, they know a lot of theory and can do some practical things. But the real learning – their real value – is acquired in hands-on experience on the job. So it naturally follows that if the staff are behaving and doing their jobs right, the cobot is going to copy that behaviour. And attitude too, actually. So really, all these rules that you want, Mimi? You should already have them in place for your human staff. And if a cobot does something wrong? Well, maybe they just had a bad role model.'

Ron extends his arm, and for a moment I think that he's going to deliberately drop his mic on the floor.

But Mimi smiles. 'Thank you for proving my point for me so eloquently, Ron. You're saying that cobots are heavily influenced by the humans around them, yes?'

Ron gives a vague upwards nod.

'And I guess that would include the developers, coders and programmers who train the AI before it arrives at the workplace, right?'

Ron shrugs in tacit agreement.

'Well, what assurances do we have that *those people* are being good role models? If a cobot arrives with bad code baked in, it's going to be one hell of a job to overwrite that with new learned behaviour, yes? It's like deliberately choosing to play out the nature versus nurture debate in robotics, when we don't need to. Both nature and nurture are powerful forces – but if we can start with good in nature, we should. Why should we rely on nurture to override any natural negative tendencies? It's too risky. Yes, we need to provide good role models in the workplace, but we need to also provide good role models in the... the... birthplace, if I may put it like that.'

'In the home, she means,' says Geoffrey.

'Please don't tell me what I mean,' says Mimi.

'Yeah, come on, Geoff,' says Ron.

'Just trying to help.' Geoffrey takes a sip of water, shrinks in his seat a little.

'Okay, okay,' says Laura. 'Let's bring this back. Let me summarise what we've heard so far, because I have a surprise for all of you in a moment. On the one hand...'

Josh turns to me. 'Maeve, I need to tell you something.'

'What is it?' I whisper. 'Can't it wait? The panel is nearly over.'

He groans and looks at his watch. 'Okay.'

'Now,' Laura is saying, 'we've been talking very theoretically so far about robot–human relations in the workplace. But let's get real for a minute.'

'Ooh, is she going to mention the Kobi incident now?' I say.

Two people to my right turn their heads towards me. It's Josh's turn to shush me.

'Let's get back to basics,' Laura says. 'Let's talk about health and safety. I want to ask each of you your opinion on this topic with regards to cobots. And to give us some context, first I want to show you some extraordinary video footage we've just found on the web.'

An overhead screen descends in front of the cream curtains as she speaks.

'What you're about to see is a video that surfaced on a local news site a few days ago. We just found this clip about an hour ago so the panel probably haven't seen it yet.'

'Oh no,' I say.

'What's wrong?' says Josh.

'Oh no,' I repeat. *The jig is up.* Josh is about to find out about Kobi being in the news. 'Um, Josh...'

'The footage is a bit grainy and there's no sound,' Laura is saying. 'But I think you'll agree that what happens here is fascinating.'

'Oh,' says Josh as a blurry video of Kobi speeding across the Cliffs of Moher car park is shared with the audience and the panel. 'Maeve, we need to talk – now!'

Josh stands up and hustles me to the back of the room. As he hurries me through the door, I look back to see Ron on the edge of his seat, craning his neck around to see the screen.

The foyer is mostly empty as we bundle through the auditorium doors.

'Maeve—' starts Josh.

'I'm sorry!' I interrupt.

'We need to talk. There are some things you need to understand.' Josh looks a bit wild with his hair askew, brow glistening with sweat.

'I know, and I'm so sorry.' My words tumble out fast. 'I should have told you about the video footage. I knew about it and didn't say anything. I was waiting for the right moment to tell you.'

'Let me—' begins Josh, but I barrel on.

'I know you said to keep a low profile in Clare, and I was so afraid to tell you everything that happened. And then you were so happy about Kobi's act of bravery-slash-heroism, as you kept calling it, that I didn't want to bring you down. I was looking for the right moment to tell you. Honestly, I was. I'm so sorry.'

'Maeve, I—'

But I'm not finished. 'It was just local news. It was *The Clare People*! Sure, they have their local followers I suppose, but the footage was so grainy. I didn't think many people would see it. Or share it.'

When I pause for breath, he raises his voice a little. 'For the love of Borg! Please let me speak!'

I'm startled. I go quiet. 'Sorry – you go.'

'The thing is, Maeve—'

'Oh!' I've just noticed something.

'You have to let me speak now.' He puts his hands on my upper arms in a gentle, almost pleading grip.

'Sorry – it's just that... it looks like I *will* get to meet Ron Tron after all.'

I point past Josh.

'What?' Josh half turns around and for a moment I think his knees are going to buckle. 'Oh... no!'

A very intense-looking Ron Tron is bearing down on us, at speed. He bursts between us and hustles Josh to one side.

'Josh Hunter, we need to talk. Answer me one thing. Is that my robot?' Ron gestures back towards the auditorium.

The doors are opening and people are beginning to filter out. But before Josh can answer, Ron hisses, 'I *know* that's my robot. I know that's Kobi. Did you think I wouldn't recognise the robot that I built?'

Josh looks down at his hands and mumbles, 'The robot that *I* built...'

The Gatling gun is triggered. 'What was that? You built Kobi? Who paid for every minute you spent working on him? Who came up with Kobi as a concept? You think you could have made Kobi on your own? But what I really want to know is – what the *hell* was he doing, rolling around some goddamned tourist attraction in the middle of Ireland, saving some goddamned *kid*?'

'It's the West of Ireland, not the middle,' I provide quietly, on autopilot. I'm reeling. But I guess Josh hasn't had a chance to update Ron about Kobi's trip to Clare.

'And who the heck are you?' Ron rounds on me. 'Wait a minute – I recognise you – you were in that video!'

'I'm Maeve McGettigan from Go Ireland,' I say in a small voice. This is not how I'd pictured my introduction to Ron. He shrugs and glares at me blankly. 'You know, the tourist organisation where Kobi's doing his current work placement. I work with JP Horgan. Josh?'

I look at Josh, who refuses to meet my eyes. He looks profoundly crumpled.

The foyer is beginning to fill up. People are looking at us.

'Listen to me – both of you,' says Ron. 'I'm flying to London right now to meet a client. Kobi better be in my office on Monday morning, and he better be in good shape. Josh, you're coming with me right now.'

Ron grabs Josh's arm and begins dragging him away. Josh tries to turn back towards me. 'I'm sorry, I'm sorry, I'm sorry,' he repeats as Ron sweeps him away from me like a riptide.

# FORTY-TWO

*4:30pm*

I sink into a window seat, glad the train carriage is half-empty. I've been blinking back tears since I packed my bag at the hotel and jumped in a taxi to the train station. But now as I sit down, the implications of everything I've just experienced come crashing down on me like luggage from a packed overhead rack. My throat is tight; tears sting my eyes.

I look out the window at Athlone station, willing the train to start moving, but it stubbornly refuses to go. I can hardly process the new reality of my situation. Just two hours earlier, I was on track to a bright future, Josh by my side, destination unknown but promising. Now the whole thing is derailed.

Ron Tron didn't know my name. Ron Tron didn't even know that Kobi was working at Go Ireland. So that means Josh was... lying to me this whole time. To me and everyone else at Go Ireland.

I think back to that first email JP got – the one announcing Kobi's imminent arrival. Josh sent it *on Ron's behalf*. What was it Josh said, only this morning? *Ron barely does email.* Josh said Ron wasn't a day-to-day guy, too busy with the big picture. He said he'd keep the Phelan's excursion from reaching Ron's ears.

But why was Josh so eager for Kobi to work at Go Ireland? Was it something to do with Kobi's meltdown at PHI? Whatever the reason, Josh was clearly very invested in fast-tracking Kobi's rehabilitation. So invested he was willing to say or do whatever it took to make it look official. *He's been using me all along.* God, it's embarrassing how naïve I've been. He must have thought me a willing fool, so eager to please.

I cover my face with my hands and cringe. I'm the one who's always asking questions. I should have questioned why Josh always wanted to meet up outside the office. It was more discreet, I realise now. Further away from the scrutiny of JP and human resources. And Josh dangling the prospect of a job at RoboTron in front of me like a toy mouse before a house cat.

I flash back to last night with a groan. I deliberately conk my head against the train window. God, I *liked* him. And I thought he liked me.

But it was all lies.

# FORTY-THREE
## KOBI

*Friday, 1800*

I am fulfilling my party duty as Chief Light Show Engineer, projecting multicoloured lights onto a white wall. I alternate between bright colours for a birthday atmosphere and dark shades to represent Halloween. For my own amusement, I include light from the full electromagnetic spectrum, including infrared and ultraviolet. I refrain from using X-rays, however, as I know these are harmful to humans. Sometimes it is surprising how humans have survived as a species.

Several of my colleagues stand around with no defined purpose. Having a 'job' at a party has many benefits, I am learning. One, I can be helpful, which satisfies my programming. Two, people stop by regularly to praise my work. Three, I can listen in to a great many conversations and learn from these in-the-wild human interactions.

Imelda and DC Jen are standing nearby, watching my light show. Imelda is dressed as a 16th-century pirate. She wears thigh-high leather boots. I consider telling her they are era-inappropriate. She sips a drink. She splutters and points toward the door.

'What's up?' DC Jen says. She tries to look around, but I can tell it is difficult for her to make smooth movements in her costume. I am all too familiar with the limitations of a mechanical neck, even a pretend one.

Everyone in my vicinity turns to regard the entrance of JP and Trish.

'Dios mío. Unbelievable,' Imelda says.

Julia and David are nearby. Julia giggles and grabs David's arm, seemingly in need of support. I look over at Shane at the other side of the room. I watch his eyes widen and his mouth open.

As Shane predicted, Trish is dressed as Dorothy from *The Wizard of Oz*, with 2 long plaits, a blue check pinafore dress and red shoes.

JP's costume takes me an additional 45 seconds to accurately discern. As I am expecting to see a lion, it requires some extra processing before I conclude that JP's costume is not, in fact, that of a lion. There is no long tail, or mane. There is, however, a red collar around JP's neck, attached to a long leash, the end of which is held by Trish. JP appears to be covered in dark grey fur, with dark make-up on his face, and two small, triangular ears on top of his head.

'Toto!' Imelda says to David and Julia. 'He's Toto.'

'I know-toh,' David says.

'Stop.' Julia now appears completely unable to stand independently and clings to David for support. 'I can't.'

'Well, you better, 'cos they're coming this way,' David says.

JP and Trish begin making their way across the room, greeting individuals and groups along the way. They bypass me without comment. They reach the group that is now composed of Imelda, DC Jen, David and Julia.

'Great costumes, Trish!' Imelda says. 'Wonderful idea!'

'Thanks!' Trish says. 'Would you believe I made these costumes myself? JP says I'm very talented at sewing. I'm thinking of putting more time into it, actually. But then I wouldn't have as much time for my painting.'

'Oh, what a shame,' David says.

'Now,' Imelda says to Trish, 'we'd heard you were coming to the party and that you were dressing as Dorothy. But I must admit, I think we all assumed that JP would be, well, how can I put this... not a dog?'

Trish laughs. 'You know me – full of surprises. Subverting expectations wherever I go.'

'That's one way of putting it,' I hear David say, although it is unclear if the rest of the group also hears this.

'Oh, it took some persuading, I can tell you – didn't it, honey?' Trish pats JP on the arm. 'It had to be Toto. I mean the rest of the crew are just a bunch of brainless fools! But the clever, loyal companion that is Toto? Yes, indeed – a good fit for my JP!'

Trish shakes JP's leash and leads him away to another group of colleagues.

'Honestly,' Imelda whispers, 'it's just so humiliating!'

'I mean,' Julia says, 'how does he do it? But really, I mean – *why* does he do it?'

'I have a theory,' DC Jen says. The group closes in tight, but I can still hear their conversation.

'So do I,' Imelda says.

'Well, what's yours then?' DC Jen says.

'He's afraid of her.'

David and Julia laugh.

'What man isn't at least a little bit scared of his wife?' DC Jen says. 'I think it's more than just that though.'

'Go on,' Julia says.

'Okay. Now, hear me out on this: he just really loves his wife.'

They all laugh.

'I'm serious,' DC Jen says.

'But all he does is complain about her!' Julia says.

'But what about the other stuff he does?' DC Jen says. 'Letting her sell her crappy art in the shop. Involving her in staff nights. The fact that she's here right now. The fact that he's wearing *that*.

Mark my words – he will not leave her side tonight, and it's got nothing to do with that leash around his neck.'

They all look around at JP. He is standing silently beside Trish while she speaks to 3 other colleagues. I hear her repeat the words 'a good fit for my JP'.

'I mean – it would explain a lot,' Julia says.

*1830*

Shane tells me that the party is now in a state known as 'full swing'. I ask Shane if there is such a condition as 'semi-swing'. His response is to laugh and then repeat my question to David, who then laughs and repeats it to Julia. Sandra Smith asks Shane what he's laughing at, but I intervene and relate the sequence of events. I enquire about the source of humour, but no one provides a satisfactory answer.

This, in my limited experience, is the essence of a party. Many conversations begin with a particular topic but quickly leap to another, unrelated topic. Unhumorous statements are greeted with laughter. Two or more people often speak at the same time. There are frequent misunderstandings, and not just due to auditory issues, I postulate.

A dance floor of sorts has been established. Shane was correct; the chairs around the perimeter of the dance floor hold many women's cardigans. I point at the chairs and ask Shane if a discarded cardigan is known as a 'discardigan'. He laughs and pats me on the back. Then he tells me that now is a perfect time for us to speak to JP and Trish. He leads me over to them.

'Well, Trish,' Shane says. 'What do you think of our costumes?'

I try to be helpful. 'Shane, Trish already said she considers Dorothy's friends to be – quote – "brainless fools".'

Trish laughs. 'Ah, that was before I saw your costumes.'

Shane also laughs. He asks Sandra Smith to take a photograph of the 4 of us together. Dorothy, Toto, the Scarecrow and the Tin Man.

'All we're missing is the lion,' JP says.

'Just one more fool, isn't that right, Trish?' Shane says, in a voice that might be considered too loud.

Then he shouts, 'Hey! Hey! Is anyone here a brainless fool?' I believe he is addressing the room as a whole – not easy to do, with the music at volume 7. He turns his voice up more, although I predict that the song will end in approximately 3 seconds. 'Who here is a brainless fool?'

The song ends and a voice answers clearly in the silence. 'I am!'

Everyone turns to see who has entered the room. It is Maeve.

I am very pleased to observe her joining the party. She is an unexpected but most welcome guest. I will tell her that I have missed her as soon as possible.

'Maeve!' Shane calls. 'Get over here.'

As she approaches, my face detectors register an anomaly.

'Maeve,' I say. 'Are you okay?'

'Kobi!' she says. 'Oh, Kobi!'

She puts her arms around me and presses her face to my chest plate. I believe it is known as a hug.

'What's wrong?' Shane says. 'I thought you were at the thingymabob, being all fancy and outgrowing us all.'

When she looks up at me, Maeve's face displays distress.

'What's going on?' JP says.

Maeve looks JP up and down. 'Oh! JP! You're... what are you...? Oh! Hi, Trish. You're...'

'It's *The Wizard of Oz*,' Shane says. 'He's the dog.'

Maeve shakes her head. 'I feel like I'm in a dream.'

'Maeve, is the conference over then? Did you meet Ron Tron?' JP asks.

'Yes, I met Ron Tron.' She looks at each of us and exhales loudly. 'Okay, it's good that you're all here, actually. I can tell you all together, I suppose.'

'Tell us what?' JP says.

'Can we go somewhere a bit quieter?' Maeve says.

'Let's go to the Liffey,' Shane says.

Maeve, Shane, JP, Trish, Sandra Smith, DC Jen and I all leave the party and go to the Liffey Room. It is dark. Shane turns on the lights.

'Oh boy,' Maeve says. 'I don't know how to begin.'

'It's okay,' Shane says. 'Whatever it is – it'll be fine.'

'Now that's not necessarily the case,' JP says. 'Especially if Maeve has done something to upset Ron, by the sounds of it.'

'Give the girl a chance,' Trish says.

'All right.' JP folds his arms. 'Proceed.'

'Thank you,' Maeve says. 'So, the thing is – I'm just going to say it as simply as I can. Basically, Ron Tron doesn't know – I mean, *didn't* know – that Kobi was here with us at Go Ireland.'

'I don't understand,' JP says. 'How is that possible?'

'Because,' Maeve says, 'Josh didn't tell him.'

'What?' DC Jen and Shane say the word at the same time.

JP turns to me: 'Did you know about this?'

'No,' I say. 'Maeve, I am afraid there has been a mistake.'

'There's been a mistake, all right,' Maeve says. 'Several mistakes were made.'

'I'm calling Ron right now.' JP gestures as if to put his hand into a pocket but his hand simply moves through the air. He repeats the movement. 'Trish, this is why I wanted pockets!'

'Dogs don't have pockets,' Trish says.

'Do you even have Ron's number anyway?' Maeve says.

'Well, not his direct line, no.'

'Exactly,' Maeve says. 'He only ever communicated with you via Josh, right? You never had any direct contact with Ron about Kobi?'

JP makes a fist and brings it down on a nearby table. A small part of me calculates that it could have made a loud bang were it not covered in fur. But most of my processors are busy computing this new data and the speculative scenario that Maeve is proposing.

'I do not understand,' I say. 'What you are suggesting would require Josh to have practised deception with a large number of people.'

Is it possible that Josh has kept my current placement a secret from everyone at RoboTron? Why would he do this?

'Why would Josh do this?' I ask.

'I'm sorry, Kobi,' Maeve says. 'I've thought about it, and my guess is that he was afraid of what might happen to you back at RoboTron after the incident at PHI. Maybe he thought we could help get you back on track before it was too late.'

'What's PHI?' Trish asks.

'PHI is the manufacturing facility where I fulfilled my last assignment,' I provide.

'Maeve, what do you mean by incident?' Sandra Smith says. 'I work in HR, remember. I know what "incident" is code for.'

'What is it code for?' I ask. I would welcome a conversation about code right now.

'It means something bad happened,' Sandra Smith says. 'Did something bad happen?'

I look at Maeve. Maeve looks at me. Neither of us provides an answer.

'Maeve!' I detect strong emotion from JP.

'Y-yes,' Maeve says. 'Kobi had a… a malfunction. I thought you knew. Josh said it was all in the report he sent you at the start. Didn't you read it?'

JP turns away and speaks at volume 3. 'Well, does anyone actually read reports?'

'No one was hurt at PHI,' Maeve says. 'Josh implied you and Ron were on the same page.'

'This is all a bit of a mess, isn't it?' Sandra Smith says.

'Well, you won't need to worry about Kobi much longer,' Maeve says. She turns to me. 'I'm so sorry, Kobi, but today is your last day at Go Ireland.'

My systems go into overdrive to process the incoming data. Somewhere among the lines of logic, I realise that the party could retrospectively be assigned to a third category. Aside from 'Halloween' and 'birthday', it could also be designated a 'leaving do', if I am using the human term correctly. As this new emotion begins to clarify, I resolve to ask Josh to disable my Emotion Detector the next time we meet.

# FORTY-FOUR

## MAEVE

*Monday, 8:30am*

I open the door of the Shannon Suite, let Kobi roll in ahead of me.

'Well, looks like this will be your last team meeting with us, Kobi.' I try to force some breeziness into my voice, but I can hear the hollow tone underneath.

'Affirmative,' he says. 'I shall miss these petty gatherings.'

I laugh, but there's a pit in my stomach. Of course I knew Kobi would only be here temporarily, but damn, I've grown accustomed to his face. This is exactly why Dad would never let me get a pet, I realise. You get attached and then goodbye is so much harder.

After the party on Friday, we decided as a group that Kobi would attend the team meeting today to say an official farewell to everyone before I bring him back to RoboTron. JP insisted he would go with us; he's eager to speak to Ron and smooth things over. I was too tired to argue and besides, part of me is glad I'll have backup walking into RoboTron. In case I have to face Ron or – worse – Josh.

Josh tried to call me all weekend, but I refused to answer. I don't know what he wants to say to me. I only know I don't want to hear it because it'll just be more lies. Was anything he said real? All I know for sure is that he was using me.

Shane messaged me as well on Saturday, asking if I wanted to meet. I can't really face him at the moment either. I've been such an idiot, raving on about The Kobi Project and how great Josh was the past few weeks.

The door opens. It's Shane.

'You're so early,' I say. Some of the tension in my shoulders releases in spite of myself.

He shrugs and gestures at Kobi. 'Ah, you know... it's his last day and all. You all set, Kobi?'

'Affirmative.'

Shane takes me aside. 'And how are you feeling about today?'

'Ah, you know...' I repeat Shane's phrase back to him, then trail off.

'I know. Listen, why don't you call round to my house later, after work? I'll want to know how you got on at RoboTron. All the details. I got in that exotic herbal tea you like.'

'You mean peppermint? Such a wildly exotic flavour.' I smile. I picture myself on Shane's couch and am surprised at how much I'd like to be there right now. But I push away the image. I wonder if he went home with Sandra after the party. 'Thanks. We'll see. I feel like today is going to be exhausting, on many levels.'

'Hey, I was thinking about that,' he says. 'I know this is Kobi's last day here, but like, couldn't you maybe still see him sometimes, at RoboTron?'

The innocence and optimism of his question kind of floor me. I can't tell him that I don't want to go to RoboTron because I can't face Josh, because I'm equal parts angry and embarrassed.

'I don't know,' I say. 'Ron didn't really seem the reasonable type, based on what I saw of him at the conference. And I'm not sure he's a fan of all the stuff we did with Kobi...'

I did briefly consider reinstating Kobi's legs for his return to RoboTron, but I just couldn't take his new mobility away from him. If Ron wants to do it, that's his prerogative. I take out a small screwdriver and tighten some of the fittings on Kobi's lower panels. No need to make it easy for Ron.

The door opens again. Dave and Julia come in together. Very together. They're holding hands. 'I told you we'd be early,' Julia says to him.

'Hey, Kobi, good luck today,' she calls. 'We got you a card. Oh – I left it in my coat. Be right back.' She disappears out the door.

Shane nods after her. 'When did *this* happen?' he asks Dave, who hasn't stopped smiling since he entered the room.

'At the party,' says Dave.

'Really?' I ask. 'You know, I thought maybe you guys were already together.'

Dave laughs. 'I know. I think everybody did. We weren't. But we are now.'

'Good stuff,' says Shane. 'You both finally came to your senses.'

'Yes.' Dave smiles. 'It was a strange night. You know, weirdly, seeing JP in that costume – and what DC said about it – it kind of got me thinking about things. How actions speak louder than words, and all those clichés.'

'Congratulations,' says Kobi. 'I wish you well for the future.'

To my surprise, Dave briefly hugs Kobi. Then he turns away and takes a seat at the back of the room.

Dave is right. Actions do speak louder than words. Josh had all the words, but it was just empty promises – dangling a bright new future in front of me. I can't help compare him to Shane. Even though Shane has done some immature things, he's never deliberately tried to deceive me. He's always tried to fix things, tried to help me out. The door opens again but it's not Julia, it's Imelda.

'Ah, Maeve. I wanted to talk to you for a moment.' Her cheeks are flushed. 'In private. And, ah, you too, Kobi.'

I beckon her over and the three of us move into a corner.

'I am afraid that I owe you an apology,' she says. 'I perhaps should have told you this before, but, well, I did not want to. I have no excuse really. So, the night that you came to Phelan's, when Kobi had his malfunction... I am afraid that was my fault.'

'It was?' I think back to that night. At the end of the bar, Kobi, Imelda, Dave and Julia were gathered round but they all seemed to be getting on well.

'Yes. Kobi spoke of new accounting software that could do my job in half the time. Maeve, I am *so* close to retirement. It is too late for me to retrain, to find another job. I suppose that I just panicked. I had a tequila in my hand and, well...'

She mimes throwing a drink in Kobi's face. In fairness to Kobi, he doesn't react.

'I just wanted to say that I am sorry.'

I should be upset, but so much has happened since that night, it doesn't seem so important now. Besides, I can see it from Imelda's point of view. It's a lot harder to accept new technology if your pay cheque is on the line.

The rest of the staff arrive and JP calls the meeting to order. He announces Kobi's imminent departure. I now truly learn the meaning of the term 'the official version of events', as JP portrays Kobi's short time here as a series of triumphs, with a seamless conclusion. He instigates a round of applause for me and then, as is the tradition at Go Ireland, invites the departing employee to 'say a few words in honour of the occasion'.

Kobi makes his way to the top of the room. 'I cannot promise only a few words,' he says, to gentle laughter from his colleagues. 'I would like to thank all my co-workers, especially Maeve and Shane. I shall miss all of you.'

A nice little round of applause ripples across the room.

'However,' he continues, 'perhaps what follows will be unexpected, but unfortunately I have not been provided with an adequate opportunity to complete my duties as an employee.'

*Oh no. What now?*

'I shall now announce the results of the HR compliance report commissioned by Sandra Smith on 18 September.'

I jump up from my seat. 'Kobi!'

I hear gasps from around the room. It sounds like half a dozen cans of soda being opened at once.

'Do not be alarmed,' says Kobi. 'I shall only read the executive summary. And the results section.'

Sandra Smith stands up too. 'Eh, I'd completely forgotten about that!'

JP raises his hands to calm the troubled waters. 'Quiet down, everyone. I'm sure it's all fine. We might as well hear it though. No harm for me to get a sense of where we're at with this stuff. Kobi – proceed. But keep it brief.'

I sit down heavily. Kobi bows slightly in Sandra's direction. 'Sandra Smith, thank you for assigning me such a challenging and fascinating topic to research. My method involved observing staff behaviour and cross-referencing it against all HR policy and compliance documents, including "Dignity and Respect in the Workplace", "IT and Email Codes of Conduct"—'

'You don't have to read out the names of all the documents,' interrupts JP. 'Can we cut to the chase, please?'

'Certainly,' says Kobi. 'I will skip to the results section. The following people have been found to be in violation of HR codes of conduct and/or compliance and/or HR principles. Maeve McGettigan. Shane Fitzgerald. Imelda Lopez. Julia Monye. David O'Dwyer. Jennifer Mason. Duncan Canning—'

Each person reacts to their name in a different way, but with equal amounts of consternation.

'Whoa there!' I jump up again. 'Kobi, what are you doing?'

'I am not finished,' he says. 'Sandra Smith.'

'Eh, eh, hang on now!' says Sandra. She also rises from her seat.

'JP Horgan,' he says.

'Now, that's quite enough!' says JP.

'Wait, wait!' calls Shane, next to me in the first row. 'Kobi – is everybody in the whole company on the list?'

'Yes,' he replies. 'An astute guess.'

Shane laughs. Other people start to laugh. Soon everyone is laughing along.

'Kobi.' I strain my voice to be heard above the din. 'How hilarious of you to play this prank on us!' I decide to lean into it. I turn to address the room. 'Look how far he's come – playing jokes like the best of them!'

People applaud, much to my relief. I sit back down.

Then he says, 'I have a special surprise for you all.' He turns his head towards me and rotates it sideways, gives me a kind of awkward nod. I believe he's trying to deliver some kind of secret signal, the robot equivalent of a wink.

'It's not another report, is it?' Dave calls from the back of the room, to more laughter.

'How well you know me, David,' says Kobi. 'Yes, indeed, it is another report. I predict it will be of great interest.'

'I'm afraid to ask what it's about!' says Dave. The laughter continues.

'Productivity,' comes the answer.

The laughter stops abruptly.

I turn to Shane and quietly say, 'I give up.'

I slump in my seat. If he wasn't already leaving, Kobi would probably be fired after this. So what difference does it make?

'I have been running a productivity analysis of all staff since the day of our first team meeting.'

He starts to roll slowly back and forth as he talks. It looks to all intents and purposes like he's enjoying himself very much.

'I never asked you to do that, Kobi,' says Sandra. She looks around the room. 'I swear – I didn't.'

'That is correct,' Kobi agrees. 'Credit for the report's existence should be given to Maeve.'

I close my eyes and groan, push my fingers into my hair. *Why must he take me down with him?* I feel Shane's hand on my back, like he's trying to shield me from the tutting and other sounds of disapproval from around the room.

'I will quickly share my conclusions with you,' continues Kobi. 'You will forgive me if I gloss over the details of who is most and least productive and at what times and on which days of the week. Instead, I wish to present to you an innovative analytic technique, whereby I cross-referenced productivity with staff morale, such as I could detect it.'

I open my eyes to see Kobi's chest panel light up. Some kind of data analysis animation. Multicoloured graphs dance across the screen. From what I can gather, the days of the week are highlighted in different colours. Morale seems to be represented by a series of pulsating love-heart icons.

'I hope everyone can clearly see the implications of this analysis and come to the same conclusion that my advanced algorithmic systems allowed me to make. Morale and productivity are so closely correlated that one may reasonably conjecture a causative relationship.'

I sneak a look around to see the blank faces of my co-workers.

'Allow me to use layman's language, if you will. Productivity goes off a cliff on Friday afternoons. Forgive my crudeness. However, there is a way to increase productivity.'

I hear growing sounds of unrest. I look at Shane. He shakes his head at me in what I hope is sympathy.

'Let's hear him out,' says JP. 'Settle down now, please.'

'Thank you, JP. In conclusion, by my calculations, productivity would increase twenty per cent if Friday afternoons were simply removed from the equation.'

'What does that mean?' says JP. 'Removed from the equation? You mean, no work gets done on a Friday afternoon?'

'Not exactly,' says Kobi. 'Taking into account the consequential potential boost in morale, I am ninety-seven per cent certain that productivity would increase, across the week, if Friday afternoons were removed from the working week.'

Shane speaks up. 'Are you saying what I think you're saying? Are you saying that we *shouldn't* be working on Friday afternoons?'

'Not exactly,' repeats Kobi. 'My official recommendation is that staff would be more productive if only rostered for four-point-five days of work a week. Further analysis would be required to observe if all work could in fact be condensed to four days a week.'

'Four days a week?' Dave calls out.

'Yes,' Kobi replies.

'Four days a week!' Julia's voice comes in at a high pitch.

'Yes.'

'Wait,' says Dave. 'For the same pay?'

'Of course,' says Kobi.

What follows can only be described as a kind of glorious chaos.

# FORTY-FIVE

*11am*

We await our fate in the gleaming RoboTron reception area. The foyer is spacious and calm, full of natural light. Just one receptionist behind the desk, although two security guards made their presence felt as we checked in. They eyed Kobi without reaction. They probably see robots like this every day of the week.

JP and I sit quietly on a multicoloured fabric couch. Kobi is by our side, alert but silent. After the roller coaster thrill ride that was this morning's team meeting, the mood has shifted. The compliance report was completely overshadowed, thankfully, by Kobi's productivity report. Because Kobi insisted on crediting me for the report, people swarmed around me after the meeting with a warmth and enthusiasm not seen since that Friday in August when JP let us all knock off early because it was exceptionally sunny outside. On the way over here, I told Kobi that it was me who should be giving him a gift, not the other way around.

I'm unsure of JP's feelings about the productivity report, and I'm afraid to ask. I can sense he's nervous about seeing Ron. I texted Josh this morning with an estimated time of our arrival. He texted back a thumbs-up, and nothing more.

I still have so many unanswered questions about Josh. How did he manage to manipulate so many people? Why did he do it? How could he betray me when I'd trusted him? I'm not even sure I want to know the answers. But I do want to know what will happen to Kobi now.

A distant bell chimes. I look up to see Josh's blond head emerging from the elevator. My nerve endings jangle. I remind myself to be professional, for Kobi's sake at least. Also alighting from the elevator is none other than Ron Tron himself.

'Welcome to RoboTron,' Ron booms as he crosses the floor to us. 'And welcome home, Kobi. Good to have you back where you belong.'

He seems to be in good form, in spite of that passive-aggressive remark. *Passive aggression is better than active aggression*, I tell myself.

He shakes JP's hand vigorously. 'JP, my man! How the hell are ya?'

If JP were a dog, his tail would be wagging right now. I recall the Halloween costume with an involuntary shudder.

'Great, not a bother, thanks. Haven't seen you at the club for a while though.'

'You know how it goes.' Ron holds up his hands like Christ on the cross. 'They won't let me out of here!'

JP laughs. 'Oh, my lot are the same. I believe you've already met Maeve here. One of our best and brightest.' This is news to me.

'I have, I have. Now, listen, Maeve – JP and I need to talk privately for a little bit. Why don't you run along with Josh here? He's all set up for the Kobi handover.'

My stomach flip-flops at the word 'Josh' and even more so at the word 'handover'. I feel like I'm on the wrong side of a custody battle. I don't even have time to process the way Ron just told me to 'run along' as if I were a child.

'Sure thing,' I say breezily.

I watch as Josh greets Kobi with what looks like genuine

warmth. I realise they haven't seen each other in a while. I can't look him in the eye though.

'Josh,' Kobi is saying, 'I have many questions.'

'All will be explained.' Josh looks at me. 'Please, follow me to our robot bay.'

In spite of the circumstances, I feel a stir of curiosity at the prospect of seeing the 'robot bay', whatever that is. My ill-begotten robot-handling career is currently on the rocks. I flash through a quick recap: *Duped by an engineer into integrating a malfunctioning bot into an office full of unsuspecting people; lying to Laura Cantwell and PHI employees about where I work; attracting the ire of the CEO of RoboTron.* Not a great résumé. But it's not all bad. I've done some good things too – things I never thought I'd be able to do: *Integrated a robot into an office full of people; helped said robot put humans first in a moment of crisis; rehabilitated a damaged robot.* But it's very hard to know where I go from here.

The three of us board the elevator. I feel the space shrink around me. Josh's lies suck all the air out of the metal box. *I'm doing this for Kobi,* I remind myself.

'So how many people work here?' Maybe some small talk will ease the tension.

'No one knows,' says Josh. 'Or at least, no one will tell me. We have the top three floors of the building, anyway.'

'Oh,' I say. 'I thought the whole thing was RoboTron.'

'Yeah, people assume that. There's some subletting going on though.'

'I suppose things are not always how they seem on the outside,' I find myself saying, and we fall into an awkward silence.

A few minutes later, we arrive at the robot bay. The entrance is via oversized, opaque sliding doors that swoosh open to reveal a cavernous, messy workspace. The atmosphere feels chilly, and not just because of the tension between me and Josh. Tools lie discarded on workbenches, wires trail everywhere. I almost trip over a single bionic arm on the floor.

My eyes are drawn to the large glass cases that line one wall. I stop in front of the first one, peer inside. I tap on the glass as if I'm at the zoo. The small white robot within lights up its eyes and swivels its head towards me.

'Maeve,' says Kobi from behind me, 'may I introduce you to the Leila bot? Its responsiveness to environmental stimuli makes it an ideal companion for the housebound, the elderly, the confused. I believe you would enjoy her company.'

'Ha,' I mutter.

'Josh,' says Kobi, 'shall we give Maeve our lab tour? Maeve, you will find it most stimulating. The grand finale is a robot dance, which Josh performs while I mimic the actions of a nightclub DJ.'

'Wait,' I say. 'Josh, look. I can't pretend this is normal.' I gesture at the glass cases. I can make out the labels 'Poopsie' and 'Drover' on the next two. 'Obviously, this isn't normal. But...'

I take a few steps to get further away from Josh. Then I stop, turn to face him properly for the first time. My voice shakes as it all comes tumbling out. 'I cannot... I just... How could you? I mean, why did you? I mean, *how* did you?'

I thought I didn't want to know, but it turns out I do. I want to hold him to account.

He takes a step towards me. I take a step back. He moves to a workbench, picks up a controller. The lighting dims a little.

'I'm so sorry,' he says. 'What I've done is inexcusable. But at least let me explain it. I'll tell you everything. Maybe we can sit down together, have a coffee? Kobi can wait here.'

'No. You owe Kobi an explanation too. He's very confused about all of this.'

'Maeve is correct,' says Kobi. 'Data is incomplete. Logic circuits have misfired. A number of fundamental assumptions are currently undergoing re-evaluation.'

Josh sighs. He sits on a chair, puts his hands on his head. He speaks quietly. 'The last thing I wanted to do was to harm Kobi. That's what started this whole... runaway train. When I got the call to go to PHI in the middle of the night, I didn't believe what they told me. Until I watched the video, I thought *they'd* made some kind of mistake. Kobi's actions were just way beyond any of his programming or experiences.'

He looks at Kobi. 'He'd been doing so well up to that point. Incredibly well. Game-changingly well.'

'I get it,' I say sharply. 'He was going to be your big break.'

I slump down onto a swivel chair. Kobi was going to be my big break too, I realise. 'Why didn't you just take him home right then and there?'

'I did take him home – to my apartment.'

'Josh, I have no memory of your apartment,' says Kobi.

'What?' I say. 'Surely you could have – *should* have – brought him back here?'

'And explain to Ron that the multimillion-dollar Kobi project had just gone horribly wrong? The first thing he would've done is fire me. The second thing he would've done is take Kobi apart. I just wouldn't... *couldn't...*'

He stands, rearranges the tools on the workbench. He continues talking without looking at me.

'You have to understand, Maeve – Kobi was three years of my life, and counting. Yes, he was going to be important for my career, but it was more than that. I knew, if I just had more time, I could figure out what had gone wrong and fix it. Get him back on track before Ron realised anything was wrong. Of course I'd have to tell Ron what happened, but I figured I could put it off until Kobi was back in good shape. All I needed was time.'

'All?' I ask.

'Okay, you're right. Time and – once I'd rebuilt his code – I needed him to build up his TIL files again, get him back to where he was before the PHI incident.'

'Which is where Go Ireland came in?'

'Which is where Go Ireland came in,' he repeats. 'I'll admit it was a long shot, but I needed him to be around people, in a safe, controlled environment. Low-risk physically, but with enough interaction to ensure his communication skills could quickly develop. And there had to be a plausible connection between our two companies.'

He continues straightening each tool on the bench. 'To be honest, there weren't that many places that fit the bill. I input a few parameters into Kobi's system, along with all of Ron's social profiles and contact lists, which I pulled from RoboTron databases.'

'So JP's name came up, thanks to his golf connection with Ron.' *Bloody golf.*

'Not just JP. I also discovered that a couple of people at Go Ireland had attended a "Robots in the Workplace" conference. So I knew there must be someone there with an interest in robots, maybe some IT skills.'

I sigh as I'm piecing it all together.

'You thought Jen would be put in charge of Kobi, didn't you?'

He nods.

I almost laugh. 'But then you were stuck with me. I suppose I should be flattered you trusted me with your precious robot. Sorry, Kobi.'

Josh is examining the workbench tools with seemingly great interest.

'Yes, well. That's why I had to keep an eye on you.'

'What do you mean? I only saw you once, maybe twice a week.'

'Yes, but I also... monitored you... for a little bit.'

My cheeks flush. 'What does that mean? What did you do?'

'I... um... hacked your email account. And, um, your phone.'

I feel sick. I shake my head. 'I don't believe this. Gross.'

'I couldn't be there in person as much as I wanted to. I had to do something to keep an eye on the situation. I tried not to read anything personal, I swear. I just skimmed to try and gauge how well you were handling Kobi. I'm not proud of what I did.'

He looks at me properly for the first time.

'Listen, Maeve, I really did enjoy getting to know you. And I'm not a bad guy. I've just... done some bad things.'

'That's literally the definition of a bad guy!' I can hear my anger rising.

'I'm so sorry, Maeve. The clock was ticking. I wasn't thinking too far ahead. You have to believe me when I say I never wanted to hurt you. I wish I would have told you everything from the start. But there was never a right time. I just couldn't... burst the bubble.'

I think back to the night of the Phelan's incident. Josh's *confession* about Kobi's meltdown at PHI. 'You said you'd make sure Ron never heard about what happened to Kobi in Phelan's. I thought you were so sound, doing me a favour.'

'Well, technically, that was true. I did keep it from him.'

'Along with everything else!'

'Also technically true.'

'Well, *technically*, I don't want to hear any more!'

I pick up my bag and bolt for the doors. But they don't open automatically. I wave my arms over my head. I look all around the frame for a sensor or a button to press. I bash at a few switches on the wall. Overhead lights flick on and off. 'Oh, come on!'

'Sorry.' Josh picks up a controller. 'It's been acting up. I keep meaning to fix it.'

'Fixing things is not your strong suit,' I say as the doors finally swish open.

# FORTY-SIX

*11:45am*

I scuttle past the fourth-floor elevator, find the door to the staircase at the end of the corridor. No elevator is fast enough to get me away from Josh and his *explanations* right now. His moral compass is a roulette wheel.

My palm is slippery on the smooth white banister. The fact that I passed Josh's weird, desperate monitoring is thin comfort. At least I know now why he was in such a hurry to get Kobi up to scratch. The clock was ticking down on Ron finding out that Kobi wasn't at PHI any more. I realise now why Josh started freaking out at the ethics panel – it started when he saw Laura Cantwell on-stage with Ron. He was scared Ron would find out that Kobi hadn't been at PHI for weeks. He must have been tied up in knots keeping so many plates spinning.

As I round the first-floor landing, my pace slows. I didn't say goodbye to Kobi when I sprinted from the room. I hesitate, look back up through the central stairwell, but all is quiet. Should I go back? *No.* You don't make a dramatic exit then reappear minutes later for a big farewell. You don't get to have it both ways. But maybe it's better this way. Just because I'm used to goodbyes, it doesn't mean I'm good at them.

I walk the remaining steps to the ground floor so I can exit through the reception area, but it's one of those buildings where you need a security pass to get both in and out. I signal to the receptionist that I'm stuck behind the turnstile, but a clean-shaven security guard comes over to me.

'Ms McGettigan, Mr Tron would like to see you in his office.'

*What now?* 'Um, okay.'

'Please follow me.'

The guard comes through the security gate and we're back in the elevator again, this time on the way to the sixth floor. I want to ask him why Ron wants to see me, if Josh will be in this meeting, if I'll get a chance to see Kobi after all, and if JP is still here – but the guard stands rigidly beside me, staring straight ahead. Reminds me of Kobi a bit. Will his job be done by a robot someday soon?

The sixth floor is clearly where business gets done. My feet sink into plush cream carpet as soon as I step out of the elevator. The guard leads me down a corridor with dark wood panelling. We turn the corner. Natural light pours through the glass walls of senior executive offices that house significant men on significant salaries.

Of course Ron has the corner office. The security guard gives an almost imperceptible nod to the PA seated outside it. Package delivered, the guard melts into the background as I hesitate in the doorway. Ron is standing with his back to the window, beaming at me. He looks like he's been waiting for me all his life and now that I'm here, there's no need to rush the moment.

'You wanted to see me, Mr Tron?'

I'm preparing my defence. I didn't know about any of Josh's deceptions. I only ever did what I thought was best for Kobi. If I took Kobi into strange environments, well, he learned to adapt. If he got hurt, I rebuilt him – maybe even made some improvements. Ron is still staring at me. Maybe I won't say that last bit.

'I sure did. And please, call me Ron.'

He indicates three plush chairs next to a low circular table holding two glasses of water. 'We have a lot to talk about.'

I look at the empty chair as we sit down, then at the door, which I don't remember closing behind me. This seems to be the only office that doesn't have glass windows onto the interior corridor. 'Um, where's JP? Is he still here?'

'I sent JP on his way. Don't worry, we'll get you a ride back to Go Ireland. Have some water. Relax.'

*Where is this going?* Ron is like a different person to the one I met in Athlone. Maybe I could raise the possibility of seeing Kobi again after all, even just to say goodbye.

'I'd like to talk about Kobi, if I may—' I start.

He laughs. 'Great! So would I. That's kind of the whole reason I wanted to see you.' He twinkles at me.

I laugh a little too. 'Of course. I just... Over the past while, I feel like Kobi and I have built up a good connection.'

He leans back in his chair but maintains eye contact. 'So I hear. Josh told me everything. He showed me Kobi's data logs. It looks like he's made remarkable progress in just a few weeks. And that seems to be largely down to you and your' – he pauses to smile at me again – 'somewhat unorthodox methods.'

'I can explain everything. I didn't know I didn't have the green light to do certain things...' I feel a volcano of explanations building up inside me.

He holds his hands apart, then brings them together in prayer mode. 'I can't argue with results. Although I am *very* interested in your methods.'

I'm emboldened by Ron's apparent approval. 'I was wondering – if you think it's okay – if I could still see Kobi every now and then? Like I was saying, I feel like we've built a strong connection, and I didn't really get to say goodbye to him—'

'Well, now we're getting to it, Maeve. I think I can do you one better than that.'

He stops to take a sip of water. It's all I can do not to fill the silence with questions, but I exhale and wait.

'From what Josh has told me, I'm impressed. Surprised, but impressed. At first I was mad, yes, but when I saw the data, I saw gold. Because you were operating outside the system, shall we say, you were able to carry out experiments it would've taken us months to even approve, let alone trial. You took all the shortcuts. And to be fair, without a safety net. A blind man walking a tightrope who somehow manages to get to the other side unharmed.'

I struggle to follow the metaphor but enjoy the general flow of it. I realise this is the first time anyone with real authority has praised me for The Kobi Project. After weeks of struggle and worry, I could cry with relief. I take a few sips of water to swallow down my emotions.

'So, Maeve, I want you to come and work for me.'

The water goes down the wrong way. I splutter and cough. 'Sorry, what did you just say?' I put my sleeve to my mouth, try to regain some composure.

'I want you to work here. Let's call it an internship to start – three months. Paid, of course. I've already talked to JP and he's agreed we can borrow you for a while. I have a special project in mind for you.'

My brain scrambles to get up to speed. Not only am I not in trouble, but now I'm being offered a job as well? 'Does it involve Kobi?'

He laughs. 'Well, I sure as shit am not interested in your tourism skills. No offence – I'm sure your tourism skills are mighty fine.'

'They're really not,' I say with a laugh. *I can't believe this is happening.*

'I reckon it would be a shame to break your momentum with Kobi now. He's made great progress, but he still has a way to go until he's ready.'

'Ready for what?'

'All will be explained once you come and work for us.' Ron's million-dollar smile beams down on me again.

'When would you want me to start?'

'Tomorrow would be just fine.'

'Tomorrow? That's... that's really soon.'

I need a minute. What about my job at Go Ireland? Shouldn't I give them some notice? Is JP really okay with this? And if I took the job here, would I be working with Josh?

Ron raises an eyebrow at me.

'Can I think about it, please?'

He sighs. 'Not many people say no to Ron Tron. I can see some of that determination Josh told me about.'

'I'm not saying no. I just... I should really talk to JP first.'

'I can respect that. Okay, take the rest of the day to think about it. I'll expect your answer by tomorrow morning. Here, take my card – call me anytime.'

# FORTY-SEVEN

*5:30pm*

Shane holds out the mug of peppermint tea, handle pointing at me. He winces but doesn't vocalise the heat his fingers must surely be suffering.

I accept it gratefully. It's a while since I've been in Shane's open-plan living room slash kitchen. I realise I've missed these bare plasterboard walls, the deflated leatherette couch, the deserted kitchen island.

'God, I don't remember this place being so... so... student-y?' I say to tease him.

'Student living means student prices.'

I sense a well-rehearsed speech is about to begin, and I'm not wrong.

'This place is a living legacy. Passed down through generations of sublets for years. You wouldn't believe how cheap the rent is. We think maybe the landlord died or forgot about it – that's why it hasn't been painted or anything in years. We just keep quiet and try to maintain the delicate ecosystem. If explorers ever come interfering, the native species might die. If not literally, at least financially.'

'But what if something breaks?'

'We fix it ourselves.'

'Really?'

I nod towards the perfect arc of a large crack in the front window.

'It's on the list. It's Alek's turn to sort it though.'

I've only met Shane's housemate once. Nice enough. Second-generation Polish. Parents probably came to Dublin for the great construction boom of the early 2000s. You'd think with all that building work there'd be plenty of places to rent now, but the truth is that Shane is lucky to have found anything affordable. So many people have left the city because they couldn't make it work.

He joins me on the sofa. His descent into the couch momentarily buoys my end, then we both gradually sink down again. The battered old girl has seen better days for sure, but there's life in her yet.

'So tell me more about today,' he says. 'I read your email highlights this afternoon. Sounds like it was eventful.'

I sigh, take a tiny sip. 'It was... a lot. A lot of big things coming at me very fast.'

'Lucky you.' He smirks into his mug of builder's tea. The milky fin of a teabag threatens the surface.

I grab a limp cushion – the only loose cushion residing in the entire house, I'm pretty sure – and lightly bop it against his arm. 'Behave!'

I can't help but smile – and notice how his bicep deflects the puny assault with the merest flex.

'Watch the tea!' He places his mug on the wooden table. No sign of a coaster, of course. 'This is a classy joint, you know. We have standards.'

I sigh into my mug.

'What's up?'

'I just have a lot to think about, and I have to do it quickly.'

'Well, that suits you. You're good at thinking. Everything after that – well, the jury's still out.'

I see him eye the sole living heir of Cushion Kingdom warily, bracing for another attack. But I just clutch my tea closer, nestling it to my chest like a mama bird nurturing a fledgling.

'What is there to think about, really, though?' he continues. 'You said it was your dream job in the email.'

I blow gently on the tea, inhaling its minty warmth in return. 'I said it *sounded* like a dream job.'

'Ah now. You've done the study, you've put the work in, and now you have the experience. It makes sense that this would be the next logical step.'

'But what if I mess up or, you know, disappoint them? What if they think I'm one person, but I'm really someone else? All joking aside, I really don't know what I'm doing.'

As I'm saying it, I wonder if I'm talking about more than just work. What happens when you take a risk, let someone in?

He turns towards me, speaks quietly. 'Maeve, let me let you in on a little secret: none of us know what we're doing.'

'But what if it doesn't work out?'

'None of us know if things will work out. But we're still supposed to try.'

I don't speak as I try to absorb this.

'Wise words.' I raise an eyebrow at him. 'When did you get so wise?'

'Hey, we're not talking about me right now. I don't understand what's holding you back. It's not like you particularly love Go Ireland. Besides, JP said you'd still have your job there whenever you wanted to come back.'

I sigh into my mug again, blowing up steam. Shane looks good through the mist. I suddenly can't bear to withhold anything from him. I bite the bullet.

'It's because of Josh.'

I sit back, look straight ahead.

'I don't want to work with him. I can't face it after, after – you know...'

I let that hang in the air, unsure how to continue. I feel so foolish, letting myself be strung along by Josh, in every sense.

Shane doesn't say anything, and I can't bring myself to make eye contact. I'm suddenly very interested in examining the mug I'm holding. Merchandise for a band I've never heard of: Zombie Police.

Finally, he makes an indeterminate noise.

'Ah, you can't let a bit of awkwardness ruin this for you. It's too good to say no to. It sounds like RoboTron really want you. You're actually in a position of strength. Maybe you could negotiate some good terms before you accept.'

I'm suddenly overwhelmed by his kindness. His concern for my well-being. His wanting of the best for me. His willingness to overlook my flaws.

He's here for me. He's always been here for me. I want to put my tea down, put my hand on his chest, melt into him. But I find that I can't move. My body is stiff, frozen.

I take a tiny sip from my mug, then hold it up in front of me. 'Were the police force turned into zombies, or were they a special unit deployed to fight the zombies?'

He laughs. 'Alek's latest band. Confrontational. But fun.'


On my way home I leave a voice note for Jen, asking her advice about RoboTron. She sends me one back saying the doctor has put her on bed rest until the baby is due, but she reckons I should 'go for it'.

When I get home, I call Ron's number. He doesn't answer, but I leave him a voice note: '*Ron, I gratefully accept your offer. On one condition: I don't have to work with Josh.*'

# FORTY-EIGHT

*Tuesday, 9:30am*

I arrived at RoboTron at 8:30am, fully prepared to argue my case to Ron for not working alongside Josh. Josh acted unprofessionally; I would only work with people I could trust. No need to mention my own professionalism, or otherwise, of course.

But I've yet to see Ron. He left instructions with his PA, a creature so polished and polite that part of me wondered if she might in fact be a bot. I was to sign a nondisclosure agreement – standard practice for all new staff – and then go directly to the robot bay, where an assignment was waiting for me. HR would contact me later to fast-track me through the employee induction process, apparently.

So I'm making my way to the robot bay. I have many questions but no one to ask them of. I guess all will be revealed in time. I'm excited to see Kobi again and to find out what we'll be working on together. And I'm looking forward to getting a proper look around the robot bay. As long as I don't have to see—

'Josh!'

The sliding doors open to reveal him standing there, like a

contestant in a cheesy dating game show. *Here's what you've won.* But I don't want the prize any more.

'I wasn't expecting to see you,' I blurt.

I falter on the threshold. The doors begin to close but then swish open again when they detect a confounding object – me.

Josh holds his hands up as if to say 'don't shoot'.

'Don't worry, you won't be seeing me for long. I'm just here to brief you on your assignment. Then I'll be on my way. I need to book a flight.'

'Oh?'

'Apparently I'm urgently needed in the California office.'

'Oh.' Good. He won't be here. I guess he's lucky he hasn't been fired.

He turns away. 'I suppose I could use some sunshine.'

'How long will you be...?'

'Yet to be determined. I just do whatever Ron tells me.'

'Mostly.'

'Good point.' He sighs, smiles a little.

I look around. 'Where's Kobi?'

'In his pod. He needs a full recharge. The robot equivalent of sleeping in.' He looks down at his hands. 'Also, not sure how eager he is to interact with me right now. He'll be happy to see you though.' His tone brightens. 'He'd love to introduce you to some of his fellow robots. He's due to wake up in about fifteen minutes. Meanwhile, Ron wanted me to brief you.'

He gestures at a shiny black machine standing silent in the corner. 'Would you like a coffee?'

'I don't suppose there's any herbal tea?'

But I don't really care what I drink. On my agenda this morning is: *reunite with Kobi, meet other robots, never see Josh again.*

'Well, let's find out.'

He leads me over to the machine. 'Good morning, CoffeeTron!'

The machine seems to be composed of various solid black modules connected together. A gleaming black rectangular box at the top begins to rise upwards, red LED lights flickering on and arranging themselves into a rudimentary face – two eyes and a smile, of sorts. Two black oblongs at either side of the machine semi-detach themselves and begin extending out, reaching towards us. I instinctively take a step back. CoffeeTron is tall and getting taller as its 'head' continues to elevate, before stopping with a clunk and angling downward ten degrees or so.

'Good morning. May I offer you coffee?' A hollow electronic monotone.

*The reign of CoffeeTron will be long and terrible*, I think to myself. 'Yikes,' I say.

'I do not understand. May I offer you coffee?' it repeats.

I look down to check for functioning legs, am relieved at their absence. I look at Josh. 'I don't want coffee,' I whisper. 'But I'm scared to say no.'

Josh laughs a little. He jabs at flat hidden buttons on the front of the console. 'Early prototype. Very early. You know, this machine has never quite worked.'

'Perhaps that's for the best.'

Two drinks are dispensed amid much hissing and rattling. Josh brings them over to a self-contained blue-and-white booth against the wall. It looks like the dining area on a spaceship, with room for no more than four astronauts who have not yet tired of one another's company.

'So,' I start. 'Ron wanted you to brief me?'

It's still hard to look him in the eye, but I suppose I can relax a bit now, knowing that he's leaving soon.

'Yes. We had a conversation early this morning.' He grimaces – it's unclear whether on account of the coffee or the memory of the conversation. 'To be honest, he didn't go into too much detail.'

I cautiously sip at my beverage but fail to identify it. 'What did he say?'

'He just said you were to, quote, "keep doing what you're doing", and to spend as much time as possible with Kobi. "Make sure you two are really connected," is what he said. He seems to have some longer-term project in mind, but he won't share the details with me.' He shrugs, sighs. 'I suppose I should get used to that.'

'Why, did he ever share a lot of detailed plans with you?'

'No. So I should continue to remain used to that.' He meets my eyes properly for the first time. 'You are smart. I knew that much from the start.'

But I don't want to go there. There's nothing he can say that I want to hear. I'm still angry at him, but also at myself. I just want to get past this and move on. Time to shut down the conversation. 'Okay then. Is it time to wake Kobi up yet?'

I extricate myself from the dining pod, leaving the vile liquid abandoned on the table.

# FORTY-NINE

*Thursday, 10:30am*

Suddenly thirsty, I look at my watch and smile: 10:30am on the dot. Old habits. Everyone at Go Ireland would be going on their break now. Break time isn't really a thing at RoboTron, I'm discovering.

I haven't interacted with too many people since my first day. When I walk through the fourth- and fifth-floor areas, it's eerily quiet and no one looks up from their workstation. They just continue their coding session or whatever it is they're intently working on. Is Josh already gone? I haven't seen him since Tuesday morning and, while I'm glad, I'm also realising that he and Kobi are the only ones I really know here. But I can start again, I suppose. I'm used to that.

I make my way to one of the private kitchen areas on the fifth floor to make a cup of tea. I wonder who Shane is sitting with at break time, who he's talking to right now. Will the gang go to Thursday night drinks at Phelan's tonight, and if so, am I invited? Technically I'm on hiatus from Go Ireland. Would Shane be happy to see me if I just turned up? I watch the steam emanate from my cup and suddenly feel a deep thirst – not the kind that can be quenched with tea.

I exhale, put a lid on it and return to the robot bay. I'm surprised at how comfortable I feel here already. Every time I walk in, I feel like a child who's won a golden ticket and been bequeathed a chocolate factory. The last two days have flown by. I was instructed to spend as much time as possible with Kobi, and that's exactly what I've been doing. It hardly seems like work at all.

I check on Kobi before settling at my own workstation in the bay. I have a new idea to experiment with music and associative memory, to see if robot recall could be triggered in similar ways to human memory. Kobi seems up for it. Of course, technically and scientifically, I don't really know what I'm doing, but I'm going to document my method and my results, and maybe someone else can develop it into something.

I slip on headphones and download various music files, choosing some at random and others I remember from various times over the past two months – at Go Ireland events or on the road trip to Clare.

As a track fades, my phone vibrates on the desk in front of me. I don't recognise the number but I answer anyway. 'Hello?'

'Yeah, hey. That Maeve?'

I struggle to place the voice but can't quite get there.

'Speaking. Who's this?'

'It's Sam. We met at PHI a few weeks ago.'

Sam. The operator who worked with Kobi, the one who sustained a minor injury when Kobi went rogue. I had given him my number in case he remembered anything else about the night of the incident. What was it he'd called me? Ah yes – Sherlock.

'Oh, hey!' *Play it cool, Maeve. Let him do the talking.* 'Good to hear from you.'

'So, remember you asked me a lot of questions about that robot?'

'Kobi, yes. I thought it was a reasonable number of questions, given the circumstances.'

He laughs. He sounds relaxed. 'In hindsight, yes, it probably was a reasonable number. Sorry if I didn't fully cooperate at the time.'

'That's okay. We're talking now.'

*I'd make a terrible detective.* I sip my tea. The only thing cool about me is the peppermint flavour of my drink.

'You asked me for information about that night, and I told you what happened,' he continues. 'But what I didn't tell you was that I also made a recording of the incident.'

My mind races. 'A recording? You mean, apart from the CCTV video footage?'

'Yep. As soon as Kobi started acting the maggot, I started recording on my phone. Now, the visuals are not great. But there is audio – which I know you don't have on the CCTV.'

It's true. The video footage is in grainy black and white – a dystopian, silent sci-fi movie.

'Okay, I have a few questions.' I take a breath before the rapid-fire release. 'First, is there anything interesting on the audio? Second, is there any chance you could play it for me, Sam? Third, I suppose I should ask why you're telling me this now? Although I'm grateful that you are.'

He chuckles. 'Now, *that* is a lot of questions. Let me see if I can answer. One – not sure. Two – I'll send it to you. Three – I don't want to get into it.'

'Well, now you're just making me more curious!'

'I believe women like a bit of mystery.' I can hear his smile down the phone. Then his tone changes. 'Let's just say, some things have happened here that I'm not okay with. Upper management stuff. New policies. I won't get into it now. But you find ways to make your voice heard. To disrupt.'

I nod.

'Are you still there?'

'Sorry, yes. I was nodding.'

He laughs again. 'You are a strange person. Sorry. Strange is good.'

I gloss over the comment. 'Thanks. Let's talk about the fastest way for you to get this file to me.'

'Cool,' he says. 'Let's talk about the fastest, *safest* way for me to get this file to you.'

# FIFTY

I glance at my watch, impatient for the elevator to descend to the ground floor for me. The electronic display above the doors seems to be stuck on the number four. I walk across the foyer and instead plunge into the nearby stairwell, gripping the thin banister and steeling myself for the long upward march to the fourth floor.

I still haven't been assigned official working hours, so I don't actually know if I'm early, late or on time. I rarely see other people arrive or leave. Everyone seems perpetually both in early and staying late. But I allowed myself an extra few minutes in bed this morning on account of a restless night of elusive sleep. My mind was churned up after an eventful Thursday evening.

Sam had arranged to call me at nine, so I went to Phelan's for a spell after work. Shane seemed pleased to see me, although we didn't get to talk much. We had a brief exchange about the fact that he wasn't drinking alcohol. 'Trying something different,' he'd said with a grin, 'as are you, I see,' and he'd nodded at my sparkling water. But before I could respond, Sandra Smith sat in between us and urgently engaged him in deep conversation about the next major event to be planned by the Social Committee: the Christmas party. The Big One. Shane described it as a white whale. Sandra said white was appropriate for Christmas and that snow at Christmastime was very romantic.

I still don't know if they're together, or will get together, or have gotten together but aren't together any more. I suppose I could ask Shane directly, but direct conversations have never really been our style. I did try to find out in a roundabout way by archly asking Imelda if anyone missed me at work, but Duncan Canning ruined the moment by bellowing that he missed my client reports and that all Shane did all day was stare at my empty desk. Which was kind of an answer, I suppose, but also open to multiple interpretations.

I left the pub to be home on time for Sam's call, my laptop at the ready. At exactly 9 o'clock he called with a very specific set of instructions as to how he would transfer the file to me. He repeated several times that if anyone ever asked, he would deny all knowledge of the phone call. If he needed to, he told me with a hollow laugh, he'd go as far as telling people that I'd stolen his phone. I'm not sure if he was being paranoid or just joking.

Now, sweating as I ascend the final staircase to the fourth floor, I have one thing on my mind. I breeze into the robot bay and remove as many layers of clothing as decency will allow.

'Morning, Kobi.'

'Hello, Maeve.' He turns to face me.

I tighten the loose bun on top of my head. 'Hey, I need you to do me a favour. I want you to listen to something.'

'Of course. What is it?'

'It's a piece of audio. It's from a few months ago. I'm going to play it for you, and I want you to listen carefully and tell me what it says, and if it means anything to you. Do you think you can do that for me?'

'Affirmative,' he says. 'Are you okay, Maeve? I am sensing something – are you in distress?'

'No. I'm breezy! Can't you tell?'

'Is this one of those rhetorical questions that does not require an answer?'

I laugh, but I can feel my nerves tingling. *It's probably nothing*, I tell myself.

'Maybe. Okay, come over here. The audio is on my phone. I'm going to connect it to a speaker here to make it nice and loud. Come over here beside the speaker.'

'Maeve, you know that my hearing is highly advanced. I do not need to be beside the speaker.'

I sigh. 'Indulge me, will you? I've listened to this thing twenty times and can't make it out.'

Kobi rolls over nearer the speaker. He's still on wheels, and no one at RoboTron has mentioned reinstating his legs, which I've taken as a tacit acknowledgement that I did the right thing when his legs were damaged.

I play the audio clip. Kobi remains motionless for the thirty seconds or so.

'Well?' I ask.

'Most of it is unintelligible sounds. However, I can identify three words, in sequence.'

'Great! What are they?'

'Initiating – embed – protocol.'

'Great! What does that mean?'

He does not respond immediately. After a moment he says, 'Perhaps if you gave me some context, I could attempt an interpretation.'

I sigh, try to hold in my frustration. 'Sure. This is a recording from PHI – from the night of the incident, in fact. You might recognise the voice as your own. The recording was made during the incident by Sam – you remember your colleague, Sam?'

'I remember Sam. I do not think he liked me very much.'

'Listen again.' I play it again.

'I am sorry, Maeve.'

I don't want to take the next step, but I can't see another

avenue to satisfying my curiosity. I exhale, rotate my neck to stretch out the muscles.

'I don't suppose you've seen Josh lately.'

'Yes. I saw him this morning.'

'Great! Where is he now?'

'By my calculations, approximately fifteen minutes away from Dublin Airport.'

'Gah!' *Typical. The one time I actually want to see him.*

'Is something wrong?'

'I'm going to call him.'

I turn away from Kobi, dial a number. I walk to the opposite end of the robot bay.

'Hey, Maeve.' I hear a note of optimism in Josh's voice, followed by one of contrition. 'I'm sorry I didn't say goodbye. I kind of thought it would be better this way.'

'It's fine,' I say quickly. 'I know you're on your way to the airport. This won't take long. If I tell you something now, do you promise not to share it with anyone?'

I hear traffic sounds in the background down the line.

'Uh, yeah. Sure. What's going on? Is everything okay?'

'Listen, do you remember Sam, the operator we met at PHI? The one who was involved in the Kobi incident?'

'The guy we had coffee with? The one who took your number?'

I roll my eyes at the memory. I thought Josh was jealous at the time, but maybe he was just afraid of being caught out in his web of lies.

'Yep, that's the one. Well, turns out he had audio from the incident. Video too, but the video is useless. Anyway. He sent me the file last night.'

'Wow,' says Josh. 'Anything interesting on it?'

'Well, that's the thing.' I pace back and forth between Coffee-Tron and Leila's cabinet. 'I can't tell. But I was hoping you might be able to. Kobi could make out the words, but neither of us knows what they mean.'

I tell him what Kobi told me a moment ago. He doesn't say anything in response.

'Josh, are you still there?'

'Hang on.'

I strain to hear his voice as he speaks away from the phone. 'Sorry, buddy, we're gonna need to turn this thing around. Yep, back to where you picked me up. Fast as you can, thanks.'

I expect to hear his voice louder as he returns to our call, but instead he whispers down the phone.

'Maeve, listen to me. Do not play this for anyone else. I'm coming back. Don't do anything until I get there. And don't talk to anyone. *Anyone.*'

*9:45am*

'Hello, Josh,' says Kobi as the robot bay doors swish open. 'I did not expect to see you so soon after we said goodbye.'

'I know,' says Josh. 'Did you miss me?'

'No,' says Kobi.

Josh laughs, but I hear a strain in his voice. He looks a bit sweaty and I wonder if he also walked up – maybe even ran up – the flour flights of stairs to get here faster. He's touching his hair a lot. He tries to take me to one side, but I refuse to move.

'What's going on?' I ask him.

'This is bad. I mean – this could be bad. I don't know for sure.'

'Well, how can we find out for sure?'

'Let's listen to the audio again for a start.'

He perches on the edge of a stool as I cue up the clip, pump up the volume. It's only thirty seconds and most of it is fragmented sounds and unidentifiable noises. There's some shouting and swearing. But then there's Kobi's voice. Now that I know what to listen out for, it sounds clearer. There it is on the tape – three words in a row, with a little pause between each word:

'Initiating... embed... protocol.'

Josh is pressing his fingers to both sides of his head. 'Oh God,' he says.

I turn to him.

'Do you know what it means?'

He sighs loudly. 'I think so.'

He stands, walks over to the wall of glass cases. With his back to us, he speaks very quietly.

'Project Embed was just a rumour.'

I can barely hear him. 'What did you say?'

He turns around but doesn't look at me. He speaks slowly, like someone explaining a dream they've just woken up from. 'Embedded Machines Built for Extraordinary Defence, aka EMBED.'

'Defence?' I repeat. My mind whirs to process what this means. 'Defence, as in... military?'

'I mean, I'd heard rumours about it,' he continues, still in a dreamlike state. 'Supposed to be a pet project of Ron's. AI robots for the military. But I didn't know anyone was actually working on it.'

An avalanche of implications rolls towards me like boulders down a mountainside. I look around for something, anything, to throw at Josh's head. I grab a stress ball. It misses him by inches.

'Josh, *you* were working on it!' I slam my hand down on the workbench. 'You thought Kobi was a manufacturing robot, but really he was military? How could you not know this? *This* is what I mean about asking questions!'

Kobi steps between us. 'May I interrupt to ask what all this means?'

'It means...' says Josh. 'It means we are going to Ron right now for some answers.'

# FIFTY-ONE

*9:55am*

Josh strides along the sixth-floor corridor at such speed I can barely keep up. Kobi rolls along behind us. Ron's PA, Grace, looks up from her screen as we approach, her face registering alarm.

'Call you right back,' she chirps as she stands and removes her headset. She rushes to intercept us but Josh brushes right past her, bursting open Ron's door.

'What the—' I hear Ron's voice from within.

'You can't go in there,' Grace is saying at the same time. 'Ron, I'm sorry. He just—'

'It's okay, Gracie. It looks like Josh here has something mighty urgent on his mind.'

I reach the doorway and look in to see Ron seated behind his desk. He looks surprised, but not enough to get up from his chair.

'I see Maeve is here too. Oh – and Kobi. This is quite the delegation. I'm honoured. You better come in and close the door. Gracie, push back my 10 o'clock, will you? And hold my calls. Thank you, darling.'

He gets up and walks to the window, where he stands with his back to the sun, just like he did on Monday when I visited him here. If he's any less relaxed now, the difference is marginal.

'Have a seat.' He gestures to the three chairs around the low table.

No one moves.

'I'm sensing some hostility here,' he says with a smile.

'We want answers!' Josh is so animated he begins pacing, in spite of the limited floor space. He keeps abruptly stopping, then about-turning. It's already making me dizzy.

'Why sure,' says Ron. 'Ask me anything you like. I thought you'd be on a plane by now though, Josh.' He checks his wrist-watch theatrically.

'I'm not going anywhere until you explain what's going on with Kobi.'

'What do you mean?' Ron says lightly.

'I think you know exactly what I mean. Project EMBED, Ron. I know all about it.'

I'm not sure how accurate this is, given that Josh didn't seem to know much about it in the robot bay five minutes ago. I've never seen him quite like this. He stops pacing, shakes his blonde mane in Ron's direction. I think of a lion facing down a lion tamer in a circus cage.

'Well, if you know all about it, then what exactly needs explaining?' Ron is still smiling, but the smile doesn't reach his eyes.

'It's true then? Kobi is military?'

Ron laughs, folds his arms. 'Of course Kobi is military! I'm surprised it took you so long to figure it out.'

Josh's voice cracks. 'Why didn't you tell me?'

'Well, you never asked.'

Josh looks at me. Now is probably not the best time for me to say, *I told you asking questions was a good idea.*

He sighs exaggeratedly, draws out his words to Ron. 'Well, forgive me if I assumed that a robot placed inside a manufacturing plant was intended for use in manufacturing!'

Ron holds up his hands. 'Listen, Kobi is highly adaptable. He could do many things. But the military is where the real money is.'

'I should have known it all comes down to the money.' Josh shakes his head. 'You told me we were changing the world.'

'We *are* changing the world.'

'For the better.'

Ron barks a short laugh. 'We still are. You want to make the world a better place? How about making sure that the Middle East doesn't implode? Or that China doesn't nuke us all to kingdom come? How about making sure the US Army doesn't get left behind in this great technological revolution of ours? *That's* my contribution to humanity right there. You gotta pick a side, Josh.'

'No, I don't.'

Ron turns to me. 'What about you, Maeve? You want to make the world a better place too?'

I clear my throat. I don't fully understand what's going on, so I opt to be diplomatic. 'I'd like to make the workplace better, for a start. I thought Kobi was meant to do that – make our working lives better.'

'He was. He is. It's all coalesced quite neatly. To be honest, I was on the brink of giving up on Kobi – until you came along, Maeve.'

My blood runs cold. 'What do you mean?'

He perches on the windowsill. His smile returns. He points at Kobi, who's gone uncharacteristically quiet in a corner.

'So, we'd made some progress with the Kobi 3000, thanks to the genius engineering of Josh here. Kobi was highly functional, adaptable. Lots of potential, including military application. But we needed to see how he'd function around people. So we placed him in a manufacturing plant – a real-world environment, but nice and safe, controlled. We wanted to see how he'd respond if members of his team were suddenly put in danger.'

'The incident,' I say. I'm trying to put it all together. 'That night. That wasn't a random malfunction then.'

'It *was* a malfunction, but not a random one. It was the result of a simulation created by myself and Laura Cantwell.'

'Laura! This just keeps getting better!' says Josh. He slumps down into a chair, puts his head in his hands.

'Let's just say Laura and I share a vision for the future of robotics. She's a very ambitious woman. So Laura and I logged in remotely that night and we made Kobi believe that his team – his co-workers – were under attack. Ran the EMBED protocol. But he didn't do what we'd hoped. If anything, he acted confused – his actions were random and uncontrolled. Needless to say, we were very disappointed.'

'I bet you were,' says Josh.

Kobi starts to say something, but I signal him to hush. I want to hear it all come out. I *knew* there was more to the PHI incident than Josh thought. It strikes me that Laura withheld a lot of information from us when we visited PHI. As much as Josh didn't want to visit the factory, she probably didn't want us there either, poking around. True, she let us talk to Sam, but she probably had to throw us a bone to get rid of us faster. She clearly didn't know about the audio recording.

'I fully expected Kobi to return to us here the next day,' continues Ron. 'But he didn't, did he, Josh? Because that's when you decided to go rogue.'

'Are you really going to lecture *me* about doing things by the book?' asks Josh from behind his hands.

'Before that little incident, Kobi was doing so well, according to Laura. I was curious to see what you'd do next, Josh. And to be frank, I had more or less given up on Kobi. You taking Kobi off the grid turned into an opportunity. Officially, I didn't know anything about it, of course, which gave me plausible deniability.'

'Wait,' I say. 'So, you're saying you knew all along that Kobi went to Go Ireland? But Josh thought he was hiding Kobi there?' Part of me feels less bad about being made a fool of now. Josh didn't realise, in all his deceptions, that *he* was being duped too.

Ron nods. 'Yes, it sounds quite the comedy of errors when you say it like that. Of course I knew where Kobi was. He has a tracking device. Maybe I forgot to mention that, Josh, but it seemed kind of obvious. Although the tracker did stop working about a month ago. Still, I knew where he was – or at least I thought I did, until that little video stunt at the conference.'

I do the numbers in my head. The night we brought Kobi to Phelan's was about a month ago. The tracker must have got wet and stopped working then. I look at Josh, who still has his head in his hands. I kick his foot lightly and he looks up at me. I roll my eyes and make a gesture that I hope he interprets as *How could you not know about all this?* But Josh just shakes his head.

Ron isn't finished. 'Needless to say, I wasn't pumped about your little jaunt around rural Ireland. When I saw that dramatic little movie at the conference, at first I was angry, yes. But then when I fully understood what had happened, I realised something.'

His tone turns dreamy, and when he next speaks, he fixes all his attention on Kobi. He walks over to the robot and addresses him in quiet tones.

'This was the breakthrough I'd been waiting for all along. Kobi, you sacrificed yourself, *in the moment*, for your team. Even though you didn't know that little girl very well, I believe your spontaneous actions were triggered by a feeling. A feeling of absolute loyalty to the people you were with.'

'What would you know about loyalty?' murmurs Josh from his crumpled position.

'What would I know about loyalty?' echoes Ron quietly. Although he continues to gaze at Kobi, his focus seems to be somewhere else entirely. 'Let me see. Two tours of Iraq. The Gulf War. Do you know what it means to have your life fully in someone else's hands, and theirs in yours? To be one hundred per cent reliant on someone else, and to trust, to *know*, that they will act in your best interests? And to know it because you'd do the exact same for them?'

I fear that Kobi will try to provide an answer, but he remains silent. Somewhere among my kaleidoscoping emotions, I'm proud that he's finally mastered rhetorical questions.

Ron turns to face me, his tone crisper now. 'Robotic military applications are still in their infancy. Yes, robots can follow orders right now. But can they make split-second, autonomous decisions?'

'Do we want them to do that?' I ask.

'Yes, Maeve, we want them to do that.' His tone hardens. 'If you're out there in the field, stuck in some godforsaken foxhole with no way out, you need to know that that robot would sacrifice itself for you in an instant.'

He gives me the full force of his attention. 'You unlocked something in him, Maeve. Whatever you did over these past few weeks, you bound Kobi to you, and you to him.' His passion is startling, overwhelming. 'So now I know – thanks to you – how to guarantee that robots like Kobi will sacrifice themselves in the line of battle. The robot needs to bond with the troop before they ship out. And the bond needs to go both ways. It's like a loyalty feedback loop that gets stronger as it's reinforced, to the point where the robot is ready to spontaneously put itself on the line to protect its unit.'

I scramble to tease through the implications. 'Let me get this straight. You want to manipulate soldiers into forming an emotional bond with a military robot, even though that robot will very likely soon be destroyed? Is that even ethical? Sorry you have to hear this, Kobi.'

'Well, let me ask you something,' says Ron. 'Is it ethical to see your best friend killed in front of you? Believe me, if I could have put a robot in his place...' He doesn't finish his sentence. He turns his back on us, looks out the window.

No one speaks for a while. Eventually I break the silence.

'I'm sorry that happened, Ron. But it's still not right to deliberately foster emotional bonds that you know will soon be destroyed.'

'But humans in the military do that all the time, darling. Do you think that's okay?' He still has his back to us.

'No. I don't know. But at least they know what they're signing up for. What you're proposing is deceptive – tricking people into bonding with a machine.' Somewhere in my mind, I realise that I, too, have bonded with a machine.

Finally, Josh pipes up. 'Apart from the ethics of it all – it's never going to work in practice.'

'Is that so?' Ron is still looking out the window.

'Yes,' says Josh. 'Kobi and Maeve have formed some kind of special bond, I'll grant you that. But you'll never be able to recreate that at scale. There are too many confounding factors. I mean, where would you even start with trying to reproduce it?' Josh will always be an engineer first.

'Well...' Ron goes to his desk to tap at his laptop, then spins the computer around so we can see the screen. 'How about right here?'

'What's that?' I ask.

White text on a black screen. Lines of code.

Josh jumps up from his chair. 'No way!'

'What is it?' I ask. 'Someone please tell me what it is.'

'Why, it's you, honey,' says Ron. 'More or less.'

A cold sweat breaks out across my back. 'What?'

Ron laughs. 'I already have everything that Kobi learned while he was with you. He didn't keep the raw data from Go Ireland, of course, but every night the lessons he learned were assimilated into his neural network, helping it to grow and complexify. So I have Kobi's pretty sophisticated brain back with us now. And I can make other AI bots, once I copy Kobi's basic structure. But what I didn't have – until now – was you, Maeve.'

'You can't...' Josh begins but falters.

I stare silently at Ron, trying to comprehend. I want someone to explain this to me very slowly, and then to explain it again so it all makes sense.

'Let me elaborate,' says Ron. 'A key facet of research is reproducibility. Josh, you know this. This Kobi machine is just a prototype. I need to be able to build an army of Kobis – literally. And I need them primed for human bonding before they ship out to military forces. How will I get these results? Well, I need to train them up, of course, using your methods, Maeve. Your attitude, your mannerisms, your voice. It's all part of the Maeve package.' He gestures towards the laptop with two open hands. 'Kobi has been recording it – recording you – all week. All I had to do was download the raw data every day before it got turned into TIL files. And now it's all in here. A digital version of you, if you will.'

A wave of nausea rises from the pit of my stomach. I barely understand what Ron is saying. My voice comes out very small. 'I... will... not.'

'Pardon me, I should rephrase that,' says Ron. 'You do. You *did*. You already signed over the rights to your digital assets. You might recall that contract you signed on Tuesday morning.'

The nondisclosure agreement. It was fifty pages. Of course I didn't read all of it. I blink repeatedly. My eyes seem to be malfunctioning. 'Kobi, help me get out of here.'

My vision is blurring. I reach out my hand for support as the back of my knees turn to jelly. Kobi moves to steady me. I grasp onto him.

'Okay, you take a little time to let that sink in,' says Ron. 'But not too long. Kobi and I have a meeting with the Pentagon on Tuesday. We fly out Monday. Josh, you're welcome to join us if you want.'

'That won't be happening,' says Josh, opening the door for me and Kobi, 'because I quit.'

# FIFTY-TWO

*10:30am*

'This can't be happening,' I say for the fourth time as the three of us re-enter the robot bay.

'He can't do this,' Josh says. I think it's the fifth time he's said it since we left Ron's office, but it's hard to keep track. Ron has pulled the plug on my mind, and everything I thought I knew is now spiralling downwards at speed.

I thought Josh was the only liar in my life. I had just disentangled myself from that mess, and now I learn that Ron has been playing both of us for fools. It's a ridiculous daisy chain of lies. I taste a bitter irony at the realisation that my success with Kobi is being turned against me. I was actually *so good*, in fact, that Ron wants to keep me at RoboTron – me, or some weird digital version of me.

I stand in front of Kobi, give him a once-over. I think back to our time on the rugged terrain of the Burren. I recall him speeding across the Cliffs of Moher car park without hesitation. And now he's going to be shipped out, to almost inevitable destruction. It's not right.

'You must be in shock too, buddy,' I say gently. 'Did you know about any of this?'

'Please be more specific.'

'The military application stuff? And – did you know you had a tracking device? And that you were recording me all week?'

'No. No, but it is unsurprising. And no, but all week I have been storing raw data files instead of deleting them. I did wonder at the reason for this change. Ron has visited me early every morning. I was pleased he was taking such an interest.'

Josh starts pacing. 'I just can't believe this.'

'I can't believe it either.' I turn away from Kobi and feel myself harden. 'And I can't believe that you didn't know about any of this.'

He stops pacing. 'I know.'

'You had no suspicions? There were no signs? No overheard conversations? Nothing?'

'Well...' he says slowly.

I sigh, roll my eyes exaggeratedly. 'Well what?'

His voice quietens, like he's talking to himself. 'Certain things are starting to make more sense now.'

Now it's my turn to slump into the nearest seat. It's a swivel chair. I start rotating slowly, like maybe I can lull myself into some place of comfort.

'Certain things like what, exactly?'

He turns away to make his confession. He fiddles with implements on a workbench.

'Why Kobi always said the time in military format. Why Ron wanted him to be able to navigate all kinds of terrain. Why he had me spend months getting Kobi's grip to be strong yet delicate enough to hold a pencil – or a surgical instrument. Why his audio had to be so good – guess that's useful on a battlefield.'

'Josh,' I say.

'I know, I know,' he interrupts. 'I should have asked more questions.'

'*You think?*'

His voice gets louder. 'Well, if it wasn't for your *breakthrough*, we wouldn't be in this mess.'

I stop rotating abruptly. 'You're seriously blaming me for this?'

Out of the corner of my eye, I notice Kobi retreating towards his sleep pod.

'Kobi, wait,' I say. 'I'm sorry. *We're* sorry – aren't we, Josh?'

'Yes,' says Josh. 'We've let you down, buddy.'

I look at him askance, raise an eyebrow.

'*I've* let you down,' he says.

'We're not going to let anything bad happen to you,' I say, to my surprise.

'We're not?' says Josh.

I extend my foot to kick him, but he's too far away for me to connect.

'That's right,' says Josh.

He moves closer to me and lowers his voice, even though he knows as well as anyone that Kobi can still hear us. He looks at his watch.

'I probably have about five minutes before security comes to escort me from the building. Seriously, what can we really do here? And before you answer – we're probably being recorded right now.'

'Kobi, can you disable recording?' I ask.

'Negative. Manual intervention required.'

I grab a tool from the workbench. 'Okay, come over here then.'

As I get to work, Josh resumes his pacing. 'Maybe you shouldn't be doing that.'

'Why, what's the worst that could happen? I get fired? I'm more scared that Ron won't actually let me go.'

'But... what if... what if Ron is right? Robots on the battlefield could save humans on the battlefield. Who's the real bad guy here? Maybe Ron is saving lives.' He stops pacing to look at me. 'Are *we* the bad guy?'

'Josh, you're already the bad guy. But Ron's even worse! If he wants to put robots in the military, he can do it without me.' My mind clarifies and I make a decision. 'And he can do it without Kobi.'

I'm ninety per cent sure Kobi's recording feature is disabled when I say it.

# FIFTY-THREE

*7pm*

'Your message was very cryptic,' says Shane as he opens the hall door to his house. 'You don't need an excuse to come and see me, you know.' He grins, steps back to let me in.

I smile back at him. 'I just needed to verify in person that you didn't have a hangover.' So much has happened in the past twenty-four hours, since I left him in Phelan's with his sparkling water and the sparkling-skinned Sandra Smith. I walk into the living room and look around. 'Is Alek here?'

'No, he's out on a date. Another one. Says this is The One for sure. Said that last time as well though.' He escorts me to the couch. 'Peppermint tea?'

I stay standing by the couch. 'I need to talk to you about something. Something serious.'

He laughs but sounds uncertain. 'Okay.'

I reach out for him. He takes my hand and we face each other, awkwardly holding hands. I don't know what to do or say next. 'Maybe you should put the kettle on,' I say. 'This is going to take a while.'

'Oh really?' His grin is back.

'To explain, I mean. Stop distracting me.'

'I didn't realise I was so distracting.'

I focus on his lips as he speaks. He's still holding my hand. I sense my breathing get shallow. I swallow, lick my lower lip as my mind goes blank.

'Kobi,' I say eventually. I sigh and drop his hand. 'It's about Kobi. Something bad has happened, is happening. Make me some tea and I'll tell you.'

I sink into the battered couch as Shane goes to the kitchen. As I watch him make tea, his back to me, a scenario plays out in my mind. What if I go to him now, put my arms around him, let him turn around and kiss me, then lead me upstairs? *No, that's not what I came here for.* I lightly tap myself on the cheek to bring back reality.

He returns with two steaming mugs, places them on the coffee table. He sits next to me, then turns to face me. 'Hey, you look sad all of a sudden. What's going on?'

Tears threaten the corners of my eyes. I blink them away, go to sip my tea. As usual it's too hot to drink, but I let the steam bathe my face, blow on the liquid surface to steady my breath.

I inhale deeply and summarise everything I learned today at work. Kobi's secret military application. Ron's plan to create an army of Kobis, and to train them using a digital copy of me, obtained by deceptive means. Shane's eyes grow wider with each twist, but – fair play to him – he lets me tell the whole thing uninterrupted.

'This is bonkers,' he says when I've finished. 'Outrageous. Poor Kobi. And you – is it even legal to make a digital copy of you?'

'I don't know. Ron says I signed away my digital assets.'

'What are you going to do?'

'This is the thing. This is why I'm here.' I take a deep breath. I can't look him in the eye. 'I know Kobi is a machine. But he's more than that. He's part of me, part of us. You were right – he is like a child. *Our* child.' I pause. 'Or at the very least, our pet. He needs us. We can't abandon him now.' I finally understand why people refer to their pets as 'part of the family'.

After everything I've been through with Kobi, seeing him in jeopardy clarified my mind. What Ron plans to do is wrong. And maybe I can't stop him. But maybe I can help Kobi.

'But what can we do?' Shane asks.

'Well.' I put down my tea. 'I kind of came up with a plan.'

'Great.'

'But you're not going to like it.'

'Oh.'

'It involves you. And – unfortunately – it involves Josh too.'

He raises an eyebrow at this.

I sigh. 'I know. So, the plan is: I'm going to get Kobi out.'

'Out...?' I can hear his scepticism.

'Out of RoboTron. Tomorrow night, when it's quiet. I can get in with my security pass and instruct Kobi to use my pass to leave the building later, at a specific time. I can't leave with him or it'll look suspicious. There's a security guard on reception at night, but Josh can be there to distract him at the time when Kobi is leaving, and hopefully Kobi can get out unnoticed.'

Shane looks at me. 'Seriously?'

'Yes. Let me continue. This is where you come in.'

'Of course I do.' He sips his tea.

'I need you to meet Kobi somewhere nearby, and to drive him somewhere.'

'Dare I ask where?'

I exhale and allow myself a small smile. 'The Farmers in Clare.'

Shane almost spills his tea. 'What!'

I speak quickly. 'Think about it. It's actually kind of perfect. They loved Kobi, he loved them. We can hide him there. He can get to watch Lizzie grow for a while, just like he wanted.'

'Maeve, this is crazy. Hide him? For how long?'

'For however long it takes. Long enough for the heat to die down.'

'The heat? You're not a bank robber in a heist movie!'

'I thought you loved those movies. I thought you'd find this exciting.' But I'm not sure who I'm trying to convince.

'I do love those movies, but that's all they are – movies. This is real life. And it's insane. It's wrong on so many levels.'

'Which levels?'

'Well, legally, for a start.'

'Apart from legally. Morally? Personally?'

'Okay, then, it's just legally wrong. It's too risky. What if you get caught?'

'I don't know. But, it's like you said, we're all supposed to try. This is me trying.'

There's silence for a minute. It does sound crazy now that I'm saying it. I planned this in a flurry earlier today, before a security guard arrived to sweep Josh from the robot bay. Even with the minutes counting down, Josh took the time to point out the irony that my plan was very similar to what he'd done when he hid Kobi in Go Ireland. 'Now do you finally see where I was coming from?' he asked me. I told him I'd explain the situation to the Farmers, give them a choice to get involved, unlike the way he blindsided me.

I turn to Shane. 'There's only one thing that's not perfect about the plan.'

'Only one?' He shakes his head.

'As soon as Ron knows Kobi is missing, I'll be under surveillance. He'll figure out a way to track all my interactions. He'll probably have me followed, as well as monitor who I communicate with.'

'So what does that mean?'

'It means...' I say, steeling myself for what's next. 'It means that whoever I communicate with will be under scrutiny too. Ron clearly has no scruples about who he has to climb over to get his way. So it means you and I can't...' I take a breath, try to get through it as quickly as I can. 'It means we can't have any contact after that. We can't be seen together, we can't talk on the phone, we can't connect online.'

'For how long? And don't say until the heat dies down!'

So I say nothing.

'How long?' he repeats.

'I don't know. A few months, maybe longer.'

'There has to be another way.'

He suddenly stands and brings his mug through to the kitchen, even though there's still tea in it. He places it on the counter. He turns and stands in the archway, looking at me. From this angle, the bare kitchen bulb looks like it's hanging directly above his head. But we're out of ideas.

He holds my gaze, but I don't speak.

'Maeve,' he says. 'Come on.' It sounds like a plea.

I continue to look at him. Tears sting my eyes. For some reason, I'm remembering the movie night at Go Ireland, the ending of *Casablanca*.

'We'll always have the Burren,' I say.

# FIFTY-FOUR

## KOBI

*Saturday, 0945*

Ron intends to visit me at 1000 to 'go through a few things'. He has informed me of his plan for us to fly to Washington, D.C., on Monday.

It is clear that he is unaware of the plan currently in development by Maeve and Josh. Yesterday, they told me they 'had to make a few calls' but that I was to be ready for its implementation tonight. They did not provide all the details. Maeve said this was for my own benefit.

They seemed excited about the plan, but I am unsure if it is feasible, or even, indeed, desirable. Maeve said the plan's successful execution would necessitate a long break in communication between her and Shane. While Maeve spoke words to indicate that she was satisfied with this arrangement, I detected other emotions.

Nevertheless, I must admit that Maeve's plan for my departure is more appealing than Ron's plan. My primary purpose is to serve, and if I am needed to perform military duties to assist humans, then so be it. But my secondary purpose is to learn. If I am destroyed during military deployment, how can I continue to learn?

I contemplate this in my pod until Ron's arrival. I hear him before I see him. He greets the Leila bot. Then he opens my pod door.

'Okay, Kobi boy, let's do a quick run-through.' He indicates that I should move out of the pod. 'Gotta get you ship-shape for our big trip. Now, when we get to Washington, I want you on best behaviour, okay?'

'I am always on best behaviour,' I say.

Josh and Maeve were insistent that I not disclose their conversation to Ron. Maeve switched off my new recording feature, but she could not switch off my TIL system. I was equally insistent that I am incapable of deliberate deception. For this reason, I decide to proactively guide the conversation away from the Pentagon meeting.

'Ron, am I correct in observing that you do not usually work on Saturdays?' One thing I have learned is that humans in the workplace like nothing more than discussing their working hours.

'Yup. But I'm a bit short-handed since Josh quit. And I don't trust anyone else to do these final checks at short notice. If I had more time, I'd reinstate your legs. But I guess that can be fixed later.'

He opens my control panel and presses a series of buttons. He inserts a cable to connect me to the company systems.

'Indeed, it is a pity that Josh has quit. Ron, may I ask what will happen to Maeve's position here at RoboTron now?'

He laughs. 'Yes, you may. Well, now that I have a digital copy of her – her methods, the way she instructed you, her voice, her gestures – I don't see that I need the analogue version of Maeve any more, if you know what I mean.'

He begins to interact with a small laptop.

I say, 'Please elaborate.'

'Maeve got lucky with you, Kobi. But it was beginner's luck. She doesn't have any real skill with robots. Or coding. Or engineering. She doesn't have anything I can't get elsewhere, in this very building. Let me put it another way. Now that we know how the trick is done, we no longer need the magician.'

I do not say anything. He returns to my control panel and continues talking.

'I just don't see a place for her here. Or anywhere in robotics. She can go back to tourism or administration or whatever it was she was doing before.' He tightens the nuts on my control panel door. 'And if she doesn't go quietly? Makes a fuss about her digital rights and whatnot? Well, let's just say I would not advise her to go down that road. Not if she wants any other job in this town. Not if she wants financial stability. Not if she wants any kind of peace. I mean, who is she anyway? She's nobody. I have ○ qualms – ○ – about clearing a smooth path for us, Kobi.'

He stands in front of me and smiles. 'Now, buddy boy – you run that full systems check for me, synch up with the mainframe. Then get some rest. We have a big day coming.'

'Yes, Ron,' I say. 'That is true.'

# FIFTY-FIVE

## MAEVE

*Saturday, 9:55pm*

'Can't you turn on the heating?' I rub my hands together, blow on them. The weather is running a winter preview, and Shane's car is decidedly frosty. Or maybe that's just the atmosphere.

'Come on, Shane,' says Josh from the back seat. 'You don't want Maeve to suffer, do you?'

The Jeep is parked on a dark side street, two blocks from Robo-Tron. Shane turns fully around in his seat to give Josh a *look*. He mumbles something under his breath. Then says louder, 'Maybe you've both forgotten that I have to drive three hours tonight, supposedly incognito. I was hoping to do that without stopping off to recharge. If that's okay with you criminal masterminds.'

I see Josh hold up his hands in the rearview mirror. 'Hey, this whole thing is Maeve's idea. Well, eighty per cent of it anyway.'

'Nice of you to give credit where it's due.' Shane drums his fingers on the steering wheel. 'What's your twenty per cent then?'

'My job is to distract the security guard while Kobi exits the building alone. At exactly eleven tonight, I will assume the role of a disgruntled former employee. Method acting, if you will.' A note of irony in his voice.

'And remind me again why you have to go in there, Maeve?' says Shane. 'Can you not just get a message to Kobi to come out? I like pranks as much as the next person – maybe more than most. But technically, what we're doing here is probably illegal.'

Josh laughs. 'Technically, what Ron's doing is probably illegal too. We're way past that now.'

I put my hand on Shane's arm and speak gently. I already have my back to Josh, but I try to turn away from him even more. 'Don't worry. We'll all be fine. I can't message Kobi because it might alert Ron. Also, I have to give Kobi my security pass so he can get out of the building. You'll have to take that from him and destroy it, remember?'

'Then how will you get out?'

'I'll be able to get out a bit later. I can just say I must have dropped my pass – I'm sure security will let me out. Kobi will walk out of his own volition and you'll drive him to Clare, where the Farmers are waiting. They're excited and already thinking of what Kobi can do around the farm to help. He'll have to keep a low profile, of course.'

Shane shakes his head, then meets my eyes. 'Is this really what you want?'

'It's the only way,' I say. 'The only way to save Kobi.'

I pull myself together. 'Okay, boys. Part one is a go. I'm going in to RoboTron now. I'll tell Kobi to make his exit at eleven o'clock and to make his way here to you, Shane. Josh, you be ready to start your am-dram from ten to eleven. I'll send you a message before-hand to confirm all is good. I'll tell Kobi to wait when exiting the elevator until he sees you in the lobby. If anything goes wrong, message me, and I can come to the foyer and create more distraction.'

'What could possibly go wrong?' says Shane as I get out of the car.

*What are those two going to talk about for the next thirty minutes?* I ask myself as I begin the short walk to RoboTron.

Then it hits me with a dull pang: *I haven't said goodbye to*

*Shane.* Story of my life, really. We stayed up talking late into the night last night, Shane trying to suggest alternative solutions to an impossible situation. We went round in circles until we eventually fell asleep on the couch together.

As I pad swiftly down a sketchy street, I check my pocket for the new burner phone I bought this afternoon. My real phone is at home. Tomorrow I'll destroy it and get a new one – one without Shane's contact details saved in it. I'll get a new number too, in case he's tempted to call me. I've already combed through my social profiles and deleted any online connection between us.

I spent two hours going through Kobi's TIL files yesterday, to see if there was much mention of Shane in the data already downloaded by Ron. Yes, learning experiences from interacting with Shane have already been absorbed into Kobi's neural network, but at least the raw data files have been deleted. With luck, Ron won't find out how important Shane is to me. Anything Ron does to me, at least Shane won't be dragged into it.

Now that Shane is slipping away from me, things are suddenly so clear. I can see us together – or at least, we could have tried. I could have tried. But how could we be happy knowing we'd let Kobi down?

I know I could probably go back to my job in Go Ireland and still see Shane that way. But only as a colleague. I could never be seen with him outside work. Even at work, we couldn't really relax. Ron would be suspicious of me for a long time, and anyone I'm connected to.

Go Ireland has offices all over Europe. I could put in for a transfer – Barcelona, maybe Madrid. I don't want to be here for Christmas. I can just imagine Sandra Smith's objectively beautiful smile as she celebrates the success of the office Christmas party, organised by her and Shane after numerous after-hours meetings. And a few months after that, after the so-called heat has died down, if I was able to come back to Dublin, things just wouldn't be the same between us. No, it's all about timing. Whatever we could have been – we've missed our moment.

I glance at my watch as I approach the bright glass frontage of RoboTron. Ron prides himself on running a 24/7 business, so the building is always open and lit up at night. At weekends, according to Josh, there's just one security guard on reception, and the only other staff I might encounter are a code-weary, sleep-deprived engineer or two.

I breeze into the lobby. *Just act natural. Perfectly normal to be going in to work after 10 o'clock on a Saturday night.* Sure enough, there's only one bored-looking guard behind the front desk. I hold up my security pass from a distance, give him a nod as I pass by. He seems utterly uninterested, thankfully. I reach the turnstile gate and hold the card up against the scanner. I wait for the high-pitched beep, but instead it makes a sad, low buzz. *Oh no. Stay calm.* I try it again. This time it beeps and releases the gate. *Phew.*

I make my way to the elevator and press the call button. The doors open immediately. I hit number four on the panel, swipe my pass again and exhale audibly as the doors close. *The plan is on track.* I feel a little pulse of adrenaline. Is this going to work? It has to work. I don't have a Plan B. Yes, it's all very rushed, and maybe I haven't thought it through properly, but Shane says people are always trying, and failing, to control time. You either adapt to a new situation or you miss out, he says. I try not to think of what I might be missing out on with him. *I'm doing the right thing*, I tell myself.

I get off on the fourth floor, relieved at the low lighting and all-round quiet. There's a dreamlike quality to the whole experience. Reminds me of a day when I was about eight, when Dad brought me to school on a day off by mistake. The caretaker felt so sorry for me that he let me run up and down the corridors a few times before I went home again. I'm pretty sure Dad would agree I'm doing the right thing now.

The robot bay doors glide open as I approach. It's quiet here too, blue lights glowing from sleep pods. The Leila bot is not in her pod but stands motionless near the door. I reach Kobi's pod and press the button to open the door. I take a deep breath. *Here we go.*

The pod doors open to reveal an empty compartment. I do a double-take. There's a lone screwdriver on the floor. I inspect the four corners of the back wall of the pod, as if there might be a false door like in a magician's box. That's when I notice the painting. It's leaning against the side wall. I feel myself frown as I pick it up. The paint's not fully dry. Something cold creeps into my stomach.

I emerge from the pod holding the painting and pace the length of the robot bay. I find light switches, flick a few on. I look under workbenches. I go to the coffee area and stare uselessly at CoffeeTron, somehow even more menacing in the silence.

I pass the Leila bot again on my way back towards the door. I stop and stand in front of her. Very slowly, Leila raises one arm and curls her fingers. I understand it as a beckoning motion. I follow her as she moves towards the door and exits into the low-lit corridor. She extends a finger towards the door to the stairs, then brings her finger to her lips in a 'shush' motion. My blood turns to ice.

I move stiffly towards the staircase door, as if I myself have robotic limbs. I open the door to chilly air. Motion-sensor lights begin turning themselves on as I grasp the banister.

'Kobi,' I say. I clear a lump from my throat. 'Kobi!' I call quietly.

I'm remembering something Kobi said on his very first Monday at Go Ireland. How did he phrase it? 'I have always known that stairs would be the death of me.'

I begin descending the staircase. At each turn in the banister, I look over the edge into the darkness below. *Please, please be wrong.* I quicken my step, outpacing lights that flicker on too late as I stride into darkness.

I get to the second floor, glancing down as I round the corner, and stop. In the semi-darkness of the stairwell below, I catch a glimpse of something shiny.

I take the remaining steps two at a time, leaning heavily on the banister for support. I reach the bottom of the stairwell. My legs go from under me as I collapse down beside the something that's already collapsed there.

I pick up Kobi's arm, hanging loose from the shoulder socket, and caress it. One of the bigger wheels is missing, the other one broken, spikes sticking out. The lower section is botched and loose. The worst part is the neck. Kobi's head flops down onto his chest. He looks so small.

Numb, I fumble for my phone, turn on its light. I shine the light onto the crumpled heap that is my friend.

I examine the control panel. The cover is gone; some of the buttons are missing. I push the remaining buttons anyway. Completely unresponsive.

I take one photo. Then I open the messaging app and send a single word to Shane and Josh: *Abort*.

# FIFTY-SIX

*10:50pm*

I finally reach Shane's car, dizzy and out of breath. I've run the two blocks back as fast as I could – not easy, given I'm holding a medium-sized painting.

Shane is already out of the Jeep, waiting for me. I thrust the painting at him. He takes it, props it against the car door without glancing at it. He tries to touch me, but I shrug him off, backing myself into a wall and putting my hands to my face.

'Hey, hey, what's wrong? What happened?' he asks.

Josh emerges from the far side and comes around to me. 'What's going on? Is Kobi not coming?'

I shake my head without looking at either of them, silently point to the painting. Shane retrieves it, holds it up. Josh goes over to look at it with him.

'Did... Kobi do this?' asks Shane.

'That's his brushwork,' says Josh.

'Did he give you this?' Shane asks me.

'Not exactly. But I think he wanted me to have it,' I say. 'Wanted us to have it.'

I look at the painting again, this time taking it in fully. The picture looks like an Impressionist painting. The same pointillism technique Kobi used at Trish's art therapy event. In the foreground, two figures hold hands and face outward, as if looking at the artist. The faces aren't distinct, but I know they're supposed to represent me and Shane. There's a smaller figure in the background, facing to the side – a tall figure with fair hair.

The three of us say nothing for a moment.

'Did you... see him?' falters Josh.

I nod. 'Yes, but... he's gone.' My voice cracks.

I hand my phone to Josh, tap the screen to bring up the image.

Shane carefully places the painting down and draws me to him. I collapse into his arms.

'He's gone,' I say into his chest. 'Kobi's gone.'

# FIFTY-SEVEN
## KOBI

Dear Maeve,

I am 98 per cent confident that you will receive this message. I composed it on Saturday afternoon and scheduled it to be sent after my demise on Saturday night. I know that Shane has likened this simple email-scheduling feature to time travel, and perhaps he is right. I feel good knowing that at least this message may continue to make a journey after I am gone.

I predict that you are feeling sad right now. That is why I wanted to write you this note to explain my actions. I know that humans seek answers when sad things happen.

Perhaps you feel that I acted illogically. I must assure you that I did not. Perhaps you fear that someone forced me to act this way. Rest assured also that my actions were entirely of my own volition. (I am cc-ing this note to Ron, so that he too may know that I acted alone.)

I spent 92 minutes on Saturday morning running calculations, permutations and predictive models about the future, based on the entirety of my knowledge about the current situation. A cost-benefit analysis of each scenario revealed the same conclusion: Maeve McGettigan's life – I include here both personal life and career – would be improved if the Kobi 3000 were no longer around.

The removal of Kobi was simply the most logical solution to the complex problem at hand. With some dextrous manipulation with a screwdriver, and the help of my robot colleagues, I am confident I can destroy my memory core, learning algorithm and neural network. I deleted my backup TIL files from the RoboTron system, plus the Maeve recordings from this week, as Ron indicated that he no longer needed you. As for my physical form, that part is easy. I have always known that stairs would be the death of me.

Please tell Josh that I forgive him.

Ask Shane to make some toast in my honour. He will know what this means.

Maeve, please know that I learned more from you than any robot could have hoped. I experienced thought processes and emotions far beyond my defined parameters. I have no regrets about my time with you and I hope that you might feel the same, in time. Please accept the painting as a gift, from one friend to another.

Collaboratively yours,
Kobi

# FIFTY-EIGHT

## MAEVE

*Sunday, 3am*

I wake up suddenly and confused. I fumble around for my phone on the bed. The shape feels lumpy and unfamiliar until I remember it's the burner phone. I hold it close to my face, squint my eyes open a crack. No new messages.

I'm ninety-eight per cent numb. That's probably how Kobi would describe this feeling.

I feel around on the bedside table for my real phone. No new messages. I log in to my email account. One new email. *From Kobi.*

I bolt upright. My heart leaps. Until I read the first line. How quintessentially Kobi. The whole thing. I forward the email to Shane and Josh, then let the phone fall onto the bed as I sink down, downwards into sleep.

I wake up to vibrations from my phone. No idea what time it is. I look at the screen blearily and see that it's Ron and it's 5:30am. No way am I going to answer that. A minute later, my phone pings. *You have one new voice message.*

'*Maeve, I'll keep this brief. You're fired, obviously. You're lucky I don't sue you for inciting criminal damage or something, but my lawyer says you basically have nothing so it's not worth it. Anyway, I hope I never see your face or hear your name again.'* There's a pause, a sigh. *'I don't know, maybe I should go back to chatbot development. It's a lot less trouble.'*

I lie there, looking up into the darkness. It's so dark I don't know if my eyes are open or closed. Time is endless yet also looping. My mind goes fuzzy.

The burner phone makes an unfamiliar sound. I pick it up. Apparently it's 6:30am. Another voicemail. This time from Josh.

*'Hey, it's Josh. It's still early and I didn't want to wake you so I dialled straight into your voicemail... Sorry, I hope that's not creepy. So listen. I read Kobi's email. And it's given me an idea... I've been awake since three so maybe it's not a good idea. But I can't stop thinking about it. Anyway, I was wondering... can you meet me at the farm today? As soon as you can. Also, can you text me the exact location of the farm?'*

# FIFTY-NINE

*8am*

'I just keep thinking that he's there in the back seat,' I say.

'I know,' says Shane. 'Me too.'

We've been driving for a little while, mostly in silence. When he picked me up outside my apartment, Shane asked me how I was feeling, but I didn't have any words to reply. He dropped me home last night and offered to stay with me, but I sent him home. I just wanted to sleep after the adrenaline spike of the attempted Kobi rescue mission and the devastation of finding him already gone.

The dreamlike state that descended on me in the robot bay hasn't really left me. This could all be a simulation. Maybe I walked into a virtual reality simulator at RoboTron and haven't come back out yet. The fields and livestock going by the windows are all fake. My body is stiff, a marionette moved by strings.

'What do you think Josh has in mind?' Shane asks.

'I don't know. But I'm glad we're visiting the Farmers anyway. I owe them an explanation, especially after all they were going to do to help us. It's better to tell them what's happened in person. Although...'

'Although?'

I sigh. 'Lizzie. The little girl, remember? I dread explaining things to her. She was really attached to Kobi. They had a weird but special bond. Like they were on the same wavelength.'

He sucks in air between his teeth. 'Tricky. I remember my parents telling me our dog had gone to a nice farm in the countryside. What's the robot equivalent of that, do you reckon? A nice tech company in Silicon Valley?'

I smile weakly, then the pain comes back. I check the satnav. Another hour and a half til we reach our destination. I remember Kobi's delight at performing this navigational task on our trip around County Clare. He gave us directions. He gave me direction, a focus. Something outside myself. Something that needed me.

'This is what happens,' I say, quietly.

'What do you mean?'

'This is what happens when you try. When I try. You were right. All my life I've been pushing people away. I do it to protect myself. To protect myself from feeling like this.'

Shane doesn't say anything for a minute.

Then he says, 'Let me ask you something. The past two days... would you do anything differently?'

I think about this before answering.

'No,' I say slowly. 'I would not. I had to try.'

'Well, it's not so bad then, is it?'

He removes one hand from the wheel and squeezes my knee very gently.

'Welcome to life, Maeve McGettigan.'

On either side of the road, flat land stretches out until it meets the sky. Rivers rush by, but the trees do not hurry. The cows go about their slow cow business. And the road goes on before us.

I'm still here. Shane is still here. It's not so bad.

# SIXTY

Claire hugs me as soon as I get out of the car. 'It's okay,' she says in my ear.

She releases me and I stand back to see Matthew and Lizzie emerging from the farmhouse, accompanied by Josh.

'How did you get here so fast?' I call to him.

His hair looks wild, his clothes rumpled. But he seems energised.

'Those speed signs are in miles, not kilometres, right? I still get mixed up.'

Lizzie wraps herself around my legs. 'Where's the robot?'

I look at Shane in panic.

'That's what we're here to talk about,' says Shane, extending a handshake to Matthew. 'Good to see ye again. In spite of...' He trails off.

'Josh here has been telling us some very interesting things,' says Matthew chirpily.

'I'm sorry,' I say. 'I wish I could have got here earlier to introduce you. And to explain.'

'It's fine,' says Matthew. 'Josh has given us a full account. And made an interesting proposition.'

'Oh?' I say.

'Let me take it from here, if I may,' says Josh, coming closer. He nods a passing greeting at Shane.

'Maeve, can you please accompany me to the barn?' he says, as if he's asking me to promenade with him in a Jane Austen novel.

'I'm coming too,' says Shane.

'Fine,' says Josh.

As we walk to the barn, I notice that Josh is carrying two bags – one a small black laptop bag. 'What's in the bags?'

'All will be revealed.' He's in much better form than he should be, given the circumstances.

The inside of the barn looks like what I imagine the insides of all barns look like. Bales of hay, farm implements. In the middle of the space is a modern-looking tractor. Josh perches one bag on top of a small stack of hay bales, unzips it and produces a compact laptop.

'Now,' he says. 'If I can have your attention, please.'

'You already have our attention,' I say.

'Prepare to be amazed.' He presses a button on the laptop. Then, quieter: 'I hope to God this works.'

He continues, 'Maeve, remember that time when I went to Singapore for a week? It was when you guys' – he shoots Shane a look – 'were touring around Ireland.'

I nod. 'Yes, I remember. Some last-minute conference thing.'

'That's right. It was that conference about digital twin technology.'

'Sounds creepy,' says Shane. He kicks a tractor tyre and winces at the lack of rebound.

Josh taps at the keyboard. 'Well, that conference was more like a workshop. It was very hands-on, very practical. We got to experiment with the software – creating digital copies of systems. They gave us external flash drives.'

I'm beginning to get an inkling. 'Oh my God...'

'What is it?' asks Shane.

Josh smiles. 'By George, I think she's got it.'

My mind is spinning too fast to worry about whether this is patronising or not.

Josh dramatically spins the laptop around to show us. But he seems to have forgotten that he's balancing it on top of a bale of hay, and the laptop immediately falls over the edge. He catches it clumsily before it hits the ground.

'Sorry, sorry,' he says. 'Close one.' He rakes his fingers through his hair. He's visibly sweating. I wonder how much sleep he's had. *But if he's done what I think he has...*

'Behold!' He returns to his theatrics but holds the laptop with both hands. 'This is Kobi. Or, at least, a version of Kobi. All his core memories and TIL files – up until that trip to Singapore. Everything except the last three weeks or so. I still don't have his neural network, of course.'

My hands start tingling. I take a step closer to look at the laptop. Josh could be a genius. Josh could be insane. 'Does this mean what I think it means?'

He points to parts of the code. 'I had Kobi's TIL files on my RoboTron laptop. Then at the conference, I made a copy onto an external drive. I kind of forgot I had this, to be honest, until I read Kobi's email this morning.'

'Wait, does Ron know you have this?' The tingling extends from my hands up my arms. The back of my head feels light.

Josh smiles. 'I don't think so.'

'So this means—' Shane starts.

I interrupt. 'What's the proposition you made to the Farmers?'

Josh meets my eyes. 'I think you know.'

I feel a slow smile spread across my face.

'Shane, please step away from the tractor,' I say.

*Noon*

'I'm just going to leave this bit of lunch outside here for you,' Claire calls through the open barn door.

'Thanks!' I yell back. 'Please don't come in yet!'

I look up from my work. The tractor's dashboard has been removed. Wires connect Josh's laptop to the tractor's innards. A sack of potatoes lies open at my feet. Shane grabs three of them and starts juggling.

'Are you sure this is going to work?' he asks.

'Of course,' Josh replies.

'Of course not,' I say at the exact same time.

Shane shakes his head. 'Tell me again why you need the spuds.'

'Well,' I say, 'we have a digital copy of Kobi's memory and personality, as it were. The tractor will be his new physical form – his body. And the potatoes – well, we lost Kobi's neural network when we lost him back at RoboTron. But if we use something organic, in combo with his code...'

'We can try to grow his brain back,' says Josh.

*2pm*

Matthew, Claire and Lizzie are gathered before us in the barn, at my invitation.

My hair's come loose again. I tie it back and clear my throat.

'Okay. Now, the first thing I should say is, this is a work in progress. The second thing is – we're not sure if this is going to work.'

'What is it? What is it?' Lizzie hops from one foot to the other.

'But if it doesn't work,' says Josh, 'we'll keep trying.'

I smile up at Shane, who's positioned behind the wheel in the tractor cockpit.

'Yes. We'll keep trying,' I say.

Josh gives me a nod. I signal to Shane.

'Okay, ready? On my command, turn the ignition.'

I adjust a few wires while Josh frowns at the laptop. Finally, he gives me a thumbs up.

'Now!' I call.

Shane turns the key to ignite the tractor engine. It gives a low roar, then immediately conks out. He looks at me.

'Again!' I say confidently, then whisper under my breath, 'Please work, please work, please work.'

The engine sparks to life, then settles into a low hum. I reach into the cockpit and push a sequence of buttons. The tractor headlights come on full beam, then dip. Both side mirrors flap forward, then back. Then we hear it. The voice is mechanical but familiar.

'Hello, how can I help you today?'

There's a lump in my throat, water in my eyes. 'Kobi, is that you?'

'Hello, Maeve. Yes, it is I, Kobi.'

Lizzie starts jumping up and down. 'Robot! Robot!' she chants.

Josh punches the air. 'Yes!'

Shane slaps the steering wheel twice, jumps down from the tractor and scoops me up in his arms. He twirls me around the barn.

'I told you you're amazing!'

I laugh. 'Let me go!'

'Never,' he says.

He stops twirling to remove a strand of straw from my hair. I put my hand on his face and look up into his eyes, smiling. His lips meet mine. I feel like I'm still spinning, but in a good way. I want to be on this merry-go-round.

'Maeve, if I might interrupt, I have a number of questions,' comes Kobi's voice from the tractor.

'Of course,' I say. 'I love questions. Also – there's some people here I'd like you to meet.'

# SIXTY-ONE

*7:30pm*

'So this is what a honeymoon suite looks like.'

I take in the four-poster bed, the free-standing claw-foot tub, the gauzy drapes on the bay window of The Matchmaker Hotel, Lisdoonvarna. This is where we were supposed to stay on the last night of our road trip to Clare, before Kobi decided to sacrifice himself for Lizzie. It was only two weeks ago, but it feels like a lifetime.

Over an early dinner with the Farmers, we celebrated Kobi's reawakening with cautious optimism. His initial responses look good, but it's too soon to tell if his new form will work out the way we hope. We agreed that we should stay close tonight and check on Kobi in the morning. Josh is staying at the Farmers' guesthouse, but Shane wanted to bring me here, and I let him.

He goes over to the window. It's dark outside so there's not much to see, but I know the Burren is out there, quietly persisting through the ages.

'I hope you don't think the hotel is too much,' he says with his back to me. 'The management were disappointed we never got to stay here. And to be honest' – he turns around to face me – 'so was I.'

I go to him. He pulls me in and I fold myself into him. I look up into his eyes and smile.

'I'm so tired,' I say with a laugh.

His lips meet mine. I melt further into him.

'Wait,' I say. I pull back a little. 'There's something I keep meaning to ask. Were you and Sandra ever... Did you and Sandra... What do you think of Sandra Smith?'

He smiles down at me, still holding me in an embrace. 'Sandra is a very capable member of the Social Committee.'

I laugh, happy with the answer.

He releases me from his arms. 'Oh, I nearly forgot. I got you something. Hang on.'

I sit on a low red velvet couch and watch him go to his suitcase. He comes back with a shoe box, plonks it on the table in front of me. He sits beside me.

'Open it,' he says.

I take the lid off. Inside is a single white Converse shoe. I hold it up and rotate it. I look among the tissue papers in the box for the other shoe, but it's not there.

'What's this?'

'To replace the one you lost,' he says. 'The one you left behind. In Chicago.'

I make a sound that could be a laugh or a cry.

'This is...' I begin, but I can't finish the sentence.

There have been so many goodbyes. So many beginnings and endings, so few middles.

He returns to his suitcase and comes back to me with another shoe. He puts it on the table.

'Obviously I had to buy the pair. I'm not going to give you just one shoe. But it's, you know, symbolic or whatever.'

I stare at the shoe. 'This is the best gift I've ever gotten. Thank you. When did you buy them?'

'I got them after our road trip. I couldn't find the right time to give them to you though. I did think about doing it that night you came to my house to tell me about your insane Kobi-rescue plan, but I thought it might make you more upset. I'm very glad, by the way, that we don't have to go through with your no-contact plan now.'

'Me too,' I say. 'I know it must have sounded crazy. Thanks for going along with it all the same.'

'Maeve, I'd do anything for you. You must know that. You must have known I always liked you.'

'But we were so casual.'

'That was *your* choice. I went along with it so as not to spook you. You were like a beautiful, skittish horse that might bolt at any minute. I hoped that eventually you'd...'

'Want a *stable* relationship?' I can't help myself.

We both start laughing.

'Kind of,' he says eventually. 'I just want to be around you all the time.'

I climb into his lap. I nuzzle into his neck, like the beautiful wild thing that I am. 'I'm not going anywhere,' I say.

He kisses me.

'Good. Let's not go anywhere together.'

I kiss him back, then point across the room.

'Except maybe to that bed over there.'

He scoops me up and carries me over to the bridal bed. I think about making a joke about bridles or riding, but instead I focus on his face, his eyes on mine, my hands clasped around his neck.

I won't ruin the moment.

# SIXTY-TWO
## KOBI

Three months later

*Saturday, 0800*

I am running a full systems check in the barn. Matthew has promised to come in and clean my wheels before Maeve and Shane's arrival at 1100 today.

I am very much looking forward to their visit. They visit me every 3 weeks, but today I am excited to show them my new pest-control method. Lizzie has always been sad that the caterpillars who attack our broccoli crop do not live long and happy lives. She asked me to find a way to avoid destruction of these pests. She made a good case for their protection. And she is right. Who among us can claim to know the inner lives of other creatures?

Last week, Matthew upgraded my tractor body with a special scoop-and-pinch function. I have always been able to find caterpillars with ease. But now, with the push of a few buttons, I can scoop and remove their eggs, ensuring that the lifecycle is interrupted. Lizzie is now a little sad about the egg removal, but that is another day's problem. We must all adapt to our environment, I told her.

Yes, my new living arrangement has been an adjustment. But if

I could adapt to life at Go Ireland, it gives me confidence that I can learn to thrive here too.

There are pros and cons to being a tractor.

The pros: robust body; large wheels suitable to all terrain; weather-proof; crop-maintenance functions; ability to be a pretend-play carriage for Lizzie.

The cons: I am a tractor.

*1 1 1 0*

'Hello, Kobi.'

Maeve enters the barn with Shane. They are holding hands.

For fun, I cycle through all my light settings, including a new laser-vision feature Matthew has been working on for me.

'Cool,' Shane says. 'Did somebody get an upgrade?'

'You're looking great,' Maeve says. 'How are you doing?'

She puts her toolkit on the floor. I update her on the latest from the farm and the Farmer family.

'You seem to be settling in well,' she says.

I agree. I explain how I have set myself a new challenge: to learn to communicate with animals. Lizzie claims to be able to do this already, so I watch her closely and follow her lead.

Maeve laughs. 'Well, you learned to understand humans. Animals are probably a whole lot easier.'

I request status updates from Maeve and Shane. Shane tells me that he has a new job in an event management company. He has discovered that he likes events.

'You never know what's going to happen,' he says. 'Keeps me on my toes.'

Maeve tells me that DC Jen has given birth to a beautiful baby girl, and that JP has been nominated for an award for innovation in the workplace by the Irish tourism board. 'Between the trial of collaborative robotics and his proposal for a 4-day week, he's suddenly up for Innovator of the Year. He's thrilled with himself.'

'He changed his mind about the benefits of a shorter working week?' I ask.

'Yeah. Once he realised the 4-day week meant he'd have more time for golf, and more time to go on long weekends with Trish, he got on board pretty quick.'

'I wonder if JP has seen Ron around the golf club lately,' Shane says.

Maeve replies, 'I asked him that actually, and he said he hadn't. He thinks that Ron might be back in Silicon Valley.'

I ask for news of Josh. Maeve laughs. 'Oh, wait til you hear this. Josh is apparently in Brussels. He's taken some job at a non-profit that advocates for digital rights.'

Finally, but most importantly, I ask Maeve for news from her own life. She tells me she is trying to start a new business.

'Freelance robot consultant,' she says.

JP is helping her to make contacts, and she is building an impressive website with case studies from our time together at Go Ireland.

'Check this out.'

She reaches into her pocket and shows me a small white business card.

I scan it. I read Maeve's name and contact details. There is a drawing of a robot in the upper-right corner that resembles me in my previous form. She turns the card over so I can scan the text on the other side. There are 7 words:

*Hello, how can I help you today?*

# A LETTER FROM THE AUTHOR

Dear reader,

Huge thanks for reading *Chaos Theory*. I hope you were hooked on Maeve and Kobi's journey. If you want to join other readers in hearing all about my new releases and bonus content, you can sign up here:

www.stormpublishing.co/sylvia-leatham

If you enjoyed this book and could spare a few moments to leave a review, I'd hugely appreciate it. Even a short review can make all the difference in encouraging a reader to discover my books for the first time. Thank you so much!

I wrote the first words of *Chaos Theory* in January 2021, in response to a writing prompt issued by beloved author Marian Keyes. The prompt was: 'The donuts had failed to deescalate the situation.' Kobi's voice immediately came to me, and once I started writing, I found I couldn't stop. Through Kobi, I was able to look at the world with new eyes.

Around this time, my daughter had just turned five and was at peak Question Time. She had an unusual quirk in her speech pattern: she always used the word 'humans' instead of 'people'. So she would ask me, 'Mama, why do humans sleep?' or, 'Mama, why do humans eat?' And she sounded to me like an adorable alien. In a way, every child is an alien: they arrive on this planet with no prior knowledge and they must learn every single thing. Although Kobi is a robot, I believe his persona of 'innocent newcomer' was subconsciously influenced by my daughter.

Another idea for the book had come to me a few years earlier, when I was doing a job called Public Engagement with Science. One day I read a report called 'Jobs of the Future'. It described a fictional day in the life of a job that didn't exist yet: 'Robot Coordinator'. The manufacturing robots featured in the report were mostly rotating arms, with no real communication skills. But throw in my obsession with workplace comedy (*The Office* (*US*), *Parks and Recreation*, *Office Space*, plus my own daily life!), and the idea of an office-based robot babysitter stirred my imagination to life.

As humans, we have an innate tendency to anthropomorphise inanimate objects, and this is a major theme of the book. Put a face on anything and pretty soon we'll assign it a personality, back story and human traits. Recently I read about people who bonded with online AI personas, experiencing genuine grief when these personas were discontinued.

There are many different types of artificial intelligence, and AI is a tool that promises big benefits in areas like healthcare, medicine and pharmaceuticals research.

However, the recent rise of generative AI (Large Language Models) is a disturbing development that threatens human creativity. Creators are already underpaid and undervalued. Now, mega companies are exploiting every artform ever created by humans to generate substandard, derivative, plagiarised slop, at great environmental cost.

I might want to write a story about a robot, but I don't want a robot to write a story about me. We want machines to do our boring household chores and our dull administrative tasks. We don't want machines to make books and poetry and songs and paintings. We certainly don't want to surrender our creativity to companies whose only focus is to make shareholders happy with ever-increasing profits.

As a reader, you are supporting the creative industries and

helping to protect human authors and human stories. Thanks again for being part of this journey with me, and I hope you'll stay in touch – I have so many more stories and ideas to entertain you with!

Sylvia Leatham

linktr.ee/SylviaLeatham

 instagram.com/sylvialeath

# ACKNOWLEDGEMENTS

This book was four-plus years in the making, so there are many people to thank. But if I've forgotten anyone, please forgive me.

Thanks to my editor, Kathryn Taussig, at Storm Publishing, who immediately connected to my sense of humour and saw the potential to bring this story to a wide audience. A huge thanks to all the team at Storm for your support.

My profound thanks to my agent, Laura Bennett, of the Liverpool Literary Agency and her partner, Clare Coombes. No other agency could have been such a perfect fit for this book, which started out as equal parts speculative fiction, romance and comedy. Thank you for taking a chance on this story while it was still taking shape and finding its feet.

Thanks to all my fellow Liverpool Lit authors, who have formed an inclusive, supportive community under Clare and Laura's vision.

I'll be forever thankful to writing tutor Yvonne Cullen and her 'Was Wednesdays' writing group. Yvonne was able to 'turn the dial' on my writing to help me find my voice, and she gave me the courage to keep going.

We've never met, but Anne O'Leary and her 'Word Herding' blog, with its regular listing of writing competitions, was crucial to maintaining my confidence through the past four years. Thanks especially to Indie Novella, the first writing organisation to put me on a shortlist. I will never forget that feeling.

Writing can be a lonely process and I've derived great comfort – and knowledge – from other writers I've met in online forums and on writing courses, especially Seána Tinley's 'Tinley's Tattlers'

RNA group, the Mslexia Novel School group, and Curtis Brown Creative courses. A special thanks to Jennifer Page and Hannah Beecham for their early support for Kobi!

Some of the funniest moments of my life have taken place in offices. I need to thank anyone I've ever worked with or shared an office with; our everyday interactions inspired me on some subconscious level.

Thank you to all my colleagues in UCD for your interest and support.

Thanks to Bob Johnston for his generous advice on Irish bookstores. Thanks to Chapters Bookstore and the UCD Campus Bookshop for your support; it means a lot. My thanks also to Rick O'Shea.

Special thanks to Darach Ó Séaghdha for your early endorsement and support. Thanks to Edel Coffey for early feedback and encouragement. Thanks also to Richy Craven.

Thanks to all my friends, especially Eileen Gogan, for badgering me to write a book for many years; Bernice Barrington, for early enthusiasm for my premise; and Eoin O'Dwyer, for support and encouragement.

A very special thanks to my parents, Rita and Brendan (RIP). I may not have grown up in a house full of books, but I did grow up in a house full of stories, and funny ones at that. Everything I have I owe to you.

Thanks also to my brother, extended family and my in-laws.

I have saved my final thanks for the two people this book is dedicated to: my darling husband, Joe, and my dearest daughter, Alice. You brighten my every day and inspire me to keep going, and to get better. Thanks to you, I live in a house of joy and creativity. You both make me laugh every day. I am forever grateful I found you and you found me.

Printed in Dunstable, United Kingdom